BOTTOM

FEEDERS

Roth

~2020~

JERRY ROTH

HELLBENDER BOOKS

Hellbender Books

MECHANICSBURG, PENNSYLVANIA

an imprint of Sunbury Press, Inc.
Mechanicsburg, PA USA

FIRST HELLBENDER BOOKS EDITION: April 2020

Set in Adobe Garamond. Interior design by Chris Fenwick | Cover by Chris Fenwick. Edited by Chris Fenwick.

Publisher's Cataloging-in-Publication Data
Names: Roth, Jerry, author.
Title: Bottom Feeders / Jerry Roth.
Description: Revised trade paperback edition. | Mechanicsburg, Pennsylvania : Hellbender Books, 2020.
Summary: Jerry Roth writes a thriller of a murderous devil hidden inside a prison.
Identifiers: ISBN 978-1-62006-227-2 (softcover).
Subjects: BISAC: FICTION / Thrillers / Supernatural. | FICTION / Horror. | FICTION / Thrillers / Suspense.

Continue the Enlightenment!

For my son, Jesse—your appetite for life keeps me young.

"Hell is empty, and all the devils are here."

~William Shakespeare

CHAPTER 1

Thirty Years Ago

Ben climbed onto his John Deere tractor, started the massive beast's engine, and listened as it roared to life. Finishing tasks was the one thing Ben did well. It wasn't in him to give up or to call it quits when times get rough. His sense of duty was why he still owned and operated farm equipment most considered a relic even by production standards. Scrapping the machine for metal when the breakdowns became more frequent was never an option. He rolled up his sleeves and made it run like new for yet another season. Farming wasn't an easy way to live, and if pressed on the issue, he wished for a hundred other ways to provide for his family. Farming was what he knew, what his father taught him, and what coursed through his veins. How could he ignore a talent when it puts food on the table?

If there was an element more important to a farmer than timing, it was a mystery to Ben. No sane farmer wanted his wife to deliver a baby the same time as the crops were coming in, but that was the reality. He prayed for at least three more weeks to get the harvest in before the little arrival. His eyes knew better, and Lily's belly was a ripe melon, ready to burst. *God's will*, he thought. The loud hum of the tractor drowned out the surrounding noise, and careful consideration went into the noticeable hearing loss the farming contraption no doubt caused. He put the shifter into gear, preparing to drop the clutch when the clouds rolled in and changed the sky from bright to dreary. The sudden change shocked Ben.

A black streak filled the once white, puffy clouds. Their foggy innards turned to the color of onyx—like ink soaking into a cotton ball. Angry clouds multiplied until the entire sky darkened everything. Ben never experienced a storm front roll in so fast. Weather-watching was always a farmer's preoccupation, and he fancied himself a good judge of atmospheric conditions. He never saw a sky so dark, so all-encompassing, giving him shivers with each glance upward.

Ben stalled the tractor, killing the engine, causing its massive frame to lurch forward one last time. He surveyed his land, watching the wind whipping the leaves in a circular motion on the large tree his great grandfather planted generations ago. The world around him was turning black in a hurry. He looked to the clouds for a hook in the sky, the first sign of a twister. He saw nothing.

Ben felt a tingling in the air that was brand new to the senses. Electricity from the wind surrounded him, pressing until he was suffocating from the ozone odor. With each breath he took in, the air became thick, clogging his lungs and constricting his chest. In a panic, Ben darted in every direction to discover the cause of his sudden discomfort. His eyes found nothing out of the ordinary except for the raven-colored clouds descending upon his small Ohio town. The hairs on the back of his neck stood up as if the electrified air became a part of him. Energy filled his mouth, causing the fillings in his teeth to vibrate. He pressed his teeth together in a clench, quieting his mouth for the moment. Above Ben, the clouds began to gather, swirling into a vortex. The center resembled a black hole sucking in the shadows and twisting around Ben's two-story home. The sight dumbfounded Ben, and it was enough to freeze him where he stood. He shifted his view from the swirling mass above to his house and back again.

"Lily," he shouted, breaking his paralysis and running toward the house. Three steps toward his home, the ground began to shake below his feet. The world turned sideways as if the sky was down, and the stable dirt was floating above him. He recalled the recordings of the astronauts floating in their space capsule. Without warning, the horizon righted itself once again. The electricity in the air became charged, and with it came an enormous roar of wind swirling around him. From the hole, torn into the sky above him, a bolt of lightning scorched its way out of the spinning vortex colliding into the tree his great grandfather planted so long ago. The trunk of the tree exploded in a cascade of sparks. A tree that stood so strong weathered so many storms and watched the entire family grow suffered a slow death brought on by flames. When lightning smashed against the tree, the impact knocked Ben off his feet. Dazed from the blow, Ben looked up from his field and watched the fire spread from the trunk to the branches. Ash floated toward Ben like fiery snowflakes in a snow globe nightmare.

Above the crackle of burning wood, a scream rose and curdled the blood within him. The tone of the cry cut into his spine with the precision of a sharpened blade. With his heart in his stomach, Ben ran to his home, trying to understand the reason for his pregnant wife's screams. Frightened legs refused to move fast enough to satisfy his worried mind. Ben pushed his way into the front door, scraping the frame as he hurried. A sight destined to scar Ben the rest of his life appeared before him as vibrant as a scene from a movie. Lily stood over their area-rug, knees locked together, and blood pooling under her until the beige colored rug turned an angry shade of crimson. The sight haunted his dreams for years to come without the clarity ever fading. When Ben reached his wife, she was shaking as he guided her onto a nearby chair. Her eyes were wide, filled with terror, and gone was any sense of reality. Ben waved a hand in front of her face and snapped his fingers.

"Lily, can you hear me? Please, Lily, talk to me?" She turned her head to him—tears rolled down her cheeks. "What happened, Lily?" She looked at the bloody carpet.

"I was dusting, and it felt like my insides were ripping apart," Lily said. Ben looked at her swollen belly and began to cry.

"Will the baby be okay?" Ben asked and not wanting an answer. Lily turned on a smile that became a cry as if her face was melting.

"Call doctor Bain. Get him now. My contractions are starting," she said, and Ben complied. When Otis Bain entered their home, he found Lily resting on their couch with Ben rubbing a washcloth over her forehead.

"Thank God you're here, Doctor Bain," Ben said while shaking his hand spastically.

"Please, call me Otis." The doctor was peeling off his coat and still sucking on a lollipop—its handle sticking from his mouth. "Can you tell me what happened?" Otis asked while starting his examination of Lily. Ben left out his suspicion that the lightning brought on her labor—deciding against the minor detail.

"She said she felt something rip...from the inside. What could it mean, doctor?"

"The act of childbirth can be painful, and there's no judging pain by any scale that's accurate," Otis said, lifting Lily's dress and shaking his head.

"She's dilated ten centimeters," Otis said.

"What's that mean?"

"It means the baby's coming right now."

"What do you want me to do?" Ben asked. Otis positioned himself below Lily's legs, hiking her skirt, and searching for the child's head.

"It's crowning. Listen to me, Lily. When I tell you to, I want you to push, okay?" She nodded. "Don't hold your breath or you'll pass out." She exhaled in a loud burst. "Just breathe natural," he said. Ben began to pace around the room, wishing he was somewhere else. "Here it comes. Keep breathing, Lily." Ben bit his lip hard, leaned over Otis's shoulder to see the progress, and looked away when the baby's head became visible. "Start pushing Lily." She grunted and let out a scream, chilling Ben's skin.

"I can't. It hurts too much." Lily said.

"You have no choice, young lady. This baby is coming right now." The head broke the human boundary. Otis pulled the baby free from its mother. "There you are. Come to Otis." Otis Bain lifted the baby into the air, making sure its air passage was clear, and then he gasped.

"What? What's wrong, doctor?" Ben asked in a panic.

"How's my baby?" Lily begged. Otis wrapped the baby in a sheet and handed it to Ben.

"You have a baby boy, but..."

"But what?"

"He doesn't have an umbilical cord," Otis said. Fear was in his voice. "Not even a spot for it."

"How is that possible?" Otis shrugged. Lily screamed at the top of her lungs, while Otis positioned himself once more.

"You have a second one coming."

"Second one?"

"Push, Lily." The second baby came much faster than the first. Otis looked at the infant with a sudden urge to vomit. He wrapped the child in another sheet. Both men rushed to the bedroom.

"Where are you going with my baby? How is it? Talk to me," Lily yelled to them, in frantic words. Otis placed the baby on the bed, uncovered the infant, and when Ben looked at his child, he winced, eyes filling with tears.

"What's wrong with him? What happened to my boy?" Otis shook his head.

"Did she fall?" Otis asked.

"What?"

"Did your wife fall?"

"No, not at all." Shattered bones became visible in multiple places.

"Something crushed him while he was inside your wife," Otis said and covered the body. Ben put a hand over his face, distorting it into a scowl. His tears fell.

"Did he…feel any pain?"

"After examining the trauma…he died at once," Otis said, looking at the carpet and wishing to disappear under the shag. Ben brought the fallen baby into his arms.

"Where are you going?"

"My wife needs to see our child." Ben walked back to Lily and passed his brother kicking on the floor. Sadness swept through Ben.

"I want you to meet your son, Lily," Ben said, with tears.

CHAPTER 2

Jenny Deville peeled the wrapping away from the margarine and set the naked stick on a tray beside the butter knife. She turned on the radio with **Tom Petty** springing to life in the background singing, **Don't Do Me Like That**, and she felt right at home. The song's attitude matched her mood, and she melted into the lyrics. Jenny relished both the early hours before the rush of the day and the quiet calm before the storm. Her hunger never seemed to align with her family's schedule—she never ate alongside her husband and son. Instead, she took meals when and where she could.

The eggs sizzled next to the bacon with the yolks bubbling from the heated pan. The walking dead stirred in another room with the sounds of drawers closing hard, bathroom doors shutting, and water hitting a porcelain bowl. Jenny's schedule was like clockwork except for the occasional prompting of a six-year-old to hurry his pace. However, that day was different—Jenny never had to move her little soldier along.

As Jenny pried eggs from the frying pan, she turned to see Zack already at the kitchen table with his legs crossed under the chair, and his arms folded in front of him. The sight of her boy sitting still and avoiding attention from her threw her off balance. For a brief second, Zack resembled a spectral vision, a shell of the vibrant child, spending his day in silly mimicry to the point of exhaustion. Jenny directed her focus on her son to make sure he was even in the same room behind her.

"*I* was wondering when you would join the living, sleepyhead," Jenny said, trying to keep her voice loose and fun sounding. "How did you sleep, puppy?" Zack's bloodshot eyes told her everything she needed to know. He wasn't sleeping, and that much was clear. She wondered if he rested an hour the whole night. Jenny tore herself away from the sight of Zack and used tongs to place bacon on a plate next to the boy's egg and toast. "There you go, sweetie, eat up." Zack grabbed the fork with his tiny digits and positioned it into his small palm. The large fork looked comical in his hand, and Jenny might have laughed if something wasn't wrong with her son. Violent shuffling broke the silence in the kitchen. Zack's tiny frame tensed as if a live wire touched his spine, causing every muscle to flex. Robert bustled down the hall and inserted each foot into a shoe. He soared through the kitchen doorway with every limb working on a task of its own.

"Hello, hello," Robert said with happiness as if he wasn't dead to the world fifteen minutes earlier. Jenny saw her husband heading for a chair next to Zack but made a beeline for her and finished his short jaunt with a kiss, lingering long enough to send a flutter into her stomach.

"Um…that *was* very nice," Jenny said. Robert found his usual place next to Zack and ruffled the boy's hair with his palm as he did every morning since he first met the child, two years earlier. That morning was different somehow, they all knew on some level. Zack gave a weak whine, to Robert, sounding like the noise a mouse might make as a shoe squashed down on it. The squeaky reaction was more than enough to rattle Jenny all by itself, but it wasn't the vocal emission stopping her in her tracks, it was his subtle movements. She didn't think Robert even caught his action, and she was thankful for that.

Jenny loved her husband, but she also knew Zack's stepfather was not good at the fine-tuned details a mother used to rear a child from infancy to adulthood. Robert was more of a wrecking ball, exploding to a problem with all the force he could muster. *If we have a kid, you will need to work on that, Robert.* What she saw from Zack was a flinch, and not much more. To the kids in a schoolyard, the flinch stood for weakness, and in Jenny's world, it stood for the same thing. Something damaged Zack—there was no doubt in Jenny's mind, damaged by something or someone. The thought wouldn't go away—it bounced in her skull like a crazed bird ricocheting off the bars of its cage.

Robert cut into his eggs, allowing its yellow juice to drain across its white body. The sun-colored yolk pooled around and under a slice of toast, washing its vital fluids across the edge of the bread's crust. Robert tore into the eggs, unaware his wife's nerves stood on end like a bare electrical wire. The two boys in her life were stark opposites as they sat next to each other. Robert ate while his stepson picked at his meal. He was eating by the technicality of putting food into the mouth.

"So, how is everyone this morning?" *Talking* was all Jenny wanted Zack to do, but Robert took the bait instead.

"My first day as a warden, can you believe it, me a warden?" Robert stabbed at the fleshy egg, slurped it into his mouth, and dribbled a fragment onto his chin. Jenny removed the food particle with a napkin and studied the napkin stain with Zack absorbing her thoughts. *I want to include you in these kinds of problems, Robert. You have a good heart, but not a soft touch.* Her real concern was to get Robert out of the house so she could deal with Zack alone.

"I picked up some soymilk yesterday at the store. Your evil plan is complete—we are now a Dairy-Free household. Your stomach will thank me," Jenny said. Her worry for Zack came in and out, much like a radio tuned between the stations. "Well, I hope you are nice to the other school kids today, and you play well with others," Jenny said to Zack, but speaking to Robert.

"I will, Mommy," Zack said without raising his head from his plate, a plate as full as it was when Jenny sat it in front of him.

"I will, too, Mommy." Robert smiled a toothy grin and kept it even as he swallowed orange juice hard, making a belching sputter deep in his throat by drinking too fast.

"So, what are you expecting, your first day as a warden?" she asked.

"Prisoners are creatures of habit, and they want nothing to do with change. It will be difficult," Robert said.

"But you love it and thrive on it, don't you?"

"That I do." Robert folded a slice of bacon, shoved it against his tongue—it disappeared inside his closing lips. Zack made one last futile attempt to place more food in him and gave up.

"I'm not so hungry. Can I get ready for school now?" He sat motionless, waiting for the answer. He seemed mesmerized by his already congealing egg.

"Sure, but what do you say?"

"Can I go get ready, please?" Zack asked, with the last word sounding muffled and distorted.

"You sure may, sweetheart," Jenny said, and Zack pulled himself, with some effort, away from the table and down the hall. She could hear his footsteps clacking on the wood stairs. "Make sure you brush your teeth," she hollered, stood paralyzed in place with her head craned, and waited for Zack to answer.

"I will, Mommy," he said after a long while in a faint, faraway voice. The sad voice frightened Jenny.

"Oh, Jenny, one more detail," Robert said. Broken from a spell—she whipped herself in a circle with her socked feet spinning on the glossy laminate. She landed in Robert's lap and snagged the end of his tie under her rump as she did. The necktie tugged him downward. He yanked at the tie to free it from her backside and felt a laugh fall from him without warning. She kissed him, letting her tongue roam around on its own volition.

"Now, what was it you wanted to discuss, my darling?" He rolled his eyes and gave a mock waving air into his face gesture.

"Where am I?" he asked *with* a smile. Jenny was already piling the plates on each other and heading to the sink.

"About my trip to Columbus. I can't make it today because of the new job." The reality of daily life jarred her back to her senses.

"It's time again, isn't it?"

"Yep," he said, thrusting the last bit of juice down his gullet. "You know what? I can try to sneak out early..."

"No way. It's your first day on the job. What kind of example would you be setting?"

"You should bring along your friend with you to Columbus to-day," Robert said.

"Way ahead of you. I'm bringing Liam." Robert's smirk began to change into a broad smile then into an all-out roar of laughter.

"Stop, stop it." Tears streamed down Robert's face. Jenny pretended to slap him. "I mean it, stop making fun of Liam." Robert curled his face up and rubbed the side of his ribs.

"I'm sorry, I just pictured Liam all dressed in feathers like some woman wrestler ready to kick ass." Jenny laughed.

"Liam is very tough, maybe not tough so much, but very strong for his size. Anyway, you need to be nice—he's my best friend."

"I know," Robert said and wiped his eyes dry, "but the only thing Liam can defend is your fashion sense."

"Liam will come for moral support then."

"That…I'll buy. If you have any problems with Morris, I'll only be *a* phone call away." Jenny tossed a leg over Robert's lap and straddled her husband, pressing her chest close to his. She circled his lips with a caressing tongue, plunged it deep into his mouth until he kissed her back. Her cheeks strained as she applied more pressure, swooning from the passion she had for her husband. Jenny sensed warmth down below and wanted to rid herself of the urge. Any other day and she would have made Robert go in a little late, but today was his first day of work. She pushed herself off Robert hard with her urges remaining strong.

"Can we continue this later?" Robert asked.

"You bet. Kiss, kiss."

CHAPTER 3

Robert Deville reached the gate of the Reclamation Correctional Facility, stopped his car, and swung the car door open. Reclamation stretched out before him like a medieval castle, built by King Arthur himself. His eyes drifted to the thirty-foot steel fences curving inward. At the top of the fence, rested razor-sharp wire meant to keep rabbit prisoners inside or cut them to shreds if they attempted a flight to freedom. Robert wondered how desperate he would have to be to take on a fence as daunting. As the thought bounced in his head, his eyes darted back to the ominous structure that housed over three thousand convicts from every background imaginable.

The prison was a four-story building built into a circle. One end of the structure flowed a half-mile around and met with the other end of the circle until the two sides joined into an enormous rectangular building. From high above, the facility resembled a giant wedding ring. The administration building had the shape of a diamond—and the prison confines shaped as the band.

Robert looked to the diamond and sensed the first pang of unease that gripped him. There was more to come, but this one was the first moment of apprehension shaping his opinion of the prison forever. Robert was big on first impressions, and he relied on his instincts every day on the force. He valued intuition as the one commodity separating the gifted officers from the nine-to-fivers who collected a paycheck, happy to kiss the wife goodnight before they fell asleep in front of the television. The world needed those working stiffs, too. It required those soldiers to get the small things done, but making the hard choices on the streets of Columbus, Ohio, required a specific breed. Robert moved up the ranks on the backs of those not willing to shake trees and watch what fell out. He didn't see his co-workers in the police department as cowards. Every man and woman put their life on the line. One difference was he didn't wait to respond to problems—he searched for them.

He had a *friend*, if you could call him that, who saw Robert Deville as an adrenaline junkie and nothing more. Robert had a way of finding the mess and cleaning it up. Whatever the opinion, what also lingered was respect. The same brand of respect forced officers in their moment of crisis to pray Robert was heading through the door right beside them. His confidence was priceless in deadly situations. More than once, it was Robert's unwavering nerve, turning an improbable outcome into a brilliant maneuver, and he understood the gift.

His ability to make hard decisions revealed the limitations of his career in law enforcement. He wanted more power and what better reason for a career change. Except he still didn't expect an opportunity thrust upon him so soon. A position as a prison warden was beyond his reach, and he knew that, too. He planned to work his way up the ladder another ten years to reach such heights.

The vast prison towered in the small town's horizon, and although the city received many subcontracted jobs, the prison was a symbol *of* what was wrong with society. Robert knew he had big shoes to fill, replacing Joseph Hughes. The warden was beloved in Pataskala. Robert was up to the task but carried some remorse about missing his opportunity to pick the old guy's brain about the running of the prison. There was a lot to learn from the old guy, but his wisdom went with him to the grave. Either way, the responsibility was his, and he would conquer this mission the same way he conquered every obstacle he had ever faced.

Robert continued to lean on his door, working on stretching the time before entering the fence line. *Are you afraid of this place?* No answer appeared to him, and the thought stung Robert with shame. It wasn't his fear that worried him—fear was part of the job and helped prioritize problems—it was the cowardice. He wouldn't forgive men under him for their yellow streak, and he was much harder on himself for such weaknesses. When it came down to it, he knew he would step inside the prison, but it was the apprehension that unnerved him.

He was working toward a promotion like a prison warden, and he knew he would reach the peak. He expected the promotion in his golden years. Then poof, there it was, decades earlier than expected. *Am I ready for this?* He put his time into understanding the streets and dealing with the locals. Studied every nuance involving negotiating with criminals, but it was the finer points of diplomacy eluding him. The missing skills seemed invaluable immersed in a world where the fist was a detriment. The position called for zero raw aggression, and a well-phrased sentence could mean the difference between getting what he wanted and getting left out in the cold. *It's a new day and a new game.*

A security guard, who made a few too many visits to Dunkin' Donuts, waddled from a nearby guard shack and bolstered a tactical position behind Robert. The guard placed a hand, dripping with sweat, on the butt of a pistol encased in a holster. The odd-shaped guard came to a stop.

"You can't park here," the guard said in his most authoritative voice. "Move it now." Robert never flinched as the guard barked his orders. Robert even fought off an urge to laugh. Men on the force would never admit it, out loud, but rent-a-cops, like the guard, were nothing more than a punchline in the police department locker room. *A lapdog yelping for attention*, Robert thought to himself. He swiveled around and shut the car door in the same motion. Before the guard could react, Robert was at eye level with the guard shack Rambo. Robert saw the fear in the robust sentry's frame. He shook like a leaf, and Robert spotted it right off. His opinion of the guard went down a notch in his mind.

"Stand down, son," Robert said. The guard reeled between his duty and his fight-or-flight instinct. "What's your name?" Again, the guard shredded the words like unidentifiable images.

"Jake Shoeman," the guard said with a growing suspicion the man confronting him wielded some authority.

"Mr. Shoeman? I'm Reclamation's new warden." Jake was at a loss for words but understood that he wandered into a minefield.

"Mister…" Jake asked in a coy schoolboy manner. Robert thought about twisting the knife further and changed his mind. There was time enough for that later.

"Robert Deville." Jake gave Robert a smile resembling an act of submission.

"Listen, Mr. Deville. I have worked here for the last two years. I don't have an exciting life. My wife hates my guts most of the time.

I have a child that is so spoiled I want to rip my hair out, and on top of it all, I think I'm having a passionate affair with food." Jake looked pitiful. "I know with every new administration—people get swept into the streets. I couldn't bear my life on the unemployment line. If you can overlook this misunderstanding, I will never let it happen again." Robert released the worm from his hook.

"I'm not firing you, yet. Because of your honesty, I will keep a close watch on you. I don't like weak people around me. There is no room for weakness in a correction facility. I can't allow you to go on the way you are," Robert said.

"Sir?" Jake questioned.

"It's obvious you're stationed out here in no-man's-land because of your build and maybe other reasons. Have you looked at yourself? You've let yourself go, Jake. I need versatile guards that can be inter-changeable. I count on all members of my team when the chips are down. Do you hear me?" Jake nodded his head. "I need to hear the words."

"Yes, sir."

"You have a week to pick a workout regimen and stick with it. I believe improving your physical health will lead to higher self-esteem and save your love life. Every single day the prisoners here are lifting weights, getting bigger, and getting stronger. How can you compete? I suggest you make a change, starting now. If you need help with training ideas, come to me. But if you ignore my warnings, then I have no sympathy." Jake remained quiet. "Do you have questions?" Jake shook his head.

"I hope you take this as a positive," Robert said. "Now, open the gate." Jake scrambled to the guard shack and opened the mechanism. The steel gate slid open—Robert drove through without a second look. He didn't intend to fire Jake. He saw a chance for Jake to be indebted to him, and he took it. Jake's life, livelihood, and pride were on the line, and Robert spared him like a decree from a king. Robert found the technique useful in weeding out the disloyal of the bunch, not to mention it sent a strong signal to the rest that a new day arrived.

The encounter would circulate through the staff before darkness fell. Robert watched the fence recede beside and behind his car. He pumped the brakes, peered through the rear-view mirror, and saw the fence closed, locking him inside. The visual did more to his psyche than he thought it would. He held his breath and imagined a prisoner's first time entering with their stomach dropping as reality collided with pure fear. He spent his lifetime sending criminals to the very facility and never imagined carrying out their punishment. The concept seemed backward to him. He was preparing to manage the underbelly of the state after the justice system found no other alternatives. Preventing the decay of a soul before they reached law enforcement was an enticing prospect to him. He needed to face the truth—there was no money or prestige in any form of the social work game. Robert pulled into a parking spot marked: WARDEN

Stenciled letters just below on the cement curb spelled out the name of the former warden: Joseph Hughes.

The remnant of the past warden shimmered in black letters. A memorial to a man that served the community for so long. All that was missing was the date of birth and death to memorialize his predecessor. He exited the automobile and looked down at the parking space as if the prison administration buried the body of Joseph beneath the asphalt. The thought gave him the creeps enough to change the course of his path across the yellow parking line. *Let's not walk on someone's grave.* An eighty-year-old woman greeted Robert as he stepped through the doors of the diamond-shaped administration building.

Robert noticed the deep wrinkles covering the delicate cheekbones of the silver-haired lady. The creases circled her eyes and sunk into the black wells beneath. Robert wondered what life experiences caused such dramatic signs of wear in a human face. He suspected the wrinkles were a roadmap burned into her flesh from some tragic event. *If that theory were correct, then this woman lived through the trials of Job.* She lifted her lips to smile, and when she did, the wrinkles shifted from one region of her face to another. Loose skin curled under her mouth and revealed a set of brilliant teeth, too white for her age. Her false teeth were distracting to his mind, and he couldn't shift his eyes. Eyelids shot up in accord with her genuine smile.

"Hello, dear," she said in an assuring voice. "I'm Agatha." She held out a hand for Robert to take. He took a moment and studied her outstretched hand. He marveled at her paper-thin skin, bunching up near her palm, with raised blue veins protruding above her pallid surface. With a grip of her hand, he felt the gentle embrace and the give of her soft bones as he pumped it with mild force.

"It's a pleasure to meet you, Agatha," Robert said and meant it.

"The pleasure is all *mine*, Mr. Deville. I've watched your career with great interest," she said.

"My career? How so?" A look of discomfort flashed across Agatha's face.

"It isn't anything creepy, Mr. Deville, I promise you that. I collect news stories chronicling men of valor. Good deeds that go beyond the call of duty always make it into my scrapbook. I have many clippings of your accolades from your years on the police force." Robert nodded, and his anxiety subsided.

"I'm flattered," Robert said.

"May I show you to your office?" Agatha asked.

"I appreciate the escort, and I'm looking for the associate warden. His name is Reginald Williams. Do you know him?" Agatha smiled and led Robert up a flight of stairs.

"The late Joseph Hughes hired me as his administrative assistant over two decades ago. About fifteen years ago, Joseph brought in Reginald. I'm a glorified secretary, which means I know my place, but I also know everybody else's, too. The two things to understand about Reginald is that no one knows more about this prison, and once you get to know him, you'll find he has a warm heart." Agatha stopped in front of a wood door with a glass window containing Joseph Hughes's name. She noticed Robert's gaze at the window.

"The men are coming tomorrow to update the door and the parking space. I'm sorry, I haven't done it before your arrival. I guess it was hard to say goodbye to Joseph. He was an amazing man." Robert placed his large hand onto her shoulder.

"I understand Agatha, and I hope you will express the same warmth for me someday."

"I'm sure I will. After you settle in, perhaps we'll have tea and learn more about each other. Welcome to Reclamation." Agatha disappeared down the stairs. Robert couldn't help but smile after the sweet lady. He opened the door to his office and shuffled into a time warp. The room held the decorations of pictures filled with fishermen—hunters in varied acts of courageous triumphs. One scene immortalized the battle between a fish and a fly fisherman in full sportsman regalia—another photo showed the visceral danger of a hunter facing a grizzly bear with his twelve-gauge rifle at the ready. Art deco style pieces decorated the rest of the room and gave the inhabitants the feeling they just stepped into a scene from *The Maltese Falcon*.

Robert noticed a large desk taking up half the room. The color of the wood was a mystery because of the flood of sunlight from the window. A dark silhouette hovered behind the large desk. Robert squinted and watched as the dark form moved away from the window to greet him. A hand lingered in the air and awaited its reciprocation.

"I'm Reginald Williams—associate warden." Robert placed a hand onto Reginald's shoulder and ignored the outstretched one.

"It's nice to meet you, Reginald. May I call you Reggie?"

"No. You may not," Reginald said.

"It's my pleasure to meet you, Reginald. I'm—"

"I know who you are." Robert's anger swelled. *Diplomacy, diplomacy.* "How you found your way into this position isn't clear." Robert strolled to the desk and found the seat. Atop a mound of crumpled paper sat a card in the center of the wastebasket. He fished out the card and read the front: CONGRATULATIONS

The card contained handwritten signatures from the entire staff. The prison director passed over Reginald. He looked from the card to his new second in command. Robert folded the card in half and moved closer to Reginald, making sure not to relinquish eye contact for even a slight moment. Robert played a part in stalling this man's rise to a warden position.

He approached Reginald like a hunter stalking a bear and waiting for a sign to strike. Robert tucked the folded card into the front coat pocket of Reginald's suit and dared his expression to change. Reginald's expression didn't change, and his stock rose in Robert's mind. As if by magic, Robert's marble expression melted into a smile so carefree that Reginald could not recall the disturbing one it replaced.

"Because I am new here, I'll give you a little slack. I'm sure you've paid your dues, and it won't be long before all your strengths and weaknesses reveal themselves." Robert moved away from Reginald and could detect a hint of fear in the air. He was used to the smell, but he didn't allow himself to enjoy the discovery. He hurried around the large desk with grace and again found the chair with a plop more reminiscent of musical chairs.

"Thank you, sir," Reginald said in a tone of submission. Robert guessed his number-two man recognized the danger of crossing him. *I'm improving at the art of confrontation.* Robert's eyes scanned the wood-grain patterns in the desk in front of him. He traced the path the subtle carvings meandered across the face of the desk. To him, the delicate carvings looked like flames enveloping the legs and rushing out of control to the top of the wood.

"Where did this desk come from?" Robert asked, transfixed by its dazzling beauty. Thankful for the distraction, Reginald joined Robert in his inspection.

"Our former warden constructed this piece. You are welcome to bring a desk in—one that you choose if you like. I'll have maintenance remove it at once." Robert raised a hand to stop Reginald.

"No." Robert, surprised by his reaction, leveled his tone. "What I meant to say is…I'm fond of the desk…I prefer it to stay." Reginald pretended to look over the desk for himself.

"It *is* a lovely piece," Reginald said. Robert tried to detect a condescending tone. "Joseph Hughes told me he built this from reclaimed wood right here inside the prison. To me, it resembles Tigerwood, indigenous to Africa or places in South America where the land was wet. Maybe it grew here a long time ago and then went extinct, who can tell. I know the wood is rare, though. Instrument makers used this wood for the sound it conveys. They say it holds spirits of the forest within its rings. It has a fantastic shimmer, doesn't it?"

"Yes, it does," Robert said. He pressed his foot against a wooden floorboard under the desk, and it gave with his weight. The wood plank dipped two inches and let out a loud creak from the stress.

"It seems there's a loose board under here." Robert started to stretch toward the object of his focus.

"Please, don't mind yourself with those worries. I'll have someone take care of it as soon as possible. Now, let me show you around the facility." Robert nodded and walked toward the door, still under the mesmerizing effects of the fiery desk.

"Lead the way, Reginald," Robert said with his attention remaining on the carved lectern. The interaction left him foggy, but the sensation was fading fast. The urge was like a mother leaving a child. Safety resonated from the desk, and he wanted to bask in its presence like a comforting fireplace. Robert shook his head, and the simple act seemed to relieve the cobwebs threatening to turn his mind to fog. *Strangle my thoughts.* The idea almost fell from his mouth until he caught Reginald's puzzled expression. Reginald bustled through the door with Robert following close behind. Reginald approached a railing continuing into a circle in front of him the entire length of the prison.

"This prison has four levels starting with the floor we are on and three more going up." Reginald lifted his finger skyward as if finger-painting in mid-air. "There is the infirmary and the offices for the administration and guards. As you can see, the mess hall is in the center of the prison, one-half level lower than the offices." Robert leaned over the rail, peered through the glass ceiling of the cafeteria, and watched a few inmates scurrying around below to prepare for the next meal. "Over a hundred years ago, when this facility was still an asylum, the center of the building contained a greenhouse. All this was open." Reginald pointed to the ceiling three stories up.

"It was open?" Robert asked with Reginald nodding.

"Like a doughnut. In 1906, the state saw fit to convert the asylum into this fine institution, and a construction crew covered the center.

From what I hear, five men lost their lives in the undertaking. Still, I imagine it was a marvel to see." Reginald smiled to no one in particular. "Hundreds of Pataskala's townspeople would come out to the surrounding meadows with picnic lunches each day and watch the construction." Robert looked away from the associate warden out of embarrassment of his gushing. Reginald walked on and up a steel staircase wide enough for two men standing side by side. Up they rose to the second floor.

"Are the inmates locked down?" Robert asked.

"That's correct. We keep prisoners inside the cells twenty hours of the day. We allow one hour for each meal and one added hour for exercise or leisure activities."

"I'm impressed with the discipline, and surprised," Robert said. Reginald nodded his approval.

"Warden Joseph Hughes was a religious man who believed that time incarcerated required quiet reflection and through isolation and solitude could an offender find understanding for the devastation their deeds heaped upon their victims."

"I agree so far."

"Reclamation prefers to segregate the prisoners by offenses when possible. The second level holds—habitual criminals convicted of robbery, assault—and drug offenders ranging from possession to trafficking." They continued to the next level.

"This place is enormous," Robert said.

"These are the rapist, pedophiles, and some mentally ill."

"Why are the mentally ill here at all?" Robert asked with urgency in his tone. Reginald furled his eyebrows.

"Some prisoners never receive a diagnosis and fall through the cracks while others…the best way to say it is their offenses were severe enough to warrant incarceration rather than therapy. As you've guessed by now, the further we move up, the worse the offenders. It was a safeguard implemented by Warden Hughes. We lock each level down from each other and the main floor. If a prisoner ever overpowered a guard, access to keys of every level is impossible. At least that's the theory."

"So, we assign each guard a key that works on that level alone?" Robert asked.

"Correct."

"So, what's on the fourth floor?" A shiver went through Reginald.

"If this were an orchard, they are the bad apples. The fourth level is Reclamation's version of death row. Reclamation once owned the oldest electric chair in the country right here in this facility. We house the lifers and the condemned side by side. Studies show releasing a lifer into the general population sometimes has dire consequences on other inmates.

"What consequences are you referring to?" Robert asked.

"A prisoner with a life sentence to look forward to doesn't have much to lose. They are missing a conscience in their daily interactions. Aside from meals and one hour of exercise a day, we allow a small group of prisoners to earn the privilege of laundry, cafeteria, and landscaping duties."

"Take me to the fourth floor." Reginald looked to Robert as if he misunderstood for a moment.

"Excuse me?" Reginald asked.

"Fourth floor, now please."

"Yes, sir." They moved up steel stairs. Reginald nodded to a guard who opened the level and swung a steel door open. The guard stiffened when the warden approached. "Lucas, this is our new warden, Robert Deville. Warden Deville, this is Lucas Muldoon. We have stationed him on this level for the past ten years. We like to keep our more seasoned officers manned at this level. Robert inspected the officer more out of habit than curiosity.

"How do you like your job, Muldoon?" Robert asked.

"I like it very much, sir," Lucas answered.

"Great. Carry on," Robert said without an upward glance. Lucas closed the steel door and locked it once more. Robert's eyes surveyed the concrete path curving left far beyond his gaze. As he began his slow pace, predatory eyes lingered on his every move. The arms, not unlike venomous snakes, slithered through the openings of the bars and rested a moment before their fanged mouths clamped onto the steel barrier. Robert concentrated on the soft echo of his footsteps against the cement and wondered how many condemned men listened to the same mocking noise the last moments of their life.

Whispers rose like tropical air and attempted to suck the oxygen from the warden's lungs. The animals paced back and forth in their enclosures, baring angry teeth. The associate warden spent the last fifteen years brushing past these criminals, and Robert noticed the depravity of the men weighing down on Reginald. He watched the slender man cower before the surrounding evil. Robert might have laughed if the sight didn't invite sadness into his own heart. Three inches of steel protected the pencil pusher from the worst specimens the world has seen. *On the outside world, Reginald was at the mercy of men like these*, Robert thought.

The anger all around solidified Robert. During his career in law enforcement, he spent a time or two in lock-up, but prison was different. The blanket of evil tried to penetrate him, throwing daggers into his skin. He stiffened from the sensual pleasure of knowing he dominated these men. As the warden, he owned them, and he couldn't deny himself the detail. A vague thought swam through his mind, and he recalled the story of Charon ferrying lost souls across the river Styx. He discovered his place, and this was his kingdom. Robert allowed his eyes to lock onto a prisoner burning into him.

Robert swayed off his trail toward the prisoner stabbing him with his eyes. He could see the prisoner's resolve weaken as the convict turned from the bars to his cot. Robert never missed a step when he fell back into line with Reginald. They continued down the caged corridor until Reginald flashed a pointed finger toward a door to his right.

"This door, Mr. Deville, is the most solemn room of this facility. I thought it most important to show you this in person," Reginald said. Robert faced the nondescript silver door resting between two prison cells. The random room was out of place. *Something is wrong about the room*, he thought. Reginald fumbled with a key ring. *Don't open that. Don't do it.* Reginald found the right key and slid it into the handle with no awareness of the silent communication by his superior.

The reinforced doorknob clicked a second before Reginald rotated it and cleared the space between the door and its frame. A whoosh of wind exited the room and blew past Robert. The air pressed against his cheeks like the hand of death. He shook his head, and his stomach churned acid, but he refused to yield to the sudden euphoria. *Abandon all hope who enter here. Enter the gates, Charon awaits.* The line from *Dante's Inferno* cascaded into his mind. In an instant, Reginald flicked a light switch and illuminated a small room.

Reginald stepped into the area first, without looking back. Robert hesitated to cross the threshold and experienced a pain in his chest that stole his breath.

"Mr. Deville? Are you okay, sir?" Reginald asked while watching the warden lean, step through the door, and topple forward to the cement below. Robert's lungs expanded inside his chest, bringing color back to the world.

"I'm fine," Robert said. He gathered his senses, raised himself from a bended knee, and stared headlong at the frightful sight—causing his heart to flutter. A butterfly flapped in his chest and then stole his breath for a second time like a dip into frozen water. A large cot sat in the middle of the small room. Four feet to the right was a glass barrier, and behind it, two rows of wooden chairs lined the room like a sinister puppet show. To Robert, the cot resembled a gurney from an emergency room. Leather straps dangled from the steel rails, bordering its thin mattress on both sides. Head and leg restraints curled and wrapped around themselves like the tendrils from the carcass of a sea squid.

"This, Mr. Deville, is our lethal injection chamber. In 1963, the Ohio legislature banned the mandatory use of death by electrocution. Instead, death row inmates received a choice between the two fates." Robert rubbed his hand across the soft wool sheets on the gurney. There was no power just as he expected, but he touched the mattress again like a person tests the heat of a hot iron. He received nothing, even though a claustrophobic panic seemed to resonate from around the tiny space. Energy penetrated him through the table—every crack in the walls oozed the mind fogging sensation. Loss and regret saturated Robert. The emotions were new to him, not unlike the chamber of horrors surrounding him. Reginald's voice came in and out and found no comfortable journey to Robert's ears.

"Around 1930, an intelligent convict by the name of Sean Spires planned a dramatic escape from this facility. Spires devised a way to cut into the ventilation shaft—he maneuvered his way across the facility," Reginald said and pointed to the center of the ceiling as if the mere gesture could dissect the concrete. "His idea hinged on a planned diversion near a guard stationed by the shaft he needed to enter. Spires practiced night after night, timing the slow burn of a candle. He did this for months until he was sure about the time it would take to burn down. Satisfied with his progress, he planted a similar candle over a flammable liquid in a strategic position in the laundry room. Spires planned the fire to erupt when the prisoners were at work and exercise and cause the most upheaval to secure his escape. But somewhere along the line, he changed his mind and chose the candle's exhaustion to sync with the nightly lock-up."

"Now, why would he alter his escape to cause more risk to himself?" Robert asked. Reginald took on a more serious expression.

"Because Mr. Spires wanted to take more lives after the fire started. The flames spread fast and propelled more smoke than fire. The smoke crept into the cells at every level, and with nowhere for the prisoners to go, they began to choke on the acrid smoke filling their lungs."

"That's horrible," Robert said. Reginald nodded in agreement.

"Guards, along with the prisoners, fought back the flames that night. When all the dust settled, over 400 prisoners died either from the smoke or from the fire. The then, Governor of Ohio, pardoned many of the prisoners—the prisoners that put their lives on the line. There were considerable fire and smoke damage throughout every inch of this building except this very room. No one could figure out the reason. But there it stood, unharmed."

"There, what stood?" Robert asked.

"The Widow-maker, the prison's electric chair. The newspaper writers *said* God was protecting the justice of this state by sparing the instrument of death."

"Is that what you believe?" Reginald shook his head.

"No. I think it was something else altogether.

"What?" Robert begged.

"I don't know. It defies reason." During Reginald's story, Robert was more like himself and happy to leave the small room and the reaction it triggered in him.

"What happened to Sean Spires?"

"No one knows. Guards discovered his escape route, but not Spires."

"What's the point to the history lesson, Reginald?" The rough treatment to his tale shocked Reginald but not as much as it would have before he met his new warden.

"Each man in here may look on the surface to be doing their time passively. Don't allow their facade to lull you. Every man imprisoned within these walls is waiting for someone to let their guard down. Spires toiled months to perfect his deadly plan. They have the disposable time necessary for patient schemes. Human life means nothing next to long-imagined freedom." Robert nodded toward the wisdom his associate warden gained through the years. A dull headache dug into his skull and prompted him to leave the room.

"Thank you for showing this to me," Robert said. With a nod, Reginald led his superior away from the room of death.

CHAPTER 4

Two Years Ago

The alarm ring was so loud Gage covered his ears over his ski mask. He wanted nothing more than to squash the vibration drilling into his head. His palms, pressing to the side of the head, helped—but not much. In confusion, Gage couldn't remember which beautiful woman behind the jewelry counter set off the alarm. He had three women to choose from, and he guessed it didn't matter. The cat was out of the bag. His cohorts slid onto a new frame of mind with the siren's blare. They slipped into what Gage feared most—animals looking to survive. A degenerate addict described Ricky, but he wasn't a killer. Gage was sure of that. The brothers, Victor and Clyde, were of a different sort. Their story was old, told a thousand ways, and the end, always the same. Violence burned in Victor and Clyde. It was their fearlessness and gravitation toward violence Gage wanted to use—he used them like a bulldozer demolishing a house.

Gage thought of himself as a gentlemen thief and understood he was born in the wrong era. The high-tech world guarding things of value made Gage look more like a man suffering from brain damage—trying to unravel the mysteries of the universe. The technology was beyond him, and he made his peace. Mastering the various modern electronic systems wasn't an option—Gage needed more muscle to coerce. He could achieve more results from a threat than ten years of electronics courses.

Gage watched movies of burglars disrupting surveillance cameras with a stick of gum or tapping into the mainframe of a computer system, from across town, and it all seemed like a fantasy. *Even if there was someone with a fantastic amount of knowledge in the world, the guy's working at IBM cashing in his stock options,* Gage told himself. He saw himself as a working-class robber, a meat and potatoes kind of guy. Disabling security wasn't in his toolbox.

Gage relied on his wits and his ability to read a person—that was his weapon. He understood how far to push someone and the discipline to pull back when needed. The tricky part came when he tried to keep his partners from turning every score into a scene from *The Wild Bunch*. It surprised Gage how fast each robbery deteriorated into a mad struggle to inflict pain and suffering. To Gage, fear and manipulation were *a* commodity. There were no personal feelings held against the owners of the establishments he robbed. Gage kept no grudges against the security officers who opposed him on each job.

Clyde shot at a speaker screaming its alarm—it pierced every ear in the jewelry store. When the sound stopped, even the patrons sighed with relief when the siren's wail ended. Gage looked over to Ricky, waving his gun at the manager a lot, as Barney Fife might if he turned to a life of crime. If Gage called someone in his profession a friend, it'd be Ricky. But Gage rewarded Ricky with a spot in his crew because his wife, Maria, liked him. People in their business avoided any real attachments, and most people he associated himself with, treated girlfriends and wives with thoughtless disregard.

To them, women were the weak links preparing to come undone and take everyone with them. A scare from the police or interrogation by enemies might land everyone involved behind bars, and Gage witnessed this more than once. Maria was not just the **woman** behind the scenes or a lover who observed the moves behind the curtain. *They don't know Maria as I do.* Maria may have known about Gage's jobs, but that's where her involvement and influence ended. Maria had more important things on her mind. She spent her hours caring for her three-month-old son Ryan. The boy matching her husband's eyes, and his crooked smile meant everything to her.

Because they moved around so much, and she was alone most of the time, she became good friends with Ricky. And after they got the news of the baby's chances of survival, Ricky took it upon himself to play cards with Maria or watch movies when Gage planned the next heist. Anything to keep her occupied from the thought of losing Ryan. Maria loved Ricky's company, and Gage loved him for the gift of his time. Gage often wondered whether he could do the same for Ricky. But his generosity toward Maria endeared Ricky to him.

Victor forced a man to his stomach in the carpeted center of the jewelry store. The amount of hair Victor pulled from the shopper's scalp to get him to the floor, disturbed Gage, but he refused to be a control freak and micromanage every situation. The store manager was a female, and Gage counted himself lucky. He bet she *had* a husband or children at home. With the thought driven home that she might not make it back to her family, she cooperated. Gage watched the store manager, dressed in a two-piece business suit, that seemed expensive, and contemplated his next move. He bet after her work-day, the store manager slipped out of her work attire the moment she got in the door with jeans pulled on seconds later. He spotted her classic beauty at once as he grabbed the tuft of her neck as if he was subduing a cat.

"You open your fucking mouth, and I'll knock your goddamn teeth down your throat," Gage screamed. "Are you going to give me trouble?" he asked. The manager shook her head back and forth and made sure Gage saw her. Gage squeezed her neck with more force.

"Say the word."

"Yes," said the manager. Victor turned to Gage.

"You want me to deal with her? She's the one who set off the alarm," Victor asked. The comment infuriated Gage. *If you handled crowd control, we wouldn't have to deal with the alarm in the first place,* Gage wanted to say, but he gave Victor a nod and continued with the manager.

"What's your name?" No reply. "What is your name?" Gage asked again.

"Cheryl," she said in a mousy voice.

"Do you love your family, Cheryl?"

"What?" Cheryl asked.

"If you want to see your family ever again, you'll help us get out of here as fast as possible. Do you hear me?" Gage asked and watched Cheryl move her head to the side while saying yes.

"Good, because I'll put a bullet in your head." Gage liked her very much. She had strength. He knew Maria would hold up as well under pressure. The jewelry expert was a problem waiting to happen. Gage needed to use harm as a threat.

"Time's ticking, Saint. It won't be long before we have company."
Gage nodded and turned back to Cheryl.

"You heard him. I want the contents in your safe. Now," Gage
demanded.

"I don't…" Victor placed his gun to the head of a blonde saleswoman and pulled the hammer back. Cheryl saw and listened to the
click of the gun. The gesture left Cheryl frazzled. Gage first scanned
Victor and drifted his head back to Cheryl. The sound fell from
Gage's mind as if he was part of a silent movie.

"I know the combination," Cheryl said.

"That's what I thought," Victor answered. "If you have any more
memory loss, your employee here will get it," Victor promised. Gage
led Cheryl to the back of the store to a large safe while Victor
watched from a distance with nervous energy fueled by anger.

"The cops are on their way. Get out now," Cheryl said.

"Keep your concerns to yourself and open the damned safe,"
Gage ordered with Cheryl turning to the safe and spinning the dial.
She looked into the air and closed her eyes.

"What the hell is that number?" Cheryl spoke aloud to herself.
Victor pointed the gun to the blonde saleswoman's chest and pulled
the trigger. The hammer fell and propelled a bullet into her skin. The
noise stirred everyone toward Victor. He watched the woman fall
with no remorse in his expression.

"What the fuck did you do?" Gage screamed.

"I warned her." Cheryl, in fear for her life, twisted the knob and
swung the door open in one motion.

"Stupid, son of a bitch. She wasn't fucking with you. She was trying to remember," Gage raged.

"I warned her," Victor continued. Gage ran to the fallen woman
with Victor and Clyde emptying the contents of the safe into a duffle
bag. A frightened stupor captured both shoppers and employees.
Gage placed his hand behind the head of the wounded woman and
lifted her onto his lap. She wasn't dead, but he guessed she didn't
have long.

"We gotta go," Victor announced. Gage looked through his ski
mask at Victor in disbelief. Tears welled as he returned his attention

to the blonde saleswoman. He placed a hand against the bullet hole as it gushed blood. The wound drained fast, and it shocked Gage.

"You will be okay. Do you hear me?" Gage asked and turned back to Cheryl. "Call an ambulance." Victor raised his gun to Cheryl. His eyes blazed through his mask.

"Don't you do it, Victor," Gage screamed and raised a gun of his own toward Victor. "You've done enough." The saleswoman made a suffocating noise from the blood, filling her throat. "Get out of here," Gage ordered with his gun sight held firm on Victor's face. Victor readjusted the gun in his palm and reconsidered his options. Sirens brayed for the first time somewhere in the distance.

"Time is running out, Victor. What's it gonna be?" Gage asked. Victor trained his gun from Gage to Cheryl and back again.

"Fuck you, Gage." Victor lowered his gun and headed for the door with his brother following.

"Victor," Gage screamed. Victor turned back. "I'll get you for this." Victor smiled and walked out of the store. The wounded woman's eyes rolled into her head. She attempted a sentence but failed. Ricky kneeled next to his friend.

"We gotta go," Ricky whispered. Gage shook his head.

"I can't leave her like this," Gage said. "Get out of here." Cheryl, speaking to a 911 operator, fell apart twice before she gave the right address. Ricky lingered by his friend.

"Just go, buddy." Gage nodded as if to say, it's okay. Ricky placed out a hand and shook Gage's.

"Maria will get your share. We'll save Ryan. I promise," Ricky said.

"Tell her… I'm sorry." He nodded, let go of Gage, and exited the store. Gage turned the wounded blonde onto her stomach. Blood drained from her mouth and cleared her breathing passage. The woman choked, struggling for air as blood began to drown her.

"Relax. You'll be fine. I promise." A male shopper lifted his sweater off his body and handed it to Gage. He pressed the wool cloth onto the wound—the blood soaked into the sweater at once.

"Stay with me. Please stay with me," Gage said. The sirens arrived on the scene and squealed to a stop. The sound of heavy footsteps thundered into the store. Gage yanked his ski mask from his head and looked at the woman. Her eyes were lifeless, with a mouth wide open. Gage closed her eyes with the heel of his palm. During Gage's last moments of freedom, he thought of Maria, at home with Ryan on her lap—waiting for a husband that wouldn't arrive.

"Why did you do this? Cheryl asked.

"I did this for my son." The world erupted with police and guns.

CHAPTER 5

Jenny wiped the counter and was getting the kitchen in order when the telephone rang. It was loud enough to interrupt her chore, but not enough to penetrate her desperate thoughts about Zack. Being alone with her son used to be a normal experience. Jenny spent every waking moment with him for the first five years of his life. Today was different—she was watching a black cloud cover her happy home. Jenny plucked the phone and shifted it to her ear.

"Hello?" she asked.

"Hello, yourself," a gruff woman's voice echoed through her telephone.

"Hey, Mom," Jenny said, not sure she wanted to talk. "I was just going to call you." The lie fell too flat to convince.

"I'm sure you were," Margaret Salvo said. "What's wrong?" Moments passed before Jenny spoke.

"It's . . . Zack. He's become distant—trapped behind a barrier. As if he . . ." Jenny broke off.

"He remembers what Morris did to you both," Margaret said.

"Yeah."

"Well, Jenny, he was young, but I bet he still holds onto a lot of baggage from that time in his life. He's scared and alone with a codependent mother," Margaret said.

"Excuse me?"

"It's a little late in the game to pretend you have no blame in the situation, dear."

"Morris was an alcoholic. What blame should I accept?"

"The obvious mistake was picking such a miscreant. Robert, however, is a real find. You should count yourself lucky for snagging him."

"I do, Mother, but that wasn't what I heard from you when Morris and I were together. I was the one to blame, the one who needed to be more understanding, to bend. Well, I bent for him, Mother—where did it get me?"

"I was a tad off with Morris, I admit my faults, but I just assumed you were the problem in the relationship, you always were so headstrong. Even as a baby, you refused to eat most foods I tried to feed you." Jenny saw counselors, took the twelve-step programs seriously, read *Chicken Soup for the Soul,* watched Oprah Winfrey religiously, and when times were terrible, attended several church services. And she still felt like a fifteen-year-old girl when she spoke to Margaret Salvo. "Have you spoken to Robert about this yet? An ideal relationship needs communication and honesty, darling," Margaret said.

"No, I haven't, Mom."

"Why not? Robert is a man who knows how to deal with things such as this. He's dealt with domestic cases throughout his career— you should listen to him—no matter what your stubborn side tells you."

"I get that you like Robert, and that's great, I love him, too. The thing is, Mom, a psychological issue of a child, isn't Robert's strength," Jenny said.

"Nonsense. He's capable of nurturing a child." Jenny swung the phone with her hand, punching the air. She gritted her teeth and put the receiver back to an ear.

"I'm not saying Robert is incapable—but the death of his parents influenced his emotional side.

"I wouldn't worry about it. Robert is a well-rounded person, and he just needed someone to bring him out of his shell."

"So, I brought him out of a shell?" Jenny asked.

"Perhaps, dear, but don't forget. You need Robert a lot more than he needs you. Don't lose sight of that." Jenny wrung the phone with her hands and pictured her mother.

"I've spent enormous time and money to discover—I don't need a man to complete me. If I'm not a whole person without a man, I sure as hell won't be whole with one. Mother, you of all people should know better than to say that, after the way, Dad left you."

"Don't you dare bring your father into this," Margaret shrieked, "he was never a man, not an ounce. Morris and your father were two peas in a pod." Jenny sat on the line and listened to her mother's breathing and wondered what to say next.

"I'm sorry, Mom," Jenny said, "I didn't mean to **hurt** you. I'm just worried about Zack." Margaret inhaled, turning into a wet sniffle.

"Think nothing of it, dear, I want your happiness. That's all I want for you." Jenny, dizzy from her mother's barrage, sat motionless, wishing she could escape her skin. A knock at the door stirred Jenny and was the distraction she needed.

"Mom, I got to go now, someone's at the door, I'll call you when I get back from Columbus, okay? We'll talk later." She hung up the phone before Margaret could utter another syllable, and she was glad. When she opened the door, she was still shaking off her mother's words. They stuck to her like pieces of a spider web, eluding her grasp. When Jenny opened her front door, Liam stood on her front porch like a love-struck suitor with the broadest grin possible. She threw her arms around him in an anguished embrace before he could react.

"There, there, sugar cakes," Liam said in a mocking voice. She slid her arms from his shoulder and slumped into an uncomfortable position. Her despairing expression jolted Liam into a sad expression of *his* own. "Oh no, what's wrong?" Jenny backed into the living room stumbling, like a child about to begin a tantrum. Cardboard boxes sat around her like an enlarged version of a child's building blocks.

"If you called me over here to help you unpack," Liam rolled his eyes, "think again, little missy."

"I just got off the phone with the dragon lady," Jenny said. Liam dropped his pretense, lunged for her, and drew her in for another hug. His cologne, warm and intoxicating, caused Jenny to melt into his knitted sweater.

"I'm so sorry, and I bet it was horrible."

"She's just so…preachy," Jenny said while scrunching her face.

"Long shot, but she might have the wisdom to impart."

"Yeah, right."

"Well, she used to love me," Liam said.

"That's when my parents believed you were straight, Liam. When they found out you were a peter puffer, they never let you in the house again." Jenny gave a malicious smile.

"They were also against prostitutes, but they let you stay in their house." Liam marked an invisible tally in midair.

"Shut up. I need you to come with me to drop Zack off to Morris," Jenny said.

"What about the Boy Scout, isn't that his job?"

"Robert will be home late tonight. He's starting his new career."

"Oh, that's right. So how long has it been since you saw Morris?" Liam asked.

"Two years ago, in court," Jenny said. "There's something else. I haven't mentioned it to Robert because…well, you know what he might do to Morris." Jenny paused long enough to agitate Liam. "I've noticed some changes in Zack."

"Changes?"

"It may be nothing, but a mother's paranoia . . ."

"Just freaking tell me," Liam said, shocking himself with his impatience.

"Zack has become distant. It's like I'm losing my happy little boy. He hasn't withdrawn from the world like this since Morris, and I started our divorce."

"Do you think he remembers those times?" Liam asked.

"I'm not sure," A shadow moved in and darkened the edges of her round eyes with sadness. "Can a six-year-old have depression or mental illness?" Liam, lost in options, answered.

"I guess it's possible, but I—"

"Wait a second," Jenny interjected, "for a while there…Zack would get quiet after he came back from his visits with Morris."

"What?" Liam asked.

"Yeah, and now it's happening *before* his visits. What does that mean?" Liam shook his head and readjusted his sweater. He guessed the possibilities and hoped Jenny wasn't considering them herself.

CHAPTER 6

Gage eyed a photo of Maria and Ryan a moment longer, placed the picture between two pages, closed a book, and sat on his cot watching other inmates pass the bars of his cell. The movement caused the natural light to flicker bright then dark in each portion of the iron enclosure. The constant reappearance of light through the bars generated a subtle strobe effect forcing him to squint until thin slits remained. Farther off, a sound rose above the usual chatter of the prison. A sound fell past the steel I-beams lining each circled floor, reaching the highest levels of the cement fortress. Gage walked to the cell's boundary and peered down at the marching group below. A roar of laughter and some shrill screaming cut through the facility.

"The new King is walking through today," a voice said from behind. Gage turned and stared at his skinny cellmate and back to the scene below.

"Yeah, they told me the same."

"What do you think he'll be like?" Eddie asked.

"Meet the new boss, same as the old boss."

"What's that mean, Saint?"

"It's a song. You don't know, *The Who*?" Gage asked. He could tell from the boy's expression he didn't. "I guess my frame of reference has changed. I wonder—when did that happen?" The sound of the crowd's chatter moved closer to them like audible dominoes igniting every cell. The first figure he saw wasn't the warden, as Eddie predicted but a guard. He came into view, stepping with his ego in his gait. Gage knew the walk, could see it when he closed his eyes at night. Correction officers were far from SS soldiers, but to Gage, the comparison was within hands reach, and he grabbed onto it, along with all the other inmates.

"We got a delivery, Eddie," Gage said.

"Not the warden?"

"Fresh meat," Gage said. A voice from a cell somewhere below soared above the rest: Fresh meat.

The excitement began to double, then triple in seconds. The air itself was full of urgency. Electricity stirred the wind with anticipation. Men who busied themselves swabbing the cement walkway, became locked in place, stiffer than any mannequin standing in a department store window. Rapists, drug addicts, and thieves of all sorts pressed their faces against the steel netting. All eyes found the slow walking line of men strolling through the facility and took on a chant filled with as much violence as raw frenzy: Meat. Meat. Meat. Meat.

One by one, the men walked through a dark doorway, a doorway that seemed to transport each prisoner across the threshold from some other realm. First darkness, then a prisoner, the pattern repeated until ten men in orange jumpsuits were marching single-file behind the guard like a horrible game of follow-the-leader. With every stride of the orange brigade, the inmates grew louder, projecting their short, stabbing obscenities at the new additions to the Reclamation facility. As the guard moved ever forward, the men to his rear carried folded wool blankets with outstretched arms. Their palms faced upwards like a picture of Christ, welcoming newcomers into the flock. Metal cups balanced in the center of their undulating bedding. The chant continued: Meat. Meat. Meat. Meat.

"Stop right there," a prison guard demanded. The group's momentum kept them trundling forward a second longer. A few produced a stuttering step, one bounced against another, and all soon stood rigid in place. Each measured a comfortable distance between the other and adjusted until uniformed.

"We will have fun with these ciphers," Eddie said.

"Must we do this with every new arrival?"

"What? It's fun, Saint?" Gage began studying each inmate in line one at a time. The dark side in him relished their fear, their vulnerability. Fear fueled the prison, and a trembling panic went through their muscles. Deep inside, all convicts feared confined spaces—the showering with each other—the aggression, the violence, or the mere threat of it.

"You were in their spot once, was it fun for you?" Gage asked.

"No," Eddie said, his voice quivered from a sudden remembrance of his first night at Reclamation.

"It's always different when it's someone else. Our empathy keeps us human, Eddie. Animals belong in cages, not humans. They are beasts waiting for feeding time—working themselves into a convulsive rage. Look at them out there." Arms jutted from the bars of many cells and lashing out at air. They thrashed their arms in and out of the metal cages like captive chimpanzees. "Don't reduce yourself to that."

"You're right, I'm sorry," Eddie said. A line of fresh meat wavered and seemed to draw-in the taunting voices, shouting in chorus. A separate, menacing evocation rose under the unified wails. The calls were sinister, personal declarations with none of the sport of the prison chant. Isolated voices were promising silent slaughter, submission through sodomy, and acts too violent to consider. The first inmate in the row was shaking like a leaf—Gage saw it right off, recognizing the terror in them all, all except one. Gage's eyes darted to the anomaly in an orange jumpsuit. His fingertips slipped around the bars and squeezed tight enough to send the blood out of his digits. Gage's knuckles curled around the metal like gnarled vines strangling its prey. A single syllable escaped his mouth. "Victor."

From behind the inmates and around the guard, Robert appeared. He adjusted his suit as if he wasn't in prison, but alone in front of a mirror. The simple, confident gesture disquieted the mob, and the chant stopped soon after. Angry shouts continued with Robert reaching for a megaphone—a guard was already handing him.

"I'm Robert Deville, the new warden here at Reclamation," Robert said and waited for the clamor to fade. The guard to Robert's immediate right snatched the megaphone.

"If you don't shut your traps, I will fuck your world up," the guard squealed into the instrument. The threat quieted the inmates.

"Thank you, Jimmy." Robert placed the amplifier close to his lips. "For some of you, I'm here to shield the fragile outside world from you," Robert shuffled down the row of men and leered into several cells, "you have crossed a line, and forgiveness isn't an option. I'm here to give you punishment and," He crossed the walkway and swiveled around to the opposite side, "time, so you can learn how to assimilate into polite society. The statistics tell me many of you will be back in here for another stay." He dropped the megaphone from the edge of his chin. "But, if I rested my career on those discouraging numbers, I wouldn't be able to sleep at night. A small percentage of you will never return. I applaud your resolve if it turns out to be you."

"Screw you," a voice howled in a cell close to Robert and caused his thinking to stall. Jimmy leaned into his warden's ear.

"If they see weakness in you, it will be difficult to maintain order." Robert nodded, and Jimmy trudged to the cell of the offender. He snapped his finger and pointed to the cell. Two other guards removed the prisoner and walked him away.

"Ten days of solitary," Jimmy yelled for all to hear.

"As you can see, I'm a fair man. But I won't tolerate insubordination to authority here in my facility. I think you will find me an amiable guy, and a man you don't want as an enemy. It's your choice which side to deal with." Robert directed the megaphone to the line of new prisoners. "It is my understanding your former warden was a disciplinarian. I think you'll find my methods are much like my predecessor. We differ in one aspect—you cross me, and time in the hole will seem like a picnic compared to the punishment I will hand out." Jimmy took the megaphone and led the warden back through the dark doorway. Another guard brought the prisoners to their new homes. Gage's eyes were a magnet on Victor.

"Who is he, Saint? I've never seen hate in your eyes, not like this," Eddie said.

"He killed my son. His name is Victor," Gage said, choking on the words.

"From the botched robbery?" Gage gave a perfunctory nod, swooning from anger so deep and pure that a shift became visible. His rage rose degree by degree before he could recognize it himself— he was burning out of control. The fundamental change did more than ignite his spirits—it ate away at his sorrow, his pain, and all the things he wanted to forget and never forgive.

"How did he kill your son, Saint?"

"My son needed surgery. My whole reason for the robbery was to save Ryan. Victor killed my partner, stole our shares, and sealed my son's fate."

"Saint, you've done a lot for me. I wouldn't have made it in here without you. I owe my life to you, but killing Victor won't bring your son back." Gage's thoughts skittered along the ridges of his gray matter, embedding fury. He no longer saw Eddie standing in front of his cot, watching him. His remarks slipped over him like water across a car with fresh wax.

"We have to act fast, Eddie," Gage said. Eddie veered to his right and collapsed on the cot next to Gage.

"What we need to do is think this through," Eddie said.

"The next few days, Victor's setting up shop and looking for protection. Not that he needs much," Gage said to a concrete cinder block two feet away.

"You act like this guy will come for you. Do you know that? If you're planning to go all the way…" An absent, distant attention became replenished with a dangerous focus in the time it took the words to fall off Eddie's tongue. Gage threw daggers at his cellmate with a glower issuing a caution.

"I didn't…I didn't mean I wasn't with you in this or whatever," Eddie said.

"I've spent my time in here like a man with a life sentence, a death row inmate treading water until they light me up with juice. But that's not my sentence. There is a higher power controlling my destiny." Gage gazed at Eddie. "There are billions of structures around the world, and someone or something locked the reason for my loss into the same concrete building. I can't say I know a hell of a lot about fate. Still, Eddie, this can't be a coincidence. Can it?" Gage asked, close to tears.

"Uh, no. You're right. It can't be," Eddie said. "I understand what Victor has done to you, and I'm sure it was a large part, but are you looking to hurt someone?" Gage wrung his hands, scraping them together in a furious display of hand washing.

"Victor took away someone I loved, and now he is in my reach. I can make things right for my son." He continued to strangle his hands without thought before looking down at his red blotchy palms.

"Whatever you say, Saint," Eddie said, beaten.

"I have a goal—a reason to live or die."

CHAPTER 7

Jake Shoeman wavered in position, shifting his weight from one foot to the next when the strain became too much. The circumference of his belly hung over his belt in enormous rolls, forming a wave of fat. His shirt rested askew, tucked in, but rotated to the left, forcing the line of buttons into a sharp downward curve toward his right hip. Robert saw all of this from his angle behind his desk and resumed his paperwork. Reginald swept past Jake several times—he was a momentary apparition carrying notarized documents and gone without a word. Jake was a dripping sponge, releasing sweat from every pore, which shone a shiny gleam along his skin.

"You wanted to see me, sir?" Jake asked. Robert never answered and never looked up from his frantic scribbling on a stack of papers. His hand shook, lurching in circular motions, moving a pen to finish his signature.

"I appreciate you waiting around until this late hour, Jake. I've made it my prerogative." Robert paused and raised his head to Jake for the first time. "Mission, that's a better word. Whether you think it's a good thing, I guess time will prove. I'm making it my task to rebuild you. To oversee your every waking moment until you reach the summit of your potential," Robert said, refocusing his attention back to a mountain of pulp where he validated another document with his signature.

"I think I'll call it a day, Mr. Deville," a voice said from behind Jake.

"Thanks for all your help today, Reginald. I couldn't have done it without you," Robert said.

"That is for sure. Night, sir."

"Goodnight," Robert said and looked to the security guard, shaking like a leaf in front of his desk. "At least I don't have to worry about having a yes man." Jake tried on an uncomfortable smile—it didn't fit, and he gave it up. "Back to you, friend. I found the time today to print out our full plan of attack." Robert motioned to the corner of his desk. He repeated his boss's motion before picking the paper up.

"That is your new bible, Jake. I outlined everything you can eat, the portion amount, and mealtimes. From now on, I want you to spend your lunch hour in the Reclamation weight room. If you don't meet a two percent reduction every Friday afternoon, I'll reduce the portions instead." He gulped with Robert spotting the reaction. "Think of this situation as a promotion, if you will. I'm transferring you in here to become a part of my security team. As of now, your life is in my hands." Robert ignored Jake's terrified expression. "Dismissed," Robert said. Jake walked out of the office, leaving Robert to stare at an empty doorway until he shuffled across the room in aggravation and shut the door himself. The doorknob snapped, and the mechanism clicked with a vibration moving through his hand. On the other side of the room sat his desk. A desk lamp threw a meager amount of light, but the grains of the wood still seemed to dance. The grains veered back and forth in jagged curves, and coming alive with a fiery illusion, whooshing from one edge of the desktop to the other.

Robert watched the orange flames with transfixed fascination. The air itself melted into an electric vitality that first burned his nostrils and then filled his lungs with a sickening acrid aroma. An unsavory poison flavor rose in his mouth. He swished his tongue against his cheeks and teeth like a broom sweeping the cobwebs out of an attic. The taste remained as potent as ever. He lumbered back to his emblazoned desk in a fog. He placed his hands flat on his desk, then snatched them away. The flaming illusion made by the lamp was a strange reality. Warmth rose on his palms into a crescendo of agonizing pain. He withdrew his hands once more.

"What the hell?" he murmured. He plodded around the desk, watching the light change, and a shifting flame rose and dove with the angle of the light. A gust of fire, as if ignited by the wood just underneath, soared higher than the rest. The fire, joined by another, and then another until the center of the desk was ablaze. Robert's eyes gained another sight through his foggy seeing. The papers sat in the center of his desk were still there, but not there. He recognized their squared outline under the undulating flames that became a python of ardency. The urge to put his fingers atop the wooden pyre seized his senses.

He was a man along for the ride, he liked the ride, and there was lustful freedom stroking his insides. It was underneath his skin starting at his ankles, but it was soon on the move darting up his legs, with a slight twinge or tickle as it skimmed past his knees. He wanted to close his eyes, allow the seductive sensation to take over, and couldn't. His eyes wouldn't budge from the desk and its fiery display. A sound ascended the empty room. At first, the sound seemed to come from a speaker. The noise came in and out as if someone put a heavy, wool blanket over a radio and removed it several times like a modern-day smoke signal.

Robert's concentration on the desk grew more critical. He moved to the front of the Tigerwood desk and sat behind it as a man might sit in a jet fighter seat for the first time, looking at the dials, controls, the flashing lights, and making sense of none of it. He guessed the clacking was more remote, a trick of acoustics sweeping reverberations close in from farther away. His eyes were stinging from the lack of moisture, but he believed it was the flames jumping from wood grain to wood grain.

Robert redoubled an effort to shut his eyelids and couldn't—eyes stuck open by industrial springs. He collected his thoughts, focusing them on a fine keenness. Tears formed from his ducts when the clacking returned. A sound, once separated by space, refortified itself into a louder and bolder echo vibrating in everything around him. It was in the walls, the floor—even the light buzzed and then incorporated the clacking into its wiring. The phantom sound whirled around Robert in a vortex biting at his ears like claws. It drew closer and closer, spinning faster and faster.

A ravenous tornado spun, circling him, and never relenting. He arched his neck to the ceiling to watch the funnel rotating around him, but nothing was there. His mouth dropped open and formed a horrifying oval, teeth glimmering, and his tongue scraped against the roof of his mouth. A stark recognition jolted him upright into his chair. The rattling sound was drifting from his open mouth. A terror rose in his throat before he spoke. The rattling, emanating from within, was lucid, more precise like the rattling of chains.

"Chains," he uttered alone in his office. Just below, clinking chains were faint but growing strength. Robert sensed it coming, and it terrified him for the first time in his life. He sat behind a burning desk, lost in a spiraling wall of resonance, and becoming a living antenna. *Antenna, for what?* A dim chatter grew and mingled with chains—chains dragged across a surface. Robert opened his jaw further, and the chatter amplified out, gliding on the air. A child's voice, low and pathetic, rose in a heaving whimper. The child emitted a sick breathless cry following every drag of the length of the chain. There was something else, Robert strained to hear it. His eyes flew wide. There was scratching.

"Mommy," a voice cried into the wind. The soprano voice, nearing a falsetto, was pitiful and begging. Robert pictured the child scratching at the walls, his escape hindered by the metal restraints. He smelled urine and feces that lay next to the small boy.

"What's happening?" Robert asked. The metal chains clinked and with it a clawing more desperate.

"Mommy, Mommy, Mommy." The wail of the child was too brutal for Robert to endure. He wrenched his lips together like the gradual turning of a vice, clamped his hand over his mouth the stop the torturous cries. The screaming went unnoticed, with the sound muffled as if the child was underwater. *No more.* Although he no longer heard the boy in the room, he was alive and well in his head, banging and bashing the walls of his brain. He didn't want it to go on—it couldn't. *It's breaking my mind.* Just when he felt torn apart from the inside, it stopped. The flames surrounded the front of the desk, parted like a fluffy dissolving cloud. After the wavy haze dissipated, a rectangular drawer glimmered of brilliant Tigerwood. Robert extended a hand, trying to pull the drawer to him by the handle. His fingertips touched the desk drawer, and the fiery haze broke up and fell away like a wilted, dried plant, and then disappeared.

Robert, stupefied by the episode, sat holding the handle and wondered if it ever happened. He yanked on the handle, the wood gave under his strength, but it didn't open. A metal envelope opener glittered under the desk lamp, and Robert grabbed it, marveling at how his mind was his own again. He loved the desk and didn't want to damage it, but he needed to know what was hiding in the drawer.

Robert inserted the sharp edge of the opener between the top of the drawer and below the desk drawer encasement. With a quick, violent thrust, the metallic opener pried and snapped a concealed latch. It crackled and buckled under the pressure with the drawer sliding half free of its prison. Robert slid it the rest of the way, revealing a book. That was too easy a description for what lay dormant for who knew how long. A better description was a bible with rich leather, a gold-trimmed binder, and thick pages. There was writing on the front of the large book's cover: *Joseph's Diary*

He touched the cover with his hands and expected it to jolt him with electricity—it didn't. Raising the former warden's journal, he placed it onto his lap and opened the cover of the diary.

It started with dreams. When I arrived at work that day, I was preparing myself for the fires needing put out. Life in the prison involved thousands of hours of boredom followed by minutes of frantic terror. I learned to judge the prisoner's mental state with all the deep interest of a voyeur watching a runaway fire with its dangerous tendrils reaching out from its edges. Waiting for when the firefighter might look away or pop out for a smoke and in that desperate, fragile moment, strike. The analogy of a firefighter was the best description through the years and the most misunderstood by my staff. Fire prevention, as I have lectured so many times, is the primary task.

My staff has a bad habit of becoming lax—with the prisoners, and careless with the procedures. Prisoners need dominating—they need it the way a child doesn't know they crave discipline and calls out to their parents for punishment. Keeping an inmate inside the Reclamation confines goes far beyond mending a broken fence to keep the clientele from blowing into the wind. A more subtle hand is necessary, and a softer touch is hard to find with most of my guards. There is a high percentage of the guards using brutal force against the prisoners as a first resort instead of the last.

When I made it into my office, my staff descended upon me with a frightening fervor making the blood in my veins circulate faster from my apprehension. I tried to calm Roger Witmar, the associate warden, and the most subdued of my staff. There was something volatile in the air that day—it was thick with a congealing fear we all breathed in through the lungs and stuck to the capillaries decaying everything from the inside. With every breath, the body was more contaminated. I focused my eyes on Roger for the first time and studied the tiny triangles that formed the edges of his mouth. Roger earned those lines through intelligent leadership and patient diplomacy. He is my most trusted ally here, and I could not function without him.

His expression sent me reeling, and I wondered what transformed an always-amiable fellow into the thoughtful wretch shaking and quivering in his skin. That's when he started to babble. He explained how the entire prison dreamed in unison the night before. I consider myself to be of average intelligence, but my pistons weren't firing in the right order just then. It was as if Roger was a talking dog that, moments earlier, broke out of a science lab. He needed to slow down, and I instructed him to take a deep breath—he listened, followed my suggestion, and began again.

Roger sucked air in, stuttering gasps, reminiscent of a child recovering from a tantrum. I watched his chest as it heaved spastically up and down. He closed his eyes, relaxed his posture, and trained his dull, gray eyes on me. What's wrong, Roger? I asked, and for the first time this morning, I wished I called in sick.

Roger said that a rash of dreams spread through the facility. A bleak and murky change crept in and around us. I sat there, turning his words over and over in my head and wondered what they meant. The idea was too alien, too abstract, and far too frightening to accept at face value. Roger knew at once his declaration didn't hit home and tried another tactic. The inmates shared a vision the night before, he explained. The dream was of fire and a dark man. I asked him if it stormed during the evening because I've understood thunderstorms caused mass disruptions in sleep. He assured me of no such weather. I was already working on my next theory when he started again. He began pacing around my desk with me behind it like a trapped animal seeking the exit.

After a moment, Roger got to the gist announcing to me that Anthony, a guard from the night shift, shared the vision. Anthony entered, squatted on the edge of a nearby chair, and rubbed his eyes with nervous energy. When he started to speak, his frame was rigid, frozen in place against the chair's back. Soon the simple act of talking seemed to thaw him. His body loosened as if he turned a pressure valve, releasing inhibition at the same time. He admitted he was at fault. It seemed he fell asleep while on duty. The occurrence happened after midnight. Sweat ran from his scalp down into one wild brow.

The vision started in a farmhouse—a farmhouse in decay. Shutters hung sideways, tottering on a few precarious nails. Aged paint puckered and crackled on the wood siding, leaving the facade of the structure resembling a sad clown with drying make-up. A screen door, warped from endless summer sunshine, swung in the breeze. The metal netting of the screen door escaped its frame and showed several snags across the front like the runs on a nylon stocking.

A hand seized the door handle, pulling it out into the night, hinges screeched with anger until he was inside, staring down a hallway. Antique farming tools rested in a skittering pattern up and down the hall walls. His footfalls reverberated on the worn wood planks of the old farm home as the intruder focused his sight to his shuffling feet and a butcher's knife. The blade glistened in the moonlight even as a dull red film stained the sharpened edge. A streak of blood jutted from the razor's edge and was the symbol of violence and mayhem. Glimmering metal swung, causing a whooshing sound accompanying the hollow echo of his footsteps.

The corridor vanished as a living room, ballooned all around him. A fireplace, nestled behind two armchairs, projected glinting red embers of a dying fire. Flames licked and devoured the remaining timber, struggling to stay alive. An animalistic urge sprung from the intruder and seemed to seep from his pores. Although no sense of his rage was recognizable, a raw emotion rose to the surface and became noticeable in his locomotion. He moved like a man whose errand was of the utmost importance as if it was necessary, brutal, or not.

Except for the shadows from a waning fire, the living room was empty. The intruder loved the chase, allowing the moment to linger if possible, prolonging it until the sensation filled his stomach and chest, and finished in his heart. His pursuit turned from a primal comatose into a convulsing fury when he found the living room empty.

Reborn by his visceral anticipation, the intruder prodded up a staircase, leaning his free hand on the rickety railing, it dipped somewhat from his weight. He plodded with care on each wooden step like a minesweeper testing every inch of a path that lay ahead. Creaks explode as maturing nails holding the step planks down moaned and awakened from their peaceful slumber.

When the intruder reached the head of the stairs, his fury was already retreating into a meager simmer. His plans, however, remained the same. A fist gripped the handle of his knife, turning it around in the moon's rays and gauging its heft. With every deliberate motion, slower than the next, the intruder's impatience won out over his skulking expectation.

He entered the small bedroom and at once noticed the sports heroes pinned to every free space on the wall. The bed was empty and still made up from that morning. The deserted scene affected him. His heart fluttered, not unlike the stories people relayed to him of mourning a significant loss. He missed his chance to deal with the boy, and there was no way to avoid the detail.

He moved to the next room, which was the master, and walked on the floorboards with caution waiting for their squeaky emanation—there was none. Two forms, one large and a form much tinier, lay next to each other in an oversized sleigh bed, extending upward and bent toward the wall. The view of the vulnerable couple renewed his urges and ignited his warm muscles to scuttle forward.

The intruder straddled the smallest form like a thoughtful young lover might, pressing his groin against her belly. He understood the urgency of acting fast but relished the danger in procrastination and thrilled in the situation's lunacy. The woman began to stir, which meant a death sentence to her man lying next to her. The intruder slapped a palm over her mouth hard enough to cause excess skin to puff and fold over his grip.

Eyelids flew open, and blue irises searched into the darkness for an explanation. A muffled murmur screamed through the intruder's hand. He shook, lifted the knife skyward, and pushed the steel into her companion's neck just below his Adam's apple. He drove the blade deep enough that the tip became buried in the mattress while the hilt sunk into the victim's fleshy skin. Choking gurgles filled the room, and blood poured from the wounds like a butchered pig. The woman's eyes began to figure out the fate of her companion. Tears filled her eyes.

The intruder removed the knife and watched the man grapple with his mortal wound. He turned to the woman as her mate was already drifting into the quiet calm. The intruder wanted so much to release his hold over her mouth and let her screams fill the night air, burning his ears, sharpening his wits. She was the appetizer and not the main course.

The little girl down the hall was the prize and the reason for the visit. And the potential fulfillment of the urge. He held the mother tight against the bed, aware of her sweat beginning to saturate the sheets. The smell of her sweat flung him into a swoon as cavernous as he had ever experienced, and still, he *fought to pull it back. She wasn't the one, and the charade needed to end before he went too far.*

The intruder snatched his hand away from the mother's mouth as if it became an oven burning and replaced the hand with his mouth. Her eyes went round. With a delicate touch, he assured and projected serenity, he slid the knife under her chin and skimmed it back away, tearing at the soft skin of her neck.

The intruder pressed harder, his mouth against hers—he tasted the blood expelled from her throat to her lips. He wanted to savor her last breath, and he did. In an instant, he was off the mother and stumbling down the hall, still lost in an enchanted moment where her dwindling energy intermingled with his enormous appetite. The best lay ahead and his feet no longer touched the floor. He floated toward the little girl's bedroom.

Anthony stopped speaking. The story was far from over—I guessed the direction the story was going, and being honest, I didn't want to hear the rest. Anthony leaned back in the grips of some inner turmoil as if the simple act of retelling the dream robbed all the energy from him. The spent guard leveled his eyes to me, and I saw for the first time his caginess in describing the vision. I asked him if he saw the prowler raiding the farmhouse during the dream.

Anthony was sure I could not have misunderstood, but I did it seemed. He carried a sad expression, but I didn't detect disheartenment in his tone. Determined to be as transparent as possible, Anthony let me know he wasn't watching the intruder during these acts—he was the intruder, seeing the world through his eyes. Anthony was a slave to the killer's urges, dark preoccupations, and a sick hierarchy of fantasies. Anthony explained how he tried, many times without success, to shift his eyes away from the murders.

I gathered he would never be the same, and the little girl's finality was a horror beyond anything he would have thought possible. Burning in his brain was the child's last moment. Along with damn near all the inmates in Reclamation.

At the start of Anthony's confession, my first impulse told me to reprimand him for falling asleep on the job, but after, I supposed he received more punishment than I could ever deliver. He walked to the door trembling as I muttered how I wished I knew who the farmhouse intruder was. Anthony froze in place, turned back to me, and said two words before leaving the office: Damon Torinson.

The name itself shot shivers down my spine and not because I knew his name, the truth is I didn't. Nor was I familiar with Damon's crimes. I didn't believe the entire facility could share in a collective dream like some strange story from a Twilight Zone episode. I thought it was a case of plain hysteria. Mania was far more frequent than most wanted to accept.

I thought the vision was nothing more than a campfire tale skipping through the facility to pass the time. Tall tales are an essential part of the fabric of prison life. Nobody hints at this in books or movies, and as far as I could tell, James Cagney never ran a sewing circle dishing gossip to other inmates before he screamed, top of the world, Ma. The fact, however, remained—these boys in here spin a yarn a mile long and say it with a straight face while doing it. The nonsense sometimes swallowed up my guards, and it distressed me. I guess that's how hysteria works, like a contagion.

My first order of business was to investigate if a prisoner named Damon Torinson existed, then throw away the premise of a malevolent creature once and for all. I didn't expect to come across the notorious man in my records, and if I hadn't, the facility could go back to their normal daily life. That wasn't the case, and normalcy would become a precious commodity. It seemed like before I put forth any effort toward finding Damon Torinson, there he was in a file, picture and all, staring at me with gloom behind his eyes. I refused to fall for believing in a supernatural boogie man.

I read the details of his conviction the way I often do when I must deal with a behavioral incident. But my heart skipped a beat—I wanted to toss the file away and pretend I never found him. He was a death row prisoner, convicted of murdering a family in a small southern Ohio town, a farming community. Damon Torinson slaughtered Betty and Eddie Williams while they lay helpless in bed. He cut both throats. Soon after, Damon ventured into their daughter's room. The girl's name was Cheryl Williams. Damon took his time with her, assaulting her throughout the night and into the morning hours. Damon drained her blood and continued a sexual assault after her death.

The descriptions were well beyond horrific, and worse still, the story was true. I was about to close the file when another sentence captured my attention. The record stated a son survived the ordeal. Reginald Williams spent a night at a friend's house and avoided the savagery his family received. I couldn't imagine what it was like to be the boy, now an orphan. My heart went out to him, and for the loss, he was enduring.

My stomach twisted into knots as I traveled to the highest level of Reclamation—it was there the death row inmates awaited the spark from a chair and the sweet escape from their horrible acts. Roger, along with two guards, ambled every inch of the steel monstrosity with me. My lone thought was protecting him from the awful details of Damon's misdeeds for the sake of his daughters, Tracy and Miranda. Roger was a dear friend of mine, and I didn't want the tragedy to touch his family. I stopped him halfway to Damon Torinson and begged him away.

To his credit, Roger protested the way any self-respecting associate warden might do. He relented to my overriding authority and waited while I journeyed onward. As we parted ways, I observed in him a weakness, a vulnerability somehow eluding my usual mental perceptions. The job didn't agree with Roger's personality—he accepted his position out of friendship, our friendship. I felt sad, deflated, and cut off as I walked away toward Damon.

I listened to the loud clap of my footfalls on the metal walkway and regretted sending Roger off. When we reached

Damon's cell, one guard found the keyhole with his key, and the other grasped the cell door, heaved it out, and open. The wind whipped next to my face as the door swung outward, displacing air. Before I laid eyes on the prisoner, a guard ordered Damon to his feet in a gruff voice demanding obedience. I entered the cell with Damon raising his head. I recalled his eyes from his photo, the way they appeared to hold the secrets of death.

Standing a few feet from him, I saw death emanating from the rest of him as if a fatal virus started in the eyes and spread throughout his structure and into the core within. I wanted to project power and dominance, yet when I fixed my eyes upon him, I realized my artifice wouldn't hold up for too long. Damon's eyes contained something else I didn't understand. My mind, trapped in a thick and arresting bog, caused me to spin my wheels with every thought. The mood persisted until Damon Torinson spoke to me. His tone wasn't what I expected if I expected anything at all.

His voice was melodic, soothing, and hypnotic. The voice dug into my brain and calmed my soul. My brainwave sputtered, then an image so brutal and so primal came into my mind. The picture was of a snake lulling a mouse with its black, dead eyes, its long cylindrical head swaying as if the breeze alone was holding its frame erect. The mouse iced over, shivering in a mass of furry trepidation. My train of thought derailed, and I reasserted myself through forceful confidence. A learned trait I discovered on the job some years back, and now I slipped the confidence on like a glove.

I took the offensive with Damon and asked him if he remembered Cheryl Williams. No reaction. Deciding on a less subtle course, my hand glided a manila folder from under my arm and let its contents scatter across the floor. Damon soaked-in the picture of Cheryl's mutilated body, and I watched it all.

Reaching down, I plucked the vilest specimen from the evidential file between my fingers and handed it to Damon. I guessed he would not take it, but he did, he repositioned it in his hands, and I waited, and waited. I watched his plastic expression for minutes. Damon viewed the nasty little scene in the photo, absorbing every nuance.

I needed to see his face falter in front of me—I wanted to witness the thin, yellow vines of guilt strangling his heart and tugging at his countenance. He said he remembered Cheryl's smell. I looked at his face, and it never twisted from regret—no walls went up, a barrier kept his emotions from spilling out into his prison cell. I knew he had no defense against his feelings because they didn't exist.

My mind shaped a moment of clarity—there was more than just death in his pupils, inside lived wisdom. I can't explain how I knew a thing like that or how it was even possible, but there it was right in front of me. My shell melted, and I articulated all my fears and all my outrage for humanity in a single, razor-sharp question. Who are you? I asked and heard the shudder in my voice. He spoke almost too quiet to hear. I'm the Devil.

CHAPTER 8

Cars of every shape and size bustled in both directions on I-70. Jenny watched the freeway traffic like bees scurrying to and from their hives. The display filled Jenny with a gloomy sympathy toward drivers showing no outward awareness of the surrounding strangers. *Alone on an island,* Jenny thought. She set her cruise control at sixty-five miles an hour and joined the drones.

Jenny caught reflections in the rearview mirror, first her own, then her son, Zack, who was scribbling on construction paper in the backseat with hands moving a blurry speed. He cradled an orange crayon between his small thumb and forefinger. The crayon, worn to the nub, and jutting from his fingers, smeared the greasy wax to create his masterpiece. "How are you doing back there, sweetheart?" Jenny asked. Zack broke his absorption in his sketch—tiny hands halted their fervent labor, and he peered up to meet his mother's eyes. The connection was short, lasting a second or two, but it was what Jenny needed. Her concern for Zack's recent state of mind started to bubble at breakfast, and minutes before dropping him off to Morris, the ex-husband, her concern began to boil into anxiety.

Liam leaned into the passenger seat and shared a pregnant glance with Jenny. Neither would have said anything in front of Zack, but the subject didn't call for a complicated dialogue. Zack fell into a disturbing spell. Watching her son in pain made her want to cry, it made her want to pull the vehicle over onto the berm, leap from the car, and with raised arms scream to the heavens. Instead, she took the Hamilton Road exit and headed right into Morris's neighborhood. Although the streets were well-known to Jenny, with them came the dark memories of living with Morris Chaney.

"Why would you name streets after a fairytale?" Liam asked, with a smile plastered across his face. Jenny wasn't in the mood for one of Liam's inane rhetorical questions, but she responded after a glimpse of her agitated son in the back. She needed the diversion.

"When they built these homes in the fifties and sixties, they always used a theme to name the streets." *Robin Hood is a good a theme as any,* she thought. "We have Sherwood middle school to your right," she said in her best tour guide voice, "named after the infamous forest of the prince of thieves."

"There's Nottingham Road," Liam shrieked like a game show contestant. "Do you know where the name came from, Zack?" Liam asked, trying to get the somber boy involved. Liam looked toward the back seat twice. Zack never broke his crayon concentration. "The Sheriff of Nottingham. You remember the bad guy from the Robin Hood story, don't you?" There was still no answer from the cheap seats. The car motored past side streets, cul-de-sacs, and courts in a blur with Liam calling out the names as they went.

"Marion, Arrow, Friar Tuck, Huntly. Why did they use Huntly Drive?" Liam asked. Jenny shrugged her shoulders.

"Beats me," she said and turned down Huntly Drive toward her ex, Morris. She cast her memory back with the sight of the older homes—spider-webbed pavement sealer, reaching out with asphalt hands on the surface of most driveways, and the solitary disregard a mature community alone provided. Lights out—curtains drawn, and eyes always turned away whenever Morris would show a moment of violence. There was never a sympathetic look at the bruises or even a considerate question prying into the desperate situation of a mother and her young child.

Often, Morris's drunken stupor continued onto the front yard for the world to witness, and still nothing. Entrance doors shut behind their screen doors—windows closed on the muggy, summer days to drown the shouting. The street locked itself down like a seaside community preparing for a storm. They battened down the hatches, reduced the sails, and ignored a small boy at a screen door crying for his tattered mother, a mother fighting for her life on the little front lawn. *They ignored. All of them*, she thought with bile rising in her throat. Her disgust was full in her eyes, and it spilled over into her focus. Her fingers forced a death grip on the steering wheel.

Jenny's vehicle trundled past familiar facades, lackluster automobiles, and over-grown lawns. The street looked to be in the last throes of its own dismal, decaying swan song. As if the universe forgot about the quiet, apathetic street. Karma, in its divine wisdom, had something to say concerning her neighbor's silent avoidance. But she felt no celestial touch, just the sad urging in her own heart to forgive. She would never forget. How could she? Still, logic whispered forgiving might put to rest the pain, vanquish the microscopic hatred that ate at her innards.

The same provoking anger that warmed her belly spread to her chest and ignited the promised deception of tranquility. Jenny knew better even as she relented to fury's pleasing black tentacles. She supposed absolution was a possibility for some. *For everyone? Would* she allow Morris to slither off the hook? Morris Chaney, the once brutal, and the forever smashed off his ass would never change. Captured in time at the crest of his consumption, Morris seemed preserved there in his entire wretched libation.

All of Jenny's inner squabbles were for nothing, and she grasped the finality of her thought. *You can't forgive someone who hasn't changed.*

The car pulled into the driveway of a modest home with the same high grass growing as tall as the lawn on either side. Her nerves were a bundle of clawing, slicing apprehension. Robert handled this part of her life, and she handed it over—no remorse for the loss. Jenny wished he was here a great deal, wished she never again saw the house she once called home, and didn't want to lay eyes on the reason for her high medical bills, mental or otherwise. And she hated turning her precious, fragile boy over to him so often. The very idea of entrusting Zack to Morris was maddening, defying all logic, and bordering on insanity.

"You want me at the door with you?" Liam stuttered. Jenny shook him off straight away.

"I can handle this. I'll be a second," she said. Before Liam made and argument, and she didn't think he would, Jenny was out of the car, helping Zack out of his seat. Zack carried his overnight bag like a soldier heading to war. The front door, with its red paint fading to pink, it was a color she chose years back. It now resembled a pink, mouth waiting to chew, waiting to devour. Halfway up the cracked blacktop driveway, the pink door disappeared inward. Like a parlor trick, Morris stood in the doorway, with an evil grin promising endless grief for her. She tried on a smile, and it didn't fit, didn't come close to fitting, so she abandoned it right off.

"There's my boy," Morris screamed from the mouth of the entryway. The combined smell of beer and liquor was in her nostrils and heading to her brain. Morris was too far away to reek of the concoction, but the odor came to her from memory as if the sight of him set in motion a strong Pavlovian response. Morris's eyes took Jenny in—he savored the rarity of her bringing the boy alone.

Standing on Morris's driveway—exposed, aware of her vulnerability, she wanted to cover her body with hands and forearms. The home's greedy tongue reached out when Morris drove the screen door open and leaned his elbow on its wood frame, both propping the door and balancing his weight at the same time. Morris's gesture was majestic as if he was a doorman at an aristocratic hotel on Park Avenue receiving elite guests instead of engaging his ex-wife. Jenny was a lion tamer pushing her son toward the lion and hoping for the best.

"Hello, Morris," Jenny said. "It's been a while." Morris smiled a terrible smile. He bared his teeth with lips seeming to hold his porcelain captive rather than cover them. He beamed his yellowed nicotine grin in her direction as if it still held the same potent masculine allure.

"Jenny lover," he said and scanned her body, "you look very edible."

"You started drinking early, I see," Jenny said before she could stop herself. But it was too late. Her indiscretion was out there, flailing about like an octopus. Eight arms and oblivious to what each other was doing. There was no excuse—she knew his triggers when he drank better than anyone. Had the Morris Chaney boot camp been so long ago, she didn't remember the rules? They were second nature, as engrained as understanding the danger in throwing gasoline onto an open flame.

But a revolt came alive in her, reared its selfish little head, and disappeared as fast as it arrived, leaving her alone to deal with the fallout. Robert was to blame—if he were there, he would have taken Morris's head off for looking at her wrong—she had no doubts. Except Robert wasn't there, just Morris, the snake was lying in wait. He remained limp and docile when Robert would drop off Zack. He bided his time, put on his plastic face for Robert, the officer of the law, and waited for the opportunity, an excuse.

Jenny recognized her lapse, and in a split-second, she prepared herself for the brunt of the penalty. She already saw Morris's edifice alter, shifting. His demeanor summoned those black clouds, the same haze encircled their marriage, as if no time passed since their difficult divorce. Difficult? The word gyrated in her mind until it lost all meaning. Calling the strenuous period in her life that drained her money, time, resolve, willpower, and faith in the courts difficult, was maddening. Morris's Cheshire grin receded to a sneer—lips parted—yellow teeth gnashed in a sick impersonation of quiet civility.

"Hi, son. I'm glad you're here," Morris said to Zack in a way a children's television show host might speak to a child. "I got a lot planned for you, little buddy." His words squeezed their way out of his mouth, sliding off the tip of his tongue, and plunking onto her son like green toxic waste. Morris opened the door further for Zack to enter, and he did it without another glance back. Jenny watched as her son ducked under an arm clutching the screen door and watched him disappear into the menacing black background beyond.

"Zack. Wait, Zack. Come here." Fear stole her breath and tickled her ribs like a child dragging a stick across a picket fence. An insane thought came to her. *What if I never see him again?* The house with the faded red door swallowed up her **pride,** as she stood watching it happen. "Zack…" The small boy trotted back into the light and stood on the edge of a fractured concrete porch, repaired in several spots.

Zack was there waiting, and the color came back to the world for Jenny. "I love you very, very much. I'll be seeing you soon, and I want you to remember," Jenny lowered her voice so that Zack alone benefited, "I'm only a phone call away if you feel uncomfortable or scared about anything, anything at all. Okay?" Jenny waited a long time for Zack to nod, and she would have stayed there until he did. She hugged and kissed him, and again he vanished through the dark doorway.

She wasn't sure why she questioned Zack, except she wanted to protect him from harm. What worried her most, what jabbed cold blades into her skin, was the passive way that Zack walked in and out of the house. The image of a paralyzed mouse, too frightened to move from the snake's advances, popped into her head. With Zack inside, Morris altered his expression like someone pulls a lever, melting his bogus front. The transition was so smooth, so effortless, and long forgotten. It recurred rapidly enough to seize her chest for protection.

"Jenny Chaney," Morris said, spitting out the words like a mouthful of putrid food.

"My name isn't Chaney anymore. I was never happier to get rid of anything in my life, besides you," she said and wondered if any backpacker who happened across a hungry bear and stood their ground survived. She was skeptical and flashed her uneasiness to Morris.

"You thought you'd take away everything from me, and I was just going to take it." Morris let go of the screen door to crash shut with a loud bang. It bounced off the frame and repeated the clap before settling motionless. Morris was a bear lurching forward—his claws sunk into Jenny's sweater tightening the fabric around her body, compressing her breasts. Her heart beat faster, and she recognized her pulse thumping in her constrained chest. Morris's paws scrambled from the folds of the sweater to the meat of her shoulders, digging into the skin. She winced from the pain and sensed warming between her legs.

"I own you, Jenny. You're mine if I say so. You hear me?" His hands moved down her arm, applying the same force. She wanted to grind her crotch on top of his knee and punch him in the face to light his fire—and enrage him to the point of yanking her into the house. Jenny imagined him ripping her clothes off, tearing at her delicate skin with his nails to manage the task, and envisioned his throbbing manhood stabbing at her loins before ripping its way inside her. She pictured herself biting his lip until warm copper dripped into her mouth. The hatred taste of liquor and sweat would fuse into the highest level of fantastic shame.

Liam shoved Morris back on his heels. The push wasn't hard, and his act of aggression was feeble, but it got the reaction he sought.

Morris pivoted on unstable footing, zeroing in on his prey with Jenny already coming around, the spell broken. A chubby, disheveled man stood upright as if an electric current ran through his spine. The hairs of Liam's beard curled upward and plunged downward, giving him an unkempt appearance that, combined with his greasy blond hair, gave him the look of a gentle vagabond.

"Think you can put your hands on me, faggot?" Morris edged closer to Liam, reached his fingers into the husky man's hair, and clasped his hands around a tangle of locks. "I heard you like the touch of a man," Morris said and slapped Liam across the face with a dull thud as skin hit skin. Liam's head flew back with a snap but held tight by Morris's firm clench on his mane. His facial expression showed his frazzled reality, eyes ajar showing the terror of helplessness.

He was powerless to resist Morris's whim, under his complete control, and the prospect petrified him. Liam was no stranger to a letdown—to being dominated or even scorned by others who objected to his lifestyle. Still, his detractors were far away voices, passing distasteful murmurs that faded into quiet denial. Morris was a different story—he was a different animal built for chaos. He embodied the lingering traditions that fed on hate, fed on weakness, and fed on fear. Morris wasn't an elusive voice that harassed from the divide of a parking lot. He was in his face bending Liam's will with his own.

Liam shifted his bulky frame and attempted to overpower Morris with his sheer weight alone, and for a brief, hopeful instant, he thought he could. Morris, the more agile of the two, rotated Liam's arm in a circle and twisted his limb until it ended flush with his plump back. He replaced his hand on Liam's scalp, this time from the back, and yanked with all his strength.

Liam fell to the ground like a rag doll missing a corner of the cement step by an inch and tumbling his large body into awkward revolutions. When he found himself sprawled on the lawn, Liam arched his neck with no fight left in his eyes. As soon as Liam fell, Jenny was tugging at his shoulder, bringing him to his feet and leading him to the passenger side of her Jeep Cherokee. Liam, reduced to a mindless invalid, couldn't open the door without help from his friend. Morris watched all of this with detached interest until Jenny closed Liam inside the vehicle and headed for the driver's side.

"If you think this is over, you're crazy," Morris said. Jenny knew more conflict lay ahead. She knew it would escalate, and a part of her was tired of running from a bully. The concern crushing down on her was her son in the lion's den, inside enemy territory. She had enough of Morris Chaney for one day and decided on the lone option left to her in a hopeless situation. She raised a hand, lifted her middle finger, and smiled. The gesture was juvenile, immature, but felt good as she piled into the Jeep and pulled out of her former house of horrors.

The Jeep sped past parked cars, leashed dogs, and swaying trees to produce a swirl of images that left Liam nauseous. He breathed deep through his mouth and clenched his jaw as warm saliva began pooling under his tongue into a threatening, suffocating choke. Jenny thrashed and batted the steering wheel—it shook and recoiled from the impassioned blows. The impact started a fire in her palm that stretched to her elbow and sent another burning twinge to her shoulder around the area where Morris's meat hooks dug deep.

"That son of a bitch," Jenny said. Her pounding hand bounced off the controls much harder than planned and with it a numbing ache that cautioned a limit. "I'm so sorry, Liam, he has no right to hurt you like that. It means everything—you trying to defend me," Jenny gripped the roundness of the wheel, and wrung it like a neck, Morris's neck, "but that bastard." Liam veered his head away from the changing scenery outside his window and concentrated on the still dashboard. The rising and diving of his queasy stomach ebbed until his breathing became more typical. "Are you okay, Liam?" Jenny asked. The saccharine quality of her concern was jarring in its sincerity. His eyes tingled as he tried directing his sight to his long-time friend. Liam forced his eyelids open, but the merging of emotion along with the air's drying touch on his corneas set off their defense mechanism. His eyelids folded shut, and the burning sting caressed his sorrow, engulfing him in the gloom.

"I'm so useless," Liam sputtered, "I could just kill myself." The dam, already cracked, surged forth its deluge of hysterical crying. The ferocity of his bawling, at the onset, equaled and overtook his saline flow of tears. "Pathetic, pathetic, pathetic," he pronounced like a machine gun in rapid succession.

Liam's unexpected, miserable cries startled Jenny and came close to piloting her off the street and onto a lawn. The front-right tire hopped the curb and ran along the concrete rim before dipping down and toppling back onto even asphalt. The thud jolted the car as a fire hydrant emerged inches next to the curb. A few more inches to the right would have separated the bumper with its protruding yellow snout. Jenny pulled the wheel, straightened the car, and then let out a scream after the crisis was over.

"Shit, that was close," Jenny said. She gave Liam a fleeting glance and decided that he was too far inside himself to appreciate the narrow escape. "Hey, darling. It's okay. It wasn't your job to fight that jerk-off. Calm down. Okay?" His howling persisted, but her words would penetrate the dark cave he hid from the world. "Please calm down, Liam. You're freaking me out."

"Me sticking around does nobody any good," he said between weeps and sniffles.

"Stop right there. You know how much I hate it when you talk like that. Do you have any idea what I would have to endure without you?" Liam shook with a hopeful expression creeping onto his face. "I would have to deal with my mother at dinner tomorrow night. Is that what a real friend should do, leave me to fend off the dragon lady by myself?"

"No," he said with sarcasm and smiled.

"Good. You can keep me company while my mother blathers the night away to her beloved Robert." The invitation was the first lifeline that came to mind, but the more she considered the ruse, the more it made sense. Reassuring Liam was not Jenny's favorite pastime, she hated the task, but it was a necessary part of their friendship. At any moment, Liam might need gentle coaxing back away from a ledge, and she would step up to keep her friend chugging and plugging along. *He would do the same for me.*

When Morris was at his worst, dragging Jenny and Zack to the brink, Liam was there. He was always listening and still waiting for his chance to step up. Most times, even before she knew the situation was dire. Besides, Liam's cutting stopped two years ago, and that event seemed impossible to overcome, and she didn't want to revisit a blackness so consuming. A phantom pain ripped into her shoulder, and she suffered Morris's clench all over again. Her mind drifted back to the compelling urge to straddle her ex-husband. The appalling memory sent blood rushing to her pubic area, inciting her again. The filthy fantasy washed over and made the hollow in her belly shudder.

"How about a distraction?" she asked. Jenny placed a finger on a radio knob and tweaked the controls. A newscaster's voice crackled to life with first a waning weather report and then transitioning into a local Amber alert. The broadcaster repeated the story of a missing boy who vanished a week earlier. A radio voice described the child's appearance right down to the clothes he was last seen wearing before the abduction. An unhappy bulletin wasn't the distraction she was hoping for, but she let the despairing information play out over the airwaves until music filled the interior. They passed the same streets out of the community that they met coming in, and they both saw the mood loosen its tight grip of anxiety. The radio announcer was finishing up when a detail caught Jenny off guard.

"Arrow Road," said the disembodied voice, "that was the last place witnesses testified seeing the child before his disappearance." The report broke off, and Jenny spotted the street sign that read: Arrow Road

"Did you see that?" Jenny asked.

"See what?"

"The sign, the sign we just passed."

"No. What sign?"

"We just passed the street the radio mentioned. The boy disappeared right here."

"It's kind of creepy. You saw the street sign at the same time. Weird coincidence?" Liam asked. Her wheels were already turning.

"I wonder if Morris had something to do with the disappearance." Liam smiled and understood that his friend showed no humor in her expression.

"I don't know, Jen, he's an asshole, but an abductor or a murderer?"

"Did you live with the man? Well, I did, and I got to glimpse his dark side. What are the chances of me seeing that sign at the precise moment of the alert? Of all the streets in Columbus, I'm right at that one." Liam furrowed his eyebrows.

"Coincidence?" She was already shaking her head.

"It's more than that. There's a reason for everything, a reason that I'm dropping Zack off today when I never do it anymore. There's a reason for Zack's sudden change of behavior. My gut tells me that Zack is in danger."

"Listen, he's acting peculiar, no argument. The thing is, Jenny, we can't just accuse him of something like this without a shred of proof," he said. She pondered his logic.

"You're right. We have to look into this ourselves."

"Okay. I'm with you." Thinking of Morris acting out something so horrific scared her. But something else stirred in her far deeper. Optimism? She forced her thoughts away from a centric revelation that kept returning. If she proved Morris committed the crimes, she might rid herself of him forever. No more visitation, no more custody battles. *No custody at all,* she thought with colossal glee. Jenny would free herself of Morris. The concept was more than she ever hoped for, and she went on hoping. If Morris was the child abductor, then Zack was within the abductor's grasp at that very moment.

Zack was alone with his father, and she was helpless to do anything at all. Liam was right, and she knew he was. Refusal of visitation led to a closer examination of the custody agreement, or worse yet, it opened the possibility that Franklin County Children's Services might try to step in and take Zack away. She worked too hard and too long and wasn't about to jeopardize her son.

"We can do this. I have friends in the Columbus Police department that'll help." Tom Petty sang in the distance about standing his ground as a defiant chorus ascended behind his vocals. Jenny tapped her finger on her window, bit her lower lip, and looked to the vacant back seat through the rearview mirror. Her heart broke for Zack's pain, a pain she observed from the outside. A glimmer of color caught her eye—the bright shine was leaning against the seat next to a twisted seatbelt.

"Liam, what is that in the backseat?" She nodded to her rearview mirror as if the backseat were in front of her instead of behind. Liam stretched and screwed his body toward a thin section of construction paper. He unscrewed his torso and brought the paper onto his lap, feeling the paper's featherlike mass.

"What is that, Liam?"

"It's a picture, done in crayon. Zack must have left it behind," Liam said. Jenny spied the work of art and made sure not to lose track of the road.

"It's creepy," Liam admitted. In the center of the construction paper rested a chair drawn in brown crayon. The chair itself looked so lifelike more like an illustration—every fine grain in the wooden structure was visible.

"That's not possible, is it?" she asked, unsure of herself.

"I didn't know Zack could draw like this," he said.

"He can't." And if he could, she never saw the evidence. Most of his artist renderings were more on the level of stick figures or puffy clouds in the simple depictions that a child often imagined. The picture Liam held between his fingers was different. Bright colored flames shot out of the chair from every direction. The subtle mixture of Crayola tones danced as if it were living fire. At first glance, Jenny thought the backseat caught fire, or maybe a light somehow reflected into the car, anything but a child's artwork.

"Is that what I think it is?" Jenny asked. Liam nodded.

"It's an electric chair bursting into flames." They both stared at the drawing for a long time and said nothing the rest of the way back to the town of Pataskala.

CHAPTER 9

Morning light poured in through both sides of the window shade with floating dust particles dancing in dawn's first glow, and the warming rays stroked Robert's cheeks until he roused from a restless slumber. Jenny lay next to Robert, dozing in and out of dreamy sleep, one that closed in around her with its fuzzy, formless embrace. The bedspread, turned down halfway off the bed, draped over the footboard, and onto the floor. Jenny, dead to the world, flung the sheet off her delicate tummy, exposing her tiny belly button. Her uniformed breathing climbed and tumbled, causing her abdomen to follow suit.

Robert swept his hand across his leg, fingertips brushing thigh hairs on the way to their destination. Fingers, suspended in the air, remained unsteady and slow to thaw from the quick awakening. They tingled as he rested them on Jenny's neck under her chin. Robert noted the beating into his palm. The pulse was strong, and he could feel the lifeblood flowing through Jenny's jugular. He smiled, and it captured his face, twisting the corners upward into a malicious smirk. His hand exuded a rigid muscularity alongside a gentle carefulness.

Robert's peaceful grasp turned maniacal, departing into madness. First, a twitch, slight in its form—Jenny deep in a swoon. Tendons worked like the strings of a marionette, shortening under the skin and destroying the space between a husband's firm hand and a wife's subservient neck.

Robert tightened his fingers around Jenny's neck. Maybe it was the horrid pressure of skin against skin or perhaps the lack of blood, not to mention the decrease of oxygen, but her eyes, the eyes of the dying flew open and were wide enough to rupture all that she saw or ever would see. Jenny's eyes met her own eyes in the mirrored ceiling above.

She struggled to verbalize her fear and outrage—the force of her husband's hold grew as snug as steel. Robert pressed his skin onto hers, scraping his fleshy shell, and awakening his excitement. With his free hand, Robert sized up her belly, measured the distance between the gentle slope of her stomach and the edge of her pubic hair. Short hairs massaged and slipped between his fingers.

Fingers moved to explore her pubic area, grazing her delicate folds before plunging into a wet opening. Robert constricted her airway further, limiting her breathing to short bursts of inhales. His largest finger sank and withdrew, sank, and withdrew. Jenny's air passage was closing, and she could feel both sides of her esophagus touching each other. The sensation resembled long hair caught in her throat— moving neither up nor down along the air canal. He grew stiff as pleasure and pain racked her body, distressing one end while gratifying the other.

Still, she lingered in the gratification of death, basking in its finality before succumbing to the possibility of a fatal orgasm, one that sucked her down into a mortal climax. Her frame stretched out and tensed, catlike in appearance. He compressed Jenny's throat until he felt the joints in his hand ache from the stress. Robert moved his other hand in and out. Robert estimated her completion by her physical reaction.

Jenny's eyes rolled behind the lids and stared toward the painful darkness of her skull. Robert's hand stroked her below the waist— she discharged a soundless scream at the peak of sexual excitation. Her body was ablaze with responsiveness and convulsed one last time before Robert pulled both hands away from his wife. Jenny inhaled right away—the air she sucked in made a loud rasping noise that sounded more akin to a banshee's wail.

She breathed in hard, filling her lungs to slow her cadence. Reality crept back in, first from the edges, then the vague haze adjusted to familiar shapes, and soon she was watching herself in the high mirror. Jenny's throat felt sensitive in a disconnected, alien way that somehow gave her an outward suspicion that her fleshy tissue was someone else's and not her own. Shaking from the event, she caressed her neck—turning with the help of her extended arms as crutches and stared at Robert's face.

"I never heard you come in last night. Was it late?" Robert leaned in and kissed the nape of his wife's neck, returned to his original position, and supported himself on his elbows.

"It was late. I would have woken you up much earlier, but you looked too peaceful to disturb." The urge to smoke captured her, starting in her belly as a white-hot aggravation and moved to her chest as a rowdy teenager complete with irrational demands. If not for quite a few unsuccessful, several embarrassing, not to mention short-lived attempts to quit smoking, she would have hopped into the Jeep and started to burn into a cigarette before Robert downed his first coffee. Jenny balanced herself on the headboard—satisfaction bathed her, inflated her chest, and allowed her jaw to rest easy with a smile.

"Why don't you enjoy doing that?" she asked. "Why won't you at least pretend to enjoy dominating me?"

"You gotta understand, Jenny, I'm not able to play like that."

"It'll help our sex life. You want to expand our sex life, don't you?" Robert nodded. "A little role-playing killed no one." A solicitous smile stole her face. "I get it. Your parents passed. I know the thought of death is different for you, but I need it this way, for now."

"You don't know how it feels. My parents went way too soon. Can't lose you that way," Robert said.

"I understand. I lost my father too soon, and I won't push anymore. All I'm asking is for you to consider it. Can you promise me that?"

"I will."

"Oh, and don't forget, my mom is having dinner with us tonight."

"That'll be fun," he said, sliding on his underwear and snugging them just above his hips. Disdain crossed Jenny's face, but she pulled the disgust back as far as she could, so Robert didn't see.

"What?" He elevated his eyebrows high enough to break from his scalp and scuttle across the floor. "I like her, she's funny."

"She's atrocious, and it's the one sign that doesn't bode well for you. You know that?"

"Stop it. Your mother isn't that awful." Jenny arched her neck, a remnant of pain flaring, then dying away, and kissed her husband. She pressed her tongue into his mouth, enjoying every ridge and crevasse of his warm wet opening.

"I love you, Robert."

"Back at you, lover," Robert said. He watched her naked body slink off the bed, each cheek undulating up and down with every step until the bathroom door hid her feminine form.

The morning became a kaleidoscope, rolling from one bleak thought to another, and corkscrewing out of his mental control with no help from Jenny's constant talk of Morris. He wasn't jealous, having any need of her ex-husband made him laugh, but she droned on. She continued describing his inadequacies, her fears, his sinful vices, and all the while his mind reverted to the chains. He heard the clinking, clattering of chain links in his head. Its resonance was comparable to the ding dong of a doorbell or the repetitious chime of a grandfather clock. The jangle of the chains seemed born inside Robert, bursting through him as if he were a fleshy speaker, it returned to him again and again—never leaving him.

The wakeful dream continued through the first meal of the day— an immense appetite at the start then reduced to bird pecks on wheat toast. Still, the vague shackle noises continued, combining with its manifestation, the child's small voice begging for help.

Robert stood in front of the facility—the concrete monster towered over him. The prison's windows were eyes, searching for more prisoners to bring inside its hungry belly. He wondered how many souls the prison absorbed. Convicts taken into its cement husk, then spitting out the men's empty shells, and gravediggers at the ready to bury the social mistakes in the Reclamation cemetery. The cycle was maddening. Civilization churned-out defunct individuals at a faster pace than Reclamation could put in the ground.

Components were missing to the equation that Robert didn't understand. Nature always created a balance, the good and the bad, the right, and the wrong. That was how Robert viewed the world, and he planned to fix the problem. He made it to his desk without speaking to anyone. They all nodded, waved a hand in salute. He chose not to respond—he didn't even offer a glance. There was one thing on his mind, and it wasn't the protocol and etiquette or the inner political beast that thrived in the Reclamation building. What he wanted, what exhausted his conscious thought, if not his subconscious mind, was the diary.

The child's feeble cries hit a nerve. Supernatural wails of the child were more in line with possession. His rational mind tried to shake the absurd thoughts from his skull, but the sad little fact remained untarnished—it happened. The part of Robert who needed to see the monster at the end of every horror movie, no matter how much the fear dissuaded him, was the same part that wanted to re-experience the phenomenon of the crying child. He needed to confirm his fears. But above all, he wanted to prove he hadn't gone around the bend. Reginald thwarted Robert's tactics of evasion by standing guard at his office door with an arm full of folders.

"We can get an early start with the paperwork this morning, sir," Reginald said.

"Your devotion to the job is impressive," Robert spoke in a tone that bit on the side of sarcasm, "I wanted to lock myself in the office with the brunt of it today if you don't mind."

"That's fine, sir." Reginald looked bewildered.

"And make sure not to disturb me."

"You might need my direction to fill out the forms." Robert's patience had reached its end. He wanted isolation to read the diary at his leisure. Reginald tried to keep him from Joseph's knowledge.

"Tell you what. I'll send for you if I run into a snag. You run along now." Before Reginald answered, Robert passed through the door. He stared at his glimmering wooden desk. The outside fell away. *For how long?* Robert couldn't gauge any certain passage of time. He knew that time didn't apply to the moments when he was in his office behind his most valuable desk.

For the first time in his life, Robert was at home. He craved the time he spent in prison and never wanted to leave. Even next to Jenny, he thought of nothing but the freedom that the fiery fixture allotted him. Perhaps this was why he awakened Jenny from sleep so early. The sooner he could get out of the house, the sooner he could get to the office, to *it*. He spent the night hours aware of his longing to return to the desk. It held the power of serenity.

Robert thought of the fabled Sirens that guarded the coast, coaxing Odysseus and his crew toward evisceration of a rocky doom. *They had no choice but to listen, and neither do I.* Their fates seemed connected somehow. He didn't know why. Yet sitting there in front of the radiant desk, he felt danger pulling him under the surface. He understood that at the lowest plane of thinking, his basement thinking. It required no complicated dissection of motive, rationality, or logic. To deny these truths was to deny one's self, and Robert wasn't about to reject himself.

"I'm here, boss," a voice said from a corner of the room belonging to Jake Shoeman. He stood on a scale, fiddling with the sliding weights, and keeping the metal indicator balanced between the small numbers. "I weigh myself every day as you asked me to, Mr. Deville." Reginald jabbed his head in through the doorway like a baby being born or a cruel version of Jim Henson's Muppets, torso visible and legs never seen.

"I forgot to tell you, sir, Shoeman arrived minutes before you, and I sent him in to wait."

"I see that, Reginald." Robert waved the back of his hand at his associate warden and watched as the upper half of his body disappeared. An idea occurred to him and seized his faculties.

"Wait, Reginald. Come back here." He stood staring at the husky guard, still pouring back into his clothes and figured Reginald never heard him until the door opened once more.

"Mr. Deville?"

"You *told* me that this prison was once a mental institute in 1906."

"Before 1906," The associate warden corrected.

"Did they, by any chance, chain or shackle patients back then?" Robert asked, unsure of his perception.

"They . . . meaning doctors?" Robert nodded. "I believe so. I've heard that when they started the renovation, they found steel restraints a level down from where we are right now." Reginald pointed to the floor next to his feet, and the gesture seemed necessary. Jake got off the scale, and Robert rounded the desk, rediscovering his chair. "That is where they placed the most violent patients for behavior alterations. At least that is the way Warden Hughes explained it to me years ago." Reginald had the look of someone who had given out more information than necessary.

"One more question," Robert said and wet his lips, "were there any young boys and girls brought to the asylum?"

"For sure, Mr. Deville. When mental problems cropped up in a child's youth, the parents, at their wit's end, brought their loved ones here, for treatment."

"Treatment? With chains?"

"A darker time in the medical field, sir. Knowledge of mental illness was scarce."

"Excellent, Mr. Williams. You may leave." Robert was sure Reginald was leaving things out, but he wanted to be alone. *Alone with the desk?* The desk was the source that swelled his need. Every urge bubbled and threatened to overflow. His intentions hinged on the selfish necessity, however ridiculous it seemed to even himself when he wasn't close to the wooden relic. "Write your weight down and leave it on my desk." *My desk?* "We'll talk about your eating habits later."

"Yes, Mr. Deville," Jake followed Reginald out. He sized up the desk like an exotic lover, eyeballing the ridges and the perpendicular lines intersecting with the horizontal ones. To *him,* the spectacle was a delight, and the surroundings were his safe harbor even as the first illusory flicker of flames blazed to life across the wood's surface. The inferno sparkled, and his eyes already adjusted. A thought came to the front of the line past others. *Could others see what I'm seeing? Could they detect the slight pupil change, the sweat forming from the heat thrown off the beautiful writing desk?* He didn't think so unless they knew what to look for, and they didn't. *You are my treasure, my sanctuary.*

He walked around the flank of the bureau, fingers outstretched, and skimming the exterior. The fire obscured his fingertips as they sank, warming him. It wasn't the raging heat of combustion—it was more on par with a heating pad set on high. The fire possessed life, with an energy dwelling in it, and he didn't doubt it was alive. It was as if the rare wood contained imprisoned souls, and instead of attempting to escape, they banded together to radiate their powers outward. Trepidation shot into his head. *Time has no meaning here. One second or ten years felt the same.* He permitted himself to linger a moment longer before forcing himself to the drawer containing *that* book of secrets—Joseph Hughes's dark secrets. Robert's eyes read the title once again:

Joseph's Diary

I sat there across from the Devil. Did I think he was the Devil, the actual Devil? I can't say I did, but he believed it, I'm sure of that. And I've been in this profession long enough to know when not to provoke someone. It doesn't do anyone any good trying to prove you're right. So, there I was in front of the Devil in my prison. Like a child knowing they have the power to pull the wings from an insect, he unnerved me in a way that upset my stillness within. Whether he could see through my cool exterior became less important. A death sentence awaited the inmate in a short time, and no matter how fast hysteria may have spread throughout the facility—no real answers explained the dream phenomenon.

Foolishness crept in as I faced down the evil man, but a man close to meeting his maker. I think I was throwing futile punches at the air itself, and it was time to put an end to the idiocy.

Jumping to my feet as if my backside rested on springs, I headed toward the cell opening when Damon spoke, speaking in a calm voice, and with diction, I didn't expect.

He enunciated every word with the labored precision of a seasoned orator like Demosthenes, the great statesman of Athens, addressing the forum. Stopped in my tracks, I turned, almost possessed. I tried to catch his lips and make out the words my ears took in. His words drilled their way into my mind:

To do aught good will never be our task,
But ever to do ill our sole delight,
As being contrary to his high will
Whom we resist.

I sat down with matching distress spinning me around, my insides continuing to spin unhindered. I resisted another look to Damon. Instead, I lifted a hand in the air palm up and left it there. It dangled until a guard leveled a manila folder on the flat of my hand. The guard was a shadow retreating like a trick of the light. I leafed through the contents of the file, maintaining my vision on the pulp, aware of his eyes, deep and penetrating. When I tore my view from the file containing tight spaced typed words, Damon was burning through me. I battled through the discomfort with all the dominance my professional status granted me over the years of civic duty.

I asked Damon, who taught him the difficult text, shuffling my eyes from Damon to the folder and back again but not seeing either in my nervous gesticulation. The passage was by Milton. From Paradise Lost, I said, trying to provoke a quick answer but attempting to control the tempo of our conversation. Just two guys at a bar, maybe at a baseball game, pal-around buddies chatting. The sociable types that reared him didn't read books and gave sideways expressions for those who did. The revelation was no surprise to me.

I knew the types. I straddled between the worlds of education and ignorance. Prison life felt as if I planted one foot on the path to destruction while securing the other on the puffy white of a cloud blustering toward celestial eternity. The opposite side of the coin never threatened the virtues of the side I held dear, it solidified my resolve and shored up my weaknesses with the true-to-life testimony of the damned. One infallible rule has served me well and always came through in a pinch—condemned men seemed to lose their urge to tell a lie. When the arrangements to meet the maker comes, and when all foolish hope in the courts ended, the true soul remained. However, right in front of me sat the anomaly, the contradiction to my experiences with all other death-row inmates.

I confronted Damon about his file, a file losing more and more meaning as the seconds ticked away. It says right here *you are illiterate, I said. He seemed unperturbed by my accu-sation. I knew inaccuracies ran through the files concerning every detail imaginable, but something stuck in my craw. Da-mon taught himself how to read while inside, and it wasn't out of the realm of possibility. The matter that sunk into my skin like a snake was how he wielded a difficult text like Paradise Lost.*

I have seen many pretenders, some hayseeds who touted royal blood, wealthy cusses, and everyone in between. This fel-low was not a pretender, he wasn't a fraud, and I began to understand his power as I felt my energy wane in his presence.

I asked him what he was doing, and he smiled at me the way a child might grin with mischief at a teacher before she rested upon a well-placed tack. We shared a mind. I didn't have to explain my meaning, he knew. A "human" was an adjective I might have never used to describe Damon. It felt reasonable to think he was a parasite or a vampire. My will—strength or a mixture of both ran off my hide.

I needed to ask Damon other things—questions might al-ways float in my brain unless I gave them their proper attention. But I was sinking fast, and I couldn't focus my thoughts to stand up. Someone needed to drag me away. I rose, staggered to the opening, and grasped my man in uniform a split second before I collapsed. My sentry helped me down the cement corridor with the other enclosing Damon into his cage, built for a good reason in this case, and I walked away from the predator. With every step I took, the poison in the air dissi-pated, and with every step the fog lifted, the zapping force lost some of its potency. I needed to rest.

When my wife woke me the next day, she said I spent fifteen hours asleep. If she attempted to convince me I hadn't been conscious for twenty weeks, I'd make no argument. I was plia-ble about anything, except Damon Torinson somehow robbed me of my energy. I never considered the idea and tossed it out at once. A more plausible explanation was a lack of sleep com-bined with overwork, and I agreed with myself. I was positive

I missed lunch, and I thought it played a factor in the sudden drain of my stamina. The alternative was unthinkable, and I put it out of my mind straight away.

What I felt after my encounter with Torinson, besides my wife shaking me from oblivion, was an invisible force twisting in and out of my skull in rapid jabs. It made me close my eyes to bear down against the pain. The thudding gained some authority over me. A slashing pain swung from the base of my skull and down my vertebrae like a xylophone played too hard. Karie was speaking to me, but I was somewhere far away. My eyes opened, and there she was, her sweet soft, white skin hovering over me, and I smiled at her—the best I could offer under the circumstances, and felt my skin tighten as my cheeks turned upward.

Raising myself, I saw the phone stretched out in front of me, for how long I didn't know. Getting the gist of what Karie was telling me, I recognized her trembling hands. She'd been holding the phone out for God knew how long, trying to stir me from the sleep of the dead. I apologized to Karie without delay, feeling out of sorts but beginning to brush the cobwebs aside.

The veil dividing work-life, dealing with rapists, murderers, and salty cusses began to fall. The acidic rainwater seeped in and mingled with my home-life, enjoying our walks, dinners, and lovemaking. I've worked so long to shield sweet Karie from the underbelly of the world. I dove headlong into every day, and there it was, facing me like a rabid dog gone round the bend. She gave me a look that I hope to never see in her face, the look of fear. She told me that Roger Witmar was on the line. His tone alone sent her into a tizzy she claimed. When I took the receiver, Karie melted back into the bedroom as if the phone itself was a poisonous snake she held out of duty but happy to pass off. I noted her furrowed brow, darting eyes, and placed the earpiece to my ear, trying to put her maniacal appearance out of my thoughts.

Roger, my associate warden, was a bundle of burning screams and screeches. I worked to calm him down for five minutes before he would talk to me. The problem with our notorious guest, Damon Torinson, reached a newer, fiercer plateau. Danger threatened other lives, and I had no choice but to rectify the situation before it escalated past anything I could do.

I put the phone down onto its cradle, tilted my head upward, and caught eyes with my wife for the first time. My heart ached at the worry that stole her beautiful expression. A malignancy broke down my door and walked into my house without wiping its feet. Roger's lack of subtlety blemished Karie, and I couldn't pull myself away from her until I promised to explain everything when I returned. The bargain was the last thing I wanted to agree to, but I saw no other way to soothe her concern.

My arrival at the facility didn't set my mind at ease in the least. Roger looked worse than my wife did, and it became clear he was not long for the associate warden job. I sat him down and talked to him in a way my father spoke to me when I was making no sense. I spoke with sternness in my voice—coaxing him in the direction I felt would yield the most effective train of thought from the frazzled man. Roger enlightened me that our special guest was becoming a nuisance to the other inmates. The dreaming the entire prison experienced the night before, continued in my absence.

The acts of Torinson grew more gruesome, more vicious, and much more elaborate than the first. A lifer, forty years into his sentence, couldn't bear to share the community vision any further and ended his own life. The old-timer was a good sort, and his sudden death carried a lot of weight through the steel and cement. I held down my breakfast by the slimmest of margins. I breathed in several times to make my body still and let the nausea pass.

Roger implored me to speak to Damon. I guessed he thought Torinson possessed the ability to turn off his night visions on command. I'm not sure which ruffled my feathers more, Damon having the ability to project nightmarish mental pictures into his neighbor's head or my associate warden investing all his faith in the powers of an evil soul. The choices became less encouraging at that moment, and I needed to face Torinson—there was no way around the chore.

Hysteria was pushing the roof off the building, and I would put all the fears to rest. I shared the same trepidation as all the fellows in the joint. The difference was, I didn't live through the hallucinations, but I knew the man was off. I didn't need a priest to teach me what it means to be a good person or to understand which side Torinson leaned.

The fright Roger displayed earlier crawled into me and held me hostage. A faraway, dreamy remembrance of my debilitation the night before scuttled in on a wave and broke across my body, leaving me petrified at the plan to challenge the fiend. The memory was real again. It was a living, snarling thing. Something inside me became a badger, undressing its teeth to an interloper threatening its young. But I couldn't listen even as I wanted to give in to its tempting siren voice.

I didn't have a plan to deal with Torinson. I can't call myself a clever man, but I have hefty instincts to survive. My undigested food rose and dove in my stomach with every step of my journey toward the prison's dream weaver. I ordered Hank, my most trusted guard, to open his cell. I motioned him in first with a rifle, and I entered right after, finding a seat as if no time separated us from our former encounter. Torinson was sitting on his bunk, staring my way, and never moved his head to focus on me.

I was sure he predicted my return so soon after the last visit. I was in uncharted territory and wasn't about to play games with this fellow any more than necessary. His eyes burned the same, and I wasted no time letting him know who was in control. I pointed to Hank, and he did likewise with the barrel of his rifle at Torinson, and I began to speak. I don't know how you drained me of my energy yesterday, but if I feel myself lose even one drop of perspiration in this cell, I will point to old Hank here for the second time, and he will tear your head off with his rifle, I said. Torinson looked at me again as if he expected me to make the power move, and looking back, he did.

I asked him how he was transmitting the dreams to the surrounding inmates. He shrugged his shoulders, and at first, I thought that was all I was getting from him. Then he made a gesture close to someone holding a fist to a mouth to clear the throat, and no sound came. Later I thought the gesture was a gesture of what someone or thing might do to impersonate a human. He said he was sorry the old-timer killed himself. His words sounded sympathetic, vulnerable, and I wanted to run.

God as my witness I wanted to get the hell out of the cell and drive home to my sweet Katie never to return. How are you projecting the dreams? He claimed he couldn't tell me, saying the dreams were part of a larger picture. A window was opening in his mind, he said. First, the life he was living and then all his past lives spanning thousands of years. During the night, remnants of his subconscious poured out and infected the prisoners, just trying to get some sleep. I wasn't skeptical, but I played the part to grease his tongue.

Damon Torinson arched his back in another counterfeit act caught by my keen eye. The fiend in front of me wasn't real. I mean, he was sitting a few feet away from me, sniffing the same air, eating the same bad food as the rest of the convicts, and the thing was pretending as if he was wearing Torinson's skin. A measure of me was waiting for him to tear his skin aside, climb out of the psychopath's hide, and smile a malevolent smile. Hank was thinking something along the same lines because he readjusted his finger around the rifle's trigger and ignored the sweat already beading on his forehead.

He compared a human's development with his own. To him, humans entered the world a blank slate, deciding who they are through instinct. The difference in his mind—at a certain point in each of his lives, he awoke with total recall. All his past lives rushed in like a flood of memory, filling him with wisdom, experience, and clarity to the greater scheme of reality which no human can know.

He talked about Jesus Christ and how he didn't know his identity until many years later. The implied link between the Son of God and this creature turned my skin to goose flesh. The worst part was I believed him. He went from a criminal awaiting the electric chair to the adversary of God whose plans and concepts went contrary to everything I believed. Wrapped into one human form dwelled all my worries for humanity. His protective shield was failing as he was telling me his life story. At least that was my initial deduction.

As I sat with Damon, my opinion of the man shifted to a blurry portrait of a human shell whose soul was black to the core. I could feel him holding back the secret powers he held over me or anyone that stood in his way.

My question was why he thought he was the Devil. I wanted to understand the origin of his belief system, leading him toward the fantasy of being the Devil. Damon was a sick individual, but half the people in America's mental institutions suffered from either a God complex or a fascination with the occult. He perked up from the query and asked if he could smoke a cigarette in my presence. I agreed, and Damon rolled and lit a cigarette as fast as it would take me to pull one out of a pack.

The tip of the smoke burned bright orange and faded as he drew the heated air into his lungs. A creature imitating a man nagged me further—I pushed it out of my mind. He said he felt it his entire life but could never place a finger on how he knew, that is until a moment of clarity shook his reasoning.

Sadness swept over him, and he allowed himself to wither in front of me. When he discovered his past lives, he saw how inconsequential his current life was to his sober eyes. Damon Torinson was a ball of needs and urges. That's how he saw himself with his newborn eyes. Even as a monster, he decided his current manifestation was a low-level being.

In his words, each form he became before his awakening was a random mix of his dormant traits—the environment coaxed out of him. From what I can gather, his father was the catalyst for his current human expressions. He stayed drunk night and day, and when he wasn't drunk, he would smash Damon through the walls of their dingy home. I asked him where his mother was while his father chucked him through plaster, and he replied she laughed a lot. She laughed to egg her husband on, and she laughed to ignite his focus on Damon and off her.

My heart went out to the guy for having a miserable childhood. He may be a victim of a lousy upbringing, and I also knew I could throw a stone and hit a convict with the same early days. I even went as far as giving him my condolences for inheriting a father as vicious and as cruel as he was unfortunate to receive. That's when he flashed me a look of sympathy. He explained he wasn't unhappy—his father, Frank Torinson, wasn't an animal. It was closer to the truth to say Frank smelled the animal in his son. Damon was something to hate and fear in equal measures. It wasn't his father he sought love or nurturing from—it was his relationship with God running through every one of his lives like an angry red thread.

My betrayal caused God to shun me, drive me away from him, and his amorous light, he said. You do not understand what it is like to bask in his love and have it seized from you like a child wrapped in the warmth of its mother's affection and the next minute, tossed into a dark wilderness, he said with tears standing in his eyes.

In a matter of seconds, his trembling facade became rigid, and he bolstered his defenses as someone might turn a key. Vulnerability powering his frame ran out of juice and left him hollow again. I want to die, he told me. Out of thousands of lives, he said that when he awoke in a body, that body was almost always in an institution or a prison.

When he saw his true self in the reflection, it was inside a prison cell. It kept him from his greater deeds left to perform on Earth. I asked him to describe the acts left undone, and he laughed. The snort was nasal, starting in his throat and finishing in his nostrils. I never wanted to hear him laugh again. It made me think of the Grimm's fairy tales, the one where the witch would snicker at Hansel and Gretel. It was the souls he wanted to corrupt. He said this in a way that made me feel like a tourist who didn't know even the most basic rules of the country. These were things he thought I should know, and by not knowing such a thing, might damn me.

The conversation wore me down. Not like the day before, but I was feeling exhaustion as I attempted to follow his wild narrative while debating its validity to myself. It seemed funny to me after our meeting, but I asked him another question to quiet the collapse of reason in my head. Being the Devil, how often do you return to a body? I asked, not expecting an answer. But Damon Torinson answered, and what he answered I wish I never heard. I believe in everyone's life—there are crossroads. And if you take a side road, you'll never be the same.

Although his response sealed my fate, given a choice, I would not change a second of my unhappy years to come. A burden of this magnitude comes to a human but once in a thousand years, maybe longer. Damon sat up straight and snuffed out his cigarette, pressing his thumb on the body of it like a naughty boy smashing a helpless ant for the thrill.

Damon said in a tone that sent a chill through me—he reincarnated into another human body every time his former carcass drew its last breath. Because his soul could never enter the thresholds of heaven, the soul could only drift miles from where his body lay dead. The concept shocked me to my foundations.

Imagining an evil soul continuing again and again to trouble humanity without someone to stop the cycle was disarming. Once he died, his soul floated to a pregnant woman. And now, he just wanted to die, to die and be reborn a new-fangled monster, a monster not yet aware of their evil destiny, but wreaking havoc on the unsuspecting world. I asked him if he could remember his last life, and he went through a story of living as a prisoner in the Reclamation correctional facility as a man named Sean Spires.

I heard the name before and thought he could never make up the name living in files. Either he was telling the truth—or he was the notorious arsonist that set the prison on fire, killing hundreds of inmates or . . . I didn't want to think anymore. Damon was the real thing. He was the Devil!

CHAPTER 10

Gage leaned next to the prison's coarse brick wall, listened as the stone surface scraped against the clothes on his back, and scanned the prison yard. Convicts scurried in disorder like children during recess. Steel posts that held up the fencing rose and plunged according to the landscape's natural dips and rises. Chatter drummed as prisoners left behind their confines for the prison yard, and they rejoiced in their last jovial freedom. The wind whispered in Gage's ears the promise of liberty that lay beyond the fences, the long-forgotten memories of independence, and the heartbreaking absence of a woman. The smell of Maria's fading perfumed body stung his recollection and caused him a nagging pain that constricted his chest.

"It doesn't look good, Saint," Eddie said. Gage fixed his eyes upward. The clouds above undulated over invisible mounds. The gray masses careened around and through each other, gaining momentum under the guiding hands of the prevailing wind.

"There's a storm coming," he said to his younger cellmate. Eddie caught his friend's eyes and followed their path to the angry, blackened clouds that decorated the sky. He wished he could rest on the billowy vapors and float up, never seen, or heard from again.

"Well, if you don't like the weather in Ohio, wait a minute." There were questions on Eddie's mind. Some were important, but most were inconsequential and held no worth except to quell the worry. The anxiety ate at him, gnawed at his crunchy bones, and risked the safety of his best friend, his *only* friend.

"Have you met the new warden yet?" Eddie asked and pretended to have the same interest in the gathering clouds. Gage shook his head, and for a long time, Eddie accepted that as an answer until his friend spoke.

"Why would I? The management doesn't like my cooking. They find their food elsewhere."

"I heard some strange things about the warden," Eddie said. Gage eyeballed a guard traipsing along the ledge of a brick-walled boundary. A rifle, like an extended limb, snuggled close to his chest.

"What things?" Gage asked as a cigarette fluttered from its pack and finished between his lips. A flame emblazoned the tip.

"The hack, Jake, told me," Eddie stretched his fingers for a drag of Gage's cigarette and got it, "that the new warden might be crazy."

"Crazy?" Gage asked, interested in the turn in the story.

"Crazy wasn't the word he chose. Jake said that he wanted to check in with him daily for something or other, and your majesty, the new warden, sat there behind his desk, staring at it." Eddie dragged a second time before handing the smoke back.

"Staring at what?" Gage drew the heated smoke into his lungs and felt his need for nicotine calmed.

"At his desk. He sits there for hours studying the lines on his desk. Can you believe that shit? And he's our keeper."

"That isn't even true. More bullshit," Gage said. Eddie shrugged, held out a thumb and forefinger like a pincher, and grasped the last of the cigarette. Escaping clouds had no regard for the humans in a pin below. "There's a storm coming. No doubt about it." The prison yard landscape moved, changed, and came alive with a predator that dwarfed all others. He was a big, stalking cat with appetites never quenched. When Gage saw Victor walk past a group of convicts, he separated himself from the pack at once. Gage's face went white, and he understood the emotion of hatred and fear as the sentiments fused into a single terrifying compulsion.

"He's out here," Gage said. Eddie stiffened. He checked out the crowd for Gage's distress until his eyes locked onto Victor.

"I see him."

"Good, you've seen him, now look away," Gage said with some venom.

"Sorry, Saint." Eddie snuck another peek of Victor as if the attraction to stare was too alluring. "I understand what Victor and his brother did to you. What I haven't figured is the limit of this guy. Is he a threat to us? I trust you—I do. The thing is…plans we're making are permanent." A hulk of a man sauntered next to Victor, shook his hand, and gave his new friend a hearty belly laugh that made Gage cringe. Even from a distance, the beast of a man towered over Victor.

"When I first hooked-up with Clyde and his brother Victor years ago, Victor told me a story that I never forgot. The story woke me up sometimes as if knowing it darkened me, or maybe it darkened my vision of the world. It shook my early belief. Is there good in people?" Eddie nodded along in all the right places, wanting to look back to Victor, but refrained. "Victor and Clyde's dad came home drunk almost every night and beat them to within an inch of their lives sometimes. He did that four times in a week when he got drunk." Eddie shifted with discomfort.

"His drug of choice was tequila. Later, Victor would tell me he remembered dark memories when he drank tequila. The aroma wafted into his nose, and before he could even stop it, he was back in Detroit, smelling the tequila on his dad's breath. He chose not to order it anymore to escape the vivid brutality of the recall. He didn't delve too deep into his decision to abstain, but the physical abuse seemed forever mixed with the acrid scent." Gage lit another cigarette and inhaled its pungent stench.

"The way I understand it, their father, Lucious, alcohol wasn't the reason for his evil deeds. From what Victor told me, he was a better person when he was drunk if you can believe such a thing." Eddie reached for the cigarette, and Gage held it tighter, delivering it to his pursed lips. "Lucious got it into his head that his boys weren't tough enough for the cold, hard world out there. He believed it was his duty to toughen the boys up so they could take care of themselves when he left the Earth. One day, he comes home from his factory job with Doberman Pinscher puppies, one for Victor, and one for Clyde." Gage hot-boxed the remaining cigarette and stamped it under his feet.

"Lucious made each boy train their dog to do ten tricks of their choosing. Six months was all he gave them to guide and nurture the pups. And I remember this most of all. He said that the true reason for the chore was to decide which of the boys would follow his orders without fail. The one who didn't, well, they didn't want to find that part out." Eddie's vision fell back to Gage's subject across the yard.

"There they were, two boys, one nine, and the other ten years of age feeding, caring, and loving their precious pups. They put in countless hours to teach their pets tricks topped with truckloads of encouragement. I'm sure until that sweet gift—the boys thought their daddy didn't care at all. But this chore was different—they saw the old man's heart, and both wanted to please their pops so much that they would often use flashlights to continue the pup's training into the wee hours of the night." Gage tried to smile.

"Well, time passed, and in the blink of an eye, the six months were up, and the boys couldn't wait to show their daddy what they taught their pride and joys. Lucious asked Victor what he named his dog with Victor responding, Hercules. What can he do? Show me. Lucious continued to urge the boy. Victor sent Hercules through his paces, and the Doberman responded without hesitation and completed all the tricks on command. Victor glowed from pride the boy never enjoyed his entire life. After the boy finished, Lucious turned his attention to the younger of the two, Clyde. He endured the same questioning, the same benign spectating, and watched as Clyde's happy little dog breezed past all the trials with no sweat." Eddie listened with great interest.

"The two shared a happy smile at what they accomplish in a short time. That's when Lucious sat his boys next to their dogs. You did what I asked you, he said. But what I am testing is your loyalty to me. I want you to kill your dogs, he said in a steady tone. With a glazed expression, Victor and Clyde stared up at their daddy. Go on now, you sons of bitches, don't make me tell you, again. Lucious screamed." Gage paused.

"The dogs began to suspect something was up as they began to shiver and growl. Clyde wrapped his child-size hand around his dog and broke its neck. A soft yelp fled from the wrecked dog before it lay dead at his feet. Victor looked up at his daddy as if the gruesome act from his brother never happened and shook his head to his daddy. I can't do it, he said. I know, Victor. It's my way to find which of you is the weakest of the two, and you are it, Lucious said. He leaned over the boy and twisted Hercules's neck until it was dead. Victor heard the small bones in the canine crackle until no sound remained. Lucious spent the better part of the next five years focusing his attention on the weaker son Victor, to harden his resolve.

I'm not sure what's worse, a boy who has it in him to kill his darling or the one taught to endure the act. Years later, the brothers wouldn't need alcohol, like their dad, to summon any demons. Their souls were more callused from the tough love delivered in their youth." Eddie didn't believe the story, but he knew Gage did, and that's what mattered. Eddie's evasive eyeing of Victor found an audience. Victor stopped in his tracks, zoomed in on Eddie, and whispered into his large friend's ear.

"Shit," Eddie said.

"What? Eddie, what's wrong?" Eddie turned white—blood emptied from his face. "Are you okay?" Eddie shook.

"I couldn't help it."

"Damn, Eddie, what couldn't you help?" Gage asked. Eddie moved his lips with no words passing the mouth's threshold.

"He locked eyes with me. Victor's coming this way, right now." Gage turned on rails and saw for himself. "I'm sorry, Saint. I was too curious to look away." Gage hoped that Eddie was wrong and that Victor wasn't heading his way. The confrontation was unplanned, too soon. One glance dashed his hopes.

"Calm. Do you have a shank on you?"

"Yes," Eddie admitted.

"Get it into your palm." The order turned Eddie to stone. "Now, Eddie." Eddie leaned a shoe flat against the brick facade behind him, inserted a finger into the heel, fishing out a small metal blade, and presented it to the light of day a second before closing his hand around it.

"They're coming, Saint."

"It's okay, relax. Do nothing until I say. You hear me?" Eddie made no answer. "Goddamn it, Eddie. Are you with me or not?"

"Yes, I'm with you."

"If you hesitate, we're fucking dead." Eddie tensed his body. "Be cool and follow my lead. We don't want it to go down out here. More than likely, Victor is too smart to bring the thunder in plain sight. But in case I'm wrong, do as I say."

"You got it, Saint."

"You broke the cardinal rule," Gage said. Victor reduced the expanse of the prison yard at a maddening pace. Gage pondered his next move with no time to come to any satisfactory conclusions. Gage clinched his hands, released the tension in his grasp, and little by little secured his hands into rigid balls. Victor tottered between Eddie and Gage and swiveled onto the path leading to Eddie, the smaller of the two. Victor's action resembled a ram preparing to batter its foe with its horns. He drove his forehead forward, cutting the air with his skull. Eddie closed his eyes, expecting a painful crunch—a swirling assault or violation in his personal space. Victor stopped his onslaught in midstream, staring into Eddie's eyes.

"You eying me?" Victor asked. Eddie slunk back to the brick wall guarding his back. The sharpened shiv, forgotten in his trembling hand, clung to a sweaty palm. "You either mean to kill me or fuck me." Eddie shrank on his bones like the limp consistency of clothes on a wire laundry line. "Which is it, boy, you sweet on me?" Victor winked at Gage, backing away from Eddie. His gigantic accomplice took the spot in his absence. Victor leveled his vision to Gage. "So, here's your new Ricky." Victor tilted his head the distance from Eddie's hair to shoes for effect. "He doesn't have the sturdiness of the original," Victor said.

"Victor," Gage said in the shape of both a question and statement.

"Oh, you haven't met my new friend." He waved a hand, palms out, like a used car salesman presenting the year's new model. "This is Reven." He nodded on cue.

"I've seen him around," Gage said.

"You're the Saint," Reven said.

"Saint for short. There are no pretenses here in the concrete jungle. We're all friends," Victor said.

"Are we friends?" Gage asked.

"Sure. Reven caught a chain from a Supermax facility on the West Coast. He belonged to the brotherhood until he got picked up for murder here in Ohio. So far as I can tell, he's good at lifting weights," Reven contracted his muscles in his three-hundred-pound frame, "and breaking bones."

"Sounds like dirty work," Gage said.

"I got an old lady on the outside. Checks make it to her doorstep while I'm in the service of Victor. You know how it is, you go where there's money, Saint," Reven said in a tone that startled Eddie with its harsh, gravelly quality that suited Reven's rough exterior.

"You hear where he got the name Saint from?" Reven shook. "It was years ago when we first started together. We were traveling from one city to the next working the game. It happened during a robbery in Dayton, Ohio—Gage took a guard's gun and pointed it into his face. You could taste the fear that rolled out of the guy's sweat. We got away with fifty-five thousand dollars in jewelry that day without firing a single shot. Two weeks later, that same security guard that looked down the barrel of his gun got a package in the mail. Inside a cardboard box was the same gun taken in the heist and two hundred dollars for the stress. Gage knew that the security guards paid for their revolvers. The rest of us in the gang used to laugh at those acts of kindness."

"You know how long it takes to save up for a gun when you're a working man?" Gage asked.

"I don't," Victor replied, "I'd just take it." Victor smiled. "That's where Gage got the nickname, the Saint. No one calls him that except for the dregs of society, the very worst souls around, so I'm sure the name won't elicit too much honor," Victor said.

"Did he suffer?" Gage asked.

"Did *who* suffer?"

"Ricky. Did he suffer?" Gage's face tightened by a scowl like the skin of a drum as his bottom row of teeth met his lower set.

"My victims never suffer, unless I mean them to suffer. Saint, I haven't forgotten you, boy. You kept your mouth shut and held the bag for us as the law swarmed. I have more money out there waiting for you, Saint."

"How about my son Ryan, I've often wondered how he suffered his last days," Gage said. Victor stepped back away from Gage and placed his hand on Reven's chest. Reven did the same.

"A tail would slip between this boy's legs if he owned one," Reven said.

"You see that, Reven?" Victor asked.

"See what?" Victor wrung his hands like two sponges in search of liquid.

"I offered money to a thief. I offered, and he changed the subject."

"That's right, he did," Reven said.

"It isn't a good sign. When a thief doesn't want money, it means one thing. Saint has a purpose, and maybe it's a belief he would die to protect. Either way, he's a danger to me."

"I'm sure you're right." A siren blared above the chatter, and horseplay of the yard. The guards corralled the inmates toward the prison doors like cattlemen bringing in the bovine.

"We'll continue this later," Victor said.

"Yes, we will," Gage agreed. Victor headed toward the pack of cattle and wrenched his neck back. "I think you hitched your fate to the wrong wagon with that one there." Victor pointed at Eddie, who shivered in his skin. "I thought you had a better eye for talent." Victor returned to his path, as Reven fell in line behind, eclipsing his superior with his immense size, and disappearing into the crowd.

CHAPTER 11

In the kitchen, Jenny turned over the salad in a wooden bowl, dressing spread with every turn of the utensil. Her mind scattered from one topic to another but always returned to Morris. *It's up to me to do something*, she thought. Liam scooted in behind her—his rough corduroy pants rustled from his heavy thighs, and uneven steps, giving his position away.

"I know it's you, Liam." Liam wrapped his arms around Jenny and squeezed, the smell of her shampoo filled his nose. *She* melted.

"Ah, hum." Liam and Jenny turned to the sound and found Robert staring with contempt. "Are you making a move on my wife?" Robert asked with eyes that burned with anger.

"No, not at all. I was giving Jenny…hugging her." Liam fell silent. Robert flashed an angry expression.

"He's just messing with you," Jenny said. She punched Robert's chest. His eyes rolled with the edge of his mouth, turned up toward a smile, but not quite making it.

"I'm kidding," Robert said with eyes that told a different story. Liam searched the kitchen for a chore to occupy his nervous energy.

"Thanks for inviting me to dinner."

"It's our pleasure, Liam." Coldness remained.

"Yeah, you're always welcome here," Jenny added, stroking Liam's weary nerves with her sweet sentiment.

"Well, you better hurry dinner," Robert said and tried on a smile. "Your mother's getting impatient in there." Jenny shrugged but still lunged for the food, heading straight to the dining room without pause. With Jenny gone, the smile melted from Robert's face. Liam squeezed past Robert, tilting his heavy frame backward to avoid contact. Robert stood in place until the dining room hummed with subdued pleasantries.

"So, Margaret, it's good to see you again," Liam said.

"Yeah." Margaret extended a hand for a bowl of corn just out of reach. Robert moved the bowl closer.

"There you go, Mom."

"Thanks, dear."

"Do you remember me?" Liam persisted. Margaret scooped a helping of corn onto her plate, the juice from the corn soaking into her bread.

"Yeah, I remember you. You were the funny little boy with the lisp."

"I never had a lisp—" Jenny shook her head to Liam.

"Mom, do you want some milk? We got soymilk."

"I don't want either. I want some iced tea if you don't mind."

"We got that." Jenny poured a glass of tea while keeping her eyes on Robert. "Honey, there is something I meant to ask you."

"What is it?"

"It may sound weird, but does your prison have an electric chair in use?" The question caught Robert off guard. Jenny pushed herself from the table, jogged into another room, and was back holding a piece of construction paper. "Zack drew something the other day when he was in the car with Liam and me." Liam nodded as if he was a witness on a stand. Robert's big hands reached for the construction paper.

"What picture? What are you talking about?" Margaret asked in a way that meant Jenny needed to involve her in the conversation. Jenny put a finger in the air, and the gesture quieted Margaret. Robert turned the paper over and over in his hands. The chair appeared to be on fire. He perceived something else just beneath the crayon flames.

"Zack drew this?" Robert asked.

"Yeah. So, you have this chair in your building?" Robert already shook off her question as she was finishing. The wood grain disturbed Robert.

"No. We don't electrocute inmates anymore." The wood grain of Zack's drawing matched the wood grains of his desk. Robert was sure of it. His hands began to warm from the slight touch of the fiery chair.

"Damn. I thought it meant something. It doesn't look like a kid's picture, though does it?"

"It doesn't," Robert said. "You mind if I take this?"

"Sure. Why do you want it?" Robert, lost in the image, didn't answer. "Robert?" Jenny nudged the soft nape of Robert's neck. "Honey, you okay?" Jenny's high voice broke the fog from his mind.

"I'm fine." He folded the construction paper into quarters. "I'll ask the older guys at the facility about the prison's old electric chair."

"I think talking about electrocution is making your mom woozy," Liam said.

"Woozy. I'll show you woozy, boy." Margaret drove her hands into her purse as if she was preparing to sink her entire body into the leather bag. She pulled out a square, black device no bigger than a television remote control and aimed it at Liam. "You ever see one of these before?"

"It looks like a stun gun," Liam said.

"No, it's a high voltage stun gun. If you say I'm woozy one more time, I'll send fifty-five thousand volts chasing through you. You believe me?" Liam gave her a solemn nod. "Good." Margaret shoved the weapon back into her purse, sipped her tea, and stabbed her fork at her kernels of corn. Everyone looked around to each other before Robert burst out laughing.

"I love you, Mom," Robert said through tears of laughter.

"I love you too, sugar."

"That reminds me, Jenny, I have to go into work tonight."

"What again? The prison is taking too much of the time reserved for me."

"Things will smooth out soon. I promise." His sole thought was the warm safety of his desk and the unread pages of Joseph Hughes's diary.

"Your husband has an important job. If he needs to be there, then there's no need to argue."

"Mom, please stay out of it."

"I'm just saying that neither you are your gentle friend here realize what it takes to run a prison."

"And you do, Mom?"

"No, I don't," Margaret said. "I know my place. Maybe you should find yours," she said in a whisper.

"I can see why your husband left," Liam said. The comment sent a hush from end to end.

"What do you know about my husband? Or about marriage? Your kind—nothing but outsiders in our culture, practicing your sodomy. Do you think God isn't watching? He's watching, boy. He's watching and waiting for the chance to fry your ass. You're seated across from a woman who lives in society, enduring the good and the bad. I can't escape my duties like some flimsy degenerate who mocks principles and morals valued by decent people."

"Decent people? More like self-righteous," Liam said.

"I can tell you now, or you can find out on your own. The group that dwells on top always seems self-righteous to those who live at the bottom. Sodomy isn't procreation, and if you can't produce anything, then you are what my Aunt Tillie would call a nonentity."

"Screw you." Jenny stood up from the table, ran to Liam, and pulled him from his seat.

"Come on into the other room for a second." Teardrops balanced themselves in Liam's eyes.

"Screw you," Liam repeated as Jenny led him away from Margaret Salvo.

"I was trying to warn him, Robert." With Jenny and Liam gone, Robert smiled at the older woman. Liam paced around the kitchen. His thick legs rubbed together.

"She has no damn right to talk to me like that."

"I'm sorry." Liam moved faster, causing the corduroy to scrape from the friction.

"Don't work yourself up. Did you hear Robert? He'll be at work tonight, and I'll need you with me when I investigate Morris. I can't do this without you, Liam." His pace slowed to a jittery walk. "Besides, who will be my Hardy boy while I'm Nancy Drew?" He stopped and grinned.

"I was hoping to be Nancy Drew. She's far too colorful for you to pull off."

"We'll get rid of these two and nail that bastard to the wall."

"I would like that," Liam said. Jenny hugged him and felt a pang of sadness for her friend.

CHAPTER 12

Jenny and Liam sat in detective Scott Sedge's Caprice Classic. The engine idled, missed several times, and roared to life as Sedge mashed the gas pedal with his boot. The aroma of long-ago smoked cigarettes, spilled coffee dried into the upholstery, and rancid cheeseburger wrappers drifted throughout the car. Paper of every shade jutted from the driver-side visor. The paper, along with some envelopes, looked strangled in the crack between the eyeshade and the car's liner. *Paperwork, the life of an officer,* Jenny thought.

"Thanks for seeing us, Sedge. Won't take a lot of your time. I need your help," Jenny said.

"You know I would do anything to help, but we could have done this over the phone."

"No, not at all. Robert is a cop like you, and I didn't want him to discover what I was doing."

"I'm flattered you see me in the same category as Robert, even if it isn't true." A murky layer of condensation covered the windows and grew with every breath that the three took. Jenny scrutinized the forming haze, not sure where to lead the conversation.

"What I'm about to say to you must stay between us," she said, flashing an expression that offered no doubts about her sincerity.

"I can do that." Sedge stuck a finger into his cigarette pack, probed for a remaining gasper, and put it to his lips. "You mind if I light?" They both nodded from the backseat as the detective burned the tip of his smoke.

"I . . . we think my ex-husband has something to do with these missing children cases." Sedge took a long drag on the cigarette. "Jenny, I know your past with Morris. The guy was a tool, and if I had a half-hour alone in a room with him…well. The guy's a lot of things, and a killer is not one of them. I've done this job for a long time, Jenny. Morris is a coward who juices his self-esteem by hurting women." Smoke swirled in the stagnant air and vanished into the cloth liner above.

"Sedge, I'm not asking you to arrest him. What I am asking you to do is get me copies of the info you have of the missing children and allow me to nose around." Sedge gave her a crazy-eyed look. "Far away from Morris. Scout's honor." Jenny folded her hands together like a saint praying for forgiveness.

"I can't…just can't do that…sorry. Jenny, if you got caught with Columbus police department property. I would lose my job, not to mention my benefits, and Haley might even consider leaving me if all that happens," Sedge said.

"We won't get caught with it, please, Sedge," Jenny's tone was desperate.

"Can't do it." Sedge swung his hand to the ashtray—Jenny stopped his momentum, snatched the dwindled cigarette, and placed it into her mouth.

"You made me do this." Jenny inhaled deep. "You owe Robert, and by proxy, you owe me. I have to call in the marker."

"That isn't fair."

"I'm desperate. My son's life is at stake here. I may never discover he's a child abductor. The thing is, Sedge, he's a rotten son of a bitch—my son is with him as we speak. Please, Sedge."

"Okay. I'll see what I can do. Wait here." Sedge said and slammed the car door shut. Jenny watched his footfalls on the steps leading into the Columbus police station before she attempted to talk.

"Yes, yes, yes, yes," Jenny screamed in the cramped confines of the car. "Who's the man? That's right—I'm the man."

"Robert's very lucky then if you're the man," Liam said.

"He is, and I am." Jenny's outburst ended, and they sat looking at the police station entrance and waiting for Sedge's return.

"So, why does he owe Robert anything?"

"Robert told me he saved Sedge's life once during a domestic violence call."

"That's crazy," Liam said.

"Tell me about it." Jenny saw Liam for the first time. "Are you okay? I mean from tonight."

"You want to get a scoop?" she nodded. "I hate your mother."

"Join the club."

"I hate her, but she's right," Liam said.

"The woman hasn't been right about anything in her life. Well, she introduced me to Robert. She got that right and nothing else."

"I am an outsider. No matter what I do, the gay lifestyle is the life of an outsider."

"Are you going to let her sink her hooks into you?"

"Listen, her words come from ignorance and hate…the thing is she's right. Gay was never a choice. I haven't even come out to my parents for Christ's sake. People like your mother…they make me feel alone in this."

"You're not alone, and you have me."

"When I was young, I suspected I was different, and all I ever wanted was to just fit in with everyone else."

"Every kid's that way, and I was that way," she said

"The only way for me to fit in was to pretend I was something I wasn't. Then came the realization that pretending was giving into others. I masqueraded as a straight man, and it still haunts me today. I can't live a life trapped between the lifestyle I want and the sexuality I need."

"The world's getting there," she said.

"I just don't have the strength to fight all that hard." Liam picked at the sole of his shoe, rubbing the tread with his palm. "Jenny, you are the best friend I've ever had, and that's why I can tell you this…when I talk about killing myself, you think it's a cry for help." Jenny started to speak as he put up a hand to hush her. "A part of it is a cry for help. I'm like everybody else trying to find a connection, a person to say—you're worth so much."

"You are worth so much," Jenny blurted out.

"It's not all a cry for help. Sometimes I want to do it."

"Please stop this." She moved closer, saw the sweat beading down his jawline, and flung her arms around him.

"You are not going anywhere. I want you to call me wherever or whenever these feelings strike you. Do you hear me? I want a promise from you so you can never leave me without at least a goodbye. If you ever cared for our friendship, you'll make me that promise." His shirt hung askew from her sudden embrace. He tugged at a sleeve, pressed the wrinkled creases with his hand, and glanced at the police entrance.

"I can't make that promise, Jenny."

"If you don't swear to me, I will never talk to you again. I mean it." Her words swam in his mind, flushed him with love, and the knowledge that she was worth keeping a promise.

"You'll be the first to know, Jenny." Her apprehension ebbed, her heartbeat that was pounding fast, began to slow to its normal range once more.

"Thank you." The door of the police station opened, and Scott Sedge lumbered past the threshold. A few strides and he was sitting in the driver's seat like he never missed a word. He sat motionless, not seeing past the cloudy windshield, and not trying.

"If I give you this," A folder hung over fingertips, cardboard dangled in the muted light shone from the dashboard, "it can damage my reputation." Jenny extended her arm over the seat, spreading her fingers and clasping the folder.

"I appreciate this, Sedge. I do. We both do." Jenny craned her neck, eyes opening wide.

"Yes. Your help means so much." Liam was back in the game.

"I'm doing this for Robert. He has it coming. Besides, the whole department hasn't come up with much, and I don't expect you to do any harm. A condition I'm placing on this favor is that you don't take matters into your own hands. I'm always a call away."

"We won't do a thing without your authority, I promise." Jenny slid the folder under her arm, pushed open the door, and waited for Liam to climb out past her. The folder didn't have much weight, but she felt its value just the same. She swung the door as Sedge spoke once more. She caught the door with her knee before it finished its trajectory and leaned into the opening.

"When the time is right, let Robert know that we're even...about everything," Sedge said.

"I will. Thanks, and tell Haley I said hey, okay?" Jenny shut the door, backed away, and met Liam in her Jeep.

"Did you see his face?"

"Yeah, so?"

"He just looked sad," Jenny said.

"Sedge broke the law, Jen. For *you*, he went against his code." She turned the ignition, and the car growled to life. She flicked the heater on to kill the brisk air that nagged her bones.

"It was something else. That pitiful expression…it hurts my heart. There was something he doesn't want to tell us."

"We're talking about missing children. I'm sure there's a bunch he's leaving out."

"Let's see what he got for us," she said. Her fingers skimmed the edge of the folder, fluttering the corner, and revealing a healthy stack of papers inside. She flattened the folder on her lap, slid the lever that operated the dome light, and panted at her discovery.

"Holy shit," Liam said. Lining the inside of the folder were photos.

"This can't be. Do I see this right?"

"If you are, then so am I," Liam said. Each photograph was a close-up of a boy near the age of six. Their smiling, happy grins in kindergarten pictures belied the tragic circumstances that led them into the shabby police file.

"Can this be?" Jenny asked.

"They all look the same. I swear to God they look identical, Jen."

"Right?" Twenty pictures, fastened with staples clung, to the perimeter, highlighting blonde hair and round, soft eyes. "These poor boys. They're just babies, babies like my Zack."

"They could be brothers to Zack. The resemblance is too close." Her sight leaped from one image to the next, fierce anger shattered the misery that attempted to seep into her heart.

"This is too much for a coincidence. The abductor chose these kids for their appearance," she said.

"He has a type, an example that he admires and stays close to when finding a new victim," Liam said.

"Zack." Jenny buried her face within her hands, a whisper of sobs escaped her, and she cried as if no one was around. "My instinct screams Morris. He's the one close enough to Zack for this kind of fixation." Liam rifled through Sedge's paperwork, scattering handwritten notes, and witness depositions on either side of the folder. "Here is the first." Liam slid a sheet from the rest and handed it to Jenny. "Toby was the first victim of Morris. Look below." Jenny scanned the documents, eyes darting back and forth until they found what she was looking for on a page.

"This address is in Morris's neighborhood," she said. Liam nodded, his gaze never leaving her.

"We need to make a trip into Morris's neighborhood—into Sherwood Forest."

CHAPTER 13

In the car, Jenny remained quiet as her thoughts turned over and over. Still, she kept them locked away from Liam and herself. She knew the dark streets of the Sherwood community were perfect for Morris's crimes. Streetlights lined the neighborhood closer to the main roads while the inner lanes never made it into the city's budget for lamp installation. *No one would see him come or go.* The Jeep rolled to a stop in front of a house among the modest row of homes.

"That's it, right there." Liam pointed to a house, darkened by time, neglect. Liam imagined children, enthralled by the rumors, daring each other to cross its porch to achieve immortality. All the while, never knowing they almost became the victim.

"They found Toby here two years ago. Are we going inside?" Liam asked, hoping the answer came back negative.

"We have to, Liam. What if our answers are inside?" Before Liam protested, she was out of the Jeep and removing tools from the back. Her hand felt around in the trunk's dark compartment, brushed next to a flashlight, and rotated her palm around to fit its form. She brought the business end of the torch to her face and clicked it on.

Jenny led, and Liam followed to the back of the abandoned home. Overgrown weeds, wild plants, and flowers strangled the broken slate path that escorted them to the back door. The carcass of an alley cat lay beside the stoop with worms crawling in and out. Jenny shone the light on the putrefied feline and stopped short of vomiting on the steps.

"Disgusting," she said in choking gags. "Take this." Liam grabbed the crowbar, placed it between the door and into its casing, and pried. Wood splintered as the thin frame split, freeing the door from its encasement. The door swung open on a squeaky hinge.

"You okay?" Liam asked

"Yes, I'm fine."

"We have to get inside." Liam took the light and made his way into the shadowy kitchen. Buzzing flies circled an unseen food source, and the smell of decay worsened as they shuffled further into the eating area. A bead of light shone on water trickling out of a faucet. Its thin stream glistened.

"Does the file say anything about the crime scene, like where it was?" Jenny asked, somewhere off in the darkness. The absence and comfort of usual radiance began to dig evil talons into her brain. "You need to check the file. I think this was a bad idea."

"Give me a second." He directed the beam of light to the paper in his hand. "One more second." Jenny was losing a battle with her nerves. She stepped forward, and the moon became visible in a broken, curtainless window. She inhaled the musty, mildewed odor of rotting wood—relieved she could at least view the outside. Her heartbeat slowed, not much, just enough to keep her from running for the door.

"Come on, Liam." He shuffled the order of papers.

"Here it is." The beam quivered in his hand.

"They found the body in the basement." Liam moved forward, and she followed away from the soothing moon. Back inside the darkness, Jenny hated the idea that a dead body once shared the same space or that Liam used the word "body" within such blackness. Liam started around one corner and found a dead-end of bedrooms, closets, and a bathroom that made him stop.

"We have to backtrack."

"Great, that's just what I wanted to do, spend more time in this hellhole,"

"Sorry, it's my first time here, and it's dark."

"Just get us there," Jenny said, fighting for composure. Fast-food containers blocked their trail as they passed the living room for the second time.

"I bet these came from squatters," Liam said, kicking cardboard hamburger cartons to one side.

"Good to know." Liam shot the flashlight to a corner of the kitchen where an ominous door stood.

"I think that's it." The brief sight of the door caused her stomach to plunge to the ground floor.

"Maybe we should go back to the car. We shouldn't be here."

"We're already doing this, Jen. I won't be able to go down there if you freak me out. So, please calm down." She nodded for no one to notice. He gripped the door and measured the leeway in the turn that a door without a locking mechanism possessed. The awareness that there wasn't a lock filled him with unexpected pleasure. They descended the wooden staircase one step at a time. First, Liam illuminated the next perilous footing for reconnaissance and then moved with an unsteady step. The act became a terrifying version of red light, green light.

"We're nearing the bottom," Liam coaxed.

"I don't like this. I don't want to be here anymore."

"One more step." Liam guided her down with a balancing hand. "Can you feel that?"

"No, what?"

"There's something down here with us." Liam turned the flashlight in every direction as if he were training a rifle on a prowling animal. Cinderblocks sprouted, jutted, and reached out for them at every angle.

"I don't see anybody," Liam said.

"It's Toby. I know it is," Jenny said.

"Toby, the boy murdered—" Liam didn't finish. He stabbed her with a shine of his light. Her eyelids squeezed together tighter than a swollen doorjamb.

"I'm not about to do this alone, open your eyes." He watched as she obeyed. "There is nothing down here." He searched the cellar floor until he spotted something unusual. "Did you see that?"

"See what? I saw nothing," Jenny said. Liam moved to the far edge of the basement with Jenny watching the beam diminish in the distance.

"Where are you going? Liam?" A fearful tone returned to her voice.

"Right here. Either follow me or wait there." Her movements were slow in the beginning and then jerked her body in motion in a straight line behind her friend.

"I'm with you." Jenny studied the focus of Liam's attention. "What are we looking at?"

"Steel chain links—broken all over the floor." Liam plucked the gnarled scraps of metal and positioned them onto his palm. "The police department must have cut these." He dropped the links, and they clanked with a heavy thud on the cement floor. "God, look at those." Two short chains sprouted from the surface and seemed to grow from the cement itself. "They cut Toby out of these chains." Jenny kneeled onto the basement floor, almost lying on her stomach as if she were watching a television program.

She lifted her open hand over the ends buried into the cement. It threw off heat. She moved her hand away from the top twice as a child might test a candle and pushed her hand onto the chain restraints. A flash started under her chin, a dull pain, like ice cream, left too long in the mouth. It soon swallowed the entirety of her face, running along her delicate jawline, and devouring her substantial cheekbones that sat high on her face. The pain forced her face upward into a smile that was frightening, unnatural in its queer imitation, causing her muscles to contract.

"He's here. Please don't leave me, Liam."

"I'm not going—" There was a sound, faint but loud enough to cut Liam off. He recognized the squeaky hinge of the basement door. He stilled himself to let the noise rise in the wind and carry itself to his ears. His heartbeat drummed along, rhythmic cadences stirring his stomach and throbbing in his throat. As all sound faded, the basement door crashed shut—wood splintered against wood—echoing from one brick wall to the other. Liam aimed at the open staircase with his flashlight, using instinct rather than any thoughtful intentions.

Footsteps, loud and hollow on the wood planks, rang from one step to the next. Down the stairs, footfalls thudded from the invisible assailant. The light jittered in his hand to find no trace of the person making the walking reverberations.

"Who's there? Show yourself," he said. The clatter continued until the bottom step roared with sound and then faded away. Liam stood silent, watching the darkness for any movement. Jenny's voice swelled, and she screamed something Liam couldn't make out.

"It's burning my eyes," she said. Liam tried to move to her.

"Stay away—stay back." Liam froze.

"What's burning your eyes, Jenny?"

"I can't see you anymore."

"Follow my voice," he cautioned.

"Where did all of this light come from?" Liam looked at the flashlight, resting in his hand. "There are floodlights in every corner. Were they always here?"

"Jenny, I'm coming to get you."

"No. I see him now, Liam." He didn't want to ask. "I see Toby chained to the ground. He's yanking at the chains." Tears wash out her voice. "He's clawing at the floor. I see the blood pour from his fingertips." Liam aimed the flashlight to the ground near the remaining chains and spotted the claw marks with their thin scratches, making a brighter color in the stone.

"I see the claw marks. They're faded but still there." Jenny ignored her friend's interjection.

"Jesus, Liam. Toby is staring at me. He can see me." Jenny started to cry.

"He's not there, Jenny. It's in your mind." Liam didn't believe his own words.

"I'm not your mommy. I can't help you, Toby," she said. "Stop calling me mommy," Jenny screamed and put her hands over her ears. "You get away from him, you son of a bitch."

"Who is it? Who do you see?" Liam asked.

"He's just a shadow," she whispered so the entity wouldn't notice her.

"Look at his face. Don't look away. He can't hurt you. Just look at his face." Jenny squinted at the dark figure, and he seemed to grow darker. Cuts began to appear in long stretches on Toby's back. His cries filled her ears, filled her mouth, and to her horror, she discovered the sound originated from inside her.

"He's killing him. Stop him."

"I can't, we can't," Liam said. A second flash, one brighter than the first, erased her vision.

"It's over."

"What was that, Jenny?" She shook her head.

"Before I found out I was pregnant with Zack, Morris tied me to the bed—beat me, and raped me. He starved me until I didn't have the strength even to focus my eyes. He repeated this cycle for a week. I don't think I called it rape then…it was my fault somehow." Jenny didn't finish.

"You saw him, with Toby? Morris?"

"I couldn't see anyone there, but I'm sure it was him, Liam. I know it was him. He can't get away with this."

"He won't, I promise." Liam thought about the cold air outside, the moon shining high above the horizon, and progressed to the steps clasping Jenny's arm. "We'll get him."

CHAPTER 14

The dreams the prisoners are experiencing as a group have shifted from one generation to the next in backward order like the television show, This Is Your Life, but spanning thousands of years instead of one brief lifetime. Damon wasn't exaggerating—he wasn't trying to frighten me with obscure occult practices. He told me nothing but the truth. I couldn't take the truth any more than a soldier coming home from war could take hearing the news of his faithful wife straying in his absence. Reality sank-in slow—perhaps I might have saved a few more lives if I would have acted faster. Self-doubt is better suited for others, a historian, or someone who can pass judgment out of hand without knowing what I know or going through what I have.

More inmates died by suicide this week. I have attended so many services as of late—I can deliver the sermon myself. Tears for human life are running dry. I'm now an empty husk following the rituals my job decrees—our head infirmary physician, Carl, passed-out medicines with the promise of a good night's sleep. Damon's projected dreams affected the sensitive inmates in a harsh degree compared to others.

The problem came later when the doped-up inmates couldn't wake from their nightmares. By the morning, the drugs wore off, and the dreams damaged the poor fellows. We came to find out the ability to stir from their night terrors was their last defense. When they woke, they could do little more than mumble and drool. My heart went out to those mindless creatures devoid of reality.

I ran out of options. That was the primary reason I took my life into my own hands, and I owed it to the prisoners who experienced torture well beyond their crimes. I called my wife Karie, and I tried to explain to her I needed to sleep over for work, and I knew I would have to spend the next morning baring my soul to calm her fears. My guard cleared the cell next to

Damon's and brought along Anthony to secure me during the night. He didn't look like he owned the resolve to take on the task, but his loyalty to me kept him from refusing.

My new cell was cold and dank from years of moisture. I leaned on my bunk, watched as Anthony sat in a chair just outside the bars, and in the middle between my cell and Damon's. He propped his rifle across his knee, each end teetered until it steadied itself, then leveling flat.

I stretched out on the thin bed, listening to the springs expand under me. I heard whispers and quiet conspirators closing in through the bars. Anthony looked in often, squinting to check on my slumber, hoping I wouldn't doze. A brick wall divided me from Damon, and still, I felt his gaze.

My skin crawled from the dark thoughts dwelling in his head a few feet away. I needed to know, to experience, to fill myself with the danger Damon posed to the world. Everyone affected by the dreams changed, some a little, and others ruptured down to the core. I wanted insight without consequence. I realize it sounded naïve—I believed I was invulnerable to whatever awaited me in the Deceiver and the Father of lies.

The gray coldness of the cell walls closed in around me, and I understood their power to dominate firsthand. I despised how they made me feel but relished their existence, their protective quality. I had an important job, I never doubted, but I was too late by the time the convicts traveled my way. Bringing wholesale refuge to the population turned my thoughts inward and convinced me to test fate. There was a risk, more profound and far more sinister waiting inside Damon. My plan to enter his dreams and waddle around like a pig in a stile was beneath me. Uncharted consequences lay ahead, but I never strayed from my course.

At one moment, I increased my leg's reach over the thin mattress—each muscle flexed and stiffened under my power. My body, racked with exhaustion, never crept further from sleep than in that instance. I noticed a water bug as it scampered from behind the toilet. Its legs undulated, antenna twitching, and it moved in a sudden spurt back behind the commode. The next moment, the icy block walls vanished. I must have drifted off to sleep.

My claustrophobia from the cramped cell gave way to my body floating through clouds. The billowy vapors living miles above the Earth surrounded me like my grandmother's hand-made quilts. White mist skirted by my cheeks, with its cold haze dousing me with its ghostly form. Before I could gauge my speed, I was out of the clouds, descended from a great height, dropping downward in vast distances at once, my fall slowed just as panic sped my heart into an irregular rhythm.

My body jerked from gravity's amazing force. However, it wasn't my body running the show—it was Damon's. I was inside his powerful frame, inhabiting it with no more control than a parasite living in its host. I peered from his eyes, concentrating my mental focus, and attempted to train my vision on the horizon.

My effort was useless as I was a slave to his whims, locked into him without recourse. Through his sockets, I saw the land unfold below me in mountainous ranges and long continuous desert plains, seeming to go on forever like the oceans kissed by the shores of every continent.

The enormity of the expanse humbled me. My sight darted within Damon's vision to fix on a landmark and came up empty. I made no sense of the nightmarish predicament—my instinct was in disbelief that any place on the Earth was devoid of a human population. What I was looking at felt wrong, out of place, and desolate. The terrain appeared unused. I was an archeologist, glimpsing an ancient site for the first time.

A euphoric state grew, swelling in my chest, or Damon's chest. His pride contracted his muscles, steeling his body for whatever lay ahead. He mastered the power of flight, and I questioned whether I was a bystander in Damon's past indiscretions, or I wandered into Damon's subconscious, like Edgar

Allan Poe's poem, A Dream Within a Dream. I wondered if Damon bent and twisted the laws of physics to his evil will. The thought penetrated my resolve, toyed with my weaknesses, and forced me to examine my beliefs.

My hearing reclaimed its dominance as the sound of air packed my ears with the thrashing, displacement of wind. The whispering noise made me think of pumping my five-year-old legs, lifting my arms in the shape of an airplane, and scattering pigeons willy-nilly. In childhood memory, I stood in the middle of a sea of filthy birds, their wings flapping to form the unnerving sound of death in their swirling feathery currents around me. I locked onto the fearful experience and tried to push the thought to the back of my mind.

We soared high above the planet. The absurdity of our height stoked my anxiety, impelling my unease to its most perilous climax. Somehow, I knew I wasn't in any danger, yet what my heart assumed, and my mind protested never came together into rational thought. I accepted the reality presented, dragging myself from the vagueness of Damon's dream world as I stared through the human portal.

As I was getting a bearing, the air around became heavy, thick enough to choke Damon, lodging itself in his throat with every breath. The alarming bird sounds returned, and I waited, wondering what could follow. The flapping increased, the air solidified, and I wanted off the ride. I needed to escape, praying for anywhere but fastened to this monster.

Damon's eyes glanced down without worry, and I saw the ground coming up to meet us. It came fast, too fast, and I understood why the atmosphere seemed to drain from around us. The bird clamor, I discovered, pushed the air away from us, and this was what gave us enough drag to slow before we hit bottom.

A few hundred yards from our landing, I could see the desert ground circling the foot of the mountain. The walls of the mountain rose high above. In some areas, the pitch jutted straight up, and then it leaned back toward the center a mile upward until the ground ran sideways to a plateau resting on the summit above the mass of rock.

The platform seemed human-made, sheared smooth across the size of a football field. Damon touched the platform's surface with the tips of his toes, coming down on his heels as soft as a feather. If the surface were concave instead of even, I'd have likened it to a spot where Roman orators might speak to the gathered public. The view alluded to an earlier time, a time when serious beings decided important issues. My mind captured the concept of an ancient race, men who fought for their survival when the world was young, and their choices scant.

The flapping revisited with far more force, carrying with it a vibration, shaking the bedrock underfoot. Others were descending all around us. I wanted to scream, to scream inside Damon's body to get away, to dash before it was too late. The creatures didn't wear any clothes. My eyes recognized them as human and not human all at once, like some atomic horror movie where fallout combined the attributes of two different species.

Their bodies, men and women, looked both strong and lean, approaching the caricature of what a human body should appear at its best. The sculpture, David carved by Michelangelo centuries ago, rattled in my brain, and I questioned whether these beings inspired him, the same creatures he attempted to bring out of the stone.

The first difference I noticed in the creatures was the odd material wrapped around their backs in bleached white lumps. I first thought the pieces resembled arms, larger than the two sprouted from the shoulders of every other person I knew since birth until a stripped-down understanding shattered my wall and showed me the light. I mistook the form for arms. The eerie sounds like pigeons, to my weary mind, dissolved into wings. Each of the creature's wings extended outward, reaching the size of a man and moving as independent as the fingers of a hand. *Wings moved up and down — feathers stretched and contorted—attached to their backs were the spines of the wings.*

Each wore dissent in their black eyes—resembling large marbles as black as midnight. The creatures darted fearful expressions toward one another. Every face, slender and sculpted, watched Damon. Fear and distrust stole their defiant stance and gave them the look of children, feeble in their resolve.

The creature closest to us spoke through pursed lips of rosy red. The sound of his vocalization was unknown to me. He emitted a series of strangled articulations, drenching me with a horrible dread. I watched his tightened lips and saw for the first time the implementation of his shrill speech. A red tongue, a shade darker than his lips, poked from his mouth—sniffing the air like a serpent. The organ of speech oscillated back and forth like the wings of a hummingbird, shimmying. They neither extending further from its shelter nor retreating after he finished each sentiment.

With every pause, the tongue stood still in the air, thread-like flesh widened to separate tongues forming a forked shape at the end. The tips of the split tongue fluttered in the wind like antennae with the ability to smell, or taste, or maybe discern.

I wanted to scream, and I might have given myself over to a scream if I thought rescue was possible. The lone comfort that kept my mind from separating, like the creature's hideous tongue, was the vision wasn't happening in the present. Whatever I was witnessing didn't have the immediacy of real life. The whole experience seemed like a disorienting fogginess of déjà vu. Although I saw through Damon's eyes, I remained safe from all the wicked consequences accompanying the vision.

Distracted by the serpent qualities of the creature, it soon dawned on me—I understood his hisses and rattled clamoring. I didn't know then, and I haven't understood since, but the nonsense sounds filling my ears turned into words in my brain, singing a sweet song. His speech wasn't the common words, and I was like a deaf child understanding the essence of a story through a few careful signed gestures. Before I tapped into what he was saying, I picked a name from within the language. Damon didn't sense any malice from the confrontation, yet what I sensed was the intimacy a conspiracy alone provided. The situation evolved into something far more significant than they planned.

They leveled all hope upon Damon as the deliverer. He never shrank back from the duty. But what I felt in him was a subtle acknowledgment of impending failure. He disguised his notions of certain ruin with a sarcastic smile and a defiant voice, and he never faltered, never gave one inch of ground even with the entire burden heaped on him.

The wind began to pick up, and I saw the feathers of the creatures bristled from the cold chill swooping across the mountain peak. A female of the group wrapped her arms around her body, sheathing herself from the biting frost, and hoisting her head skyward. White clouds, I waded into a moment earlier, grew dark as if someone spilled viscous ink into its billowy contours and allowed it to seep. A word, hard to distinguish in a blowing gust, sailed past. Watchers, the wind spoke. I knew at once the wind gave a name, and it referred to the winged creatures, the Watchers. They looked from one face to the next and back again. The stolid expressions of the Watchers reworked themselves into a state of worry I never conceived possible.

First, the female, and then a male Watcher closest to Damon, raised their wings above their shoulders. The simple act put me in mind of a sleepy toddler stretching before sleep overtook it. A couple more Watchers joined in the movement. What I perceived to be common agitation grew in the Watchers.

They lifted and lowered their wings with a fury that tensed every muscle in their potent bodies. Wings flapped, the wind kicked up, and weaker feathers became dislodged by the *whirlwind. The Watchers tried to leave the ground, escape whatever reprisal awaited them by the voice that spoke their name, an entity that wielded enough power to carry words on the very wind. Wings became a blur in Damon's eyes, yet the group of Watchers never broke off into the air. Disbelief expelled from their faces until resignation settled in and softened their furious thrashing.*

Damon never attempted to move from his spot. The wind, energized by fear, batted the Watchers back and forth like an invisible hand pushing and pulling their bodies as their feet remained rooted to the mountain's bedrock. The female of the bunch began to cry out in long moans as her body elongated, stretching up and out by the force of the wind. Her wails increased, causing her tone to tighten into a high shrill and stopped altogether when the lightning started. Damon searched skyward in the electric storm for its cause, finding no connection between the looming clouds and its violent volts.

The lightning continued at a faster pace forming a wall and encircling the Watchers within it. The brilliant light was soundless, to my surprise. Damon watched the electrified boundary, and I thought I detected pride in him as he witnessed the miraculous occurrence.

The Watchers abandoned their useless struggle—their hairless bodies shivered as the barricade of lightning elevated the air temperature too fast to reckon. Next, the oxygen got sucked out of their lungs, and I felt Damon gasp when his chest flattened against his ribs. The electrified wall was bright enough to sting the eyes. The Watchers spun their gaze from the light to their feet, saving their vision and hoping the dreadful anomaly would cease, and they could flutter to safety. Their prospects fled like a narrowing tunnel with a keyhole escape. Just when they thought the light of their confinement might burn through to their brains, a high-pitched hum rose, cut into their eardrums, and vibrated their bones.

The droning pressed on and seemed to clatter Damon's teeth. His serpent tongue sputtered from his mouth, licking his lips, and convulsing with the monotonous hum. The moment the hum reached its lofty peak, the desert fell silent. Glossy black eyes turned from side to side inside frightened heads. They searched for the cause of the hum, and the reason it ceased. The flood of adrenaline coursing through Damon began to spill out to the other Watchers. A female Watcher cried out for mercy. Mercy, from what? The wind, the storm? I knew there was something far more aggressive in the air than a sudden storm.

The terror I witnessed in the expressions of the defiant little group, huddled in a circle, made me wish for a sudden return to the hum. When the silence broke, I thought I was dying, or Damon was dying as I lay inside him. The noise stirred feelings in Damon. The sound was a voice—strong and never wavering. I began to cry. My soul cried out toward the heavens for sweet release. I prayed to see with my own eyes what could make such a beautiful sound. The words seemed to bounce into Damon's ears, caressing its way in, and planting a soft seed before dissipating.

The language wasn't English. I don't know what language it was, yet I understood every phrase, every nuance as if I spoke the dialect my entire life. In the dialect, I felt joy, pain, hatred, lust, and a mingling of hundreds of other emotions fading in and out of each other like a child's kaleidoscope transitioning from one hue to the next. The Watchers spoke, but the sound never came from the lips. I knew the voice was using the "old language," or at least that was how Damon thought. It was a divine language—predating every spoken dialect.

From Damon's eyes, I saw for the first time the origin of the heavenly voice materialized in the air. I didn't understand the apparition—looking back—I still have a hard time putting human words to the sight. I guess it's like a Cro-Magnon man trying to wrap his mind around a television or the sounds *sputtering from a radio. At first, I thought I willed Damon's attention to the spot, and I soon realized he was more transfixed to the spot than I was. Thin air began to ripple like the ripples on a pond.*

Ripples came from inside the air—the space in between the particles of oxygen and hydrogen—never seen by man. A magician's trap door might be a better example. The trap door looked like a sturdy wooden door but kept a secret from the eyes. Within the space in the air, the ripples came together in tight little wrinkles and spread out further from each other to allow for the melodic words to tumble from the trap door. A dog whistle came to mind as I saw the high pitch sounds forming patterns. The shapes existed there all along, and my human eyes just then recognized them. The voice possessed a sweet, dreamy quality.

Struck with fear, the Watchers trembled. A shadow began to form into a speck—the shadow increased until it was near the size of a building. The phantom's dark color faded from a gray fog to an ethereal white cloud floating atop the ripples mixing with them as a face emerged.

There's no way to describe the face—I often tried to recall the features afterward and failed at the exercise. I got a glimpse of his face and felt a rush of warmth and the same sensation filling Damon's chest with the glowing heat of morning sunshine. In less than a blink of an eye, Damon turned away, leaving his inside cold and hollow from its absence. I longed for the vision once more and couldn't fathom why anyone would turn from something so inviting. My heart begged Damon to turn back to the glowing warmth. He didn't, and neither did the rest of the Watchers.

Their faces showed the paint from the brush of shame. Black eyes darted everywhere, avoiding the mesmerizing display. I could feel the longing for the comfort of the dark visage inside each of the Watchers. Their need was far stronger than mine, and my uncontrollable urges shifted to sad empathy for the torture the creatures endured for so long. They wished for the apparition, and now they hoped for its departure.

I glimpsed the being and wanted to see what lifted my spirits with profound ease. No one could muster the courage to level their gaze the being's way. I feared the beautiful face, bringing so much sudden joy to me might elude my eyes forever when Damon did the unexpected and craned his neck toward the solidifying cloud. A mist surrounding the face seemed to react to Damon's defiance. The cloud took form and arms appeared, first in rough shapes, like a child's rough sketch of what an imagined limb resembled, then the arms became clear to the eyes with a solid body joining right after. I couldn't say the being, formed in front of us, was extraordinary, but it was just the same.

The immense man towered over us like a porcelain statue come to life, and he possessed a pull on me I couldn't put my fingers on. It didn't click just then what my fascination was with the two-story creature until much later. One way to describe him was charisma, filled to the brim with it, and all I wanted to do was bask in his light.

When Damon spoke, the air fell from my chest. I could no longer breathe, or Damon couldn't, rather. I attempted to gauge whether the mighty creature was compressing Damon's body, or it was Damon's excessive fear restricting his breath. What I could measure was Damon's anger. It was a forest fire raging below the surface, piercing the air from the threshold of his mouth with every stabbing word. Damon was a child angry with a parent and unwilling to back down.

Damon told the being he was no longer a part of his group. From that moment forward, Damon survived in the pleasure of disobedience. I waited for a response from the creature and found nothing amiss in his expression. He promised to defy his former master with every squeeze of his hands and every thought in his mind.

Damon pointed East toward a green dot on the horizon. He revealed his intentions to the Watchers, and the mighty creature rested no longer. He doubled in size before us, and yet my eyes couldn't detect his growth. I thought it was a trick of the senses, but there he was, larger in stature. His melodious voice changed to a sound scrapping the ears like razors. Venom came alive in the creature's words. He warned against interfering in the lives of humans. The reality of the situation threatened to knock me—Damon off his feet. I was facing God!

CHAPTER 15

The bedroom was dark. Some light came in through the blinds from the moon's glow, but not enough to illuminate Jenny's surroundings. She lay there, not awake, and not asleep. For *her*, it was the most liberating time of the day. She had no responsibilities—no worries squirmed their way into her thoughts. It was also the shortest part of her day. Her sunrise dreams were of the sweetest nature.

In Jenny's dreams, she has self-esteem that is plump and with no visible scars. She still has her youth, her future, and not a trace of stretch marks. Not that stretch marks bothered her, and no one complained. It's just the fact that they are there, and they are something else she can't change in her life—reminders of the side effects of living. Even before she opened her eyes, the slumbering world began to melt. The slim, stick-like high school Jenny faded, and the sturdy, weathered Jenny slipped into the vacated spot.

Her physical appearance ebbed in, but her bright-colored fantasyland still clung to her. In the distance, she heard the clinking of the chains of a swing set. Without the image coming into her dream mind, her memory recalled the old elementary swings of her youth like a dream within a dream. Her mind's eye constructed a childhood swing—worn blue strap seat with the thick knotted steel links. Traces of rust gathered across the chain's skin from years of harsh Ohio weather.

Jenny pictured the chain's lofty climb toward the claw hooks that sunk into the belly of a chain-link, holding it prisoner. Some bigger kid folded the top portion of the swing's chain down so that the swing sat higher. With the steel hook, piercing the chain, and the remaining links flopping against itself. She heard more of the chain chime, and this time the noise didn't match up.

A moment later, the chain flopped. Clink, flop. Clink, flop. The out of sync image put a strain on her thinking. Her dream went from peaceful, easy-going to a labored mystery she needed to unravel. Clink, flop. Clink, flop. Clink, flop. She synchronized the sound of the swing's chain like a person might turn the television channel when the remote batteries have sung their last song. It was no use—she couldn't satisfy her conception of the image and dropped it away altogether. The clinking sound continued. Besides the clinking, she felt her heartbeat, pounding harder and faster.

The first stirs of panic awakened in her as sleep's paralysis continued to recede. With each passing second, the clinking chain grew louder. Soon her only thought was waking, getting out of the dream turned nightmare. During her bad marriage to Morris, Jenny often found that nightmares would invade her sleep, pushing them away during the day and becoming a prisoner to them at night.

The problem she faced was there was no dream to escape. Blackness and the clinking sound. *What is that sound?* The noise repeated into the black abyss of an empty background. Her heartbeat doubled its intensity, her breathing increased, and perspiration drenched her skin. The foggy edges of reality were coming to her, and *that* gave her hope. Contained in her hope was the trickery all dreams shared, revealing a lifeline to drag it away by the unconscious mind. The closer she arrived at waking, the louder the chain would clink and rattle. *It was trying to suck me back in.*

She soon realized that her ears were hurting, a hurt that came from the constant clamor. The noise rose to an unbearable pitch. She imagined herself covering her ears, and there she *was* sitting up in her bedroom. The darkened space stretched out in front of her, and to her shock, her ears were under extreme pressure. Both palms pressed against the ears hard enough to leave marks on her hands. She removed her grip slow like she was testing the air for alarm bells. The room was silent.

Jenny leaned toward Robert and caressed an empty mattress. With the nightmare already fading, she darted her eyes to Robert's side of the bed and then rebounded them to the digital clock that read: 4:30

"Where in the hell is he? Late night at the office, I guess," she said in a whisper. Her thinking was her own again, and the first thought was of a smoke. She slid her bare bottom across the cotton sheets—reaching for her nightstand and the pack of cigarettes. Jenny pulled the pack, arched her back against the headboard, pushed her knees close to her chest, and cradled them. In a flash, she placed a cigarette on her lips with a light igniting the tip.

Smoking cigarettes always beat her. She wanted nothing more than to give up the habit forever. Jenny tried hundreds of times to kick them, but when things got tough, they held her hand. They were a crutch that yellowed her teeth and killed a little every day. What she also accepted was they kept her sane, they let her think, and sometimes that short moment was all she needed to rejoin happy society with PTA meetings, soccer practices, and neighborhood watches.

Jenny inhaled a deep drag, holding the smoke in her lungs for the nicotine to permeate her body—to give her the quick rushed she desired. She exhaled, smoke dribbling out of her mouth, forming a smoky curtain in front of her face. The smoke danced in the air, and she watched with little interest until it took shape. At the start, the smoky mist resembled clouds with their abstract quality, a creative mind made into shapes. Creativity was no longer necessary, as the mist took on a solid form complete with legs, arms, and head. Accusing eyes stared back at Jenny from the corner of the room. The apparition was so disarming that her first instinct was to jump into the air. Instead, the surprise sent her head back, meeting the headboard with the base of her skull.

Jenny closed her eyes and felt the strain from the force. For a moment, she second-guessed his existence at all. Her eyelids fluttered from the stress, and she wondered if she would open them again. She never wanted to open them—it seemed foolish to dare—but she pried them open. The smoke dissipated, and the vivid shape of a figure sitting in the corner faded back into the scenery. Although the prospect of someone or something watching in her room was frightening, she was regaining her composure as it began vanishing before her eyes.

She inhaled on the cigarette and blew it out in the same violent manner. A thick cloud of smoke returned to the air between her and the corner. In an instant, the figure was back and as complete and present as anyone she ever saw. The sight was too much for her to take. She lunged back, threw the bedsheets over her head, and waited.

The sheet threads loomed big in her eyes. She studied the pattern and noticed the silence—nothing stirred. She sensed the presence, but that was all. Jenny wanted nothing more in the world than to keep the cover over her head, fall back asleep, and forget the strange occurrence ever happened. Still, she wanted to know for sure and decided that she wouldn't hide. Her plan was like a Band-Aid—torn away from the skin all at once. 1…2…3 She paused then, ripped the cover away.

She popped her head and craned her neck toward the corner. In the wafting smoke, an inch from her face was another set of eyes. They burned with pain and anger. Although he had no weight, the figure was on her chest. The posture was horrifying to her senses. Legs folded underneath, crouching down with piteous hands out. To Jenny, it looked like a rat's posture before tearing into food or maybe a praying mantis devouring an insect. The sight was jarring but slipping away again.

Before Jenny could decide or even control it, her mouth was open, her neck was lifting her head high, and a terrifying scream erupted from her throat. The figure disappeared even as the sound departed from her mouth. Its absence played no part in her mental state, she couldn't stop the wail if she tried, and she never did.

Jenny took in air and belted out a scream twice as loud as her first. Her lungs expanded and burned as she expelled the breath along with a banshee scream. Time lost its importance as the cries continued. Shaking brought her around again or at least quieted her screech, for the moment. Liam's big hand was on her shoulder, nudging her back and forth until the color of the world came back to her. Liam scanned the empty room.

"What's wrong, Jenny?" An absent expression heightened his anxiety. His shaking stopped the screaming, but it never brought her to where he was.

"Something's in here," she said, close to tears. Liam's skin began to crawl. They were alone in the room, but he would not argue with her.

"Who's in here?" She didn't answer.

"I don't see anyone, Jen," Liam said with a touch of sadness in his voice.

"In the smoke, it's in the smoke," she said.

"What smoke?" Liam's tone gave away his impatience. A thin strand of smoke spiraled up. Liam followed the smoke trail to its origin. A burning cigarette sat between Jenny's fingers with its hot tip smoldering close to the flesh. Liam snatched the rest of the cigarette before it met skin. Jenny nodded her head toward the foot of the bed.

Liam looked at the empty spot at the bottom of the bed. A robe and an extra blanket lay there in a crumpled pile. He hesitated a little longer, took in smoke from the cigarette, and blew toward the bottom edge of the bed. The smoke exited in a blast and accumulated, settling over Liam's target area.

The mist quavered, solidifying, and outlined the figure's form. Like magic, the shape of a small boy appeared where there was nothing. Liam shot off the bed, pressing himself against the doorway opposite the apparition. He went from a skeptic to a man of total belief in a short span when he saw right off that the boy was no photographic representation. He blinked, appeared to breathe, and swiveled his head to acknowledge both Jenny and Liam.

"Mommy?" The boy cried with his voice, not matching his mouth movements.

"My God, it's Toby," Liam said.

No sooner had he talked than the smoke disintegrated, and Toby along with it.

"Liam, the smoke," she said. He reacted quick, plucking the ashtray off the nightstand, placed the cigarette inside, and scooted it under the spot Toby materialized. Smoke floated to the ceiling bringing Toby back. Curiosity replaced Jenny's apprehension. Fear captured Jenny, but with Liam there, she didn't feel alone with the supernatural presence.

Even with the child's contorted face of pain, Jenny saw the visitation as a sign, a miracle, somehow celestial. It meant that there was something out there besides them. They weren't an accident. Jenny got the proof she so desired. Night after night, she would pray that things could get better and that the horror of Morris would not touch her or her child, and every prayer session brought her farther away from anything spiritual. After Jenny gave up hope, she saw the face of God in the form of a child dead and buried. The murder case was growing cold—the headlines stopped making the news, and the town would move on with their lives. They might forget about Toby, but she wouldn't forget.

Jenny had tons of reasons to want to punish Morris. She held onto her unhappy grievances, all personal and heartbreaking. They were her fuel to get her up in the morning and keeping her going through each day. Morris made her from selfish hatred. To say that Jenny thought of killing Morris was an understatement. The idea always ran through her mind. She pictured the gun pushed into the side of his temple, watching his eyes turn round with fear. In her best fantasy moments, she smelled shit as it loaded his pants. That was a favorite image that mixed vengeance with guilty pleasure to give birth to an ugly joy. The sensation started in her stomach—moving up and out as if expelling a deep breath. But, a death like that would never satisfy.

Thirty seconds of self-examination, followed by a quick and painless death, was far from enough. The sight of Toby allowed her the opportunity to put aside her obsessions of revenge. The chance to save more helpless children from Morris's grip was an act of redemption, washing away her selfish desires and replacing them with noble ones.

"How do you explain this?" Jenny asked. She watched the flickering in and out. The translucent mist showed Toby and the room behind him.

"I can't. You brought him back from that basement—Toby tagged along with us," Liam said. He moved to the bed with caution, sat down next to Jenny, and held his breath like a bomb diffuser waiting for an explosion.

"There's more meaning behind this," Jenny was not ready to let go of the magic of the miracle, "Toby is showing us something." As the words fell from her mouth, the child's form flickered, and then blinked out.

"Whoa, whoa, whoa, what happened?" They searched in the dark with frantic movements. "We won't hurt you, Toby," Jenny spoke to the air, "come back. Bring him back, Liam."

"I don't know how to do that. Wait, a minute—" Liam darted from the bedroom.

"Where are you going?" Jenny called after him. When Liam returned, he held a bundle of incense in his hand.

"This might work." Jenny's eyes lit up.

"You're a genius," she said with giddy exuberance. Liam placed a rubber band around a bundle of incense and put an open flame to the tips. Flames burst from the ends, turning hot, and becoming ashen smolder. Smoke streamed from the multitude of incense sticks, building a thick wall of smoke.

"I thought we might need more smoke," he said. Jenny nodded as they both watched and waited.

An hour passed before they entertained thoughts that the entity might not make an encore.

"Thanks for being here tonight. Making this trip is hard without Robert," she said, scooting over on the bed, resting her head on his chest, and watched the incense trails dance.

"So, where is Captain America tonight?"

"Out protecting the world, I guess," Jenny let out a discreet sigh.

"You don't care for him much, do you?"

"I think it's the other way around," he said, not making eye contact.

"Robert would kill me if I told you this—he came from a modest upbringing. Working-class parents, his mother was a school-teacher—the whole thing." Liam nodded. "Well, on Robert's tenth birthday, there was a fire. It started on the second floor of his childhood home. When his birthday rolled around that year, his parents allowed him to paint his bedroom any color he chose as a birthday gift. As his parents slept, Robert worked late into the night painting.

When he called it quits for the night, Robert headed down to the couch and away from the paint fumes." The story enthralled Liam.

"What he didn't realize as he drifted off to sleep was that the paint thinner rags that he used to clean the brushes were both left next to an electrical outlet. Later at the scene, a fireman said that the old outlet must have sent out a spark which ignited the rags and a thinner can." Jenny flicked her lighter, letting the flame grow then lit a cigarette. "The flames in the house burned fast—first burning the adjoining wall that separated Robert's room from his parents. In the blink of an eye, the fire was inside the master bedroom."

"Did his parents sleep through the fire?" Liam asked in a nervous tone. Jenny shook her head.

"Robert awakened to the crackle of wood, the snapping of heated glass, and their screams. Robert rushed up the stairs in time to watch his parent's bedroom door burst into flames. He stood there in front of the blazing door and listened to his parents tell him they *loved* him one last time." Tears filled Jenny's eyes as she paused. Liam followed suit. "He survived that night, and every March 13th, he goes off by himself to be alone to grieve that tenth birthday." Jenny stopped, looked out at the smoke again. She took in her smoke and added to the cloud with her exhalation.

"Jenny, I did not understand," he said.

"You couldn't know.

"Listen, Liam…I know Robert comes across as a little abrasive." Liam raised his eyebrows with mock outrage.

"A little abrasive?" Jenny tried on a smile that didn't fit too well.

"From what I've heard, his mother was a saint . . . the thing I'm trying to say is . . . he has issues, he has his hang-ups, and I have even been unfortunate enough to witness some of his prejudices." Jenny lifted herself eye to eye with Liam, "But I also believe with all my heart that losing a mother and father, will put some obstacles in your social development. Robert is a generous, committed man. Trust my judgment on this—I lived with an evil man before him, and I know the difference. Give *him* a chance, Liam. For me, please," she said, wiping tears away. Liam pulled her close, wrapping her into his arms.

"I am *so* sorry, Jen, and I trust your judgment, **and** from this moment on, Robert and I will get along. *That*, I promise." They sat on the bed, holding each while Jenny continued to cry.

Jenny sat up straight on the bed. In the pit of her stomach, a swooshing began. It was soft at first, then rising with the pressure of small dragonflies—buzzing and bouncing off the fleshy walls.

"Did you feel that? Something's happening." Liam nodded. He relied on her senses and knew her connection with Toby.

"It runs through my body as it enters our world." Liam rocked on his feet and waited with exhausted patience. Liam perceived none of what Jenny described, except he detected a sudden drop in temperature in the room. It was a subtle decline at the start and moving toward chilly. True to her word, Toby was appearing. With the help of the bundle of incense, the apparition was more formed than before.

"It is Toby," Jenny said. His face was visible, matching the pictures in the police investigation folder. Toby sat there, frozen in that horrible moment—a grimace seized Toby's face as if he was dealing with an agony somewhere far off. They both watched Toby react to unseen hands. His body undulated back and forth from a barrage of blows issued beyond the room. Jenny found the reenactment hard to take, and the helplessness tore at her heart. A lump developed in her throat as she spoke.

"Pay close attention. There's something we're meant to see." Toby's hair was dirty blonde. Sweat caused the front of his bangs to matt down—he was nude except for a pair of underwear. Jenny spotted the superhero Underoos, Spiderman, like the ones her son wore. Dirt caked Tobey's olive-colored skin, with scrapes and bruises covering his entire body. The urge to avert his eyes came over Liam in a rush. He didn't want to see anymore.

"Look at that. Right there. You see that?" Jenny asked. Her finger pointed toward a leather device under Toby's chin. Liam squinted, rubbed his eyelids with his fingertips, and focused.

"I think it's a dog choker." Toby reached out—blocked by chains that held tight. He fought against the links and relented to their strength. His red eyes looked as if they cried for hours. Jenny saw that he neared the end of his struggle. Toby was wearing toward total submission. *That's what Morris had in mind*, Jenny thought. Small hands extended outward for salvation. No one heard, and he suffered alone in his last moments. Jenny was a silent bystander to the events until Toby locked his eyes on hers and reached for her.

"Mommy?" The sight was devastating. She wondered if he could see her and settled on that it didn't matter. Either way, it was too much for her to bear. She moved toward him.

"Mommy, is that you? Help me, Mommy," Toby cried. A shadow crept up behind him, causing his voice to fill with panic.

"Stay away. Mommy . . ." The choker clamped down, and his voice cut off. Jenny threw her arms around the boy. She fanned the smoke away with her approach, and Toby disappeared. She looked for the little suffering boy and found nothing left.

"Help him," she spoke through tears of outrage, "I know that shadow was Morris. We have to save him."

"We can't save him. It's too late. This vision is the past," Liam said in a sweet tone. "Does Morris have a dog?" Jenny thought about the question with a malicious smile taking over.

"Yes, he does. We need to get in his house and find that dog choker."

"That's crazy, Jen. We can't go into his house, that's way too dangerous."

"No, listen to me. If we find that choker, there will be some blood or DNA left from his victims. If we find that evidence, we can lead the police to him," Jenny said.

CHAPTER 16

I've read the bible many times and even caught his spirit sitting in a pew at church. Those were hollow forms of worship standing in front of my savior. Again, the rage bubbled up in Damon, the conflict between my joy for God and Damon's ocean of anger drowned us both inside.

Renewed defiance sprung free in Damon. It infuriated Damon that humans received the gift of free will and the ability to procreate the same as their maker. He questioned God why he pushed the Watchers to the side by rewarding the humans. Genuine sadness overwhelmed the rebellious Watcher. He wanted love from God, and the rejection he lived with was as strong as his need to be close to his Lord. The air stilled as the expression on God's face softened for his creation.

God spoke, and every Watcher turned away. God talked to Damon even as he spoke his words to them all. He didn't create humans as a slight, God promised to the Watchers. Although humans were creating offspring, he emphasized that they knew the divide of their maker while the Watchers never left his side. The Watchers swooned from God's loving words. The sight of the Watchers giving up the rebellion hardened Damon as he dared to interrupt God even as he spoke of forgiveness.

Damon roared above the wind—lungs burning, his throat closing in around the foul air he pushed up and out. He alluded to his intolerance of slavery, which God called closeness. Damon made a promise of his own. He promised with the gift of procreation—humans would all but abandon God. If humans can bring life into existence, what need is there of a master? Damon questioned. He fortified his rebellious tone, saying he would spend every moment destroying the bond of God and his creations. God nodded his head to show respect to his Watchers. He reached out his hand. For a moment, Damon's urge to take God's hand was incredible. Damon fought the urge with every fiber in his body, his soul.

The immediacy of his passionate refusal sent a shock wave through his large frame and somehow found its way to me far away inside a small prison cell. Turning away from his God was almost too much for any being to bear. But there he was struggling, disobedient with every muscle designed by his Master. The great father's hand slunk back, causing Damon's body to shake in place to keep his hand from lunging outward. So be it, God said to the Watchers in the circle. Damon attempted to turn his head away from his Lord and instead froze where he stood, or at least that's how I perceived the event until I realized each Watcher remained still.

I listened for the wind to pick up and cascade through Damon's ears. There was silence. For a second, I thought the world ceased to exist—trapped in Damon's immobile body looking outward at the still landscape. I regained my composure with focus coming back to me, and I concentrated on the face of God. It was beautiful. The lines, the creases, every wave of his hair gave meaning. I wondered if every human face drew out such meaning. The answer was beauty existed in every human face, even if I never stopped to look upon it. In the heightened state, I saw beauty in every feature. An eternity froze in time with nothing except God's face to watch. It seemed like the greatest gift I could ever wish to enjoy.

As I was drowning in the Lord's presence, I began to discern that my Lord, unlike the world with the Watchers in it, moved free. He faced me without moving, watching Damon's face with interest. I couldn't shake the feeling he was seeing me hiding behind Damon's eyes. The whole idea was ludicrous. I understood the events as memories stored away inside Damon's mind or his spirit, soul, who knows what. Either way, I never believed it was happening in real-time. How could it be? I was inside Damon sharing his experiences the same as many other inmates. Just like me, they felt the Lord's emotions. Still, the feeling God was looking at me continued.

The debate raged in me for minutes, hours, who could know for sure. In the middle of my mental discourse came a voice so sweet, so alluring It reminded me of the first loving moments when I realized that I fell in love with Karie. The comparison was a weak grasp by my mind to understand what I felt. My passion for Karie fell so short to the love I perceived in God's face. Shame stung me when I understood how little my wife aroused my passions compared to the Lord. An equal mixture of pleasure and torture rose in my chest until I could take no more.

Then he spoke. I recalled God's lips moving with sound soaring from them, and I was sure his body wasn't making the vocal tones. His voice was far too musical to come from flesh and bones. The sound more suited an instrument, a Stradivarius perhaps or some apparatus able to bend or twist the air itself to form a sound so melodic that my ear convinced me it was an illusion.

My mind tried to unravel the puzzle and then fell in upon itself. God said he loved me, and I was one of his most prized creations. Thrown by his declaration, it was quite a shock to the system to hear someone express such love for me like a father gushing on a cherished son. Words of love are rare from strangers, but he wasn't a stranger, he was my maker, my father. And my soul took substance as he breathed eternal life into me.

Even as God's words found their mark, I wondered if he gave praise to humans as his most prized creation. No sooner than the thought popped into my head—he was already assuring me, his praise was for me alone at that moment. His accolades elevated me, setting me apart from the rest of humanity, and filling me with more pride than I ever imagined. I am counting on you, Joseph, he said in whispering speech. He told me he has a journey in mind for me, and the task promised danger, carving a path of devastation with my winding road. He told me some of my loved ones are in harm's way, but I would persevere if I kept hold of my faith.

His vocal cadence intoxicated me, leading me like a rodent following the pied piper. His words did not fall from his mouth. Instead, they glided outward, reassuring my fears with every syllable uttered. I would have walked off the highest, steepest cliff to show him my reverence. He told me Damon Torinson was born many times in the past, and Damon would continue to plague the Earth. What can I do to serve you? I asked in my mind and didn't think he could hear me, but God listened to my inner voice, and more than that, he heard my conscience ring to life.

God was inside my head, crawling, almost rummaging around inside there. He could do anything he wanted to me, and I sensed my vulnerability as I have never imagined. The experience filled me with fear, but I also experienced a profound level of relaxation. I could feel his touch inside my mind, yes, and it was like the warmth of a hand cozy inside a glove. He showed me his power while removing the malice.

What bewildered me most was the way his thoughts entered my consciousness. His thinking was too sophisticated for me to wrap my logic around. Describing God did not differ from explaining the inner workings of a pocket watch to someone who has never seen one. My understanding bordered on the impossible. His language came to me in words, phrases, and sometimes images—floated in the air like so many fireflies, bright and random, or at least I perceived them as random. My brain was like a frog's tongue plucking the words and images from thin air and bringing them inside.

I marveled at how efficient God's language was, each word chosen with enormous forethought, containing, so much weight. Adding words would dull the meaning. When I spoke to people every day, inevitable mix-ups, miscommunications, and crossed signals of all sorts happened. Talking with God wasn't like that. Men are sometimes deceptive, and God isn't.

My emotions guided my understanding. His higher form of communication linked my mind, heart, and soul, culminating into a simple feeling of peace.

He spoke to me of destiny, a purpose I would share and pass down through my lineage. My time of serving him would bring upon me a heavy burden, formidable opposition to my convictions, my morality, and even my faith. He said he created me for the tasks ahead. And after me, my traits would follow with my children and their children to come to fulfill God's wishes. It was awe-inspiring to realize I had a purpose. Every person on Earth must have questioned why they existed. Here I was with an answer. I was to stop Damon Torinson.

I caught an image from God, or it was one of his recollections he allowed me to glimpse, I wasn't sure, but in this image, I witnessed the moment he created me from nothingness. First, I saw darkness and then a bright light enough to blind me if I was there to see it. I fooled myself into believing it was the big bang that created the universe, it wasn't, it was me, and I knew it to be me. I soon realized creation didn't have depth or size. God held no more importance of planets and stars born over me. In his eyes, everything shared importance. That was comforting to me—we all played a part in equal amounts. Our massive sun, billion times my size, holds the same life-force I carry inside me. The discovery stunned and exhilarated me.

I bathed in his light, listening to his melodic voice. My mind's frog tongue snatched his language from the sky. I took my training wheels off, and he sang his words at full speed, and I was excited I could maintain my focus.

He continued describing the dangers of Damon, but it wasn't Damon's name God spoke to me—the name I gleaned from him was Moloch. Damon used so many names through so many lives—a moniker meant nothing. Damon was as good as any to call him. Right off, I noticed Damon's overwhelming pride was my edge to use against him in battle.

It wasn't the details of Damon that frightened—it was the intent behind his acts that alarmed me in a way that came alive inside. I guess I never wanted to believe I was the last line of defense for humanity, even though I was a warden. Sure, some prisoners I knew would never again see daylight, and I took pride in protecting my community from their savageness. Still, I never saw myself as a gatekeeper for the depraved. I saw myself as a junk dealer or a restorer.

Some salvageable people came through the gates of the Reclamation. Evil didn't define all the convicts—some got tossed bad breaks, bad childhoods, and made terrible decisions. Even the most heinous crimes didn't involve demons. These men committing crimes suffered from severe mental disorders, but each still just a man.

Damon possessed what I feared most when I began my career as a warden so many years before. His pleasure came from defiling God's greatest creation. Spawned from hatred and jealousy, he undermined God at every turn, flaunting his power to lead men away from the light. No remorse lived inside Damon. His every defiant moment gave him a small slice of vengeance he so craved. Like a child scolded, he went on with his tantrum, hoping his beloved father would see him once more. The remedy to quell his pain and loss hid in the acts of inflicting pain and suffering on others.

God's words slowed down to a crawl, and my mind was snaring them at a more deliberate pace than before. My head was weary from his warnings—I wanted to linger in my moment with him longer. I wanted the time to stretch on like the open highway of my youth. I feared it then, and I must admit, I fear it still today. What if I forget the encounter, or it fades as a vivid dream does in the light of day? With its immediacy dissolving until you wonder if it ever happened at all.

The wind began to kick up against Damon's face, and I started to panic, a panic tearing into my bones and pulling my tendons tight around my frame or Damon's. It was as if I reverted to my childhood in the course of a few seconds. He was a parent leaving me, and I couldn't bear it. I attempted to close my eyes—Damon's eyes, but they remained ever watching. The urge to scream began to pool inside, first in the pit of my stomach, and then the runoff filled my lungs with a thick, acid urgency.

Just as a screech entered my throat, God spoke, telling me I would always remember this, and I would never be alone, and I would see him again someday. This assurance quieted my anxiety at once. The color came back to the world, a world untouched by man. I thought the fear returned when I soon realized it was Damon's fear I was experiencing. God turned from me toward the Watchers with burning eyes.

The Watcher's bruised and battered faces hid none of their terror. I gave you immortality, Moloch, God said with genuine anger in his voice. The ground shook with each word. No form shall ever hold your shape again, he added. To the rest of the Watchers, a vortex of wind spun around each one. Their eyes searched for escape and found no way to depart. Shrieks rose above the sound of the wind as the vortexes closed in on each form.

The circular body of the vortexes hardened to a solid substance as the circles spun faster. Each vortex squeezed tight— the screams rose. Teeth gnashed, eyes bulged, and jaws clenched as their bodies began to collapse inward.

The Watchers became compressed—loose at first and then withering into the whirlwinds. Their bodies stretched, becoming half their former size as the whirlwinds pushed down like a vice, and broke into thousands of smaller pieces.

The diameter of the funnel clouds changed to the size of a baseball bat and jutted skyward fifty feet. Revolutions of the vortexes slowed, leaving no limbs, no blood, not even dust. The rebellious Watchers ceased to exist. With the winds gone, silence took. God turned his gaze back to the last remaining defiant Watcher, Damon.

As God spoke, Damon averted his eyes to the place where his friends once stood. Witnessing their destruction rekindled his fire and his resolve. My beloved, my first creation. Destroying you is destroying a part of me. Instead, for your villainy, I will cast you out into the world you so despise. Your jealousy of man has threatened the balance of heaven and Earth. Will you speak to save yourself? God said in a tone that never wavered.

Damon matched his maker's intensity but still avoided eye contact. Whether I live or die has no bearing on my convictions, Damon said, hands clenched. Where there is light, I will find darkness, where there is joy, I will bring suffering. You have elevated your humans above me, and for that, I am against you. Before you strike me down, may the children of man turn away from you as you have turned from me. That will be your curse.

Without warning, darkness fell upon the Earth. A few meandering stars watched overhead. The fertile soil under Damon's feet rumbled, shook, and undulated. God knocked down Damon to a kneeling position. The image of God faded from sight.

I felt his presence as he watched. Damon rose to his feet with a posture of disobedience—wings outstretched toward the heavens. An invisible hand severed his white wings from his back. They fell to the ground next to his feet. They lay there benign, useless to the world. Pain and outrage spilled out onto Damon's face but showed no signs of surprise.

The ground broke into loose particles, shaking Damon back and forth on the uneven surface. Knowing his fate caused Damon's stomach to churn. A few yards behind Damon, the ground bubbled until a mound of dirt protruded. The mound grew into a hill until a wooden hand broke through the dirt, reaching upwards for the sky. A dim light revealed the hand for what it was—a tree branch. The small branch continued up with larger branches following, and soon the thick trunk of the tree was standing upright as if it stood there a century.

Damon struggled to move, and this time with wings gone. The wooden branches, bending into hand-like digits, grasped his body. The mighty tree took on human-like flexibility, wrapping itself around Damon's arms, legs, and torso. It was useless to struggle, but Damon did. With Damon secured in its grasp, the tree sank into the loose dirt.

For the first time, real fear captured Damon's expression as he was halfway into the Earth. Damon summoned all his remaining strength and roared up to heaven. Your children will suffer at my hands—he spoke as the tree along with him disappeared underground. The last sight I saw was a blue star above us as dirt blocked the sky.

CHAPTER 17

If there was such a thing as a good time while in prison, for Gage, it was the first hour alone in the kitchen. He relished the solitude that opening the galley early in the morning afforded him. Not too many inmates will get up as early as Gage, and his preparation time was precious. If he tried hard, he sometimes imagined he was opening a restaurant outside the prison walls, maybe even his own. Gage flicked a switch on, and neon tubes buzzed to life one after the other in the Reclamation kitchen. The cooking area, containing stainless steel preparation tables, also held thirty-five ovens—and many more cooling racks.

Gage thought the fantasy was a good pastime, enjoying its escapist quality. Still, he often had a hard time conjuring up the preferred reality when he wanted. The prison dominated his mind so much that freeing himself from it was as difficult as escaping his physical confines. The walls contained a dark nature that soiled his spirit and extinguished all hope no matter how small. In no time at all, the kitchen, quiet as a church, buzzed and bustled with inmates. But for the moment, Gage inventoried, cataloged, and reordered in peace. The shackles weren't off, but they were looser.

Gage scribbled onto his clipboard and checked serial code numbers when a sound softened his concentration. His conscious mind fluttered from the noise and returned to the task. Over his writing, a subtle squeak broke through. It was likely a mouse—he spotted many. Vermin of all kinds filled the prison. Gage pivoted his torso, *turned*, and faced Victor standing so close that if he wanted to strike, Gage couldn't have defended himself.

Victor wore a grin that told Gage he was not a threat, at least for the moment. He was much thinner than Gage last saw him on the outside. Although he was a big man, nearing two hundred and fifty pounds, he looked gaunt to Gage's eyes. Victor was always prone to dancing with cocaine. He tangled with every drug, but Gage knew cocaine to be Victor's drug of choice, and it explained his rapid weight change. Gage found Victor's eyes, noticing the deep black circles that decorated each socket. *A side effect of a lack of sleep caused by looking over his back*, he thought.

"I thought you were a rat," Gage said.

"Some have called me much worse."

"How did you get out of your cell?" Victor leaned back against a rack of knives. Their shine made him take a second look.

"These will be useful. Have any ever come up missing?" Gage tightened the grip of his pencil hidden behind his back. His face remained blank.

"They count the quantity several times a day. The screws would toss every cell in this joint to find even one lost from that rack." Victor strummed the handles with his fingers.

"I needed to talk to you alone, Saint. You've heard things I've done. and I'm ready to tell my side." *How you killed my son, my friend, and my marriage?* "First off, about the jewelry store heist, I fucked up." *You're a psychopath.* "I was tweaking, and I got overzealous with the employees. If I didn't kill that woman, you wouldn't be in here, and I would have made a lot more money for the last couple of years. You were the brains of the operation, and I see that now. That decision cost me tons of money. You shut your mouth, took the rap, and you're doing your time for me. Don't think I forgot that, Saint. I owe you one," Victor said. *I owe you one, too, Victor.*

"You don't owe me a thing, Victor. It was my choice to stay back with the woman at the heist. I have no one to blame but myself." Victor relaxed his posture as Gage gave his absolution. The immense space of the prison kitchen seemed to shrink, closing in and confining him with all the hatred he felt for the man that stood in front of him.

"Ricky's a different story," Gage's body tensed, "I would have shot him again today if I had the chance," Victor said in a tone so level that the topic sounded like he relayed changing a tire instead of killing Gage's best friend. "It pained me to kill him, Saint. You know me, and you know that. After the heist, I took the score to our fence, and when I went back to get the money, they told me Ricky got there first and took it all." Victor's face showed surprise.

"He showed up with his shitty gun waving it *around*, and with only half my money. The thought boils my blood. Anyway, I caught up with him two days later and put a bullet through him," Victor rubbed his head as if the sorrow of the situation just hit him, "I can't let it become the Wild West out there, Saint. If I allowed Ricky to get away with stealing that kind of cash from me without retribution, then every asshole from now until the grave would get the same foolish idea in their head. It will not happen."

Gage couldn't argue. The delicate partnerships in their line of work called for either trust or fear. If Victor lost one of those ingredients, life would become very difficult. No matter how well Victor told the story, it just didn't ring true to the ears. *Ricky didn't dare cross you over money. It wasn't in him. No, you killed him in cold blood*, he reasoned.

"I agree. You had no choice." Gage fought down the bile that rose in his throat.

"Good. Because I need you now, we were great together. Admit it," Gage nodded.

"I have a year left on my manslaughter charge. There is not much we can do as a team on the inside," Gage said. Victor was already shaking his head.

"That's where you're wrong." Victor lit up with a smile wide enough to force his ears to move. "This time, the judge gave me a heavier slap on the wrist for armed robbery. I can't sit in here that long."

Gage guessed what was coming and didn't want to hear it. "Rumors say an inmate escaped Reclamation when it first opened—there are ways to get out. You have the brains, Saint. Why should we rot in here when you possess the knowledge to set us free?" There it was—the opportunity that Gage was waiting to find. He pretended to mull it over. "Get us out, Saint, *and* I promise to make up for our past. We'll get you back with Maria." *If you say Ryan's name, I swear to Christ, I will stab you in the heart with this pencil.* "What do you say?" Victor's desperation rose.

"I say okay." Victor almost jumped into Gage's arms

"Yes, yes, yes, yes, yes," Victor screamed and got control of himself.

"One condition."

"Sure. Whatever you want."

"I plan this alone, and I'll *let* you in on the details only at the moment of the escape." The ultimatum took the wind from Victor's sails, but not all the way.

"Okay." Victor **turned** and extended a hand. Gage would rather shove Victor into an oven. *Into an oven.* An idea occurred to Gage as he shook the snake's hand. After the encounter with Victor, Gage was reborn. The air that filled his lungs sustained him again, and the sunlight that cascaded through the prison windows began to nurture. He enjoyed the warm tentacles radiating onto his cheeks. Mingled chatter of his co-workers in the kitchen seemed to transform from a constant drone into exuberance. Everything was new again—the food smelled better—each dull routine took on a greater meaning, and Eddie was the first to notice the change.

"What's with you today?" Eddie asked while mixing a healthy amount of potato flakes into a mixer to make mashed potatoes. He flicked a switch, and the huge beater turned in place, and then soon rotated around the stainless-steel tank.

"I have to—" Gage looked **around** for ears, "help Victor with an early release." Eddie's passive expression turned angry.

"Are you kidding me?" Gage shook.

"Don't have many choices," Gage said.

Eddie was stewing in his juices. He couldn't believe Gage meant to help someone as vicious and heartless as Victor, and it boggled his mind. It was easy to see the attachment Eddie shared for Gage. When Eddie arrived in prison, he was as green as they come. Gage saw Eddie's vulnerability as a positive and not a weakness to exploit. When Eddie first walked through Reclamation's gate as a new fish, he had an enormous target on his back, and a few ugly customers came at him in the beginning. He endured his share of gruesome moments on the inside, and to *him,* the moments can't help but change a man.

The hardest part about prison for men like Eddie was the mind-numbing repetition. It's always the small things that break down a man. Sometimes it's the spiritual breakdown while other times it's the mental side. It's difficult for a man to except someone telling them when to walk, talk, eat, and sleep. The irony lies in the reality that most convicts are not creatures of habit. They fight all constraints, searching for their pleasures, their fortunes, and their depravity. Convicts must wrap their minds around their sudden conformity, and Eddie was no different.

"Do not help that son of a bitch," Eddie said. Gage tossed chicken breasts from an aluminum tray into boiling oil. The chicken snapped, popped, and sizzled from residual water left on the skin. The excess water evaporated, bringing the erratic frying sound to a balanced sizzle. Eddie placed himself in between Gage and his next task.

"Are you not talking to me?" Gage moved to sidestep his bunkmate with Eddie jumping into his new path. "Saint?" Gage, slow to glance up, met Eddie's eyes. "After you help Victor escape, he will kill you," Eddie said. Gage moved past him, cutting vegetables on a chopping block. Eddie's eyes went big.

"I know what you're planning. You don't intend to do your time—you want to follow your son," he said. Gage flinched. "You loved your son, Saint, but don't do this. Suicide isn't the way to get to Ryan." A shadow passed over Gage's head, and his mood darkened. "Listen, you're hurt. If you want to snuff the pain for the last time, I understand. I won't even try to stop you. Don't do it like this. It's not right for him to do you in—he's already taken everything away from you." Gage relented with a gentle smile.

"It is nothing for you to worry about, Eddie. Your stretch here is almost over. The rest will go by fast. How I go out of this world isn't your concern," Gage said with a smile and returned to work. A normal day, if there was such a thing at Reclamation prison, dealt with confrontations, and heightened reality. For Gage, his day was always a blur. Some events stood out the way a soldier might remember sparse chunks of things from a battle. The edges and corners that make up the total picture of clarity dissolved. His mind, along with his thoughts, traveled a hundred different directions. Seeing an end to it all was thrilling. The prospect opened a window and let the air back into his small, confined world.

Walking down the first-floor row, Gage was oblivious to all the inmates locked into their cells. Out of the corner of his eye, Gage saw a cell open. He continued walking while thinking the cell must belong to some floor cleaner, and sure enough, Gage noticed an inmate mopping the cement walkway. There was a peculiarity of seeing a cell left open, **and** the ominous feeling lingered. The voice inside his head fell further into the background when he witnessed a sight that stopped Gage in his tracks.

Walking past him was Warden Deville. He was strolling as confident as a person enjoying a day at a park. The warden's swagger caught Gage off guard. The man was fearless, and that was the most disturbing part. Everyone that walked through any prison gate went through a period of change. From the lowest convict to the most seasoned guard, each dealt with their anxiety inside a prison. There were no exceptions, at least none that Gage ever witnessed.

When Gage saw a single guard walking with the warden, it shocked him. Jake Shoeman was the guard and not a very good one, in his opinion. A year earlier, a prisoner overpowered Jake during a routine bed check, leading to a standoff. The inmate surrendered soon after, but the prison got a black eye, and they demoted Jake to the exterior of the facility.

Alarm bells rang in Gage when he spotted the inmate mopping the same area that he already finished. The mopping prisoner hovered in front of the open cell. Jake did nothing more than glance toward the inmate. The inmate didn't **let** his eyes off the two prison officials. *Oh, shit. I can't get involved.* Two strides from the open cell and the mice were within the cat's claws. *Look up, Jake. Look up.*

Jake never looked up as the inmate pushed Jake with such force that his body soared backward into the open cell. The inmate slammed the cell door shut with Jake inside. With the mop, the inmate clutched the warden around his neck, pressing the bar hard against his throat. Warden Robert tried to scream but opened his mouth in surprise. Jake hopped back to his feet, rattling the cage door. He screeched for help from anyone who would listen.

Gage peered down two roads. One road led to becoming an outcast, while the other led to a tormented conscience. If the inmate was using the warden for an arbitrary list of demands or bringing to light grievances, Gage wanted no part of his little play. If his motives were born out of a dark idea to kill someone important to raise his status among the other convicts, then Gage couldn't allow it. The inmate pushed the mop stick further against the warden's neck.

The last thing Gage wanted was to become a blip on the warden's radar, yet the alternative seemed unthinkable. It was one thing to look away as a convict got his and understood the score, but a warden was a different story. He might be the biggest asshole on the planet, fudged his taxes, maybe even passed homeless children on the street without helping, but none of his indiscretions compared to the men all around him. The question *was*, could Gage live with himself if he let the convict put the warden down like a dog? The answer kept coming back: No. His focus narrowed to the width of a laser beam. Gage passed Jake in the locked cell, and his screaming went on. His legs were in sync with his brain, moving quicker and with a purpose.

Gage stepped up face to face with the convict and the warden. Robert's face turned a bleak shade of blue. The convict's first response to Gage's approach was more in line with a friend joining for a smoke. He didn't feel threatened, and he expected no interference.

"Let him *go*," Gage said. Shock took over the convict's expression.

"Who the hell are you?" His grip never faltered.

"You are about to find out." The convict weighed out his options. His mind was trying to unravel whether to continue his attack on the warden or pounce the interloper. For the moment, the newcomer seemed more of a threat. Gage measured the amount of a growing audience by the howls that joined the chorus. The attacking convict crunched the numbers and released the warden to the cement floor.

"I'll deal with you in a minute, Boss," he said. Robert gasped for air with the color returning. Gage saw the convict's demeanor toward the warden. He planned to kill *him*, and all doubts about his intentions disappeared. The convict made a move most street fighters make, rushing toward his opponent. Gage saw his advantage.

Gage stepped to one side and brought down his foot onto the side of the convict's knee. He could hear the snap of his kneecap even above the roar from onlookers. The convict wasn't ready to quit. He hobbled to Gage with a mask of anger more intense than before. Gage raised his clenched fists. When the convict swung, Gage was ready for the blow. Instead, Robert kicked down hard on the convict's good leg. He went down fast. Robert turned his attention to his rescuer.

"What's your name?" Robert asked. Gage was reluctant to answer. "Gage."

"Thank you, Gage." The warden looked at his guard, Jake, cowering in a cell. He didn't hide his disgust.

CHAPTER 18

Security guards filled Robert's office, lining the wall. The chattering guards gazed toward Robert for the meeting to begin. Robert swiveled in his chair, found the weak floorboard, and pivoted his foot on the plank to make a slight squeaking sound.

"Where are you, Jake Shoeman?" The warden's nervous movements made his underlings anxious, just watching him. A few guards rocked in place when Jake bolted through the door.

"Sorry that I'm late. Did you already start the meeting?"

"No, we've been waiting for you." The guards passed uncomfortable glances. Suspicion sank in when Jake saw his training scale sitting in the middle of the office.

"Is that your Lunch?" Robert asked. Jake looked down at his brown paper bag and nodded. "Bring it to me," Robert said. Jake lumbered over to Robert's desk, and for the first time, he saw and felt the other guard's eyes burn into him. Jake sat the paper bag on in the center of his boss's desk and left it behind like a mother giving up her child and took a step back.

"You'll decide when you go home to your wife—I'm punishing you for your negligent display of securing me today, and nothing is further from the truth. The discipline that I show you today comes from the most enlightened part of me. I want you to be a better man, a better guard, and a better husband. You *will* improve." Robert reached for the paper bag and spilled its contents onto his desk. Robert lifted a bundle over his head. "What's this?"

"Submarine sandwich," Jake answered. Robert removed the sandwich from its wax paper cocoon. Robert scraped the meat, cheese, and lettuce off the bun and onto the wax paper.

"This won't do." The warden tossed the bun into a trashcan next to his desk. A slight snicker rose from the back of the room. Robert's head popped up, nose flared, and anger grew in his eyes. The laughter died away. "A twenty-ounce bottle of cola. The water fountain here will do you some good." Robert flung the soda into the trash. "An apple and that can stay." Robert moved to the next item. "One bag of potato chips." Robert smashed his hand hard onto the bag collapsing its air pocket and reducing the chips to crumbs. He slid the chips off his desk with a swiping motion of his hand. "Use your head, Jake. Fat people above everyone else understand what they should put in their bodies." Robert looked to the men in the room and back to Jake. "Now strip."

"Excuse me?" Jake pretended that he didn't hear Robert, but he caught every word.

"I didn't stutter. Strip down to your bare ass, and get on the scale," Robert said. Jake moved like someone lost in a dream.

"Let's not be bashful. Every man in this room has undressed in front of other men in locker rooms." Robert's expression dared Jake to disobey his orders. Jake began to comply. He unbuckled his pants and let them fall to the ground. Reginald, who was sitting to the right of Robert, lowered his head away from Jake.

Some guards who felt Jake's shame also looked away. But most were far too intrigued by the spectacle to miss the opportunity. When Jake removed all his clothes, he revealed an enormous protruding stomach that hung over his privates. From his upper body hung long pendulous breasts, which he tried to hide with his arms like a centerfold covering up for the mystique alone.

"Get on the scale," Robert said with impatience. Jake took baby steps until they ended on the scale. Even the most shocked of the guards turned back to see what Jake's weight added up to, with curiosity getting the best of everyone. Robert stood up and walked to the scale to get a better view. He studied the results.

"You lost a pound," Robert said. His face showed total disappointment. "Not to worry, Jake, next time you walk in here, you will have lost a lot more. You can *go*, Jake." Robert scanned the other faces. "You're all dismissed. Jake hurried to gather his clothes and what remained of his lunch. He resembled a rape victim, shaken, disheveled, and on the verge of tears. Robert was already heading toward his desk when Agatha stepped into the doorway. Guards scattered out around Agatha and out of the door.

"Mr. Deville? Oh, Mr. Deville?" When Robert turned, she showed a gentle smile plastered across her face.

"What can I do for you, Agatha?" His smile wasn't so gentle. If she noticed, she never showed it in her countenance.

"I was hoping you would have that cup of tea with me now," she said in a sweet voice.

"I don't have the time right—"

"Also, the matter I need to speak to you about is urgent."

Agatha took hold of Robert's hand and ushered him into her office. The room contained a fireplace, lounge chairs, and a silver tea set. All that was missing, by his recollection, was a bear-skin rug stretched out between them. The ambiance in the room was soothing, and he felt relaxed in a way that he would have never expected to find inside a prison. He looked at the pictures of smiling faces that lined the walls of the parlor. The warmth of a family stared back from every corner.

"They are some beautiful kids. Are they yours?" he asked out of habit. Agatha's demeanor changed like butter melting on a stove.

"You know how it is. I've watched other children grow with none of my own," Agatha said. Robert detected her nervousness but was still thinking about his desk and the diary that lay waiting inside. Its secrets were waiting, and he was busy having tea with an old biddy.

"The children in these frames are full-grown—with lives of their own, now," she said with sadness. Robert's patience was wearing thin.

"Why do you have me here, Agatha?" She never diverted her glance from the picture frames.

"I wanted you to see something." Agatha walked across the room and plucked a worn photo album from a shelf. The front of the album was leather-bound and worn on one side from constant handling. It looked old to Robert and intriguing.

"Take a gander at this," she said like a car salesman. Agatha opened the book like it was a precious relic. The first thing that came into view was Robert's own eyes staring back, and it shocked him.

"What the hell?" He couldn't hide his surprise.

"I started this book many years ago. I'm a fan. This picture was my first," she pointed to a photo with Robert in a police uniform in a bear-hug embrace with another officer, "that was when I first discovered your name. You just saved your partner's life in that shootout." Agatha turned the page without warning and pointed toward another photo.

"You're surprised that I have a picture like that, aren't you? You'd be surprised what you can get on the internet. My collections have tripled since the internet." Robert saw himself in an elementary school photo from when he was eleven years old. It was astounding to him she even knew the internet existed.

"I have your Boy Scout events, senior pictures, merits from the police department—you name it," she said. Someone who kept a scrapbook of his life and accomplishments was flattering and creepy. He felt the diary's call, intoxicating in its overwhelming pull. Agatha saw his subtle clenching, which meant that he wanted out and onto his day. She tipped her silver teapot sideways and poured steaming tea into a small cup and handed it to Robert. He regarded the cup as if it were an alien artifact that didn't belong in his grasp.

"Thanks for your hospitality—" Again, Agatha interrupted.

"The real reason that I wanted to chat was that I wear a lot of hats here at Reclamation, and one—Human Resources. It's the toughest of my jobs, but I'm sworn to fulfill my duties." She sipped some tea of her own. "I heard some guards remarking that you were intervening with Jake Shoeman, and I am appalled by what I hear about your punishments." Robert's hands were shaking, and not from an antsy need to leave the Victorian parlor, but from anger. An emotion he understood at last.

"I don't think it is any of your concern, Agatha." Robert sipped the tea for the first time.

"I beg to differ, warden—" It was Robert's turn to interrupt.

"When I want your advice, I'll ask you. If I want you to mend morale, build character, or ensure the safety of my guards, I will ask you." His voice rose a few decibels within several syllables. "Now, I promise that I'll leave the bureaucratic bullshit to you," Robert gave her a condescending smile, "and you leave my men's training to *me*. Do you understand?" Agatha's face tightened.

"I do."

"Good. I have real work to do." Robert slammed down his tea, spilling a portion. He was out of the door before she sopped up the mess.

Robert sat behind the glow of his desk. His body emanated with a pulse of a power indescribable to his conscious mind. *So much for diplomacy*, he thought. He pulled the diary out of a drawer and snapped the book onto the top of the fiery desk. He watched with wondrous delight as the blazing skin of the desk wrapped the book into itself and ignited it. The act of placing the book on the fire-consumed desk was superstition, but a part of him believed that it would engulf the pages inside. He adjusted his foot, found the weak floorboard, and made it squeak by applying some pressure. Messing with the floorboard was tonguing a sore in the mouth—and he couldn't stop.

The book danced with flames, and he thought he should already know, but he asked himself anyway. *Did I go home last night?* The answer eluded him. A brief spark of concern for Jenny came and went. Robert was where he wanted to be, and all other worries would have to wait. He began to read: ***Joseph's Diary***

When I woke from Damon Torinson's visions, I was reborn. Nothing was the same after the event. The shackles of a humdrum life vanished. It is hard to describe, but the air smelled cleaner, the colors brighter, and the hearts of men didn't seem as dark in the way a toddler might do something bad and not know the consequences of its actions.

That was what I brought back from the night visitation— men weren't evil, just misguided like a child. Working as a prison warden for so many years meant witnessing the depths and cruelty men dished out to one another. Now I saw the prisoners through new eyes, and it was the best gift I ever received. The shared experience rejuvenated me for another twenty years. I didn't know before the dreams, but I was running on empty in the faith department.

As a warden, I was going through the motions, treading a path of least resistance. But I am awake now. As I walked past the rows of cells embedded in concrete, I sensed a change all around me. All the prisoners that were fortunate enough to be sleeping when I was, witnessed a similar vision—shared the same hopeful insights, and saw God's hand for the first time. A decade of correctional rehabilitation was no match for a moment in God's presence. I hadn't a clue, but I was witnessing a miracle. The event changed these men. I soon came to realize I gained brief access to a kind of spiritual fountain of youth.

Thoughts about my friends, family, and my enemies I've collected over the years bubbled to the surface. I wish I brought them there to take on the change as I have and let my Katie share in my vision of our maker. Above all others left off the list, I so wanted Roger to join me. He was a dear friend through so many tough years, and as of late, he was falling short on hope and faith. Roger's seven-year-old daughter Miranda met with a diagnosis of inoperable brain cancer. The burden of her inevitable death has ravaged the man to an unrecognizable husk of his former self. I expected to receive his formal resignation anytime, and I so dread the arrival. He's done some much for me, he's been my rock, and I missed my chance to ease his mind. My invigoration allowed no waste of time. I needed to face Damon.

As a guard escorted me to Damon's cell on the top floor of the facility, the prison seemed safer, somehow in a sedated, languid spell. The guard opened the cell, and I bounded in as if reunited with a long-lost relative. Damon sat on the end of his bunk, smiling a strange, disturbing little smile.

Damon asked me if I witnessed his past, and I told him I had. He seemed to know the answer before I gave it. Damon continued to smile, and I wanted to return it. We shared an event so monumental—maybe soldiers in wars might know the bond formed from extreme circumstances together. I reminded myself, regardless of Damon's exterior, he was the most dangerous man on the face of the Earth. He was complete again with thousands of years of wisdom at his disposal. I walked past him and sat down on his bed next to him.

My guard was not too happy with my seating choice, raising his gun, and lined his sight on Damon. Maybe I sat there next to him without fear because I possessed the knowledge that he was once upon a time, a faithful servant of God in the most literal way. In my mind, he was no longer the mindless butcher wrapped in Damon Torinson's skin. He was no longer an unknowing creature like a rabid dog oozing foam from a diseased host. No, there was now a driver at the wheel. He wasn't a thoughtless projectile propelling itself outward, and all the while feeding off his baser urges. No, he knew things. A reaction came over me to direct the guard to lower his gun, and I let the urge pass. An opportunity was an opportunity.

You know yourself again, I said, and he nodded. I knew him now, too, I added, and wondered if he recalled the awakening from every one of his lifetimes and asked him. He said he did, and with each awakening came the sad rediscovery of God's vengeance. The most difficult part of each life—remembering God's face, he relayed. I'm sure you can see it too. And he was right, I could. Underneath it all, the sights, the sounds, the running inner dialogue was a longing to see his face again. He let me know the longing would never go away.

That prospect seemed daunting in the light of day. I told him of God's warning, and when he died, his spirit would enter another woman's body, but there was a limit to the distance his spirit could travel from his last body. Damon didn't seem surprised in the slightest. I explained to him because I knew his secret, even after his death, I would stop his reign of terror. He was skeptical of my assurance.

The early morning sun spotlighted his wan smile. Unease took over his manner. He knew I was in on the game, and he could no longer start a new life without watchful eyes. Damon was on death row, destined to die, then his spirit flashing back into the community to wreak havoc, but I was not about to let that happen. Ohio would not electrocute Damon under my watch.

I think he sensed my revelation. His body tensed, and I knew that the real battle between us had begun. He knew that the body of Damon Torinson imprisoned him, and the demise of the body would send him back into the world. Then, from out of nowhere, it came to me. I wanted to give him a reason to live, a mission, a challenge, and I didn't have to look too hard to find his weakness. It was the same weakness that ushered in his fall from grace, his pride.

He couldn't win, and I revealed this to him. That with all his experience, he could not overcome the obstacles stacked against him. God's command placed him in my capable hands. My plan was already working. His calm demeanor melted in a flutter of body ticks as he spoke. He promised my destruction if I persisted. I remember saying he couldn't do anything while he was under my watch. He laughed a laugh so vile I shook from real fear. He swore to me his reach traveled far beyond his metal bars, and he would soon show me his power. It was my turn to laugh.

Confident in his fate, I exited his cell and asked him to do his worst. I ordered my escort to remove anything from his cell he could harm himself with and to have a guard stationed outside his cell twenty-four hours a day. I walked away from Damon Torinson—sure I accomplished my goal.

What I'm about to write is the hardest thing I have ever put to paper. After my last shared vision with Damon Torinson, Roger Witmar, my associate warden and most valued friend, left Reclamation behind. I did not blame him for his decision, but I was still in need of his friendship and his sound advice, given throughout the years. He told me that for the sake of his daughter—he needed to move on.

That week Miranda was to undergo an emergency surgery that would remove a malignant tumor threatening her life. The doctor assured Roger that opening her up would cause cancer to spread, but according to him, there was no other alternative. He wanted to be with his daughter on her last days, and my heart hurt for him. It was morning during a busy workday, but I asked if he needed me to take the day off to spend some time praying together. He refused, and I told him if he needed me, he should call Karie or myself anytime night or day. I said goodbye with sadness and wished him well.

I remember leaving the facility in the usual manner. Roger's sudden departure still lingered in my thoughts. I wanted so much to bring Miranda back to her father. The anguish he must have felt losing someone so close to him seemed unbearable. Those thoughts dogged me on my drive home.

The funny thing is, I don't have a vivid recollection of any drive home—I have a solid hold on that one. The warmth in the air that night was like a blanket fresh out of the dryer. Even the breeze blowing into the car gave the heated slap of summer. The yards on the main street of Pataskala, Ohio, bustled with fruit stands full of produce sold by local farmers.

I wanted to stop and pick up a few vegetables for Karie. She loved fresh tomatoes to eat while we sat on the porch. She would slice, salt, and eat them as fast as they hit the table. But that day, I just wanted to go home, spend some time with Karie, and sit on the porch swing watching Raylen play in the yard. Work captured my primary focus. He was growing up so fast, and I never saw him grow from one inch to another.

When I pulled into our gravel driveway, I expected to see Raylen pumping his legs from the tire swing connected to the oldest tree by the house. The tire rocked unattended. I stopped the car in front of the house, noticing dust clouds rise from the disturbed gravel under my car tires. As I exited the car, my eyes searched the porch for Karie. She almost always sat by the door peeling potatoes or sipping on iced tea, waiting for my arrival.

That night the rickety porch was empty. An ominous sensation washed over me. For a millisecond, Damon Torinson's image flared in my head.

I walked toward the house in a daze as if I wasn't in my body but Damon's, sharing a dream again. Frightened by a nagging intuition, I made a fist to see if my body was my own, and it was. Ahead I saw spots of brown on the steps leading into the front door. My brain cells popped. When I got closer to the steps—they were footprints leading away from the front door.

What I thought was a shade of brown was the copper color of drying blood. My heart paused in my chest. I started to enter when I saw more blood in the shape of fingers on the screen door. Dear God, I thought to myself and hurried inside. The footprints continued toward the back of the house. I observed how the copper imprints of shoes grew closer together. Whoever left those marks on the floor were not in any hurry to leave.

I began to follow the trail when I heard a noise. It was subtle at first, but it grew louder. The sound was a whimper, weak, and muffled. It was coming from upstairs. It was Raylen, and his words were inaudible, but I could tell it was him. I stared down the hall toward the footprints disappearing around a corner, then back to the staircase that led to my son.

Frozen by two paths—one leading to my child in peril and the other—a bloody path that led . . .

My feet moved to my helpless and screaming child. I inspected the steps and banister for any traces of blood and found none. Taking the stairs two steps at a time until I reached the second floor, I heard the whimpering much louder coming from my bedroom.

A chair that always rested in the hallway now stood against the doorknob of my room. The chair's purpose of keeping someone inside, crystalized. Weak thuds came from the other side of my door. Who knew how long Raylen pounded away calling for help—which never came. With all my strength, I tore the chair away from the door, breaking a leg off. I tossed the *hobbled chair to one side and turned the knob. It spun in my grip.*

With all my might, I swung the door open to see my five-year-old stretched out on our hardwood floor—his eyes, red from crying, with knuckles bruised from hitting the door. I pulled him into my arms. I wouldn't say he hugged back as much as he melted into my form. Trying to console him without knowing what he saw or heard, I gave him a quick examination and found he was complete and intact. He was in shock or at the least worn-out from the ordeal, but okay.

I walked around the room, holding his hand, making sure the room was safe, and no one other than the two of us remained inside. It all checked out. I asked Raylen what happened in the house, and I half expected him to describe Damon Torinson. I pictured him escaping Reclamation and making his way there to deliver destruction. Instead, what I heard from his mouth was far more startling. He said Uncle Roger broke into the house. Raylen explained how Roger hit mommy hard and brought him up to my room. He told Raylen to cover his ears, but Raylen hadn't covered his ears—he said his mommy was screaming so loud.

Red-hot rage took over me like a descending fog. I told Raylen I needed to find Mommy. He didn't want to leave my side, and after more reassurance, I told him to hide under his bed, and I closed the door behind me to begin my search for Karie.

I listened to the creaking of the stairs as I went down, listening harder for Karie. Any sound would have sent a rush of relief to my brain. The intruder, Roger or not, could still be in the house. Were the footprints there to throw me off? Was Roger doubling back to wait for me? There was so much blood. I pushed the thought from my mind—I didn't want to think for the time being.

When I reached the bottom of the stairs, the copper footprints stretched-out before me like an evil breadcrumb trail, I didn't want to follow. If it weren't for the chance to save Karie,

I would have taken Raylen and headed the opposite direction through the front door away from the horror. There was no sound from any direction anymore. Even Raylen, with his constant whimpering, went quiet.

I crept along the trail, trying not to make the floorboards creak my arrival. All at once, my heart sank. The bloody footprints changed to thick blood streaks leading from the counter to the steps. The streaks came from a human, the size of my Karie. Sliding the vulgar thought from my head, I was sick to my stomach. I walked beside the large wet streaks. My emotions took me from worrying if the invader was inside to praying—he stayed behind—I wanted to unleash my fury on him.

The bloody streaks went through the kitchen and curved right into the laundry room. That was the last room, and there was nowhere in the house to go. My anger, horror, and curiosity wrapped into a tight ball. I wanted to know for sure as I swung open the laundry room door. I have never been one prone to spells of fainting, but when I opened the door, the blood left my heart, leaving me weak in the knees. Using the doorframe to keep from toppling forward or falling straight down like a building imploded from its center, I tried to catch my breath.

I attempted to gather my bearings, and after the full shock of the sight hit me, I fell to the floor of the laundry room, and I cried. The streaks of drying blood pooled in front of Karie. Roger arranged her like a dime-store mannequin, looking not quite the way a human form should. Karie's back arched upward.

My eyes followed her lines to her pretty face. Her face aimed up with the pained expression frozen from her last seconds of agony. Her mouth formed a round shape like a statue sculpted for eternal screaming. I thought her eyes looked lifeless until I realized Roger plucked them from their sockets. The darkness of the empty sockets resembled black eyes. I started to gag, convulsing on the floor, and vomiting my afternoon lunch all over the floor and myself. My throat stung from acid and bile. My eyes began to water from my regurgitation, and I didn't want to wipe them, I didn't want to see anything anymore.

I forced the front of my hand across my lids, pulling the salty wetness with it. I thought my mind was playing some sick trick on me. It wasn't, and I saw the reality of Jenny's arms. Someone severed her arms from her body at the shoulders. That was the reason I thought of a store mannequin. He sewed her missing arms onto her back, one on each side of her shoulders. The Watchers came flooding back. He positioned my Karie to look like a Watcher with her eyes gone to represent their blackened eyes, and her arms stretched out on her back like angelic wings. This scene wasn't Roger's idea—it was a message from the Devil himself!

I wouldn't know how to put it into words just how hard it was to return to the Pataskala detention center days after Karie's brutal death. I don't think I was alive in the strictest sense. My nerve endings felt so dull. If I got a punch in the face, I would have felt nothing at all. The grief of losing my wife was battery acid eating away my insides until I was hollow. I operated on basic functions alone.

I passed through the detention center doors. Some sad eyes looked straight at me, some eyes avoided my gaze, and others, even old acquaintances, pretended not to see me. I asked for the officer that arrived at the scene. From around the desk, he came with an expression as somber as if his wife died along with mine. I asked the detective if he was positive Roger committed the crime, and I knew him a long time, and he couldn't have done something so horrific. The officer's gentle demeanor never faltered. The detective never wavered in his duty. He looked me right in the eyes and said Roger turned himself over to the local authorities and made a full confession concerning his part in my wife's death.

According to Grady from the dime store, Roger left Reclamation, went into the dime store, and bought a Polaroid camera. He then went to my house and killed Karie. I asked what the Polaroid was for, and the detective couldn't say. I told the detective it was a mystery why Roger would do this a day before his daughter underwent life-threatening surgery. The facts didn't add up to anything I could hang my hat on. There was a huge piece missing from the puzzle.

The department held Roger a hundred feet away in the back, and I needed to see him face to face. The detective refused right away, but I pressed. Being a warden in a small town afforded me a lot of influence, and I flexed every muscle of my influence on the detective. I don't believe a thing in the world could make me budge from the detention center and a visit with Roger. The detective relented, and I was on my way to the back.

When I walked in front of Roger's cell, I could tell he pictured Karie standing right beside me. He burst into tears, convulsing to get the sobs out. Roger shrank back from the metal door as if electricity ran through the bars. I wanted to see if he owned a soul. His eyes wouldn't meet mine. *Why?* I kept asking. He cried louder, but I persisted. I never ceased the questioning until he screamed out his answers as if spewing vomit. *I had no choice*, was his answer to me. *Why, why did you have to?* I asked.

For my daughter, he told me and went on. *I begged God to save Miranda, and each time I did, her condition worsened*, he told me through blubbering tears. His body jerked with every intake of air. I ignored his fits of crying and renewed my focused questions. *Why Kill Karie?* I asked in the best way I could without revealing my total hatred for him.

Roger tried to stall his convulsive cry and succeeded by saying he gave God a chance to save Miranda, but he refused, so he went to the only man on Earth who would listen, Damon Torinson. His confession shocked me beyond all my reasoning. He said he went to Damon and asked him to spare his daughter, and Damon accepted his request at a high price.

Roger was to Kill Karie under Damon's strict guidance. Damon instructed him when, where, and how to finish her. I couldn't believe my ears.

I had things I wanted to say to Roger, but I couldn't. He was the same person I've known my entire life, and he wasn't. It was as if a light switch went off inside him. He was identical to my old friend, apart from killing my Karie. Somehow Damon Torinson unplugged his conscience long enough to commit a horrific act and bring him back ruined on the other side. I wanted to believe that so much, to put my faith in the notion, but his face revealed something else. His eyes—red and irritated—his nose felt the rub of a handkerchief far too often and revealed a shine on the tip.

The urge to reach through the bars and shake him came over me. I saw myself slamming him into the cage over and over until the lone thing holding him upright above his shoes was the strength of my grasp. He hadn't slept since the murder, and I recognized it right off. I took two steps back away from him so as not to follow-through with my dark obsession to seek my vengeance.

Standing across from him and needing questions tested my resolve. Roger received no outside contact from that point. The people of Pataskala loved Karie, and they felt no pity for Roger.

My eyes soaked-in his anxious posture—waiting for the right time to ask his question, a question I already knew would come. I told him to ask me. Roger stepped back and fell to a sitting position on his cell cot, defeated. I spared him the anguish of granting himself the courage to ask. Miranda just came out of her surgery, and I asked him if he wanted to know her condition.

Roger nodded his head, looking to the floor, the wall, and anywhere to avoid my eyes. I explained that the doctors removed the tumor, cancer did not spread, and she made it through. Roger forgot himself when he heard the news. As if we met at a church social rejoicing the miracle. He smiled, letting his eyes dance over my face, a face with no trace of happiness for his good fortune. He wasn't smug. I don't think I could handle any sign of smugness. What I detected from Roger was a satisfaction, an absolution from his selfish choice. Damon promised him the life of his child if he took my Karie's life. The Devil's pact satisfied him. It overjoyed me knowing Miranda would live, and I told Roger how I felt. My sympathetic words quieted his expressive face. I said I spoke to the doctor, and he wanted Roger to know he was wrong.

Roger looked puzzled. The doctor said there never was cancer in Miranda's body. She would have survived the surgery either way. The doctor said he was sorry he made Roger think her condition was as grave as he first suggested. Roger's happy facade melted, and he again looked away.

I spoke with a hint of rage floating just below the surface. I told Roger he put his trust in the Devil. He couldn't wield the power of life and death the way God can. He knew Miranda would not die in the first place, and he used your love for her to force you to kill. Now you've lost your soul. Miranda will be fine, and you will never see her without bars obstructing your view for the rest of your life. I said all this, and he began to cry.

Seeing Roger's tears didn't bring me joy. Nothing would bring Karie back, no matter how much pain I inflicted on someone. Even if that someone was my beloved's murderer. When I walked from his holding cell, I never looked back. Karie's death was his burden now, and I gave it over to him to keep for the rest of his life.

My palms felt sweaty when I open Damon's cell. He was waiting for me as usual, along with a "told-you-so" smile. None of my thoughts greeted me with any comfort. I stood face to face with the one creature I wanted dead even more than Roger, who committed the act, but who was a pawn in this Devil's game. Damon started by saying he warned me his reach was immeasurable, and I realized the foolishness of attacking his power. My pride killed Karie.

I thought I was so much smarter than Damon, and I believed I had power over him. Underestimating a creature alive so many years on Earth and living so many lives showed my failure. Damon had wisdom I couldn't calculate. He didn't need to see the future to understand men. The problem was, I learned this lesson too late and at a high cost to my son and me.

Hating a creature like him did not differ from hating a bird for flying or a fish for swimming. Doing evil, causing pain, and sinning for the sheer pleasure of sinning was a part of his nature. My hands throbbed. It took me a few to realize my nails dug into my own hands. I released my clenched fists before he could discover my agitation.

He spoke with confidence, saying he wondered what went through Karie's mind as an old friend came into her house and inflicted such an act. Did she think Raylan was next? The torture she must have felt in her last moments, Damon said with a smile. I don't know how I combated my fury, but I managed not to rush him with the white-hot vengeance of a husband's love. I know he saw the anger well up inside and spill out before I reeled it back.

Damon flicked his bangs with his fingertips, and several strands flew from his forehead. He walked from me to his bed and slid one hand under the thin mattress and pulled out what looked to me to be a card. As he reversed directions toward me, I could hear the wind move from the guard standing behind me, training his gun on Damon. Without hesitation, the guard would cut Damon down with a word from me.

Damon didn't seem to mind at all as he handed me the card and waited for me to react. The card was smooth in my grip—glossy texture—I rubbed my finger on the surface. I looked down and saw a photo, a Polaroid photo. It was the murky blackness of its back. I turned the instant picture over and saw the sight I hoped to never see again except in my nightmares. The image was of my Karie, lying on the floor looking up to the camera with a dull, faraway look, but not dead, still alive. Blood was already draining from her mouth, yet her limbs remained in that timeline. Her eyes pleaded, begging for Roger to show mercy.

This photo was Damon's price, his trophy he expected from my associate warden. Roger cut up my Karie, went home to clean up, went back into the prison, and handed over the photo to Damon as payment before Miranda's surgery. Damon asked Roger to capture that precise moment in time. Tremors wracked my body from the inside. I crumpled up the picture in my hand. I never wanted to see it again, or anyone in the world to see it. My arms contracted to strike down Damon before my brain's electrical impulses summoned the command.

My fingers curled into balls, and on autopilot, thrashing Damon's face in frenzied repetition that kept me from hearing the guard's shotgun click as he watched over me. I pummeled him with more love for my wife than hatred for him. With all my strength, I bashed him until my arms went numb, but I continued to flail. Damon was an inch from his life ending in his cell. Karie's face flashed in my mind, and I threw myself away from Damon to the concrete floor. I labored to suck in air—trembling hands caused the rest of my body to shake out of control.

Damon didn't move as he lay on the floor, and I didn't expect him to. In my way, I spared his life. I didn't allow him to live because of any pity I felt for him, which there was some. He didn't die for the sake of Karie's memory, and all the other victims, he could hurt if I ended his life. I glanced at my hands and saw blood jutted through cuts on every knuckle.

As the adrenaline waned, and the anger subsided, I guessed Damon expected me to react as I did. What he didn't expect was mercy. Damon wanted out of his current body—to disappear into the world—and resume his reign of terror. I started a game with him—I had no way of winning. I knew right then I needed to isolate Damon. He was a threat to anyone he encountered inside the prison or out. Locked away and kept safe, *even from himself, became my sole solution. That's a hard trick considering Damon's electrocution loomed.*

Robert shifted the diary to within arms distance, fanned the pages, and stared at the tattered remnants. Robert recognized several pages sheared from the binding. Joseph didn't want the information to get out. Robert tapped, pressed, and twisted his foot down on the weak floorboard to find an answer.

Anxious fingers turned and found more pages with writing past the torn-out ones. The absent pages stung Robert. He was sure those pages were important. If they were important enough to tear out, **then** they were something he wanted to see. His fingers shuffled to the remaining pages after the torn-out ones. His eyes darted toward the writing, but his mind couldn't shake the missing few.

"Where are you? Why were you thrown away?" Robert tried to unravel the mystery. He began to read on with the lingering enigma nagging: *Joseph's Diary*

My scheme to keep Damon alive seemed to exhaust every connection I ever made in the state of Ohio. I faced the daunting task of keeping Damon from the electric chair when so many loved ones of his victims couldn't wait to see him fry for his crimes. How was I to make it look as if he died from the chair and still lock him away for safekeeping?

I know now, I cannot fake his death by electrocution. There are too many eyes upon this high-profile case. Too many people are relishing his death and want to see him sent to hell where he belongs. I guess I'm one of them—no one who wishes for his death more than I do. A large part of me wants to retire from Reclamation, let electricity do its work in Damon's body, and try to forget all this ever happened. Anything was better than returning to a building that held the person responsible for my wife's death. The facade of the Reclamation is a grim reminder of the evil in this world. Because of the newspapers, I am the warden whose second in command murdered his wife. I notice the stares and the whispers in certain settings.

My long career of serving the public wiped away, pushed aside by the sensationalism of the tragic events surrounding me. By a technicality, I had options, but when it came down to it, I meant to keep Damon alive. I obsessed until a plan came to me like a thunderbolt. I couldn't wait until the day of his execution to fake his death. Too many things could go wrong. And if I waited until the final day to stage Damon's demise, I would have to involve too many people in the scheme. There was no way I could keep so many loose lips from talking about Damon. No, I intended to fake his death long before his execution.

My plan rested on waiting for the death of an inmate—the same age and build as Damon. The crux of the charade was finding an inmate with no family. I didn't think I would find the right inmate before Damon's final days. Fate had something to say about my dilemma.

Two weeks before Damon's date with destiny, a young fellow by the name of John Portis fell on the steel staircase and broke his neck. John was a career criminal with no family. He moved around the country so much before his incarceration that he left no visible ties of his existence. I saw this turn of events as a sign God had a hand in keeping Damon contained.

The years have passed since those days, and my health is failing me. I have Damon imprisoned under the Reclamation facility, and my options are not good. I can leave it to fate, and when I die, let Damon waste away, or can I find someone to burden with his care? What I chose, I'm not proud of, but in the memory of my Karie, I will let Damon starve to death after my passing. Humans will once again lose sight and control of this evil soul, but I must exact my vengeance upon Karie's slayer. I hope those who will someday read these words will have pity on my last decision and believe I have spared them the crushing burden of looking into the face of pure evil.

-Joseph Hughes.

Robert's jaw dropped, and soon after, so did the diary to the desk-top. It made a loud, clapping noise that a book with some weight can make. His obsession with reading the old warden's thoughts was a guilty pleasure. The voyeuristic aspect of getting a glimpse into an older man degenerating into flights of fancy entertained him. Shocked by what Robert learned, he wondered what led to Joseph's madness in his last days. His indulgence in reading the diary made him feel like a co-conspirator—or knowing what the former warden did, made him an accessory to the crime after the fact. Sure, the jour-nal was the ramblings of a demented man, but that was what gave Robert such delight.

Reading about Joseph sinking into insanity without knowing him or experiencing it himself was fascinating, but his situation changed. For all Robert knew, there was a seventy-year-old-man starving to death just under his feet—dying as he was reading the ravings of his punisher. Did Robert believe Joseph Hughes captured the Devil? He didn't—the whole idea was laughable. The question was, did *he* be-lieve Joseph thought he caught the Devil? There were no doubts on that score. He remembered hearing chains during the night, and it occurred to him that maybe there was some credence to the diary. There was one way of knowing for sure. Robert picked up the phone and dialed Reginald's number, and looked at the diary, resting on his desk.

"Reginald . . . the time doesn't matter . . . I need you in my office at once." When Robert hung up the phone, he thought about the scandal that could follow such an atrocity committed by Joseph Hughes. He needed to handle the situation with delicate care, and he *would* handle it.

CHAPTER 19

Darkness set in. Robert's office seemed formed from shadows. Forms that bent, curved, and created the desk, chair, and the pictures on the wall. When Reginald arrived at Robert's office at Reclamation, Jake Shoeman sat in a waiting room chair. Jake had a nervous way about him like he didn't know if he should sit, stand, or run for the door. Reginald couldn't blame him considering the added attention Robert blessed him with as of late. Still, the man was a box of tremors and ticks. It was overwhelming just remaining in his presence. Reginald was the first to speak.

"Where is Robert?" Jake rubbed the back of his head until his hand found the nape of his neck. Jake's agitation made Reginald's skin crawl. Jake looked as if he wanted to jump out of his skin, and if it were possible, Reginald believed the young guard would have done just that.

"He stepped out for a second." Jake looked with trepidation at his watch and the late hour. "He said he'd be back soon. Do you know the reason for the meeting?" Jake was a man searching for a life raft, and Reginald allowed him to paddle in the frigid water a while longer before answering.

"I don't know," Reginald said. The answer didn't calm Jake's apprehension.

The vagueness of the reply fueled his unease at receiving a summons to the office at such an odd hour. They both sat facing each other like condemned men waiting next to the gallows. The tension was too much for Jake. He opened his mouth to speak, trying to cut the frosty blanket that bundled the two when a creak rose along with footsteps followed by Robert.

Reginald readied a series of questions to throw at Robert when he saw his face. It was cold, white, and translucent under the eyes, revealing blue blood-vessels that bulged as if under extreme duress. Reginald would have guessed that his superior was a ghost haunting the prison.

"Are you okay, Mr. Deville?" Reginald asked out of impulse. Robert's mouth opened to speak, but nothing came out. An invisible force seemed to keep the words hidden deep in his throat. He shook his head.

"Please, sit down, Reginald," Robert said. Reginald never saw Robert's composure anything but strong as iron. The sudden change made his stomach drop three levels. Reginald sat while Robert stood over him in a fatherly pose. He placed his hand on Reginald's shoulder, squeezing and releasing like a rhythm.

"I know how much you care about Joseph." To Reginald, the statement was out of place—like the continuation of a conversation rather than the start of one.

"I did . . . very much." Reginald was uncertain. Robert gave the associate warden a smile that didn't fit.

"Your past has caught up to you, thanks to Joseph." Reginald looked puzzled. He didn't hide his confusion.

"What do you mean?" Robert let the smile drop with Jake watching his mood turn sinister.

"Joseph took you in after your parents died," Robert said.

"How do you know that?"

"I know all about you, Reginald. I also understand your brush with Damon Torinson," Reginald went stiff. "Damon caused your heartache and Joseph's. It was his actions that united you two." Reginald's facade melted and tears soon followed.

"Who told you all this?" Reginald asked. Robert saw him relive his dark past in seconds and patted Reginald's shoulder.

"Take a moment . . . catch your breath," Robert steadied his gaze onto Jake, "I'll be with you next." Jake nodded. "Are you a little better?" Robert asked. It was Reginald's turn to nod.

"We might have inherited a scandal," Robert said.

"How so?" Reginald asked and sounding more composed.

"Did Joseph ever speak to you about your family's killer? Did he ever speak to you about Damon?" Robert saw Reginald squirm once again.

"He did."

"So, he told you that Damon Torinson was the Devil."

"Yes."

"And you believed him?"

"I was just a child when he killed my entire family. Yeah, I considered him the Devil."

"I get that." Robert paused. "Did you presume he might still be alive?" Reginald was already shaking Robert off.

"That's impossible. Damon died in a prison accident. I saw the picture myself."

"Can I ask you something? If you found the Devil, would you let him slip through your fingers?" Reginald stared through Robert. "Joseph chose between releasing him to the world or keeping him close—*he* kept him safe within these walls." Reginald's gears were moving, trying to work out the puzzle in his mind.

"You're saying that Joseph faked Damon's death. Why? For what reason?"

"He thought killing Damon would send him out there in the world to spread evil or more destruction. I suspect that he tried to spare humanity some pain by burying Damon alive under this prison. Trapping him here in the same body for as long as he could."

"You're saying my family's murderer is under us right now?" Reginald asked. Robert nodded as Jake listened with awe.

"What am I entertaining here?"

"Maybe nothing," Robert threw his hands into the air, "and maybe there is a seventy-year-old man held underground because a former warden suffered delusions that his atrocities were the act of Satan."

"Why come to me with this?" Reginald asked with sorrow.

"First off, you're my second in command, and there is no doing anything without you either knowing or finding out, and second, you had a right to learn the truth considering how personal this matter is to you." Reginald nodded with sadness. "I want to be clear about my feelings on this matter. I don't think Damon Torinson is the Devil. If he is down there, he won't be breathing fire or rotating his head three hundred and sixty degrees. And if you can remove your personal bias, and I don't blame you if you couldn't, this is textbook cruel and unusual punishment for anyone, including the Devil." Reginald fell silent. "If there is anyone down there, we are in trouble. For now, all of this will stay between the three of us. Is that understood?" Robert took their noncommittal mannerisms as an answer.

Reginald had a distant expression in his eyes like a man existing in two places at once. His mind was miles away from Reclamation, making the trip back to reality with every word. Robert wondered if Reginald's mental journey fell back to his family murders. He questioned how long a man could hold that memory and settled on forever. Robert thought of his demons that wouldn't go away and turned to Jake.

"I'm not sure you are the man for such a monumental task, but I'm counting on you to guard Damon Torinson with your life," Robert said.

"Why me?" Jake asked. Robert studied Jake, all the while, searching for an acceptable answer, and fell back on the truth.

"Because, Jake, you're disposable. If you leak anything about Damon Torinson, your work record is enough to ruin your credibility," Jake nodded as if he suspected the speech was coming. "You are on the last career stop—no more chances, Jake. I would call guarding this man your most difficult mission. I have little faith in you. And if you look around, the other men feel the same. So, I'll make you a deal. If Damon is down there, you can work here as long as he's alive."

"And if he isn't down there?" Jake asked with impatience. Robert shrugged his shoulders.

"Well, then I hope you'll have the class to have your resignation on my desk by the end of the week. Robert extended a hand to Jake. Reginald escaped his distant place to watch the exchange with wonder. Jake shook Robert's hand.

"Let's go find out. Shall we?" Robert asked.

Robert walked down the dark corridor that led to the back of the facility. Reginald and Jake followed close enough to bump him if he were to stop. The prison took on a different atmosphere when the sun went down, falling into an eerie murkiness. Reclamation was a different animal, and Robert discovered *that* the first time he entered its gates. Eyes seemed to watch, and he never felt alone within the walls. An irrational part of him imagined lost souls pacing the prison—a lifetime of misery echoing every misdeed.

A beam of light washed out into the dark hall from a flashlight, revealing a single doorway that led to a stairway going to the basement level. Two other streams joined Robert's, and none was steady enough for the task. Their beams jittered, bounced, and shook at the target while illuminating. Even with the unstable lighting from those in the rear, the large steel door materialized with the light. The large scale of the door gave onlookers the impression that it didn't belong. It was a fire door that kept fires from spreading above to below.

"Before the turn of the century, fires were more common and very difficult to put out with great success. A door like that was a defense against the onslaught of an inferno," Reginald *said*. The door itself was dirty but not unused. Robert clicked the flashlight off, slipped it into his coat pocket, and reached for the door. In the center of the door was a steel wheel connected to two steel rods.

The door reminded Jake of the hatches on a submarine. The wheel didn't require a full rotation to click the latches and move the rods. Robert felt the coolness of the wheel in his hands. In one swift movement, Robert jerked the wheel counterclockwise, as if he was turning a car into oncoming traffic. The rods followed the rotation of the wheel and snapped the latch open. The clack of the mechanism echoed in the hall.

"That got it," Robert said, pulling on the handle and testing the weight of the door before adding more strength to accomplish the task. The steel monstrosity opened slow in its frame. The depth of the door was well over four inches. Robert imagined Damon trapped behind its skin. Even armed with loads of power tools, the door would never budge. *Once you are in, you are in*, he thought. The door emitted a low, rusty squeal. Flashlights became more erratic in their owner's hands like the door was a giant jaw preparing to swallow them whole. The door finished its swing with a thick acrid odor rising in the air.

"What is that smell?" Reginald squinted and pressed a palm against his nose to dampen the stench.

"A hundred years of moisture, mold, and decaying brick," Robert said as he clicked his light back on and led the two down the brick stairs. The onetime straight edges of the concrete steps began to crumble, leaving random pieces of debris piling on the steps leading down. When they reached the bottom, they saw that they were in a large room. To Jake, the place resembled a nurse's station. Along every wall rested medical equipment, gurneys, and unidentifiable metal tools.

"This is where the insane received treatment," Reginald said. Jake jumped from his voice in the dark. "Back when we didn't understand mental illness, some men, women, and children lived miserable lives that ended down here," Reginald said.

Robert recalled the child's voice and the clanking of chains that accompanied the screams for help. He scanned the darkened room for any signs of a child's body alive or otherwise. He craned his neck in every direction expecting a child to pop out from the shadows. Each twisted metal chair, table, or medical hardware took on a life of its own and reached out for him.

"I don't see how anyone could survive down here for so long. Almost fifty years?" Jake asked.

"He had help from Warden Joseph," Robert added as he pushed a rusted-out chair from in front of his path.

"There's no real reason to assume there is anyone down here, Jake. And I'm sure we won't find anyone tonight," Reginald said. Robert slowed his walk and gave Reginald an accusing glance before continuing to an open doorway at the far end of the nurse's station.

"The holding cells are through there." Reginald pointed and realized that no one could see his hands. He flashed his beam toward the holding area. Robert breathed-in the stale air. The air smelled of deteriorated metals and pollutants from an era that didn't have much concept of what stray chemicals could do to a human body. Robert bet Damon was down there. A small sound, the soft scrape of metal on metal, interrupted their movements.

"Listen," Robert said. His eyes darted back and forth, searching for any trace of movement.

"Rats, likely," Reginald said.

"Be quiet," Robert demanded. All three men stood still tuned to any noise. The clink of metal on metal returned.

"That way," Robert said and pointed to a steel door that stood open. It was the same kind that resembled A submarine hatch.

Another entry that resembled a screen door blocked the open doorway. It wore the mesh of a standard screen door, but the woven metal was solid steel instead of the typical aluminum. They created the solid door for prisoners to gaze out or guards to peer in, but also have the strength to secure a prisoner with no problem. On it was a slot meant to pass trays of food in or out.

"What if he is in there . . . and it is the Devil?" Reginald asked, grabbing hold of his warden. Robert pulled his arm from Reginald's grasp and motioned—Jake pulled a gun from his holster and clicked off the safety. Robert tilted his head as if to say discussion over. Reginald stepped behind Robert, placed his hands on a metal lever, and joined Robert swinging the screen door outward.

"Are *you* sure about this, Mr. Deville?" Jake asked while steadying his gun. Robert nodded and wished he brought *his* gun. Instead, he aimed his Maglite into the holding cell. The first thing that he noticed was a yellow couch that he was sure came from the sixties. A table sat next to the couch with an art deco-shaped lamp atop its surface. The room seemed trapped in decades past like a replica of a bachelor pad owned by Hue Hefner. The room was a time capsule stuck in the wrong era. Robert skimmed his light to his left to find a roll-top desk. In front of the desk was a man leaning forward with his hands over his face. The posture was one of exhaustion or boredom. When Reginald saw the outline of the man sitting in front of the desk, he dropped his light from surprise. He sprang into action, scooped up the light, and directed it onto the top of the stranger's scalp. The three moved in the way hunters would cut off the escape of the animal they stalked.

"Keep your gun on him, Jake," Robert said and moved closer with the light in front, guiding the way. Reaching out, Robert grabbed the man by his long, black, curly hair and lifted his head.

Two eyes shone in the light, causing them to reflect like a cat. Reginald jumped but stood his ground. Robert released the man and took a step backward. The man lifted his head on his own accord and sat upright as if he awaited their visit all along. Robert expected to find a man in his waning years, but what he got was a younger man in his late thirties. What they discovered left them dumbfounded.

"Who are you?" Robert demanded. There was no response. "Answer me. Who are you?" No answer followed. "If you don't answer me . . . so help me God I will . . ."

"Don't use that name to me. Ever," the stranger screamed. The outburst shocked Jake to his core.

"Fair enough. What's your name?" The stranger looked from Robert to Reginald and stopped as if he recognized the associate warden.

"I'm Damon," he said and smiled. Reginald saw the raw insolence in Damon's face and could not look at him any longer. The associate warden trained his eyes on Robert.

"You killed my parents, my sister. You are a monster." Reginald continued to look eye-to-eye with Robert avoiding Damon's gaze. The harshness and anger in his eyes almost convinced Robert he was talking to him, "and I should kill you now where you sit," Reginald said, clenching his teeth so hard Robert was waiting for one to snap out of his mouth and slide across the floor.

"You were absent that night with your family. I missed an opportunity to meet you. How have you been?" Damon asked. The words were mocking. Reginald lunged for Damon as Robert expected he would. Instead, Robert was there to meet the associate warden.

"Jake, take Torinson up to my office and wait for my instructions." As Jake moved the prisoner, Robert turned to Reginald.

"I get how you're thinking—we don't know who or what we are dealing with yet. Hold your anger a little while longer. Can you do that for me?" Reginald shook his head. Robert placed an arm around Reginald to lead him away, and Reginald squirmed at the touch.

CHAPTER 20

Gage watched the shadows pass in front of his cell door. It wasn't yet time for lockdown, but the moment was fast approaching. There was a frenzy in the air that accompanied every lockdown. He watched the pacing begin as the inmates congregated around their cells, then sick anticipation of the inevitable confinement. There is no easy time inside, but the few moments before lockdown symbolize the real panic of prison. The artists that conjured up images of fear in books and movies seldom experienced it themselves. Solitary hours took their toll on a convict. Before Gage witnessed it himself, he feared the interactions with other inmates.

What the books don't write about is the childlike need that most, not all, but most prisoners have for socializing. They don't want to be alone. They hate living in their skin, living alone in a cell with nothing but their thoughts. Gage understood that uncomfortable feeling well. He sat on his bed—guards secured him and the rest into their cells for the night. Gage thought about Maria, and to his surprise, his imagination never wandered into sexual memories. There were fantasies, but Maria was different, and she represented his perfect woman. The pedestal he placed her upon rose so high that he could never join her, and she became untouchable to Gage. The one fantasy he allowed himself with Maria was the same one that replayed in his mind when he was at his lowest. The security blanket that picked him up when everything seemed too bleak to go on. His fictional premise involved coming home from the robbery safe and handing her the money necessary to help Ryan. Gage never wanted to be a hero for anyone except her, and he let her down. His prison wasn't the cell—it was reliving his failure on an angry loop—tormenting him like razors cutting at his skin.

The dying woman from the robbery flashed in his mind, and he smothered the recollection at once. Even his self-pity found a limit. He remained vigilant about not revisiting such somber topics for fear that he might fall into a swoon so deep, so all-encompassing that he couldn't climb from its alluring grip. Gage drifted between his thoughts and a book. A flicker from the corner of his eyes, saw Eddie come into the cell. He broke away from his novel but still didn't look up at his friend. Gage searched for the sentence he last read when Eddie spoke. He was out of breath, a characteristic that Gage never witnessed in his friend. The old saying, *I never run unless I'm being chased*, came into his mind.

"Hey, Saint," Eddie said, waiting for Gage to greet him. Not receiving the welcome, he sought, Eddie continued to talk into the raised book in front of Gage. "I have done something stupid, Saint." Gage looked up and threw his book aside. It bounced on the bed and fell to the cement floor. The chatter of the prison rose as the guards began securing the cell doors and the inmates inside them. Gage stood from his cot and walked over to Eddie. In Gage's eyes, his friend was a feather in the wind, swaying in the breeze. He walked around Eddie in a semi-circle, studying him like a doctor might inspect a carrier of an infectious disease.

"What did you do, Eddie?" The younger cellmate gulped hard instead of answering as Gage wanted. The clamor of the guards yelling "lights out" built momentum as it headed toward Gage. "What happened?" Gage asked, looking to Eddie until he returned a gaze.

"What I did, I did to protect you," Eddie said and broke free from Gage's stare.

"How did you protect me?" Eddie wanted to escape from the cell but saw the guards approaching to close him in for the night. Eddie, trapped together with Gage, swallowed hard to clear his throat.

"I took care of Victor for you."

"What does that mean?"

"Listen, he would screw you over, and now he won't get the chance," Eddie said.

He moved to his bunk, slid a pack of cigarettes from between the mattress, and jerked one into his mouth. Eddie lit a match, dragged it across the tip of the cigarette, and squashed the flame in the blink of an eye. He took in the smoke deep as if he were winding down from a hard day instead of fielding questions from his friend. Gage looked like a pressure cooker ready to blow its seal and spew food in every direction.

"Tell me everything," Gage said. Eddie allowed himself one more drag before speaking.

"I squealed on Victor."

"How? For what?" Eddie searched for a clever answer and gave up.

"I told a screw that a knife had gone missing from the kitchen. They don't know it yet, but there's one under Victor's mattress." Eddie breathed-in the cigarette so fast that half of its body became hot ash.

"How can you be sure he has a knife under his bed?" Gage asked.

"Because . . . I put it there," Eddie said. Gage pounded his fists on the brick wall and covered his face in disgust.

"Eddie, what have you done? Why are you so stupid?" Eddie showed his offense in his expression.

"They'll put him in solitary confinement right off the bat," Eddie said.

"What about when he gets out? Have you considered that?"

"Yeah, I have. When the guards toss the cells to find the knife, the guards will not only find the knife but half of the contraband from other convicts throughout the prison. There will be some angry men ready to do him some harm for his stupidity."

"*His* stupidity?" Gage asked. Eddie put out the cigarette.

"Trust me—this will work." Eddie smiled. Gage shook his head.

"No, it won't work. Not in this place. Something always goes wrong." Gage moved to the cell door just in time for the guard to close it in front of him. The guard smiled as if they were sharing some knowledge, and maybe they were. Gage swung around to face Eddie with fire transforming his face.

"You don't have a damn clue what you've done to me," Gage said. Eddie looked shocked.

"I've done nothing to you."

"You have. I just spoke with Victor about what would happen if a knife from the kitchen came up missing, and then soon after, a knife ends up under his bed."

"I bet someone will get to him first. What do you think?" Gage shook his head and found the corner of his cot.

"No matter what your intentions were or how you hoped it would turn out, it won't go down that way. That I'm sure of." Gage reached his hand out. "Give me a smoke." Eddie handed Gage a cigarette just as the grumbling of guards tossing the cells began the wave throughout the prison. Soon after, noises erupted in each cell, toilets flushed. Inmates flung merchandise out of their cells, passing contraband to avoid getting caught with anything illegal.

"And so, it begins," Gage said. He smoked his cigarette in silence, waiting for guards to toss Victor's cell.

The night was torturous for Gage. He watched it unfold, and he knew Victor would zero in on him. Sleep's merciful hand never touched him through the night. He lay awake, listening to the sounds of the other inmates and wondered what treasures the guards on their hunt for the knife found. *This surprise inspection will stretch solitary to its capacity by the morning*, Gage thought.

The day seemed to fly by like images on a screen until Gage made it to the yard. He did what every other convict did after the guards tossed the cells. A missing inmate meant they were in either solitary or the infirmary. Gage hoped to see Victor leaning against a wall, unaware of the betrayal performed by Eddie. His head and eyes were going in separate directions attempting to find him.

Instead, Gage found Victor's muscle, Reven. He stared back at Gage with no intentions to look away. In the wild, it was a gesture of dominance, and Gage took it the same in Reclamation. As an alternative to waiting for a confrontation, Gage walked across the prison yard. All eyes burned on Gage, which meant that the word was out that the eventful night was all his doing. Gage kept his eyes trained on Reven his entire walk. He was careful not to look away, not appearing vulnerable. Reven recognized Gage's backbone but showed little of his admiration.

"You need to speak to me?" Gage asked.

"I do. You know why, so I won't waste any time recapping. My boss isn't happy with you. Victor has some alone time for the next couple of days, thanks to you. Last night's inspections caught many powerful inmates off guard and lost a lot of merchandise. Those people made inquiries—you want to know what they found?" Gage wanted to know more than anything and nodded. "A little bird sang that your boy Eddie came in and out of Victor's cell. You can't make a move in here without somebody's eyes taking note."

"It wasn't him—it was me," Gage said in a voice that made others standing around take notice. Reven glanced around and back to Gage.

"Don't you worry so much. Victor knows who pulls Eddie's strings. He wouldn't have the guts to make a move on Victor without your guidance." It was *better* knowing that the responsibility fell his way for the treachery. "The problem—however, is that Victor needs you to fulfill your promise to him. We will punish Eddie for your deeds."

"Listen, we can work something—" Gage said with desperation in his voice.

"You see? We have your attention now," Reven said with a smile. "This is inevitable. Even if we wanted to let this slide, which we don't—others are calling for Eddie's death. If we stood by and did nothing. The stench of weakness…"

"I know a way—"

"Save it—already set in stone. Eddie's death will make Victor a hero with some heavy hitters in here, and the slate will be clean between you and Victor. Everyone wins, except Eddie. And don't forget that you brought him into this." Gage's body tensed without an attempt to veil it.

"You will have to go through me." Reven nodded.

"You have the advantage of having Eddie in your cell, but you can't protect him forever. We'll get him. You can count on that."

"We'll see," Gage said through clenched teeth.

"Yes, we will, and again I have to warn you that if Victor gets out of solitary and you have made no preparations on your mutual project, it won't please him." Gage moved closer to Reven and pushed his nose against his.

"I don't care to make Victor happy, and if Eddie goes, you'll follow."

"Good luck to you," Reven said. They each walked away.

The prison cafeteria was near capacity. Hundreds of eyes didn't seem to have the same sting while Gage was at work—while he was in his element. For the time being, he didn't have to concern himself with how to defend Eddie. When he was in the kitchen, cleaning up messes, or serving the line of men behind the counter, Gage was invisible to the world. Although the cafeteria was at a constant roar, it always blended into a comforting hum that melted away all of Gage's problems.

He jumped right in the middle of the service and helped scoop food onto the waiting trays. Before he found his groove as a server, a hush fell over the room. The prison noise changed from a low roar to quiet as a church in seconds. Gage looked up from his serving station in time to see Warden Deville leading a prisoner through his line. The screw, Jake Shoeman, followed behind with a shotgun.

The man they were leading was tall and thin. *There is something about his eyes*, Gage thought. *They possessed something. Was there wisdom in the eyes?* He couldn't be sure. The prisoner wore the same clothes as the rest of the inmates, but he was different. Gage believed it was the way he carried himself as if he had nothing to worry about, that he had the whole thing figured out. A man like that seemed dangerous to Gage. A guard shoved a plastic food tray in the strange inmate's hands, and he moved from station to station collecting food until he reached Gage.

"You are Gage, right?" Gage snapped back to reality by the warden's voice. "Are you going to serve him?" Gage nodded and scooped up food with a large spoon and dumped soup in the stranger's bowl. Robert motioned Damon to move on, and he did without a word. "I meant to speak to you, Gage. After your shift, I want you in my office. Okay?" Gage nodded, with no hesitation.

"Yes, sir." Gage looked to his potato soup and saw that it had curdled. He raised his head, snapping back to Damon. "What the hell?" Gage spoke to himself, and he pushed a ladle through the spoiled milk-based soup. He watched Damon go to a table all by himself with Jake observing him eat. A shotgun at the ready.

CHAPTER 21

Gage stood in front of Warden Robert Deville's door, waiting to go in. He sat there with apprehension. What Gage feared most was the erratic behavior that he witnessed in wardens throughout his time inside. With every minor meeting, a convict's life was in the warden's hands. A fight with the wife, an over-starched shirt, or a sore back might cause their mood to swing. Rumors of overzealous wardens might be an exaggeration, but there is truth in every tall prison tale. Gage extended his arm in front of the glass pane that spelled out the warden's name. His fist, frozen in the knocking position, hovered next to the door until a voice startled Gage back to reality.

"You may go in. The warden is waiting for you," Agatha said in a pleasant mothering tone. Still shaken by her sudden appearance, Gage twisted the door handle, pushing the door aside and took a step. Robert looked from his desk and waved Gage inside. He wrestled with the door handle once more and secured it shut.

"Please take a seat," Robert said. The congenialities made Gage nervous as he sat. Robert worked away on something while Gage watched him scribble his name on legal papers. *Making me wait is another use of power*, Gage thought. Robert made the last stroke and looked at Gage.

"Sorry about that. You wouldn't understand the amount of paperwork that comes along with the title." Gage pursed his lips and smiled. Robert shuffled one pile on top of another and slid them to the side like a magic trick. Robert's hands came together in the shape of a prayer and then folded them into each other with fingers interlocking like a basket.

"I meant to bring you in since our situation together." Robert smiled without one returning. The warden opened a Manila folder and glared at its contents. "So, they call you Saint?" Robert never looked up.

"Some do."

"Your file is remarkable. You are in here for manslaughter with a little less than a year left on your sentence," Robert continued to scan the documents as if alone in the room, "the victim was shot—and you stayed with them instead of running from the scene. It says here that you received a reduced sentence because a bystander at the robbery testified that you didn't discharge your firearm. That's amazing. It doesn't change the fact that you committed a serious crime. It says tons for your character, and that's what I'm looking for in an inmate," Robert said.

"You're looking for me?"

"Maybe. Your wife's name is Maria, and you have a son named Ryan." Gage felt the pang of nausea with his stomach dropping.

"My son passed away," Gage said.

"I'm sorry for your loss." Robert read on. "That's unusual," Robert said and studied the files further.

"What is?"

"You haven't made a phone call since you've been here, and you refused all your visitors. Why would you do that?" There is no answer. "The reason I ask—supportive relationships from the outside can raise the odds that a convict can rehabilitate. Whether you stay out when the time comes isn't my current problem. I got another idea in mind for you, Saint," Robert's smile returned. Gage was uncomfortable in his skin as he awaited the warden's intentions. "You saw the prisoner I escorted to the cafeteria today?" Gage nodded. "Supposedly, his name is Damon Torinson."

"Supposedly?" Gage asked out of reflex. Robert didn't seem to mind the snap question.

"Let's say he is a curiosity, and I'm sure he will stick out. Some inmates will come for him. I want you to protect him, Saint. I want you to shadow him, get to know him. Find out what makes him tick."

"I'll do what I can to help, warden . . . the thing is . . . I spend my time in the kitchen—I also got a cellmate of my own. I'm not sure how it will work out," Gage said. He hoped that the matter would end with the subtle excuse.

"Leave it to me. I will assign Damon to the kitchen, under your supervision, and I had Damon moved into your cell," Robert said.

"My cellmate is Eddie—" Gage said with a panic that was growing more intense by the second.

"I moved Eddie into a laundry detail. Don't worry—he'll bunk with a common thief, no one too dangerous." Eddie was a target for attack, and Gage knew what that would mean to his friend.

"I don't want him, I want Eddie," Gage said, raising his voice, and forgetting himself. Robert never blinked more than normal, keeping his composure.

"Gage, I know it's in your nature to protect Eddie, and that's why I chose you for this favor. And that's what it is, a favor. I have the power to pull strings to get your time here shortened if you do this for me. Eddie will be fine, I promise." Gage was shaking his head. "There isn't a choice."

"Warden, please." Robert looked down and started on another pile of paperwork.

"Warden . . ."

"Dismissed, Saint," Robert said with indifference. Gage understood the consequences of the warden's decision and fell silent. He turned and left more depressed than when he first arrived at Reclamation.

Gage walked from Robert's office to his cell like a man heading to death row. All eyes were on him, including the guards, telling him more with a passing glance than he ever wanted to know. An urge to fill his lungs full and scream at the onlookers came over Gage, and he fought with all his might to resist. What captured Gage's attention when he reached his cell was a guard waiting just outside with a rifle. The guard was Jake Shoeman.

Eddie already had a box overflowing with his personal effects. Because of his frazzled demeanor, Eddie didn't notice Gage standing outside the cell. He moved to the opening without an upward glance. Gage grabbed Eddie by the shoulders, stopping his progress. The physical contact didn't rouse Eddie from his stupor.

"You can't leave, Eddie," Gage said almost to himself rather than his friend. Eddie never looked up.

"Got no choice, Saint." Eddie was a man that accepted his fate. He walked past Gage showing no emotion for his longtime friend. Gage turned to Jake.

"I saved your ass when the warden got attacked. You remember that, don't you?"

"I do, and I thank you a lot, Saint," Jake said.

"You can thank me by putting a kill on this move."

"I can't do that, Saint." Jake began walking with Eddie. Gage went to stop Jake and changed his mind.

"Can you keep this from happening? Eddie will be in danger," Gage said. Jake halted his progress and stared at Gage.

"Even if I wanted to help you, do you believe I hold that power, that I could supersede a decision the warden made?" Jake shook his head. "Besides, you already have a new cellmate." Jake motioned into the cell with his head, and just like that, Eddie disappeared from the equation. *I save the warden's hide, and this is my reward.* Rage built up inside Gage with no outlet for the fire that roared. When he turned to the cell, he saw his outlet leaning against the brick wall. *He thinks he can use me as a bodyguard. I'll snap his goddamn neck. That's what I should do.* Gage moved toward Damon with purpose when he spoke.

"Every warden's the same, aren't they?" Damon gave a smile as if Gage wasn't racing toward him at all. It was the smile that did the trick, causing Gage to stop in his tracks.

"Who are you, and why are you so important that they shuffled prisoners all over the building for you?" Damon moved to a bed and sat.

"The warden thinks I'm the Devil," Damon said. Gage's frame loosened from the exchange.

"There's a devil in almost every cell of Reclamation." Damon shook his head, allowing the smile to drain away from his face as if it were never visible.

"Not *a* devil, *the* Devil." Damon folded his hands in his lap. "Robert believes I'm the fallen angel Lucifer himself come down to Earth to destroy mankind."

"And what do you say to that?"

"Devil or not, you're stuck with me." Gage seethed when Damon's logic hit home.

"It doesn't mean I have to like it," Gage said.

"No, it doesn't."

CHAPTER 22

Jenny placed the phone receiver to her ear. The faint sound of Robert snoring in the other room rose and fell. She wondered about her husband's disappearance for the last couple of nights. Jenny guessed she would get the answers she needed, but Robert was in no condition to do anything but pass out when he arrived last night.

Jenny had a sharp twinge of unease enter her mind for the first time since she met him. She planned to give him the benefit of the doubt even though her mind played insecure tricks on her. The thought came and went like a drive-by shooter, sneaking up on her, blasting her with its evil ideas, and driving away, leaving her frazzled and unsure. To her discredit, Morris was never what Jenny believed him to be until it was too late. She wasn't a good judge of character, but Robert was different. He was the best, most honest person she ever dreamed of meeting. Her mother bringing them together was the greatest gift ever given by the woman.

Jenny looked around to her spotless kitchen and wondered what it meant—staying home, scrubbing, cooking, and cleaning to have him cheat on her? The phone began to ring on the other end, and it seemed ominous to Jenny. Her first reaction was to hang up and forget she wanted to call. She searched her feelings for a plausible reason to fear contact with Zack's teacher and found nothing. As the phone continued to ring, Jenny pictured Mrs. Jenkins with her dirty blonde hair and her pear-shaped figure. She was younger than she imagined when she met her at parent-teacher conferences, but she owned the look of a teacher. *She appeared scholarly*, Jenny thought. The phone stopped ringing. Jenny expected a voice message taking over where the ringing left off. Instead, a women's voice filled the receiver, small at first—then her words flooded into her ears.

"Hello? What can I do for you?" Laura Jenkins asked with such warmth that Jenny drowned in her kind tones. Each word tumbled in her mind until she almost forgot why she called.

"Mrs. Jenkins?"

"Yes?"

"This is Jenny Deville. Zack's mom." Silence captured the line. "Hello? Hello?" No answer from the other end.

"Are you there, Mrs. Jenkins?" Jenny heard breathing.

"I'm here," Laura said. Jenny didn't know whether to speak or hang up. She wondered if she committed some breach of etiquette by calling a schoolteacher at home.

"Is this a bad time?" Jenny asked.

"Hello, Mrs. Deville."

"Is something wrong?"

"No, I'm fine." More silence filled the air.

"The reason I called Mrs. Jenkins is . . . well . . . I wanted to talk about my son's behavior at school. I have noticed a change in him that has startled me enough to call you. Have you seen anything out of the ordinary with Zack? Has he been moody, fighting, reserved?" Jenny waited for a long time until Laura answered.

"I've wanted to call you, Mrs. Deville."

"Jenny, please call me Jenny."

"Jenny. I've debated for the last two weeks whether I should contact you. Then...you're on the other end of the line. It frightened me to hear your voice, Jenny," Laura said.

"I get that. So, why were you going to call?"

"I think we should meet," Laura said with desperation in her voice.

"I think the phone will be fine—"

"No, we have to meet in person . . . there's something I have to show you, Jenny." It was Jenny's turn to pause.

"Okay."

Jenny turned on the car radio, adjusted the volume, and scanned through the stations twice. Her nerves kept her from enjoying any selection—instead, she thought about Laura Jenkins and what she wanted to show her. Liam left her home late in the night before Robert arrived, and now, she wished he joined her to visit Zack's teacher.

She was flying solo, and for now, that felt like the right thing to do. Besides, even though she knew that Zack's behavior was far from his fault, Jenny was in the middle of a mild case of shame. She told herself it was silly but couldn't shake the emotion. When Jenny pulled up to Laura's house, the butterflies in the pit of her stomach grew from slight to bordering on panic. She came there to find out about her son, and that was the very thing she feared most, finding out something so wrong that it might change her opinion of her little boy. She understood that more than likely, whatever his behavior stemmed from was Morris's involvement—still, she had to be the one to pick up the pieces.

Jenny took a deep breath, exhaled, and pushed the door open. She hurried up a stone path that led to the front door. Laura's home was a ranch that looked tidy. A white picket fence lined her well-manicured yard. Jenny could tell that the schoolteacher took exceptional pride in the exterior of her home. She guessed that was why she cared so much for her children—she didn't let the small things slide as so many others often did. As she looked from the stone footpath to the door, Laura was waiting in its frame. It was clear their meeting meant a lot to Laura, and her expression showed no signs of happiness.

"Hello, Mrs. Jenkins," Jenny said with nervous energy.

"Call me, Laura. Please come in." Laura waved her in, and it was too late for Jenny to back out even if her anxiety screamed for her to run for the car.

When Jenny walked through the doorway, she felt an uneasiness that she hadn't experienced since her encounter with Toby in the basement. She tried to shake the dread, but it wrapped around her like a blanket, weighing her down with each step into the young teacher's home. Jenny's senses were uneven as she looked around the schoolteacher's house. She still felt the heavy hand of death surrounding her like a fog descending into her lungs with every breath.

She watched Laura scurry about getting a pitcher of lemonade, pouring it into glasses, and all without speaking. A steady sound of chains rose, distracting her from the kinetic ambling of her host. Chain clinking sounds started in the living room where they both sat, but they turned inward, hearing the clinking resound in her skull. The clinking became rhythmic like the beating of a heart. Jenny scanned the room for the source of her distraction and spotted a roll-top desk sitting in the corner. An orange lacquer glaze shone from its oak exterior.

"I wanted to call you sooner, I did . . . I couldn't bring myself to pick up the phone," Laura said while handing Jenny a cool glass of lemonade. She reached for the glass, and from the corner of her eye, she regarded the desk again, hiding secrets in its wooden belly.

"Thank you, Laura," Jenny said, enjoying the tart of the lemonade.

"I want to start by saying that I think Zack is a sweet, intelligent boy, and I see no hint of malice in him," Laura said and took a drink of her own. Jenny braced herself for the worst, placing her drink on a wooden coffee table.

"What do you have to tell me, Laura?" Slight impatience bled through her words. Laura didn't seem to pick up on her guest's anxiety.

"It happened two weeks ago during reading groups. I was leading one group when your son stood up. I guess he was standing there for a long time before I saw him. Other children in his group said that he was swaying in place as if asleep. However, his eyes were wide open, staring as if he could see another world through the walls. His movements were a reaction to something unseen to us." Jenny watched Laura's face contort with every gesture it took to describe Zack's movements in the classroom. "He looked into all our eyes, not seeing us, and he said that *The Deceiver* would once again come into power. Moloch would again be free, and if we didn't stop him, he would destroy the world with his influence." Laura stopped and allowed herself a swig of lemonade before continuing.

"Moloch? Who's Moloch?" Jenny asked. Laura was already shaking her head.

"I don't know. After that, Zack didn't see us at all. He stepped up onto his school desk in the middle of the classroom and screamed to the heavens that God is watching what we do now. That it will be our lack of faith that will hide his identity from us—that if we do not use God's eyes, we will not see who or what he is until it's too late." Laura's speech mesmerized Jenny. "After that, Zack stepped off his desk and sat in his seat. By the time I got to him, he had laid his head on his desktop and fell asleep. I wasn't sure what to make of it—figured he was sleepwalking or acting out a vivid dream. I roused him from his desk and walked him to the nurse's office to check him over. She told me he was tiptop and to let him rest in her office until it was time to go home. I wrote the event off as a weird dream until this week."

Jenny needed to understand Zack's plight while her nagging desire pleaded to get away from Laura. There were things that a person didn't want to know, and everything Laura offered belonged under that category. She held onto the hope that something good could come from their meeting, yet her intuition told her otherwise.

"What happened this week?" Jenny asked more out of reflex than curiosity. Laura bit down on her lip, placed her glass on the coffee table, and stood up. Her locomotion was slow and deliberate, and even though her movements were minimal, her outward appearance unsettled Jenny as if the schoolteacher carried dark knowledge. Laura took two steps forward and stopped and then started back up again. The scene reminded Jenny of a glitch in a video. Soon enough, Laura's feet took her to the roll-top desk standing in the corner. She reached into her jeans and pulled from them a set of keys. She shuffled through them several times as if she didn't want to ever open the desk. Jenny shared her apprehension.

As Laura slid her small key into the desk's locking mechanism, Jenny pictured something alive pounding on the inside, testing the desk's strength and waiting to get out. Laura turned the key, then rolled the desk front up and open. Jenny half waited for a poisonous snake to leap from the inside and clamp down on the schoolteacher's neck. Instead of a snake, she reached inside the belly of the desk and pulled out a pile of yellow construction paper. She handled the pulp like valuable documents.

Laura, with the construction paper, walked toward her guest. Jenny's aversion to the paper was strong. She didn't know why, but she felt as if they held power over her. She pushed herself back into her chair without realizing her actions. Laura pushed the papers into her lap, wanting to shed the burden of holding them.

"Take them," Laura said. Jenny's natural reflex to grab what her host handed her took over. They felt icy cold in her grasp.

"What are these?" Laura backed away, sat down in front of Jenny, and didn't say a word.

"During our Art period, the children can paint or color anything they want. It's their opportunity to express themselves—however, they see fit. I don't even look at each of their pictures—I instruct them to pack them up in their homework folders and send their artistic endeavors home to their parents. Last week I made a change when I saw what your son drew."

"What kind of change?"

"I ask the children to pass them in."

"What did he draw?" Laura nodded her head toward the papers.

"Look." Jenny slid a sheet from the top and brought it up to eye level. On the construction paper was a charcoal relief. The quality of the portrait done in shades of black and gray went well beyond the ability of a young child, yet there it was. The eye for detail was astounding. After a moment holding the picture, Jenny realized that she was holding her breath. She let out air all at once like a balloon when a child releases it into the sky.

What frightened Jenny the most was how realistic Zack drew the picture. She blinked twice to clear her eyes and soon found that her sight didn't need adjusting. Zack's rendering was so bright, so vibrant, so well-drawn that the picture looked more like a window resting in Jenny's hand. She swore her eyes were playing tricks on her as she waited for the image to move. It didn't, and she was glad for that. She saw with shock and horror the perfect representation of Toby created by her own child's hands.

In the charcoal scene, Toby was in the basement where Jenny had her visions of the small boy. He was how she remembered him, except his clothes were too fresh to resemble the poor creature from her vision in the basement. His face was pristine if you overlooked his puffy eyes, no doubt crying from his capture. Shackles grasped each arm and leg, tethering him to the basement's concrete. At the top of the drawing, in the distance, a floodlight washed out some subtle details. In the left corner, absent of the light, a shadow formed.

She raised her eyebrows and squinted to make the form clearer. Attempting to focus didn't help her cause, and the picture remained blurry. She moved her thumb to get a better look, but just touching the figure on paper gave her the creeps. All at once, Jenny saw the form of a man, and it seemed familiar to her. She couldn't tell for sure if the dark outline of the man was Morris, but she knew the outline just the same. She thought of how Zack said he knew a baseball player was at-bat by their swing. There were hints or clues in a stance—in his frame. She stared at the shadowy figure until her eyes burned, hoping that the mystery of the identity would reveal itself to her. Laura studied Jenny, studying the drawing.

"You don't seem that surprised to see the boy in chains. Do you know anything about this?" Laura asked, bringing her voice to a tone as casual as she could manage. Jenny heard the schoolteacher and didn't break off her focus. "What do you know, Jenny?" Laura didn't soften her accusatory tone.

"I know about this," Jenny said. Laura jumped to her feet as if Jenny just told her she had leprosy. "The boy's name is Toby." Tears welled in Laura's eyes. She wiped at them, pacing back and forth in front of Jenny.

"How do you know that? How did Zack see Toby like that? What did you do to him?" Laura's voice rose to a scream in an instant. Jenny was at a loss for words. The schoolteacher's reaction gave away her closeness to the situation with Toby, and Jenny needed a gentle hand, giving out the details. "If you don't answer me, I'm calling the police." Laura made a move for a nearby phone.

"Wait," Jenny yelled to stop Laura's motion. "Give me a second to explain." Laura stopped and hovered over Jenny, hands clenched and breathing fast enough to hyperventilate. "Calm down, Laura," Jenny said. She worried about her credibility if she told the young teacher everything she learned.

"That outfit that Zack saw Toby wearing was the outfit he went missing in," Laura said, gauging Jenny's reaction, "but he was not in that outfit when the police found his body." Laura was as blunt as possible to elicit something, anything from Jenny. She saw signs of fear but not for what Laura suspected. Any wrong answer would stir-up the hornet's nest and send her into a confrontation that wouldn't bounce in her favor.

"My husband was a detective with the police department," Jenny said.

"Oh?" Laura's expression changed.

"He often brought the material home from a crime scene." Jenny felt dirty for lying—as if she were stomping on Toby's grave but saw no alternative.

"Maybe . . . still, how could Zack know what Toby was wearing when he disappeared? The police held that information close to the vest." Jenny shook her head.

"I can't explain it. It's a mystery. Zack never saw a thing, and I never did a thing. Other than Zack drawing that picture, we have no connection with that poor child," Jenny said in the most pleading tone she could muster. Laura released her death grip, fell backward into a chair, and melted out of her trance. Her adrenaline subsided, leaving her spent from its effects.

"How do you know Toby?" Jenny asked when she felt the time was right. Laura's tears remained long after the anger, flowing heavier than before.

"He's my nephew, my brother's son . . . *was* my brother's son." she looked off into the air or at nothing at all. "This tragedy devastated my brother and his family. When I saw your son's drawing, I thought I stumbled onto Toby's killer. I'd give anything to hand over his son's murderer to him. More than anything, I wanted to give him that gift," Laura said.

"I don't blame you one bit, and I would like to help you and your family any way that I can."

"Thank you, Jenny. We all miss Toby so much. We want someone to suffer for this. You know?" Jenny nodded. "The problem is the case is growing colder as more time goes by. I'm sure you would know better than me, considering your husband was a detective. The longer the case sits there, the more unlikely the murderer will see justice."

"You're right," Jenny said, realizing there was another sheet with a drawing. Looking at it would mean more heartache, and she had enough. Laura watched her scan the second sheet.

"The other one won't mean anything to you—it meant nothing to me." Jenny traced the edges of the sheet with her finger and gave it a quick tap with her nail. She wanted to throw the paper on the floor, walk out of the schoolteacher's door, and never lay eyes on her again. The problem *was,* Jenny knew she wouldn't do any of those things. Instead, she pulled the sheet from behind the first to watch with all its horror.

"Let's see," Jenny said with a lump in her throat. She touched the second sheet with the tips of her fingers almost tickling the corner. Jenny pulled the paper up and first studied the outer area, avoiding the total impact at one time and noticing it was like the same charcoal drawing as the first. The scene took place in the front seat of a car. She recognized the leather reclining car seats. The dome light gave off an eerie glow from above. Jenny forced her eyes to the center of the sheet. Jenny's stomach dropped, and so did her heart. She tucked the sheet of paper back behind the other.

"Did it mean anything?" Laura asked.

"It meant nothing just as you said." Feeling sick to her stomach, Jenny jumped to her feet.

"Would you mind if I . . ." Jenny motioned to take the papers. Laura nodded.

"I don't even want them in the house. I'm glad to rid myself of them."

"Thank you, Laura. I am sorry for *your* loss. Don't give up," Jenny said.

"I won't." The two women hugged, and Jenny walked out of the schoolteacher's house, still shaken from what she saw.

CHAPTER 23

Robert was clued-in that he would have to deal with Jenny. She was a stubborn woman, and telling her the truth was difficult, if not impossible. The truth was not Robert's problem—he planned to lie, anyway. Lying was Robert's best line of defense. Others might see moral ambiguity in lying but not Robert. He thought of a lie as useful as duct tape. There wasn't a time or situation that it couldn't benefit the teller. If done right, a lie was the most precious tool in an arsenal, he often thought. An officer knowing how to use truth or lies as a tool was invaluable. Information is power. Let other people wrestle with the ethics behind the spoken word—he had no qualms with deception.

In the few seconds that Robert searched the refrigerator, his appetite raced from hungry to insatiable. He grabbed the carton of eggs from their perch on the inside of the door. A quick hand placed a frying pan on the stove, twisting the stove dial, and coaxing an egg from the carton as a blue flame kissed the bottom of the metal. He cracked one egg after another until five in all bubbled in the skillet.

At a typical breakfast, he preferred his fried to a crisp finish, but it was no ordinary morning, and the starved feelings took over. When one side of the eggs started to cook, he wielded the spatula like a weapon, prying from the pan, and plopping them onto a plate. No sooner had his rear touched the kitchen chair than his teeth sunk into the eggs. Liquid, yellow yolk ran from the egg whites as he devoured. A soothing rush enveloped his stomach with the soft eggs filling and coating his insides. With one fire put out, he continued to eat with his mind turning to the problem of Damon Torinson.

Although reading Joseph Hughes's diary was thrilling, Robert never held much value in the narrative. He wondered if the diary was Joseph's attempt at a novel. What Robert believed most of all was that Joseph Hughes suffered from a mental breakdown.

The stress and sheer loneliness of losing his wife Karie must have caused a crack in his mind—causing him to fabricate a boogeyman. Joseph lashed out at the world for what happened to him, and Robert couldn't hold it against him. Whatever psychosis the older man was suffering from, Robert had to deal with the aftermath.

Damon Torinson, the Devil or not, was sitting in a cell. Robert had to deal with the situation fast. *How do you explain Damon's age?* He asked himself. The Damon he found under Reclamation was a young man, which meant to Robert that Joseph's insanity must have occurred in recent years. The alternative explanation meant a few decades passed, and the captive under the prison stayed as pristine as when he arrived at Reclamation.

Robert dismissed the radical idea right off. It was ridiculous, bordering on lunacy. If he were to follow Joseph's path of thinking, he would end up the same as his predecessor. As he shoveled in the last bits of egg, Robert concluded that everyone around him thought too much of Joseph, considering he suffered a delusional break from reality. He gave the old warden far too much credence by reading his diary. All of that was about to change. Robert made it his mission to find out everything there was to know about Damon Torinson if there even was such a man.

Robert ran his plate, soiled by eggs, under running water and thought of the prisoner Gage, and how he saved his life. By Robert's calculation, Gage was the perfect inside man to watch over Damon and report anything unusual back to him. He needed to convince him to report back to him. He didn't think it impossible. If he read Gage right, then it was clear Gage's weakness was that he saw himself as a good person no matter the past. Robert knew he couldn't trust him. *But I can use him.*

CHAPTER 24

Gage leaned back in his chair, curling one side of the paperback until it resembled a rolled-up newspaper. Damon was reading something of his own, but he didn't bother to examine his new cellmate. That was what the warden wanted, and he wasn't about to show any solidarity to the man who left his friend out to dry. Warden Deville was right about one thing, Damon would need protection.

During his stay at Reclamation, Gage never saw such an uproar over a convict. The one thing that there was a lot of in prison was hearsay. Rumors spread like wildfire through the facility. Tawdry details, no matter how small, fueled the motives and the actions of most prisoners. Boredom, above all other reasons, was the culprit, causing gossip to speed from one end of Reclamation to the other in minutes.

Inmates knew avoiding the daily soap opera might prevent conflict, and yet it was hard to resist. Between the bricked walls, prisoners bought and sold information every day. For many, it was a drug, filling them with an instant thrill, hearing something juicy, or being the first to let someone in on the latest news.

More than anything else, what it gave those who dealt in rumors was a sense of community, remaining a part of something much greater than a small nothing of a life. It's the closest thing to freedom that many on the inside will ever know. Reclamation owned each person from their skin down to the bone. It was their choice to give, keep, or use their knowledge. At that moment, a tidal wave of talk surrounded Damon Torinson—threatening to capsize him.

A wheel's squeak broke Gage's attention, a little but not enough to cause the meaning to fall out of his last sentence. His eyes did the work, but his brain never received the info. By the third reread, the mechanical squeal was more prominent. Gage wanted to tell Ronny to fix that wheel, to oil that thing so the rest of the inmates wouldn't have to hear him coming like an ice cream truck rolling down a neighborhood, spewing its hideous warning that it would arrive soon.

Ronny pushed his basket along the prison corridor. The wheel of his cart rattled back and forth like a grocery cartwheel that lost its direction. His cart was full to the top with mail sorted in a way that he alone could decipher. Years of hauling letters across the prison— etched upon his wrinkled face. His eyes sunk in from lack of sleep— because he couldn't or wouldn't. Every mile that he walked registered in his gnarled frame and uneasy gait. His legs looked as if they intended to start a fire as they rubbed against each other for support. Prisoners would swear the cart was pulling him rather than the other way around.

As Ronny ascended each level, a roar of chatter erupted, with many announcing the mail's arrival. Soon the noisy exchanges died away into a hush of anticipation. Mail meant different things to different people. For the new meat, mail was a vital link to the outside world that they just left behind. There was desperation in the way inmates looked forward to letters from wives or girlfriends that told them they would wait for them or parents who told them they weren't bad, and they have a place to come home to, always. For the long-timers, mail brought sadness. Mail for them dwindled to the occasional piece, around the holidays. The most devoted of friends and family never maintained their letters forever. Lovers moved on— wives remarried—siblings lost themselves in their busy lives.

If a lifer were lucky, their mother would stay connected as a spokesperson for the outside. Mothers often become the inmate's surrogate spouse, tethering their son to the community outside the walls. Gage placed his book on the cot next to him and walked to the cell door. Ronny was already standing there with a smile on his face more for show than anything else.

"Delivery for you, Saint," Ronny said. The prison postman handed Gage a few envelopes with the fluid beauty of a woman's handwriting across the front. Gage nodded without looking into Ronny's eyes. There was a rhythm to their exchange as they had done their dance hundreds of times. "See you, Saint," Ronny said and walked past the cell to the next. The cart's loud wheels squealed then faded as it went down the corridor.

Gage handled the letters in his hand like a nuclear technician would handle plutonium. Damon watched his cellmate with quiet curiosity. Gage walked to his cot, lifted the thin mattress, and pulled from under it a stack of white envelopes over six inches thick. A thick rubber band held the pile together. He slid the rubber fastener off the envelopes, added the new ones to the collection, placed the rubber band back on, and wrapped it twice. He maneuvered the stack back under the foot of his mattress and sat back down. His hands roved for the paperback.

"Why weren't any of those envelopes open?" Damon asked. His voice had a low monotone quality as if he weren't even talking to Gage. He rifled through the pages until he found where he left off. "Seems like someone wants to talk to you," Damon said. Gage tilted his book away from him to get a better look at Damon.

"The word around town is that you're the Devil. Is that true?" Gage didn't break eye contact.

Damon's smile faltered but soon returned larger than before. His eyes showed distaste for the question.

"Well, even if I wasn't the Devil, how could I deny such a prestigious title as that?" Damon forced a grin.

"Claiming to be the lord of the underworld might attract some fans, but what it is more likely to do is get you killed," Gage said.

"Then it is a good thing I have you, isn't it?" Gage looked surprised.

"What do you know about my meeting with the warden?"

"I know enough. I know you're my babysitter." Gage recognized the coolness in Damon's manner. Damon displayed the confidence a man who spent time in prison had. He was unafraid as if no hands could touch him within the penitentiary walls. Gage thought about the way the milk curdled the moment the warden brought Damon into the kitchen. There was more to Damon than Gage could see, and he understood that a wrong *step* would mean disaster.

Gage wasn't sure what to make of his new cellmate—there was much more to Damon than his appearance. He prepared himself for the question that would answer all his curiosity when a prisoner rushed into his cell. The man was short in stature but thick as a tree stump. He moved to Gage with a purpose. Wiping at his runny nose, the man wore his panic on his face. Gray, receding hair and strong glasses, gave away his age—still, his movements were of a much younger man.

"Saint, come quick." Everyone thought Stephen was the best worker in the prison kitchen.

"Slow down, Stephen, and take a breath. What happened?" The messenger sucked in air, trying to regulate his breathing to continue.

"The kitchen . . . you have to come . . . I tried to stop him . . ." Gage grabbed Stephen by the arm, pushing his face next to his.

"You tried to stop who?" Gage asked. Stephen appeared to be thinking it over.

"It's Eddie, he and I were cleaning the kitchen. It was his last day—when Victor—"

"I know who he is." Gage interrupted.

"Victor made me leave. I didn't want to leave Eddie alone. He made me, Gage." Gage let go of Stephen and headed for the kitchen.

"Let's go. *You're* coming with me, Stephen." The two men darted from Gage's cell in a flash. They ran down the corridor, dodging in-mates that leaned on the bars or against the handrail that overlooked the other levels. Gage already thought the worst, and still, he hoped he could somehow intervene. When they gained access to the kitchen, the room was dark.

"When I left, the lights were on," Stephen assured. Every dark nook of the kitchen hid Victor, who was waiting to strike. Gage listened for any sounds of a struggle *or* a call for help from his friend. Gage ran his hand along the side of the wall, fumbling for the light switch, and clicking it up. Neon illuminated the room. Both Gage and Stephen searched the kitchen for any sign of Eddie—moving fast down the rows of machinery, ducking down to see under tables as they went.

"You see anything?" Gage asked in a whisper.

"I can't see anyone." Gage shook his head. They shuffled single-file toward the back corner of the kitchen to where the deep freezers stood with enormous doors. Gage didn't bother opening them when he saw the clasps still fastened from the outside except that his instincts propelled his body forward. Gage slid up the pin that locked the handle in place, squeezed the door handle. The door began to open, and a cold burst of air escaped the seal.

Boxes lined the oversized freezer, piled to the ceiling in scattered directions. A dim, red light bulb with an iron cage wrapped around it shone from the back of the freezer warning of water on the floor in front of Gage. He stepped aside in time and watched as Stephen couldn't do the same. The older man dragged his feet through the water, and Gage noticed that the water didn't drip from his foot in its normal manner. Gage saw the liquid ooze from a shoe with the consistency of molasses. After more scrutiny, Gage saw the liquid for what it was, blood. The crimson glow of the light bulb fooled Gage into thinking the pool was clean water.

"*Watch* what you're stepping in." Stephen looked down, and when he understood why Gage was screaming a warning, he froze in horror. The pool of blood was large enough to fit a man curled up. Gage threw away his illusions. The lost blood was a death sentence. It was a frightening amount, and Gage couldn't deny his fear for Eddie. Although the blood pooled at the entrance, a small trail streaked deeper into the freezer. Above the sound of the freezer's air compressor, a faint murmur started to make its way out of the background.

"Do you hear that?" Gage asked, raising his hand to halt Stephen's progress. When Stephen stopped, the sound grew clearer. A whining came from behind a wall of stacked boxes of perishable foods. Gage dug into his shoe, pulled out a sharpened shank, and gripped it in front of him for defense. Gage wanted nothing in the world more than the opportunity to catch Victor hurting Eddie. His jaw stung from the tension he placed on it, and the pure exhilaration the prospect of retribution gave him.

They edged closer to the wall of boxes. Gage took the lead, waiting to pivot around the corner at anyone that lay beyond. Gage leaped from the side of safety to Victor's hiding place with Stephen following. With the shank at the ready, Gage rushed forward at Victor. Instead, Victor was not there. Just the motionless form of Eddie laying upon the cold freezer floor. More blood encircled him like a glossy aura.

"Eddie," Gage screamed. He bent down, tucked his arms around his friend, and lifted his weight onto his lap. Eddie was alive for the moment, and Gage knew that the moment wouldn't last. He thought of the woman at the jewelry heist that landed him in Reclamation. He could see her dying in his arms, but he didn't want to bear the memory of his friend doing the same. Jutting from Eddie's chest was a large kitchen knife identical to the one Eddie planted in Victor's cell. Victor sent Gage the message loud and clear.

"Hey, can you hear me, Eddie?" He could, but communication wasn't happening with a knife stuck in his lung. The noise they heard from behind the stacked boxes was his raspy breathing. Blood entered his wound, causing his air passages to fill with the red liquid. Eddie released a small cough that snowballed into a wet hack, filling his mouth with blood. Red trickles circled his lips and dripped to his chin.

"You'll be okay, Eddie. Just sit still. Help is on the way," Gage said. He knew that it wasn't, but he felt like the comment might soothe his friend's fear. Eddie didn't seem to notice or care about Gage's gentle assurances.

"I did it this time, didn't I?" Eddie sounded like he was inhaling helium, talking through the liquid in his throat. Stephen handed Gage a towel and averted his gaze from Eddie's death scene. Gage dabbed his friend's mouth, folding it over to wipe tears away from his eyes before the chilly air froze them solid. "Victor . . . he did . . ." Eddie tried to finish his thought, but the blood grew too thick in his throat. He spat fluid and coughed hard to gain air in his passage.

"I know, Eddie. He'll pay for this," Gage said while attempting to see his friend one last time through tears. Eddie's face was pallid, revealing how much blood left the body—appearing on the floor next to him.

"Can I help, Saint?" Stephen asked in the sweetest voice. Under normal circumstances, Gage would have smiled. Gage shook Stephen off.

"No, there's nothing for you here. Take off, Stephen. I don't want you caught up in all of this mess." Stephen seemed unsure about walking away. "I'm serious. You don't want *your* name involved in this scene. The man who did this might think you're with me."

"I *am* with you, Saint." Gage gave him the best smile he could manage.

"And I appreciate that, but you have to go." Stephen looked down at the injured prisoner.

"Goodbye, Eddie." Eddie nodded without uttering a sound as Stephen headed out of the freezer. Gage, left alone with Eddie and near death, felt akin to walking through a condemned house with all the lights off. He saw the blood pour from his wound, and he knew that his time was short. He was waiting for the inevitable to arrive.

"Victor will die for this, I promise you, Eddie," Gage said. Eddie coughed once—choking noises were deep in his throat. He hacked with all his strength causing blood to spew from his mouth onto his chest. He breathed in the air as if he were underwater. Eddie shook his head from side to side spilling blood from the corners of his mouth.

"Don't . . . if you kill Victor, you'll be sorry."

"You don't know what you're saying right now."

"I do. It's not your path," Eddie said with a watery voice. Gage understood Eddie was not in a sane frame of mind. "Promise me you won't."

"I promise, Eddie." Gage would have promised the world to his dying friend even though he intended to kill Victor even as he spoke the vow aloud.

"I know it will be hard . . . you must talk to Maria." Gage stared at his near-death friend. "She needs you. She needs to know that you are all right and that you love her—miss her." Gage wasn't ready to talk to Maria, whether his friend was living or dying. From the moment that Eddie came into their cell to explain what he did to Victor—Gage knew Eddie's fate. No matter how he tried to help, destiny tied them all down, trapping them inside with no way to run from their enemies.

"I promise, Eddie. Now, sit still." After Gage promised, a weight fell from Eddie's body, and his last reason to live went away. He closed his eyes for the last time, and Gage held him tight, feeling Eddie's chest move no more.

CHAPTER 25

Robert was where he wanted to be behind his desk. He saw the flames, felt their emanations, and all the while, it rejuvenated him in the same way an injection of adrenaline might awaken the senses. He was alive again, feeling the renewal take hold. The problem was, he couldn't give himself over to the desk as he often would with Reginald in the room. The urge to banish the assistant warden from his office and soak in the desk's radiance occurred to Robert more than once. Instead, he tapped his foot on the weakened floorboard under the desk and hoped he could manage his unusual obsession. With each push on the loose wood, he heard a slight squeak and could tell that Reginald was unaware.

Reginald sat in a chair just beyond Robert and his desk. He shuffled through two folders, both of which showed visible wear on the outside, revealing their age. They said nothing for a long time until Robert could stand the awkward quiet no longer.

"How are you holding up?" Robert asked with real wonder. Reginald first pretended not to hear his superior.

"It's hard to believe that he's still alive," Reginald said.

"I can't say that I believe it either. Is Damon safe after last night?" Reginald sat the folders on his lap in a way that told Robert that he would rather study them than speak to him.

"He's safe," Reginald said, looking Robert straight in the eyes.

"What was the final news on Eddie Fulson's death? Was it related to Damon's entrance into the population?" Robert asked.

"I don't think so. I heard some rumblings that Eddie crossed the wrong person. They never mentioned Damon." Robert sighed.

"Maybe we'll catch a break." Reginald shrugged his shoulders.

"Who knows, there's a lot of heat around Damon right now." Robert nodded. He knew the way Damon materialized in Reclamation—the rumor factory would stir. Either way, Damon was on the prisoner's radar. Robert couldn't protect him other than locking him into solitary, and he wasn't ready for that just yet. He still knew that the chances that someone might get to him for whatever reason would increase.

"If you got what I asked, let's hear it," Robert said. Reginald noticed that Robert covered up every space atop his desk.

Reginald returned to the folders perched on his lap, opened the first, and skimmed through the material. His eyes moved from left to right with his head following.

"This won't make you happy." Reginald showed Robert the inside of the folder, containing one sheet of paper with typed sentences running downward. "There's not much here on Damon Torinson. It has his age as thirty-eight. It has his weight, height hair, and eye color—no photo."

"Does he meet the description?"

"Yeah, he does, but so do millions of others."

"There has to be something I can use to identify him," Robert said. Reginald shook his head.

"Here's the report showing his death. Wait, what's this?" Reginald squinted at the sheet. "The name of the medical examiner that certified his death."

"Bingo. That's who we need to find."

"Otis Bain. He's been here since I can't remember when," Reginald said.

"Well, we need to meet with him. What else did you get?" Reginald was already reaching for another folder.

"The prisoner's name is Roger Witmar. He's eighty-seven."

"Is he still kicking?" Robert asked.

"I see no end date—must be alive. It says Roger is a lifer."

"He was Joseph Hughes's best friend," Robert said.

"Says who? Joseph never said he had a friend locked away here." Robert smiled.

"Are you sure you didn't mention it?" Robert asked.

"No," Reginald said.

"Not sure where I heard it from . . . maybe it was Agatha." He learned that the best way to throw people off his trail was to mix truth with lies. Robert didn't think Reginald bought it, but he recognized the doubt in his expression, and that was all he needed. Robert understood the benefit of secrets.

"We got a starting point. Let's go get Roger Witmar," Robert said and was away from his desk as if he broke himself from chains.

Robert walked behind Reginald as Jake escorted the two through the steel and concrete belly of Reclamation. How much at home he was becoming at the facility astonished Robert. *Others who held his job dreaded their time spent inside the penitentiary walls,* he thought. But Robert didn't feel that way in the least. He gained a thrill rubbing elbows with convicts, liars, and thieves, and never considered himself to be one of them, except he understood their aggression for life.

They were people that got what they wanted by force, and like it or not—he respected their fearless approach to living. Sure, there was a pecking order inside the prison, but outside, the men were not afraid of people, fearful of conflict, and never shied away from the world. There was a simplicity in how the convicts went about their daily lives that made Robert jealous. Staying honest wasn't easy—he also understood that you needed the courage to defy society—to take the shortcuts in life when punishment loomed.

Throughout his career, Robert used some tactics that criminals might possess to stay one step ahead. *One or two different turns,* he thought, and he might be behind similar bars. He watched Jake trundle ahead. The tight pants of his uniform squeezing his fat legs as they rubbed together, causing a swishing sound with each labored step. Robert was sure that Jake lost some weight, but he needed to stage another disrobing to keep his project guard motivated. He witnessed the unease Jake carried through the facility. He just survived as opposed to thriving in the environment. Robert wanted to remedy that issue as fast as possible. The convicts smelled Jake's vulnerability like spoiled food.

The assistant warden's almost indignant facade took a serious blow, throwing him into an agitated state. Reginald was a confident man until his family's murderer resurfaced. He felt for the man having to drudge up all the nightmare moments of his life, tracking down men who made a devil's bargain with the man that slaughtered his loved ones. Who could know how he felt?

Jake led the two men into Reclamation's infirmary. A doctor sat in an executive chair, leaning back so far that he was in the same position as if he were in a recliner. When he saw Robert walk behind Jake, the doctor pushed his body forward, leveled his feet to the floor, and almost planting his face to the cement below. His hand caught a nearby table, and it kept him from going down. He righted himself in a standing position and waited for Robert to approach.

The infirmary was the picture of antiquity. The place was better suited for civil war soldiers. He stepped into a time warp, and Robert was sure Federal money had not touched their medical facility in a while.

"This is the new Warden, Robert Deville." The doctor looked at Robert and extended a hand. He revealed a smile as bright as the sun. The doctor, sucking on the last of a lollipop, pulled it from his mouth to speak.

"So damn glad to meet you, warden. It's nice to have some young blood in here." The remark seemed funny to Robert considering the doctor was bald, wore the thickest glasses Robert ever saw, and had liver spots covering his face. "I'm Otis Bain."

"Nice to meet you, Otis." Otis adjusted his glasses, and Robert gave another saccharine smile. Otis looked from Robert to Reginald.

"What can I do for you?"

"The truth? I'm not sure. This meeting was the warden's idea. He said we needed to find Roger Witmar. You heard the name, right?" Otis's face turned red and shook his head *No* until the last second, when he nodded *Yes* to Robert.

"The records show that Roger is still alive. We tried to find him in the general population, but he wasn't there."

"That's because he lives here in the infirmary," Otis said.

"Here?" Robert asked. Otis nodded.

"Sure." Otis found his seat and looked up with a wide grin.

"Call me curious, but of all the patients that come through here, why the interest in Roger Witmar?" Otis asked while he unwrapped another lollipop and shoved it in his mouth between words. Robert found a nearby examining stool, plopped onto its top, and hurried toward Otis.

"Let's just say that Roger might have direct knowledge of a case we're looking into," Robert said in the best politician tone.

"I can't imagine how any case involves Roger. He doesn't talk to too many people, except me. If you knew Roger as I do, you wouldn't have made this visit." Robert shifted his gaze from Otis to Reginald and back.

"What year did you start here at Reclamation?" Robert asked.

"Why do you ask?" Robert moved in closer to the physician as if he were about to tell the biggest secret.

"Have you ever met Damon Torinson?" Robert asked and waited for a reaction, slight or not. Otis gave nothing away in his expression.

"I never met the man, but they told me stories of him—from newspaper reports. It was a scandalous story around Pataskala back then. I joined Reclamation just after he died."

"You said that if I knew Roger the way you did, I wouldn't visit. Why? What is his history here in Pataskala?" Robert asked. Otis nodded.

"I didn't live in town back then, but I still heard the rumors." Otis looked solemn for the first time that day. "I never met the Roger that committed those crimes that sent him here. I got to know the Roger on the inside."

"So, tell me about him?" Reginald added to the conversation.

"I believe that whatever he went through, broke him inside. He now slides in and out of reality...most of the time out."

"Can you bring him to us?" Robert asked. The old doctor dropped his line of sight to the floor. His hesitation spoke volumes to Robert.

"What's the problem?" Robert asked.

"I couldn't say that there is a problem right now except I can see one developing fast," Otis said.

"How so?"

"I became good friends with Joseph Hughes during my time here at the facility. The thing is . . . Joseph approached me the last year of his life and asked me to look after Roger—if something happened to him. He cared for the man. I guessed he watched Roger's mental state and determined he needed care full time. The infirmary is never the place to keep such people, but Joseph was my friend. It was his last request, and I couldn't refuse him that. What I'm trying to get at—I have no authority over you or the decisions you make at Reclamation. Still, I hope that you will allow me to keep the promise to Joseph and not place Roger back into the general population or a mental institute. The favor would mean a lot to me, and I wouldn't forget it," Otis said. A smile came to Robert's face. He loved having leverage.

"I tell you what, Otis, you bring him to us now, and I'll give your request serious consideration." Otis's smile returned.

"Thank you, warden. I'll go get him right now." Otis was off into another part of the infirmary. Robert gave Reginald a triumphant smile, showing his teeth as a dog might bare them. Otis returned with a graying man, grizzled from life in a cage. Roger placed a hand onto the back of Otis's shoulder as if leading a blind man. It was more accurate to say that Otis was Roger's support. Other than his walk, Roger looked very fit for his age. His eyes appeared milky white with a film over them. Robert guessed it was an advanced case of glaucoma. Seeing the glaze in Roger's eyes dejected Robert. He waved a hand in front of Roger's face and turned to Otis.

"Can he see me?"

"I can see you," Roger said. Reginald reacted as if a wax figure came to life. "I don't have the best vision . . . still good enough." The three men circled to face Roger with Robert in front of the old prisoner.

"Do you remember, Joseph Hughes?" Robert asked.

"Yes, I do. Joe is my best friend."

"You mean he was," Reginald added. Otis waved him off. The doctor escorted Roger into a chair and led the two administrators to one side away from Roger.

"As you can tell, his reality has skewed from ours. Please don't challenge him—the result might damage his mind. A year after he joined us here at Reclamation, a drunk driver crossed the median on the highway, colliding with a car on the way to church. In that car was Roger's wife." Otis licked his dry lips to continue. "She suffered from internal injuries for a solid week before succumbing to them. After the news, Roger was never the same. Call it a self-defense mechanism or whatever name you want to give it. The state came and took his two little girls and put them in foster care. His mind copes by forgetting. So, please go easy," Otis said.

Robert heard all that he wanted to hear. He saw the thread of weakness that ran through Joseph's life. He put complete trust into everyone he met during his career. To Robert, these were foolish decisions that placed everyone in jeopardy. Sure, he believed in delegating power, limited power. Still, the idea to let someone like Otis control your legacy seemed ludicrous to him. Joseph undermined protocol and broke the law allowing Roger to move unaccompanied within the infirmary as if it were in an apartment. Joseph left his reputation in the hands of some old doctor with no backbone.

Thirty seconds into their conversation, Otis gave up Roger and attached Joseph's name as the sole reason for the prisoner's residency. The old doctor made him sick to his stomach. What infuriated Robert the most, what defied all logic, and what made him want to shake Joseph's coffin was that he took such amazing risks for Roger. The madness of Joseph's choices whirled around inside his head. He couldn't fathom how he could protect the very man that killed his wife and made his son motherless.

The injustice that Otis flaunted in his face tasted too bitter to stand. The urge to take matters into his own hands was a ravenous, hungry beast that came alive inside his bones and oozed out through his pores. Nothing would have quenched his thirst as much as taking Roger into another room and bashing him to a bloody pulp. *Roger twisted the natural laws of man to change fate, destroy the lives of those around him, and then forgot all his sins?* Robert wasn't about to let Roger get away without feeling the pain of what he did.

Robert's thoughts turned to Joseph's son, Raylen. He recalled the descriptions of him in his father's diary. His heart poured out for the child in the wake of Roger's hideous acts. He regretted that Raylen never got the chance to confront his mother's killer face to face, to see the guilt flash in his eyes, to hear him beg for mercy. He denied Raylen his closure, but Robert thought of an idea that might be the next best thing. Otis was still talking with Reginald listening. Robert couldn't hide his disgust for Otis and decided not to cooperate any further. Robert motioned for Jake, who found a corner when they arrived. He unfolded his arms and met Robert from across the room.

"Yes, sir," Jake said in a military drone voice.

"Escort Mr. Roger Witmar along with us," Robert said. Otis made a move to step in front of Roger and thought better of the action.

"You have something you want to do?" Robert was daring the doctor into a physical conflict. Otis shook his head.

"You said you would consider Roger staying in my care."

"I considered it, and I now denied your request."

"But I made a promise to Joseph," Otis said.

"Otis, you are no longer Roger's caretaker."

"Wait one second—" Otis said.

"You need to be thankful I'm overlooking this offense." Robert stared down the doctor and walked away with the rest following.

CHAPTER 26

Jenny inhaled a cigarette, filling her lungs with hot, ashy air. Her chest tightened before she expelled the smoke. A gray cloud bounced off the windshield, and every other surface it connected within its path. Guilt crept in with every puff. *I'm a smoker again, so why not go with it for a while?* She knew it was the stress talking. Zack's behavior and the sightings of Toby was just the excuse she needed to pick up the old familiar, somehow comforting habit.

She placed her finger on the window control and watched as glass slid down beside her. When it was down enough for her liking, she flicked her burned-down cigarette out of the car. It was the not knowing that sent her into an agitated state. Without a moment's notice, luck could turn for Liam and her. Although she was ready to follow-through with criminal activity, she wasn't ready to accept the penalties that accompanied the risk. From outside, a cool wind fluttered against her cheeks. The weather was cold, and she liked the cold chill when she drew it into her lungs. The coolness cleansed and calmed her nerves.

For hours, Jenny worried about Liam's well-being. The talk of suicide came with the territory when you were friends with Liam. She accepted his cries for support the way someone might accept any flaws in character. While others might nag or complain, or even become critical, Liam remarked about suicide. She understood what she was getting when she was with him, but something was different. Jenny wanted to make sure that the darkness that always surrounded Liam didn't find an opening to contaminate his insides. She would reason with him all night long if it were necessary.

Headlights flashed across her windshield, and she recognized Liam in the driver's seat. She watched as the shadow of a big man strolled across the car beams. Broken light streams distorted as Liam crossed her headlight's path. The passenger door opened and closed—a moment later, her friend sat in the seat next to her with a broad smile.

"Hey, good looking," Liam said through short breaths.

"Hey," she said. The sudden happy attitude threw her into a tail-spin. Perhaps her friend was in the manic phase of manic depression, she guessed.

"Listen, Liam. We don't have to do this tonight. Morris is a dangerous man. I can handle this myself," Jenny said. Liam's face flashed with surprise.

"Are you kidding me? Helping you is the greatest thing that I can do. Toby showed himself to me, to us. I'm not letting him down." She grabbed his hand and held on tight.

"Here's the thing. I didn't know how to bring this up, and I guess I still don't." Jenny peered out into the night for an answer or a second to think.

"Just tell me, you can tell me anything," he said.

"The thought crossed my mind that you're *gonna* kill yourself." The words came out like a cannonball hitting Liam in the chest.

"How can you say that to me?" Liam felt as if he interrupted a conversation she was having with someone else.

"In the last days, we've seen some heavy things, and maybe more will follow."

"You think I'm not tough enough to see this through." She shook her head. "Yes, you do. I won't give up on you or Zack. He needs me, too." Tears began to fall down Jenny's cheeks. "Why do you think I would kill myself?"

"I have my reasons. The way you talk sometimes," she said to Liam while talking into the dashboard. "If you follow through with this all the way . . . you'll end your life."

"You're ridiculous."

"I know how I feel."

"Nothing will happen to me. I won't leave you. Do you remember my promise to you? I'll say goodbye."

"Just don't go any further with me, please," she begged.

"It's settled—I am going all the way." Jenny nodded.

"You just remember that promise." Liam nodded a second before Jenny flung her arms around him. Jenny held him tight for a long time before letting go. She wiped a tear and grabbed the paperwork describing Toby's case. Scanning the papers for anything missed, she slid the car into drive and headed out toward Morris.

After a day of worrying about Liam's outcome and making peace with his decision, she took a moment to contemplate her safety. The full gravity of her situation made its impact on her. Her hands began to shake, causing the wheel of the car to turn back and forth. She loosened her grip so that Liam wouldn't notice. Jenny's opinion of her ex-husband shifted. Still, she never came to any realization that he was anything other than a drunk, and a killer never entered the picture. She guessed that no one would imagine that someone was that bad of a person. Making such a poor judgment as choosing a killer for your partner made her ill to even think about.

She wondered how she overlooked a flaw as apprehensible as a child abductor. Sure, she saw Morris's progression from a loving husband and devoted father to an unhappy man who drank, and then a drunk who turned violent. At the end of their relationship, he was just brutal. She understood his anger, and in time even becoming numb to his sick impulsive ways.

Jenny needed to walk a tightrope—it kept her from lashing out. She saw his blackness during their unhappy married years. Still, Jenny never suspected him of being a killer even if logic said murder was the next step in violence. All evidence pointing to Morris abusing their son, not to mention the perfect suspect for the deaths of the children in his neighborhood. The highway streetlights flew by in a whirl, burning into her retina like a child staring at a sparkler. She pressed her eyelids closed for a moment to clear her vision and regarded her friend in the passenger seat. He appeared far from suicidal. Liam seemed happy for once.

When Jenny pulled next to a curb one-half block away from Morris's house, it seemed like a death sentence. She clicked her headlights off, and the older neighborhood went dark except for one streetlight that flashed and dimmed on a repeating loop. Jenny turned to Liam. She gave a soft expression that a mother sometimes gives to their child when they intend to show love and understanding.

"Nothing's in stone, Liam. You can hang out in the car and make sure the coast is clear," Jenny said, plastering a smile. The look Liam gave Jenny told the complete story, yet he spoke anyway.

"We're in this together, Jen. Whatever there is to face, we will face it together. Okay?" Jenny relented.

"Remember, we are not here to confront him."

"No danger there, I'm no hero," Liam said.

"We're here to *get* some evidence for the authorities, nothing more. We take nothing into our own hands. Agreed?"

"I agree, except . . ."

"What is it?" Jenny asked.

"If we find something horrific in there...I mean, Zack's still in there. Can we leave him behind?" She shook her head.

"No, we can't. I guess we'll see what the night gives us." Liam nodded. Jenny took out a pad and pencil and started a rough sketch of Morris's floor plan.

"This will give you a good idea of the set-up of Morris's house in case you don't remember. We'll go in from the back here." Jenny pointed toward the rear of the sketch. "The bedrooms are here, and the garage is in the front. If we find anything, it will be there. From what Zack has told me, whenever he stays with Morris, they almost always fall asleep in front of the television—in the recreation room—in the house's front, right here." She pointed to the part of the drawing that outlined the recreation room. "We'll go in through Zack's window, look around and get out. That's it," she said with him nodding.

When they walked behind Morris's house, dark shadows twisted every structure in the back yard until life seemed to spring from inanimate objects. Picnic tables, portable propane grills, and lawn tools waited for their presence, reaching out in the blackness to grab hold. The wind blew past them like a nudging creature crossing their path.

Liam surveyed the back of the house while believing every shadow was Morris waiting to strike them down for trespassing. Jenny spotted Zack's window and motioned Liam toward it with her following close behind. She pulled from her jeans a steel pry bar she brought to open a passage into Morris's home but bet the instrument would also come in handy to bash Morris's head if it came to that. Jenny slid the sharp edge of the pry bar between the bottom of the window and the frame.

She prayed for an unlocked window. A locked window meant breaking the latch and with that a lot more noise than she wanted. She sucked air in and out like a long jumper preparing to run and leap. She blew out air and brought all her weight down on the resting pry bar. The pry bar went down, and she braced herself for the popping sound that she expected to accompany the window's movement. Instead, the window glided easy up away from its frame. Liam sighed with relief. A visible light shone inside Zack's room, and she hoped Zack wasn't sleeping in his bed.

What would she say to him if he found her sneaking into his room at night? The idea alone almost made her turn back to the car except that she knew there was more at stake than an awkward moment. Jenny started for the window and stopped in her tracks. Liam's weight might give them problems if she entered first. She stepped back and interlaced her fingers, waiting for Liam to place a foot into her hands. Even with her help, Liam found it challenging to slink his big frame through the open window.

Like a dog shimmying under a gate, Liam propelled his body past the window frame. He almost fell face-first to the floor beyond. At the last second, he caught the top of the window with a hand to keep his balance. He righted himself on the inside and reached for Jenny. She tucked the pry bar into her pants and grabbed her friend's hand. Liam pulled her inside, using his weight. Both, out of breath, they panted hard standing face to face in Zack's dark bedroom.

Jenny's first feeling was that her son was lying in bed a few feet from her. Her heart skipped a beat as it would if she walked into a hornet's nest. A dim light from the closet was enough to reveal a large lump in Zack's bed as a pillow.

She opened her eyelids wide, trying to focus them in the dark. Soon, the bedroom came into view like a mirage in a desert. Jenny's heart softened when she spotted Zack's walls. She remembered painting the walls before Zack was born. It wore a light blue-sky background with a blanket of white puffy clouds that she painted by hand. She recalled how she wanted to get every paint stroke just right for Zack, even if he was an infant.

Forcing Zack to leave the house he was born in, pained her. It didn't matter that a fresh start was in front of her. Morris caused the damage in their relationship, and he got to keep the fond memories of Zack. Toys—clothes, and the sweet pictures of his first events—stayed behind with the man who caused the hurt.

During Jenny's flight into reminiscence, Liam consumed himself with whatever awaited them past the threshold of Zack's doorway. He tensed his body when he heard a disembodied voice coming from another room. The voice rose and fell so fast that Liam could almost see the animation the speaker projected. He came to a speedy conclusion that the speaker was part of an advertisement. He loosened his posture and walked to the door that led to the hallway. Jenny cast away her momentary escape into the past and rejoined the living.

"Follow me," she said with a whisper. Liam nodded, and with that, they were on their way. She moved the bedroom door inward slow to test its creakiness. The hinges hiccupped one faint creak and remained quiet the rest of the way.

All eyes peered into the hall for any signs of life. The television that blared in the recreation room threw jumbled light on the hallway wall from around the corner. She pointed to the right in the opposite direction of the television's bright glare. Liam was glad for that, wanting to stay as far from Morris as possible. He felt like he was inside a mousetrap waiting for it to snap with no notice. They crept down the hall, careful with each step to not make a sound.

Jenny recognized the picture frames that lined the walls on either side. Jenny hung each one while she was still with Morris. She felt as if she were in a wrinkle that sealed their past relationship inside for all time. Morris never moved on after their divorce. Even the pictures that proved their happy marriage still decorated the drywall. There were pictures of Jenny and Morris holding Zack in their arms, each with smiles way too big. Evidence of their past repulsed her to the core.

When they reached the end of the corridor, the path led two ways, left through the kitchen, and right through the garage. Jenny opened the door to the garage and watched Liam step inside first. With the garage door pulled closed behind them, Jenny felt safe enough to flick the light switch on. In a garage with no windows, she chanced that light wouldn't alert Morris. The state of the garage was so jarring when the lights came on that Liam knew the task was hopeless, looking at a sea of storage chaos.

Boxes stacked upon boxes, with blue Rubbermaid tubs forming plastic pyramids in every direction. They were lucky if they could find an empty patch of concrete to find a footing. Liam thought of a frog jumping from one lily pad to another, trying to stay dry.

"This is impossible," Jenny said, rifling through box after box—Christmas decorations—old athletic equipment, finding everything except what she wanted.

"We don't have time to go through all of this tonight. We have to go," Liam said.

"You're right, move toward the door." They hopped over several bags and boxes when Liam stepped on the corner of a trash bag. His footing skidded out from under him, and he slipped headfirst onto a stack of boxes that were three rows high. With the help from Liam's weight, the boxes tilted left and fell right. The crash made a noise but not as loud as Jenny expected. They both stood still listening for any rustling from inside.

"You see this?" Liam pointed to a box he toppled when he lost control. On the side of the box, written in black magic marker, read: Dominance

"Open it," she said. Liam tore the lid from the box. Jenny's jaw dropped when she saw its contents.

"This is it," she said. The box contained dog collars of every shape and size. She reached for a choker, and a restraint made of chains.

"I think we got him," Jenny said. Liam reached into the box and plucked a dog collar out as if taking a rattlesnake from its hiding place.

"This is the exact dog collar we saw on Toby. Do you remember?" Liam asked. From the shared wall between the garage and the kitchen, a thud erupted from the dividing wall.

"Move beside the doorway and turn off the lights." Although Jenny whispered, there was fear and urgency in her words. Ten feet from the door, they both went into a full-fledged run. Their feet darted from one space on the floor to another like an amped-up game of hopscotch. Liam, lunging forward, reached out and pushed down the light switch. Each found a spot on either side of the door in time to hear the handle rattle.

Jenny lifted the pry bar overhead, shaking in place with the tool hovering. *I can't believe I' doing this—killing Morris*, she thought. The handle rattled again until it started to turn. Jenny braced herself for battle as Morris flung the door wide open. The light from the kitchen shone on the cluttered mess strewn from one end of the garage to the next. Morris leaned his head into the garage, tilting and squinting for any movement.

Jenny stood still like a statue of a Greek warrior ready to strike. With help from the kitchen light, the two trespassers had no place to hide. All Morris needed to do was pivot his head to the right one foot, and it was game over. Instead, Morris pulled his weight back until his feet were flat on the floor, shutting the door in the same motion. Their chests deflated. They listened as the sound of footsteps led away from the door.

"Leave the dog collar here," Jenny whispered.

"We need this for evidence."

"If the police come here, and the collar isn't here, what evidence will they have?" Liam tossed the dog collar toward its original box. Jenny placed her head against the door and turned the handle. She peered into the hallway and saw that it was again dark and clear.

The walk back down the hallway that led to Zack's bedroom became more intense than the first trip. Liam expected Morris to jump out of the dark and pounce. The night was wearing down Liam's resolve. If he were to stand still for more than a moment, he would realize that his hands were shaking to the point of tremors.

He tried to swallow and not yet realizing that the stress caused his saliva ducts to run dry. Jenny, in comparison, thrived on the rise of adrenaline. The act of defying Morris in his home, made her feel useful and alive. When they reached Zack's door, they waited to allow the roar of the television program to hit a climax and opened the door when the time felt right. They walked through the door, closing it as they passed the doorway. Their flight instincts took over, and they were at the open window as fast as their bodies could carry them until Jenny saw something in Zack's closet that stopped her in her tracks.

"Wait," Jenny's command didn't register in Liam's mind. Exiting Morris's funhouse consumed him, and he never reacted until Jenny put her palm on his shoulder to follow. Returning into Zack's room when they were about to get away was crazy in Liam's estimation. After a lifetime of decisions, which was the last one he would ever make except that his best friend was asking, so he relented. Jenny tried to understand why she should go to her son's closet, and because a light was on was not enough. *It's calling me*, she thought.

She shoved her fingers into the door opening and pulled it wide. The closet's bare bulb washed its light on them. Liam knew Zack since he was an infant, and he didn't want to believe what he was seeing. Jenny felt no better about her discovery. Along the inside of the boy's closet door were articles cut out of the Columbus Dispatch of children, the missing children. Each article related to a child that was a part of her investigation. She scanned each picture and name of the lost or abducted boys. At last, her eyes came to the one of Toby.

"This makes little sense," Jenny said, biting down hard on her thumb to dull her anxiety. "Why would he have all of this stuff, he's just a boy." Liam stared at the items as if it were an exhibit at a museum. Zack lined the inside of the closet's walls with construction paper. Each pinned with a thumbtack. On the construction paper were charcoal drawings of children. All of them taken, murdered, and then discovered by law enforcement officers.

"These things are amazing. The detail is—" Jenny finished his thought

"Like a photograph," she said. He nodded without glancing her direction.

"It's so lifelike." As Liam studied a drawing closer, his eyes opened wide. "Some of these are showing the murder while it was happening," Jenny's eyes filled with tears as her stomach began to fill with acid, nausea taking control. Against the back wall of the closet was a map of the city streets of Columbus, Ohio. Circled and tagged in crayons were several sites. Written in every circle was a number.

"Could these circles correlate with the murders?" Liam asked.

"I don't know. Just take the map, and we'll study it later, outside this house." Liam nodded and peeled the map from the wall, folded it, and slid it into his pocket.

Jenny closed her eyes and tried to wish away the pictures, the map, everything. With eyes shut tight, she still saw the grotesque scenes playing out in the drawings in her mind. She shook her head as if the motion could shed her of its horrible reality. She wondered how Zack could draw such brutal images. Did he witness them firsthand with Morris, or did he see these things on his own? She pushed the thoughts out into a dark corner of her mind. Without notice or a conscious attempt, her thoughts disappeared. If she tried to describe the sensation, it was like a balloon floating too close to a hot light and bursting. She could almost hear the popping sound inside. Her self-defense mechanisms took over, and she was running on autopilot. She closed the closet door and headed for the window.

Liam wanted to say something comforting but knew he had to get out of the house sooner rather than later. She lifted each leg, slid them into the window opening, and let gravity pull her to the outside as if it were a daily routine. Liam was sure that he would have much more trouble duplicating her escape. He rested his right leg half in and half out of the window and adjusted his body to swing his left leg out when he heard a noise from behind. Someone grasped Zack's bedroom doorknob.

Liam tried to maneuver his body out of the window as fast as he could, but his labored movements made his attempt to exit the window even tougher. He could see the door opening when he pushed his body out of the window frame. He hit the ground *outside* in time for light to erupt *inside*. Morris was staring at the open window. Liam wasted no time, ducking down away from the light, the window, and Morris's gaze. He stood motionless for a moment under the window-sill waiting. When he looked up for Jenny, he realized she wasn't there. Sudden panic splashed him as he bolted for his friend.

In her car, Jenny fell into a trance. She passed each mile on the car ride in a fog. Liam didn't want to disturb her state any more than waking a sleepwalker, and he wrestled with the matter for many miles before he spoke aloud.

"Morris might have seen my face back there," Liam said in the gentlest tone he could manage. She stared straight ahead, watching the freeway lights brighten the car and fade away. Liam hadn't a clue where she was, but she occupied a space far away. The car ride was carried-out in silence. The miles slipped by in a melancholy haze until the 310 Exit to Pataskala appeared in their windshield. Within a few twists and turns, they found themselves parked in front of Liam's car.

They sat in quiet meditation, listening to the idle of Jenny's Cherokee. He wanted to tell her that Zack was okay, that things they found in his closet were normal curiosities. The words died in his throat. The map and drawings were not normal, far from ordinary—anything that he said sounded hollow or forced, which left him sad for his friend. Liam leaned forward to the floorboard of the Jeep and scooped up the police folder with all the missing children cases inside.

"Do you want to go over the police folder tonight…maybe look at Zack's map?" Jenny reacted as if his words assaulted her. Her outrage wasn't toward him, but it wasn't in another direction either. He felt a chill that didn't come from the outside—it sat in the driver's seat.

"I've had enough of this for today, maybe ever." She looked out her window, feeling shame. "I need some time for sleep, to eat, and see my husband." Liam gave her a smile that found the back of her head. There was no use in arguing, so he didn't try.

"You're supposed to pick up Zack from Morris's tomorrow," Liam said in a hybrid statement or a question. Jenny nodded. "I want to be there with you, okay?" Again, she nodded.

"See you tomorrow," she said without looking up or seeing her friend exit the automobile. In Liam's mind, he was a child abandoned by the side of the road. Jenny peeled away, leaving Liam holding the police folder, the map, and disappointment. He walked to his car, got in, and wondered if the night ruined something inside Jenny. Because of their involvement in matters so dark, it stained their friendship. He hoped that by tomorrow, the rough edges that the night's revelation might not be so harsh in a new day's light.

Liam tilted the passenger seat until it was flat, spread out the crime scene material, and drew his attention to the red crayon circles— spheres highlighted individual houses.

He read the crime folders for house addresses and found the connection he suspected a moment later. Each circle correlated with an address where they found a dead child. After he matched the circles to the addresses, no other connection was visible. He held the map up to the moonlight. The pit of his stomach began to tremble when he saw the circles from farther away. Small red circles formed a larger circle. The pattern seemed too simple, but there it *was* right in front of his eyes. In the center of the circle of circles was a home in a neighborhood.

His heart skipped a beat, and he attempted to catch his breath when he saw the home in the middle of the red circles belonged to Morris. On the map, Morris's home was the hub from which all the abduction cases revolved. Morris's house—ground zero for whatever was happening in the neighborhood. Something caught his eye as he hoisted the map in the air. He spotted another red circle written with a crayon beside the others. As far as Liam knew, there were no deaths linked to that address.

He shuffled through the paperwork, hoping to find a case that he somehow overlooked, but there was nothing. Dejected, he drifted his eyes back to the solitary circle and saw something that gave him some hope. Coming out of the red circle was a faint line with an arrow pointing to the edge of the map.

Liam traced the arrow with his eyes to the side of the map and turned it over in his hands. On the backside of the map was a charcoal drawing, just like the ones he saw in Zack's closet. The drawing in the middle of the map was a photo quality picture that looked so real. Liam smudged the charcoal with his thumb. He dragged one black line across another to satisfy his skepticism. He couldn't believe that Zack could draw such a realistic picture.

The picture was of a shed and nothing else. Liam had seen sheds in its form hundreds of times. The shed was a mini wood barn that an owner could put garden tools, lawnmowers, and things of the sort inside to protect from the weather or thieves. Because the drawing was in charcoal, he couldn't tell what color it was, but it sent an eerie feeling down his spine. There was something familiar about the shed, something he couldn't track down in his head. Liam allowed his eyes to skim across the paperwork once again. He searched for any keywords and found the thing that tied it all together. The heading of the paper read: Police Report Call Log

Under the bold title was the address of the mysterious house and right next to that was a handwritten description that read: Domestic abuse call - officer dispatched

The date of the log report matched the date of the first missing child report of the investigation.

"I got you now," he said. He couldn't fathom how detective Scott Sedge overlooked the glaring connection. The answer was that Sedge didn't miss it—*he wanted you to find this clue. He gave him the log report for Christ's sake.* Liam's first instinct was to reach for his cell phone and call Jenny, and then he remembered how discouraged she was when he left her. He was on his own, and he knew it. He placed the report log on top of the charcoal drawing, folded it several times, and slid them into the front pocket of his short-sleeved flannel shirt.

One street away from arriving at the mysterious address, Liam recognized the destination. There were too many coincidences in the investigation. In a world with random events, there was nothing random about the child murders, there was nothing accidental about where they all began, and it was no accident that he and Jenny got involved in the case from the very beginning. It was as if someone lifted the curtain for him to see behind the scenes.

"Why didn't I call Jen?" *She should be here*, he thought. He pulled next to a curb a few houses down and threw the shifter into gear. Like Morris's neighborhood, the lighting contained a few working streetlights, and the rest of the areas fell into complete darkness. He counted himself fortunate that the two streetlights on either side of the house from the map were out. He ignored the superstitious idea of luck and renewed his newest point-of-view that there were no accidents. Someone made sure that there were no lights to shine upon the house.

Liam opened the door and got out as fast as possible to keep his dome light from attracting any attention from insomniac neighbors. Light didn't matter to him—he intended to stay away from the house no matter what. Moving quickly down the sidewalk, he darted up the driveway of a house next to where he planned to end up. Clouds that gave him precious cover revealed the moon with its bright glow. He tried not to think about any watchful eyes and cut through a backyard to wind up where he meant to arrive.

Turning around, he looked at the house and through its eyes. Thinking he saw movement, he jumped backward out of reflex. He kept his concentration on the windows and saw nothing. Relief rushed over him. Liam pivoted on one foot, turning to find the wooden shed in the moonlit night standing right in front of him.

The shed stood where he knew it was, and it looked as he remembered it. He moved toward the shed like he was stalking his prey. He touched the wood facade and felt the years of paint flaking off with the rub of his hand.

Liam studied the shed's worn exterior. In the middle of the two adjoining doors that opened outward was a brand-new security lock. The lock was a steel monstrosity that screamed "stay out" to Liam. What it also said to him was there's something important and secret behind its wooden shell.

Although the padlock looked intimidating in its fortitude, Liam recognized like all locks it was only as strong as the latch it closed. The lock hung on a latch that screwed into the wood. With simple pressure, Liam could pluck the screws from the wood and render the lock useless. He spun around, looking for anything he could get in between the latch and the woodshed. He saw nothing that would help his cause. In a spark of inspiration, Liam remembered the jack kit that came with his spare tire. There was a kit with a four-way tire iron for removing lug nuts, a compact jack, and a pry bar for God knows what.

Locked into a plan of attack, Liam headed back onto the path from which he came. Clouds eclipsed the moon delivering darkness to Liam's senses. Every bush or tree became an obstacle that threatened to upend his progress. Heading back down the driveway, he scanned for watching eyes. He saw no movement and went to the trunk of his car. When he leaned forward, a pair of headlights appeared. The car moved at a slow pace toward his car with Liam turning his head to mask his face. He attempted to look as natural as he could for a man out in the wee hours of the night hanging around his car. The car passed him on a slow course and pulled into a spot a few houses beyond. Liam sighed and pulled the pry bar from his trunk.

The eventful night was tiring, but the possibilities that awaited in the shed fueled him—moving fast to make it back to the wooden container. He searched for just the right seam to slip the pry bar into when he felt a presence behind him. Turning in an instant, he confirmed he was alone, but he still felt the eyes of someone.

"Who's there?" Liam whispered into the night. He received no answer in reply and stuck the thin-tipped edge of the pry bar between the latch and wood, splitting the screws from the wood.

The latch broke free along with the enormous lock, falling to the ground. Liam was about to open the doors when, from the corner of his eye, a light appeared. It was the back window of the house. His instincts told him to run, and before he could listen, a shadowy figure materialized to his left. The moon appeared again, revealing the stranger.

"It's you, I guess I should have known," Liam said, with fear choking the rest of his words.

CHAPTER 27

Gage propped the freezer wide open with a five-gallon potato salad container. Stephen used the mop handle to guide a large yellow bucket with wheels. The bucket skittered from left to right out of control. It came to a stop in front of a dried puddle of blood.

"Thank you for helping, Stephen. It means a lot," Gage said. Stephen was already moving out boxes soaked through the bottom from Eddie's fluids.

"I liked Eddie. I have no bad opinions of him—it's the least I can do." Gage pushed the wet mop over an area of blood and returned it to its bucket with the water inside, turning red, resembling a wedding punch. Gage let loose of the mop and turned to Stephen.

"Have a seat for a second, would you, Stephen?" He nodded and found a box to rest on with his curiosity taking hold. "We haven't known each other too long, but you were as close to Eddie as I was." Using Eddie's name in the past tense made Gage feel dirty or somehow disloyal. "An inmate named Victor killed him. He was a wrecking ball in my life. He's had a hand in killing everyone I've loved in this world. It's personal with me, but I thought you also might have some stake in this because of your friendship with Eddie."

"What do you have in mind?" Stephen asked. Gage regarded Eddie's blood strewn across the floor. A chill crept over Gage that was far deeper than the freezer provided. He caught his mind drifting toward thoughts of his son Ryan, lingering in the misery of happy times in memories long gone. Gage forced the thoughts away.

"I'm in a unique position to scheme an escape for Victor and me."

"You're helping him get out of here?" Stephen asked with disbelief. Gage was already shaking Stephen off.

"I will kill him," Gage said with the coldest expression Stephen ever saw. "Our kitchen has the largest industrial oven in the state. A vent takes away the oven's heat to the outside—running straight up the building to the roof. The width will about accommodate a grown man." The opening intrigued Stephen.

"You want me to go with you on your escape? Is that what you're asking?" Gage shook him off again.

"This vent…leading to the roof is constructed of hardened steel. It will withstand heat *or* fire. I want to line the vent with wood to give a footing for us to climb up the flue. He won't trust me. So, I will lead Victor up the vent to the roof," Gage said.

"What would you like me to do, Gage?" He hesitated for a moment.

"The moment Victor and I burrow through the oven into the vent—shut us inside. I will have the tools ready. Don't worry about that. You must seal up the vent so that neither of us can double back the way we came."

"If I seal you both into the vent, how will you escape?"

"I don't want to escape," Gage said. Stephen began to understand Gage's angle.

"Don't think you have a hand in Victor's death. All I need for you to do is seal us in the vent." Gage moved to finish cleaning up the blood.

"Wait one minute. I'll help, but you have to tell me everything." Stephen demanded. Gage wanted to refuse outright on filling Stephen in on the plan or play coy, but he needed Stephen's help to succeed.

"After you seal us in from the bottom and I reach the top of the roof . . . I will light a fire to the wood that lines the vent," Gage said while resuming his mopping. Stephen grabbed his arm

"You intend to burn him alive?" Gage nodded.

"I will seal him from the top and open a small hole to allow enough oxygen into the small area. The flames will spread throughout the wood inside the vent—with smoke suffocating Victor while the flames burn off his flesh." Stephen pretended to mop. "I didn't want to involve you in the ugly details, Stephen."

"He was my friend, too. I'll seal you both in if that's what you want." Gage gave a weak smile.

Gage walked back to his cell. Cement and steel wrapped around him like a vice threatening to suffocate his reason. More than usual, he was under the prison's spell as if it controlled what he was planning—the building conjuring his dark intentions. He wore Reclamation's hundreds of years of misery like a bad cologne that never faded from his skin. Prison cells were dark, and most of the inmates were asleep by the time Gage finished cleaning up Eddie's blood from the deep freezer. The screws allowed Stephen and him the freedom to wipe away any trace of Eddie from the facility.

Early morning crept up on Gage when he stumbled back to his cell and realized that he had guests. Light shone, and he watched dark shadows pacing inside obscuring the view through the bars. Apprehension gripped Gage as if he were on a roller coaster heading toward the top with no way of stopping his progress.

Two men stood outside Gage's cell. One he recognized right off as the guard Jake Shoeman, the other was a stranger. He was sure that the other man was an inmate the same as him—but worn and beat up. He was a weathered man who had seen the worst parts of the facility; there was no doubt in Gage's mind. He walked back and forth inside the cell like a caged animal readying himself to pounce on Damon. Without thinking, Gage moved past the old inmate and Jake toward the cell. A nightstick found his chest. A loud thud reverberated the shallow concave of his breastplate.

"Where do you think you're going?" Jake asked, still holding the club hard onto Gage, barring him from his cell.

"To bed," Gage said as if it were the most natural response in the world.

"You wait out here with me, friend," Jake said and turned his attention back to the warden inside the cell.

Robert and Reginald rotated around Damon. Although Damon looked like a cornered animal, no fear emanated from him. Damon stood in front of them with his posture relaxed, eyelids blinking, and arms folded in a slight defensive pose that screamed defiance. Robert was the first to speak.

"We are settling this once and for all." Robert aligned his eyes with Damon's. "From what little records I have of Damon Torinson, you were in your late thirties over forty years ago. That looks like your age now. How is that possible?" Robert waited for Damon to blink, breathe heavy, anything.

Damon's demeanor never wavered, and his confidence didn't bother Robert. "I'll tell you a fact. You are not Damon Torinson. Joseph Hughes was a demented old man, and you are nothing more than an imposter." Robert waved his hand to Roger outside the cell. "This man would have your face burned into his mind if you are Damon." Robert waited for Damon to scan Roger, and instead, he gazed into his eyes. Reginald leaned next to Robert's ear.

"Roger isn't all there. He wouldn't recognize anybody," Reginald whispered. Robert leaned back and placed his lips next to Reginald's ear.

"He won't know who he is, but what I want to see is Damon's reaction." Robert smiled and motioned for Jake to escort Roger inside the cell. When Robert brought Roger before Damon, he thought he saw his body tense if only for a second. "You should know this man, shouldn't you?" Robert's smile never left. Roger moved his head from the bed, the walls, and to the ceiling as if he had no control over his body.

"His name is Roger Witmar," Damon said. Damon's recognition stunned Robert. "How are you, Roger?" Roger turned his head to the voice and fixed his gaze to Damon. "I understand that your wife had a little accident. What a shame." A genuine smile captured Damon's face.

"Who is the man in front of you, Roger? Tell me," Robert said with no answer from Roger. He fixed his eyes on Damon.

"I guess the good news is that you're still alive. Roger has two daughters—did you know that? Miranda and Tracey. Miranda's even a doctor right here in Pataskala. Maybe she's trying to improve on the Witmar name," Damon said. Roger's eyes bulged and watered as if he was staring too long into a flame.

"Have you made good on the lives you've destroyed? Is your debt to society paid in full?" Damon's smile became more defined—anger spilling over onto his face. Gazing at Damon's face did nothing to

Roger for the longest time until something snapped. A change took over Roger.

"Wait one minute," Roger said. "That face. I see it now—it's you." Damon's ironic smile deepened.

"Talk to me, who is he?" Robert asked with urgency. Roger didn't respond at all—staring at Damon as if they were alone in the room.

"It is me, I'm glad you remember old friends," Damon said. Roger's eyes filled with terror.

"I want to change what I have done. Help me make things right," Roger said. Damon was in the middle of shaking his head.

"Things in the past don't always stay there. Our experience together taught you that, Roger."

"Help me find forgiveness," Roger said. Damon's smile remained. "Only death will release you from your sins, from your choices."

"Who is he?" Robert asked in a thundering voice before turning to Damon. "Who are you?" Robert asked one last time, attempting to prod the two men. Roger began to cry in his hands and never looked up at Damon again. Robert had nothing more to say. He motioned Jake to take away Roger.

"Drop him off at the Watkins Mental Institute, now," Robert said.

"What about the promise made to Otis?" Reginald asked.

"I could give two shits about Joseph Hughes—he was a nut. Get him away from Reclamation and out of my sight," Robert screamed. Roger was wailing, and Jake was ushering him away when Robert turned to Damon.

"I can't say how you did that, but this isn't over. You hear me?" Damon nodded when a phone rang. The ring came from Robert's suit pocket. In a flash, a phone was at his ear.

"He did what?" Robert spoke into the phone, "no, no, you do nothing. I will be there in minutes." Robert pushed the off button with enough force to crack the glass. He looked to Reginald. "Something personal came up—I have to go." He craned his head toward Damon. "I'll see you soon." Robert was out of the cell in a blur.

Gage watched the whole scene with great interest, even sidestepping Robert when he barreled past as if the south wing of

Reclamation were on fire. Gage could tell that whatever decision Robert made for the graying inmate wasn't sitting well with Reginald. Several times, he shook his head in disgust—bouncing his outrage off Jake with no satisfactory solution. Jake escorted the old inmate from the cell, and Reginald followed close behind. When Gage stepped into the cell, he heard the door slam shut.

"Good to be home. What did I miss?" Gage pointed the question to Damon, not expecting an answer. "Who was that old-timer?" To Gage's surprise, Damon perked up and made eye contact for conversation.

"He's a man unhappy with his choices," Damon said. Gage lit a cigarette with a match and waved the flame out. "You got some mail while you were out," Damon said and motioned with a hand to a letter on Gage's mattress. Gage scooped up the letter, pried the bundle from under his mattress, and added the lone letter to the bunch.

"A prison stretch is a perfect place to do some reading. It's a shame that someone so dedicated as the person writing you don't get their letters read," Damon said in a voice that almost sang.

"As the warden just said, who are you?" Damon sat in a chair in one fluid motion that made him appear to be dancing.

"I am a person who knows a lot about everyone. I can help you get what you want. What do you want, Gage? In your *heart*, what do you want?" Gage listened to the words swim in and out of his mind. He couldn't help but think how beautiful Damon's promise was and how he wanted someone to deliver his desires. Looking over at Damon, he realized that he was no longer speaking, and yet he still heard his sweet, enticing voice.

"That older man that just left . . ."

"Roger."

"Yeah, Roger. You have a hold over him, don't you?" Damon's expression went blank.

"I have a hold over him. There was something that happened in our past that's tied us together forever," Damon said. For the first time, Gage fell into the depths of Damon's eyes. His new cellmate didn't belong in there with him. Gage regarded Damon as a caged bird that needed the freedom to fly.

The thought was ridiculous, and still, he couldn't shake the notion from his mind. Beneath the dark circles that lined Damon's eyes, Gage recognized pain. In the windows to the soul, he saw the suffering that Damon either caused or witnessed. The suffering made up a large part of his presence. The warden on down wanted to know who or what Damon Torinson was. Gage wanted to take up his fight. *It's not my fight*, he told himself.

"So, what do you want?" Damon asked.

Overwhelmed by a moment of weakness, Gage felt a tidal wave cascading over him.

"I want a man dead…to see his eyes right before he knows he's dead—to know that he won't get away with killing my child. I want to listen to him scream my name a second before he draws his last breath. Even if it's a day before I arrive, I want Victor to feel the heat of hell before me," Gage said through tears of rage.

"I didn't ask you what you wanted like I was going out to the store, and I'll pick something up for you. I asked you what you wanted the most. What would you ask for if you could change the natural world? If you could bend the rules that apply to everyone else? What if you were God, what would you want most?" Damon's smile returned. A thought popped into Gage's mind, and he dismissed it as soon as it came.

"I want to kill Victor," Gage said.

"Are you sure?" Damon walked over to Gage and hovered above his head, watching Gage lay back on his mattress. "I can give you something far more valuable if I choose."

"What's more valuable than revenge?" Gage asked.

"What about the love of a child?" Damon sat next to Gage on the cot like a lifelong friend.

"Meaning what?"

"I don't want you to kill Victor."

"Victor is an evil man, and the world will be a better place without him," Gage said.

"I know the blackness of his heart. Still, if he lived—the better for you."

"Sorry, can't help you there," Gage said and picked up a book, thumbing through the pages.

"Are you willing to make a deal with the Devil?" Damon smiled. "If you spare Victor's life . . . I can return your son to you."

"My son is dead and gone, and there's nothing you can do about that," Gage said.

"I can give your Ryan to you, alive and well, but you must not kill Victor. If you do…then there is nothing I can do for you."

"How do you know his name?" Gage demanded.

"I told you, I know everything about you. You're approaching your crossroads…take my offer and see your boy again. I can offer that to you—your choice." Damon hopped onto the top bunk and folded his arms around his face. Gage was in a dream-like state, mesmerized by Damon's words. Damon was no ordinary inmate, that much was clear to Gage. Still, the power to grant life and death seemed far too implausible. There was one guarantee in life for a man, and that was taking away a life. Victor had it coming, and Gage planned to stop for no one.

CHAPTER 28

When the light stirred her eyes open, Jenny saw that most of the afternoon vanished while she slept. It wasn't her choice to sleep through the day, but after the last night's events, she didn't try too hard to rise and start her morning. She missed a lot of sleep the previous few days, and she guessed that her body needed to find the balance, recover, whatever it did to function right.

Sunlight's tentacles slithered through the blinds, leaving horizontal tracks into the bedroom, and still, the room was dark. Jenny's first instinct was to reach for her pack of cigarettes on the nightstand, and the thought stung her in mid-motion. Her hand withdrew as if a snake plunged its fangs into her skin. When she exhaled smoke into the air and Toby materialized, it made her sick to her stomach. *What an excellent way to stop smoking,* she thought. *Place an abused, dead child in front of a smoker, and they would never light up with a clear conscience again.*

Her mind turned toward the poor mother of Toby. She would puff a carton of cigarettes a day just for the chance of seeing her child once more. She pulled the bedspread off her body and settled for a hot cup of coffee, and this time nothing but its blackness stared back at her. When she took her first step from the bed, she discovered something that made her happy.

Robert's pants and shirt lay wadded on the floor in front of his nightstand. He made it home at some point the night before. Jenny doubled back, snatched her cell phone from the nightstand, and headed into the kitchen. With one hand, she poured water into the coffee maker, and with the other, she dialed Robert's number. The phone rang twice until a recording came on.

"Great," she said and prepared for the beep. "Hey, stranger. We have seen little of each other." Jenny wondered about the reason and guessed they were both to blame. "Tonight, all that will change. I'm picking up Zack from Morris's in a few, getting him settled in, and I hope to spend some time with you later. I love you, bye," Jenny said, wishing she heard his voice. Robert was always her rock, and as of late, she did the heavy lifting on her own. But she had to admit that it made her feel good to think she managed the harder things in life by herself.

A cigarette jumped to her mind, and she squashed the image right off. She listened to the sizzling percolation of the coffee and hit more buttons to get a hold of Liam. The phone rang, and for the second time in a minute, she spoke to a recording. She grunted her protest and talked into the phone. "Nancy Drew, you said you wanted to come with me to get Zack, where are you? I'm leaving in two minutes, so call me back," she said with her coffee cup at the ready. Her mind was working—playing fetch with the same thoughts as she threw it back away.

Her mental avoidance took its toll, and she had to face her unhappy thoughts. She began to down the coffee even though it was burning her mouth and throat. She savored the pain, giving herself over to its escapist quality. A quick look at the clock told her she was running late. It was heading toward the evening, and she slept it away.

Jenny changed her clothes, applied make-up, and slipped on a pair of shoes all without putting her cup down. She passed Zack's bedroom and caught his unmade bed out of the corner of her eyes. The coolness of a shadow darkened her spine. Jenny pushed the feeling away and headed out the door to her Jeep. As she sat behind the wheel, the last night's events came rushing in. "Where are you, Liam?" She didn't want to face Morris alone.

The entire drive to Morris's she focused her memory on Zack's childhood, and anything that seemed out of place, any sign that she somehow overlooked. With a mother's microscopic eye, Jenny noticed signs in everything, even if they weren't there at all. She didn't trust her instincts any longer, considering that she never witnessed the side of Zack that his teacher revealed.

Blocks away from Morris, Jenny gave in to her addiction, and she reached in her purse for her cigarettes. Her hand rubbed every item and texture before picturing her pack on the bedroom nightstand. "God bless it." If ever she needed a smoke, the time was then. With one twist of her wrist, the steering wheel would point the car toward a carryout and a stimulant that helped her through retrieving her son.

She knew better. That would buy her time, but nothing would help her avoid the confrontation.

Jenny watched the sun setting over Morris's house as she sat in her car on his driveway. Liam's words began to penetrate her selfish, scattered issues. Morris might have seen him coming out of his house the night before. "Oh no," she said aloud. If he found out about her breaking into his house, what would he do? She didn't have to wonder about his violence. She sat there in the car for minutes that felt like hours, Jenny tried and refused to break her hands away from the wheel. Something told her to stay put in his driveway forever. Morris's door opened wide, and the same angry opening of the doorframe spat out her boy. He was walking just as healthy as before. Right behind Zack, walked Morris peering at the neighborhood in the pretense that he never realized she was waiting in the driveway.

Jenny squeezed the steering wheel so tight that her knuckles turned a different color from lack of blood. The urge to slam the car's gear shifter into reverse came, and then it went. Zack was lifting and tugging on the door handle. There was some hesitation—maybe a few seconds, and then Jenny flicked the switch that unlocked the door. Zack opened the door and piled into the car.

When he shut the door, Jenny put the car in reverse. Morris walked around the front of the Jeep Cherokee and pounded with a fist on her closed car window. She was pretending she didn't see him and began backing out when the pounding became much harder. She snapped her neck toward the driver's side window, and Morris motioned with his hand to roll it down. As she weighed her choices, she complied. With the window down, she understood what chances she had against an attack. Morris looked from Jenny to Zack and back.

"We need to talk. You hear me?" Morris asked. Jenny swallowed with a dry throat. *He knows what you and Liam have done*, she thought. She held her exterior together, nodded, and spoke at the same time.

"We'll talk soon," Jenny said. He stood still.

"Yes, we will," he said and let go of her car as she backed out of her old driveway and away from her former house.

The car ride home was icy. Jenny imagined the air inside the car was several degrees cooler. Zack's avoidance of conversation and eye contact, which started on the ride *to* Morris's, continued the ride *away* from him. Her initial belief that Morris was abusing Zack didn't disappear, but a new idea began to form into an opinion. Zack might have something to do with the murders somehow. There was no way he drew all those pictures without seeing something. His involvement in the child abduction frightened her more than anything in her life ever had.

Jenny had no problem sacrificing her life for Zack, except the real question was, how far would she let Zack sink—what horrors could she discover, and still accept him as her child? *Would I turn against him?* She asked herself the question over and over on the ride back home. Witnessing Toby changed things for her. The victims took most of her loyalty now.

"Did you have fun, Zack?" Jenny asked in a cracked voice, trying to contain the awkwardness. Zack stared at the passing scenery with its hypnotizing motion.

"Yeah, it was fine," he said, never budging to look her direction. Zack built a wall around himself, and Jenny sensed its construction. He was keeping a respectable distance away from his mother. Jenny was thankful he built a wall. If Zack jumped into her lap and screamed, I love you, Mommy, would she shy away herself? Her fear prodded her to shun him, throwing him from her lap like a rattlesnake searching for warmth. She didn't know how she would have reacted, and she didn't want to know.

"That's good," she said. Zack wasn't bursting to talk, and neither was she. They both sat listening to the hum of the Jeep engine until red and blue lights caught their attention. The street was empty and quiet for that time of day. She followed the flashing police lights straight down the lane ahead of her to her driveway.

Her heart skipped a beat, and she coaxed a breath from her lungs. All at once, everything crystallized. She understood what Morris wanted to talk to her about—he had the police waiting for her.

Morris caught Liam in the act, and he called the police. Zack was in the car and was about to witness his mother cuffed and hauled away.

Zack glimpsed the police lights, and in Jenny's rear-view mirror, she watched him react to the police waiting at their home. She half-expected Zack to ask about them, but he didn't. The closer the Jeep came to their driveway, the more Jenny realized that the police car wasn't setting up a roadblock—they weren't aiming guns at her tires. She could step on the gas when she reached her house instead of pumping the brakes. *I could drive by and . . . do what?* She asked herself. *Take Zack and run away to Mexico? Hide in my mother's basement?* There weren't many options left. She prayed that the scene Zack was about to witness wouldn't cause any more damage to him. Her body relented to her higher functions, her moral core.

She pressed down on her brakes and allowed the Jeep to coast into the driveway beside the police cruiser. The uniformed officers were out of their vehicle and knocking on Jenny's door. *Maybe I'll catch a break because Robert was on the force,* she thought. She watched as Pataskala's finest moved from her front door to her car. Robert was a Columbus detective—these guys might not know him from Adam—she reasoned. The leading officer came to the passenger side, looked to see Jenny with Zack, and motioned her to exit the car. She obeyed. No sooner than she exited the car door, Jenny slammed the door shut again. She put a finger up to Zack to stay put.

"Is everything all right?" She asked in her most innocent voice.

"Are you Jenny Deville?" the second officer asked. She nodded and braced and would never be ready enough.

"Liam Walsh listed you as his next of kin. It brings me no pleasure to inform you he died in the early morning hours. We identified his body from his driver's license." For a long moment, Jenny said nothing. Her heartbeat pounded through her chest, in her ears. She denied the reality of the situation as nothing seemed real, not the officers at her home, not Zack drawing pictures of dead people, not her best friend dead.

"How did he die?" she asked. The two officers exchanged glances, "How did he die?" she asked with more force.

"We can't confirm anything yet. We suspect suicide." The officer looked to his feet.

"If you would like to speak with a grief counselor . . ." The officer handed Jenny a card even as his words faded from her hearing. The stability of her world toppled like a chair that lost its back legs. Images of Liam pulsated in her memory as if he were dying at that very moment.

From the brink of denial, a picture came into view, an image of the glove compartment in her Jeep. "If there is anything you need, please let us know, and pass along our condolences to Robert," The officers nodded and were heading to their cruiser before Jenny mustered up a word of any sort. In a trance, she opened her car door, sat in the driver's seat, and closed it. She stared forward for the longest time, not uttering a sound. She leaned toward the glove compartment and pushed the button that dropped the compartment door straight down.

Jenny slid a folded paper from its hiding place and sat it in her lap. She placed the construction paper in the compartment right after the schoolteacher gave it to her. She tried very hard to forget that it ever existed, and she would have accomplished her goal if not for Liam's death. What Laura gave her that day was a charcoal drawing just the same as all the others that Zack drew.

She peered at it through tear-stained eyes. Jenny traced every line in its graphic depiction, the element that horrified her when she first viewed it in the teacher's home, and what devastated her after learning of Liam's death made her feel like she needed to try harder.

The picture was of Liam. He sat in his driver's side seat with his belt buckle still fastened. His right hand hung open and loose, dangling fingers with his left hand clenched. Although his face remained serene, just under his chin, a large gaping slit stared back at her. Blood ran down his light-colored shirt, staining it a darker shade. She closed her eyes but still pictured his image and guessed she always would.

The sad reality of him taking his own life alone in a car as if he were no more important than the steel of the vehicle or the cigarette butts in the ashtray stabbed at her mind like a hot poker torturing her loving memories. Beyond all the suffering and all the loss came an unmistakable truth. Zack drew the picture of this scene.

Jenny turned her head on a swivel, looking back to Zack. She lifted her right leg and swung it over her seat and allowed her weight and momentum to carry her over into the back seat. She aligned her body to match that of her son's. Zack watched his mother with great interest through eyes with black circles below. Her shaking hands held out his charcoal drawing up to his face. Zack reacted to his creation as if the picture belonged with his other imaginings of rainbows and butterflies. The drawing didn't bring Zack any joy, but Jenny detected an ounce of pride in seeing his work held up to the light.

"Why did you make this?" Jenny asked and got no answer from her son. "Did you recreate this with Liam last night?" She waited for Zack to speak. "Did you *hurt*, Liam?" Her voice rose. Zack fell away from her into some distant blackness inside his skin. Zack broke off from his mother's gaze, turning toward the window like a dry leaf shriveling from a flame's burn. Jenny sat, staring at the back of his head, watching the tufts of curls work their way to the left and right on his neck.

A rage, sudden and all-consuming, ignited Jenny. She grabbed Zack by his shoulders and spun him around. A hand slapped Zack across the soft fleshy part of his jawline. The clap of skin against skin rebounded inside the Jeep's interior. Her contact was hard, and the sound made it seem harder. Zack's eyes went wide from surprise.

"Why did you draw Liam dead in his car?" For a brief second, Zack didn't react.

"I don't know," Zack said, starting to cry.

"Did you see this?" Zack bobbed his head.

"I saw it in my head . . . I see a lot of things," Zack said, wiping at the tears that cascaded over the roundness of his cheekbones. "I see the ones that kill too . . . I don't like to draw them, though. They are bad. I like to draw good ones."

"Are you telling me someone murdered, Liam?" Zack sniffled hard to clear his nose and gave her a meek nod. "Who hurt, Liam?" she roared. Zack turned toward the window once again and waited for the slap to come. Jenny glared, anger rising but let the anger dissipate.

"You don't have to tell me. I know damn well who hurt Liam," she said. Jenny pushed her way out of the car and into the house. Jenny ran into her bedroom, tore open the closet, and rummaged through shoeboxes, toppling them until she found a large wooden box. Using a small key from her keyring, she opened a small lock on the box to reveal a silver revolver.

She loaded each chamber of the gun with cartridges from individual foam homes next to where the gun once rested. Jenny rolled the cylinder around until she filled each chamber the way Robert showed her months ago. The cylinder snapped as it closed. She placed the gun in her jeans, rushed back to her Jeep, and slid into her seat.

"You're going to Grandma's house for a while, okay?" Zack nodded and began to cry as if he knew what she intended to do.

CHAPTER 29

She tried several times to calm her nerves, and each time ended with her mind running a hundred different directions. It took everything she had to control her anger with Zack. When she dropped him off with her mother, Margaret, Jenny said very little. She ushered him inside her home, said a few vague words to her about a last-minute doctor's appointment, and headed back out to find the one man willing to give her some answers.

In Jenny's mind, she didn't suspect anyone murdered Liam, but she needed to know. For as long as she knew Liam, he was the boy who cried wolf. Suicide was not an off-limits subject, and often he would use his thoughts about taking his own life to gain sympathy. The weakness of self-pity didn't damage her opinion of her friend in the least. His constant cry for help was just another texture that made up the fabric of Liam.

Until Zack's teacher handed her the charcoal drawing of his death, she never thought him capable of seeing it through. He made a promise to her—he would never kill himself without a goodbye. Liam never lied to her, and she didn't think he did in his last breath.

Scott Sedge's home was an old two-story farmhouse with a wrap-around porch—a red barn in the back—a black rooster weathervane spinning at its peak. New homebuilders knew the value and quality of materials it took to construct such a home. Jenny visited there many times for dinners and parties when Robert and Sedge were partners. She stood at Sedge's doorway, looking down the long wrap-around porch. She rang the doorbell waiting and praying he was home.

Ever since the news that Liam killed himself, Jenny couldn't stop shaking. Time passed while Jenny tried the door several more times. She leaned in the window, searching for any signs of movement. When she was about to hop off the porch, a sound arose from behind. She turned back in time to see the screen door's metal frame open outward with a screech. Scott Sedge was staring at her with eyes that mirrored what she was feeling.

"I've been waiting for you to visit," Sedge said in the flattest tone Jenny ever heard. He looked back into the house as if he wanted to escape. "We have to talk out here," He pointed to a wooden porch swing, "Haley doesn't like it when I bring work home with me, and I can't say that I blame her." Jenny followed behind Sedge and found the swing and sat at the same time. The last thing she wanted was to sit when she was so wound-up. Jenny was an angry dog trapped in a cage, and she was ready to jump out of her skin, and yet she sat still with Sedge.

"I'm sorry. I realize this is personal for you. Liam was your friend. Again, I'm sorry," Sedge said with hurt in his voice.

"Don't worry about it," she said in a dismissive voice.

"Please, forgive me. I have seen death too many times in my life and some in the most severe ways imaginable. I don't see it the way everyone else does anymore. A part of me sees murder all around us as inevitable, the order of things. Jenny, I have spent my life tracking down killers and come to one conclusion. I was proud of my contribution to the world when all along I wasn't putting a dent in the world's problems. Whenever I stopped one murderer, ten more popped up where they left off."

"It sounds to me like you lost your faith in people," Jenny said while pulling the folded drawing of Liam from her pocket and handing it to Sedge.

"What's this?" he asked. He acted uninterested but studied the drawing anyway.

"Do you want answers from me?" She nodded. "If there is any truth that I've discovered in this . . . the murderer wants them found by a single person. To me, it's a matter of fate. Do you understand?" Jenny didn't, and she said so with a shrug. "I feel that you are the person who will find this killer—I almost don't want to interfere. Any part that I take in this investigation might lead you away from your destiny. But I see that you have come to me, bringing me into fate's plan. What do you want to know, Jenny?"

"Was he murdered?" They both sat in silence. "Was Liam murdered, or was this a suicide?" Jenny was ready to ask again when Sedge spoke.

"It wasn't a suicide."

"How can you be so sure?"

"You can see the cut under his chin?" She wanted to avoid seeing it, but she saw the cut clear enough.

"Yeah, I see."

"From the picture alone, I can tell that the cut was from right to left. You see it here. There is an ever so slight tear as the blade ripped the skin toward the left side of the neck at the same time it's cutting. I'm betting your friend wasn't lefthanded, was he?"

"No, he wasn't."

"I didn't think so. For Liam to make such a long cut, on his own neck, he would have had to make a very deep and fast slice with the knife. And for him to do that, it would make sense that the closed window next to him would have splatters of blood. But look at the window." Sedge pointed to the window in the drawing.

"There's nothing on it," Jenny said in surprise.

"I can tell that the cut's depth is shallow on the front of his neck and growing deeper as it reaches the left side. If Liam did this himself, the wounds would be shallower as he finished. The injury isn't consistent with a self-inflicted wound. And look, there isn't any blood on his supposed cutting hand."

"So, what happened?"

"The only plausible conclusion? Someone stood outside Liam's car window, cutting his throat—pulling the blade toward him. The killer then opened the door and closed his window to remove any visible access point."

Sedge handed back the paper to Jenny.

"There's something else," Sedge said in a muffled tone.

"What?" Jenny asked as if she were on fire, and he alone saw the flame's path.

"Look at Liam's left hand." Jenny did as he said and saw that a crumpled-up paper was visible. He was holding it with an iron grip.

"What do you think it is?" she asked with genuine surprise.

"I don't know, but if the killer missed taking it, I will find that out for you. I promise." He smiled, and she tried to smile back. "I'm not sure whose trail the investigation is leading you to . . . what I know from an insider's point of view is that the same person who killed Liam is the same person who killed all of those children," Sedge said and swung the porch swing harder. Jenny didn't hide her surprise.

"Why do you say that?" Sedge paused for a moment before continuing.

"You know from the crime scene photos as many others do that the killer secured a dog collar on the victims, right?" She nodded. "What you don't know is that each victim had their necks slit and hidden by the collars. Police investigators omitted that key piece of evidence to weed out all the whackos that took credit for the murders. Whatever you two were doing, you came close to the killer." Jenny looked down at her rocking feet.

"So, this is my fault," she said with sadness.

"It's not your fault. If anybody is to blame, it's me." Sedge stared out into the sky.

"You? How?"

"What the papers have never told . . . of the ten investigators on the case, five separate detectives saw unusual deaths happen to their loved ones when they got close to the killer. That's the same reason I gave up the case."

"You have an idea who is doing this," she said with outrage. Sedge nodded.

"I have a family to protect. Jenny, I was too weak to see this case through to the end. Why do you think I handed over police documents to you with such ease? You were meant for this case, not me. You and I are in unique positions. I have more to lose by going forward, while you...you have much more to lose by turning back. Whatever I can do to help, I will, but this is your destiny, Jenny." She watched the clouds and started to cry. There *was* more for her to lose. She lost Liam, but she still had Zack and Robert to protect.

"Thanks for all your help, Sedge."

"Keep your phone close. If I get any news, you'll hear from me," Sedge said.

"Goodbye." Jenny pulled herself from the porch swing. Her body was fighting what she planned to do next, and still, she would go through with her choice. *I must kill Morris.*

CHAPTER 30

With every bump of the Jeep's suspension, the gun pressed harder into her skin—reminding her of what she would do to Morris. Even when times were at their worst with Morris, killing him never became a plan. Walking away from him always seemed the best thing to do. Now, faced with the ugly truth, she wished she killed him before he got his hooks into Zack. She felt so stupid, so ineffectual. Liam was dead, her son scarred for life, and she needed to act.

She caught her reflection in the rearview mirror, and she turned from its gaze. The night before, she parked her car far away from Morris's house, killed her lights before they shone his direction, and found her way into his window. Jenny didn't have it in her to sneak anymore. Things changed with the death of Liam, and she would no longer pretend.

When Jenny pulled the car in front of Morris's home, she got out, lifted the back-trunk door, and found what she wanted, a small aluminum baseball bat. The bat belonged to Zack to use the year before. She meant to remove it from the car because of the annoyance of it rolling around in the back, but now she was glad she hadn't. She raised and lowered the bat with one arm measuring the weight. Jenny gripped the bat handle with one hand, patted the gun in her waistband, and headed toward what Sedge called *her destiny*.

Jenny walked up the stone path, cut in the middle of the yard, leading to the front door. She planted the stones, but never let the weeds overtake them the way Morris abandoned them. When she reached the door, she took a deep breath, pushed the doorbell with the head of the bat, and gripped its aluminum handle with both hands. She posed herself the way Zack did when a ball headed into the strike zone. The length of the bat hovered over her shoulder.

She heard the door handle snap, and a second later—Morris popped his head through the doorway. Jenny swung the head of the bat into the strike zone, connecting with Morris's mouth. She heard a crack and Robert saying—you got good wood on that one. It was always what he said to Zack when the boy got a line drive. Pieces of bone flew into the air, and she realized that it was several of his teeth hitting the ceramic entryway floor. She saw a faint hint of blood in his mouth as he fell into the living room with her following close. She didn't have to be careful because she knew this trip was one way. When she finished killing him, she might as well call the police, and that was what she planned to do. But that was for later, much later.

Sunlight streamed through the window, bleaching Morris's skin to snow white and turning the crimson that leaked from his mouth a lighter shade of pink. Jenny watched him writhe in pain on the floor, extending and curling his legs but always grasping at his ruptured mouth. Years of venom that Morris delivered, bubbling to the surface, spreading its black viscous self in between her body and her skin. Like a puppet, the poison moved her frame, controlling her will.

Once she opened that door of pain, she could no longer close it even if she wanted to, but she didn't want to. He was an insect crossing her path. Morris scooted across the carpet toward the wall. The sound he made reminded her of rubbing corduroy pant legs scraping together. His eyes wide and crazed felt the effects of the white-hot pain that broke in and took over. He saw her leaning over him, and another part of him concentrated on his mouthful of pain. He felt hot liquid running past his lips, hoping it was saliva even as he knew better.

"We both saw this coming," she said, lifting the bat above her head, "one of us would always end up killing the other. For so long, I thought you would kill me. I guess I was wrong…so were you," Jenny said. Morris wore a mask of pain with no trace of surprise in his countenance. Small droplets of blood dripped from the tip of the little league bat.

The blood made a swirling puddle resembling chocolate syrup poured over a dessert. *This scene will be a forensic investigator's wet dream,* she thought. She swung the bat down with all her strength. The full brunt of the bat's weight and force came down on Morris's foot. His foot collapsed with a crunch from the blow. The top crushed inward while the big toe was pulled out away from the rest of the toes. His foot resembled a squashed apple that no longer had its shape. Morris let out a scream that even startled Jenny into stillness.

She lay the bat on her shoulder and watched Morris's eyes tear-up—with him grabbing at his foot. He rubbed his foot as if he could heal the wound, or the shape might return the way you mend a Play-Doh sculpture. Jenny wanted to laugh, knowing that the damage was there to stay along with the pain. He was where she wanted him, which was why she took a moment to decide where to inflict her next assault upon his body. Jenny wanted to linger in her moment of punishment if she could before she turned out his lights. She chose his soft jaw as her next target. He was screaming in horror.

She wanted the whole neighborhood to hear him the way they listened to her cries for help so many years before. But she prayed no one called the police so that the rewarding excursion could last longer. Jenny re-tightened her grip as Morris flung his body on a nightstand next to the couch. He slid a brass lamp from its perch. Half screaming, and half crying, Morris smashed the metal lamp against Jenny's chest. Jenny didn't hear a snap, but she felt it just the same. Two, maybe three ribs on her left side floated away from the others.

It felt as if Morris pushed a wet towel into her lungs. Jenny fell toward the living room carpet. She felt suffocated and realized that her ribs were cutting into her lungs. She sat there trying to catch her breath when she saw from the corner of her eyes, Morris climbing on top of her, manipulating his lame foot as he went.

As Morris pressed his body to hers, crawling up her lower half as a snake would, squirming little by little. She was the perfect prey, docile, and still. Her lungs were heavy, and her head swam with confusion. One thing was clear—she made a mistake by underestimating Morris. His will to live was stronger than she expected. Her head darted around in search of the bat, flung free from her when the lamp did its damage. Her eyes saw the bat far out of reach.

Morris shimmied his weight onto her stomach, balanced his frame, and immobilized her with his size alone. His hands slid across her waist, along her breasts, around her neck, and pressing hard on her throat.

"You've had this coming a long time. You thought you could take Zack away from me. Abandon me? Now I have you right where I want you. Killing you is self-defense now that you broke into my house," Morris said. He squeezed tight around her neck, and she felt her throat close. Jenny's eyes locked onto the brass lamp, rocking back and forth on its round body. *My mom gave me that lamp*, she thought. *I never thought you'd hurt me.* The light continued to rock, casting shadows sideways from the lampshade giving the floor a frown projected from the round shape of the shade.

Jenny couldn't let it all end that way. Morris would kill her, and he would end up getting Zack forever. It was too much to bear. Morris's hands turned to vice grips narrowing her air passage further. His elbows pressed into her ribs, causing fresh pain to ignite. Her hands reached for the bat just past the length of her arm. The cracked rib disrupted her breath, causing her vision to dim.

Morris's eyes filled with a hatred that bordered on jubilation. Just as a sleepy fog began to overtake her, an idea popped into her head. It was a blinking light like a lighthouse beckoning. The idea was strong enough to wake her resolve—the gun. Her great equalizer was still resting in the waistline of her pants, between her and Morris.

Jenny's awareness of it took hold with every movement against it by her ex-husband. To reach the gun meant prying her hand into a gap of a man that weighed three times herself, all while lacking precious oxygen that her body so needed to complete the task. With her vision beginning to fail her, Jenny closed her eyes to calm her fears, quieted her mind, and focused her attention on her left hand alone.

She guided the tips of her fingers into the gap where her abdomen met his. She felt as if a python wrapped its body around her allowing her to breathe out but never back in. When she reached her hand into the crevasse, Morris's weight pushed down and blocked her hand. Jenny redoubled her focus, pressed her hand against her broken ribs. She could feel them give as if they were floating in her body and pushed her hand between the two bodies. The gun was close to her middle finger. She wiggled it around until the tip touched the butt. She forced her hand down until her fingers curled around the handle of the gun—she watched the fear explode in Morris's eyes.

By her calculations, she had one chance to get it right. Her hand pulled the gun two inches above her waistline, and just enough for her to slip her digit finger onto the trigger. Jenny smiled at her ex-husband, or at least she thought she did. It was hard to tell with her reasoning drifting away. As darkness began to blanket her, she pulled the trigger of the gun. The report was loud and almost woke her from her stupor with its shocking sound alone. It affected Morris the same way, jarring his senses, causing him to release his grip on Jenny's neck.

A bullet passed between them both but taking just a layer of denim near Morris's extremities with the blast. The bullet found a home in a wall behind. With all her strength, Jenny threw Morris off her. He swatted at the gun, knocking it away from both. She inhaled fast, restoring her lungs with vital air. The gun wasn't within grabbing distance, but it served its purpose of distracting him.

Morris, startled by his narrow escape, repositioned himself to climb back on top of her. Jenny knew that if he did that, it was over for her. There were no more second chances. She used all the energy left to her and jostled her body to the left, thrusting her hand out toward the resting bat. With luck, she had the handle on her palm with the first reach. She swung the bat around and found Morris's head—driving him back and onto the floor. He sat there blurry-eyed long enough for her to make it to her feet. She felt the burning in her chest with every breath.

Jenny took shallow breaths to minimize the stabbing sensation. She felt something cut at her lungs from the inside. The pain cried out in intervals. Although Jenny expected the hurt, she got to her feet. Jenny watched the blood trickle from Morris's head, seeing it pool onto the carpet. She imagined the mess when she opened his head and poured the rest out. Free of Morris and his weight, Jenny swiped the gun from the floor nearby and rejoiced to have its metal skin next to hers.

Morris sat in a dumbfounded stupor, staring out into some other realm. He didn't see her, and that much was for sure. She hoped that what he was seeing was Toby in his last moments of horror. How she and Liam saw him. Toby was a physical manifestation of the conscience that he lost, guilt projecting miles to her home. She didn't know for sure. The thing she was sure of was that she wanted him to suffer, to pay in every way possible.

She tested the gun's weight in her hand, walked over to Morris, and swung her hand with the gun firm inside her grip. The barrel of the gun crunched the bridge of his nose, breaking cartilage with the impact. More blood drained from him. He winced, grabbing for his nose, and returning him from his faraway destination.

"Stay with me, love," Jenny said in the most condescending way possible. "I'll give you the opportunity that you never gave Toby. I'm giving you the chance to confess your sins." The urge to repeat her strike with the gun ignited her. She resisted.

"Confess what? The way I treated you? You had as much part in our relationship as me," Morris said. He snorted in blood and spat it onto the floor.

"You think that's what I want from you? Do you think I don't know?" Her anger broke free. She thrashed the gun downward, catching his chin by an inch. There was no blood, but she would bet it stung just the same. "All of those children . . . how could you do it? Did you befriend them first, gaining their trust before betraying and killing them?" Morris looked ahead. "You took those children away from their family, out of the arms of loving mothers. All they will want for the rest of their lives is to kiss their child goodnight one last time," she said with tears streaming. "And you. You had to visit the same horror on your child—on my child."

"I did nothing to Zack," Morris said.

"I don't want to know what you did to Zack. After tonight when you're dead, I'll get Zack the help he needs and never think of it again. I've let you do enough damage to us." With Morris's eyes wide, he realized his dilemma. Jenny meant to kill him.

"You have to believe me. I would never—"

"Liar. I know the signs of abuse. Do you think you can talk your way out of this?" Morris put his hands in the air as if to submit to anything she says. His hands were shaking. "All the reason I have given you so far is enough to end your existence, but they are not the reasons. Liam is the reason." She gripped the handle of the pistol tight and thought of her friend's sad end. "Liam was the sweetest man I ever met. He would have died for me. You took advantage of him and murdered him. He was something so beautiful, and you wiped it off the face of the Earth." Her eyes were like slits.

Jenny cocked the hammer of the gun and placed it snug against Morris's forehead. Jenny closed her eyes, leaving all the choices to her digit finger. She convinced herself during her conversation with Sedge that she wanted to witness Morris's last moment. Steadying her hand, she prepared herself to finish her dealings with her ex-husband forever when she heard a sound. The sound was low at first, then grew in intensity. The sound was whimpering. She opened her eyes to see Morris crying.

"Liam . . . I didn't kill him. I never knew he was dead," he said through tears.

"Liar." She pushed the gun to his head so hard that she felt the give of cartilage in his temple. With that, Morris urinated. Small droplets appeared on his jeans at first, and soon a rush of liquid overtook his pants and ran down the bottom to the floor. His total submission made her pause.

"It wasn't me . . . it wasn't me . . ." Morris repeated like a child begging a parent not to spank them. Jenny pulled the gun back. Morris's behavior wasn't the characteristics of a killer. *Was I mistaken?* Morris continued his chant of innocence as Jenny's phone rang. When it rang, it surprised her and caused her to touch the trigger. Reflexes alone kept her from squeezing the trigger and painting the wall with Morris's brains.

Morris believed he was meeting his maker. Jenny grabbed the phone from her back pocket with her free hand and touched the face of the device to receive the call. It was an image with a text message from Scott Sedge. The text read: This was in Liam's hand. He must have wanted someone to see this, maybe you. I hope this helps!

Jenny clicked on the image, and it sank her spirits when she saw it for the first time. The picture was another charcoal drawing, this time of a shed. She recognized the tool shed at once, and the jarring nature made her forget that Morris was even in the room. She realized she was wrong about Morris all along.

The man cowering on his knees wasn't the killer. He was a weakling of a man who picked on those smaller than him. He was a frightened baby of a man. She placed her thumb on the hammer and brought it back to its starting position. As Morris cried, Jenny spoke.

"If you ever, and I mean ever, so much as look at Zack and me I will—"

"I won't, I promise, I won't," he said.

"I will creep into your bedroom at night and remove you from this damned world. Do you hear me?"

He nodded, causing his tears to fall. Jenny accused Morris, almost took his life, and was wrong. Still, she knew he would never give her an ounce of grief for the rest of their lives. She dialed the phone and listened to the message.

"Robert, whenever you get this message, I need you to meet me at my mother's home. It is a matter of life and death. Drop whatever you're doing and meet me there now. I think my mother had something to do with Liam's death. I love you, Robert." Jenny hung up the phone and slid the gun back into the waist of her pants and walked out of Morris's home like she never even had a conflict with him. She half-listened to his weeping.

CHAPTER 31

Robert pulled onto Margaret Salvo's street with many trees in the yards and lining the curbs. Mature trees blocked out the light from both nature and eyes. He visited his mother-in-law's neighborhood many times before, and every occasion was like a homecoming.

Robert wasn't afraid, just a little nervous. His nervousness was more like an itch just out of his reach. A night of open possibilities provided the same agitation. He missed those nights of adrenaline and danger so much. And although he made it to another level in his career, he wanted to sink back into the underbelly of the city where the bottom feeders chewed upon the vulnerable soft bellies of the herd.

He recognized the same bottom feeders in prison, except they weren't quite the same anymore. A prisoner was an animal pacing behind bars in a zoo, their souls quieted by their capture and incarceration. No, he wanted to face these creatures in their habitat. He longed to gaze into their evil faces and stare down their malevolence with his own. The night promised to be different, and it thrilled him to the core.

He slowed the car as he approached Margaret's house. Headlight beams shone on parked cars that lined the streets on either side of Robert's path. Less than a hundred feet from Margaret's doorstep, a figure emerged from a shadowy driveway. Robert didn't recognize the face at first with its round features. In the darkness, it looked like anyone until a beam cascaded across his body. A man headed for a car, and with Robert's approach—the figure turned his head away from the car's bright lights. All the movements took a few seconds, but in that second, Robert identified the man.

The man who attempted to conceal himself was Liam. And Liam did not possess the knack for stealth. He couldn't have looked more suspicious, more out of place if he set out to do so. Although Robert hit his brakes to slow the car as it neared the destination, he never stopped. He kept the car moving forward past Liam into a curbside spot a few houses beyond Margaret's home. He shifted the car into "Park," snapped the lights off, and turned the key to kill the engine.

Through his rear-view mirror, Robert watched as Liam embarked on his path to his car. Liam lifted his trunk, fumbled in the back for a few moments, and exited his vehicle with a pry bar. Without hesitation, Liam moved back into the shadows where Robert first spotted him. When Liam disappeared, Robert felt adrenaline leak back into his system, and he relished every second of the high.

Robert switched off the dome light, opened the car door, and strolled out into the open breeze. He breathed in, allowing the crisp night air to fill his lungs. The evening carried no real danger. Still, there was a promise for some exhilarating moments. *Patience*, he told himself. *The urges will quiet soon.* The pep talk did its job, and he crawled back into his skin. A fervor grabbed hold of his senses, moving with more purpose, smelling the musky aftershave wafting through the air. He became a predator stalking his prey in the night, searching for the man his wife thought was so important, so special.

His heart began to race with every step on Margaret's driveway toward Liam. The moon shone bright, presenting Margaret's backyard. Straight ahead, nestled next to the garage, was the wooden shed. Liam stood in front of the smaller structure touching the front doors like a lover.

Robert watched as the big man inserted his pry bar and snapped the lock away from the shed. He took two gentle steps forward, and although he was sure his movements were silent, Liam turned anyway. Robert couldn't believe that Liam heard him. *Something must have spooked him*, he thought. No sooner had Liam spun around than a light came on in the house. Robert recognized the figure in the lit window as Margaret. The light from the window was just enough to reveal Robert from his hiding place in the shadows. "Thanks a lot, Margaret," Robert whispered. With his cover blown and the moonlight flooding the backyard, Robert stood face-to-face with Liam.

"It's you. I should have guessed," Liam said. Robert took a step forward, causing Liam to step back. Robert stopped his progress. The last thing he wanted was Liam to take off in a sprint. Instead,

Robert kept his distance, circling Liam and keeping the space between them constant.

"You have the wrong idea about me. I'm only here because I got a call from Margaret," Robert said in a calm voice. Liam swiveled around to keep Robert to his front. "I was in an important meeting with a dangerous inmate when I got the call. You can imagine what an inconvenience rushing here was." Robert circled Liam quicker but maintaining the same distance. "When she called, she said that someone was walking around her back yard. In a million years, I never guessed I'd come here to find you sneaking around an old woman's house, breaking into her shed late at night," Robert said. He increased the speed of his encircling. Liam tried to keep pace by spinning himself on his heels as if they both were on a carousel.

"Margaret is not an innocent," Liam said, with anxiety.

"Who among us is innocent, Liam? Tonight, if you were to look at all three of us, you appear to be the threat. Wouldn't you agree, friend?" Robert circled him like a tiger.

"You're not my friend," Liam said. He stopped and let Robert continue to circle.

"That's right. You're not my friend. You're Jenny's friend."

"Okay, Jenny's friend. Margaret isn't an Angel. What would you like to do now?" Liam considered the question feeling the charcoal drawing of the shed still in his hand.

"I want to look into Margaret's shed." Liam tried to smile but gave Robert a pained expression. Robert stopped in his tracks.

"What will you find in there?" Robert asked.

"Let's open it and see," Liam said.

"I don't see the harm in that—if it will put an end to you stalking around her house at night. Have at it." Robert stepped beside the shed door and waved a hand to the door's direction. Liam waited a few moments to watch Robert then moved to the wooden entrance. Liam grasped the shed's door handle.

"Maybe that isn't such a good idea," Robert said. He pulled a syringe from his jacket, inserted the sharp tip into Liam's neck, and pushed in the plunger until all the clear liquid disappeared. Liam clenched the drawing tighter. The shed in his line of sight began to dim with all its edges beginning to waffle. A moment later, he saw nothing at all.

Before Liam opened his eyes, he hurt from a dull thrumming pain in his temples. The world came back to him first, like the snow on television with no reception. The edges of his vision—disjointed, bending downward like the side effects of an acid trip that went sideways. Through the euphoric haze, Liam began to make out the roundness of a face. His sight was so distorted that he couldn't tell who was in front of him or for how long. He squinted, trying to focus his eyes.

After some effort, the roundness of the face crystallized, and the soft round corners of his vision straightened. The face was a steering wheel, his steering wheel. He was sitting in the driver's seat of his car. He searched his mind for the answer to how he got there with no discernable chain of events bubbling to the surface. Liam's eyes improved as he looked through the windshield—he recognized the front of a warehouse building. He glanced at the rear-view mirror and saw empty acres behind him. He wasn't sure, but he didn't suspect he was alone in the car.

"There you are," Robert said from the passenger seat. A sudden voice shocked Liam. He couldn't turn his head. Instead, he remained motionless, unable to move an inch. He remembered the dreams when he would wake up before his body had the chance. He remembered the paralysis of his body while his mind was awake. "Don't worry, the drug will wear off," Robert said, leaning his head into Liam's line of sight. "I'm sorry for injecting you, but I couldn't have you going into the shed." Liam attempted to speak, moving his lips slowly.

"Why?" Liam asked with a slur.

"You forced my hand here, Jenny's friend," Robert said with a smile. He leaned into Liam's ear. "It's a funny drug I gave you. I found it years back. Someone told me it mimics the chemical make-up of the toxin in an Australian stonefish. Have you heard of the fish by any chance?" Liam didn't answer. "Ugly little fish. Quite a problem there, I hear. Unsuspecting swimmers would step onto the fish on the shorelines of Australia. First comes the burning in the skin and muscles, which you slept through. You are lucky for that. Soon you will begin your euphoria…compared to dropping acid. I've never done acid myself, but maybe you could tell me if it is like that?" Liam remained quiet, and Robert shrugged. "The symptoms are almost identical to the fish except instead of the toxin destroying skin tissue until death, the body's muscles absorb all the poison until there's no trace left. If I let you sleep it off, you would not know you had it in your body." Robert shifted in his seat, and Liam strained to see what he was doing.

"Why did you hurt those children?" Liam spoke slow, arranging his mouth with an effort to get each word right.

"The boys were pure. Each one came from a great home—they had parents who loved them more than anything in the world. They had parents that would have laid their lives on the line for their kids. I needed to destroy that. I had to defile that loving bond. Words can't describe how angry their happiness made me, Liam. It sickened me."

"We can get you help," Liam said through swollen lips. Robert laughed.

"It was their happiness that drew me to them. I'd see kids riding their bike or playing with toy guns, every time I passed through Morris's neighborhood. Guess that's my weakness—their innocence. I wanted to be a part of their joy, bathing in their youth. The problem, as I always found out, was that it never lasts. The moment I took them from their homes, everything went sour. So, I would resort to forcing them to at least pretend. With some, it would work for a while. It had to end the same way with them all. They can't keep the game going forever," Robert said.

"What will Jenny say about this?" Robert looked at Liam as if he were a bug.

"What do you think attracted me to Jenny in the first place?" Liam thought it over, his eyes opening wider when the answer arrived.

"Zack?" Robert smiled.

"Zack . . . he's my long-term project. He's why I get out of bed every day," Robert said with a laugh.

"Monster," Liam squealed.

"You're not even close." Liam again heard noises, and this time he recognized the shuffling of papers. Robert was going through the case files that Sedge gave them.

"Between you and me, the relationship I share with Zack has turned sour. Zack sees things other people don't. He can see my darkness, which caused me to do some things to him—I was reserving for further down the line," Robert shrugged, "The nature of relationships, I suppose." Robert continued to rifle through the investigation notes.

"There's only one person you could get this paperwork from," Robert lifted the folder into Liam's sight, "I guess I'll pay Sedge and Haley a visit after I'm through with you," Robert said. Even with the situation that Liam found himself in, he didn't like the implications that Robert made. His concern turned to Sedge and his wife.

"Sedge didn't help us," Liam said in a panic.

"Don't worry about Sedge. You should focus your energy on *your* predicament. It was fate that I discovered your little scheme to catch me, even if you didn't know it was me. Do you think I'm upset with you for hunting me? Never. I get a thrill when someone discovers me. It's the best part of the game. It's the chase—staying one step ahead of the authorities." From the corner of Liam's eyes, he saw something followed by the sound returning. Liam heard the sound as scraping. "You're not the first person I've had to stop. When I was a partner with Sedge, he suspected me for the murders back then. I suppose he didn't have the guts to bring this to light."

"You are wrong . . . Sedge didn't know it was you," Liam said. Robert smiled the same sinister smile.

"You know better than I do that he knew," Liam realized Sedge had maneuvered him but said nothing, "He used you to do the dirty work. When this is all said and done, he murdered you because he was a coward," Robert said.

"Jenny told me about your parents, she told me about the fire. I understand what a tragedy like that could do to anyone," Liam said, trying to hit a nerve of compassion.

"Your conversation skills are improving, which means the toxin is wearing off. I didn't bring another dose, so, I'm sorry but your time is up, Liam,"

"The fire wasn't your fault, Robert. It was just your parent's time—that's all. Let go of your guilt," The scraping resumed just out of Liam's sight. "Their death was an accident. We can deal with this pain if you let me go," Liam said. Robert leaned toward Liam and put his face into his hands to cry. Liam felt real relief as Robert's muffled whimper echoed in the car. Soon the whimpers turned to laughter. Robert lifted his face from his hands, revealing a smile.

"Even after you discover I'm a killer, how could you be so naïve? The fire was no accident. There was a time in my childhood my parents loved me. But they saw through me the way parents often can. From an early age, I tried to mask my true self from them, but keeping up a facade twenty-four hours a day wasn't possible. Some things always slip out. Before I was even a teenager, they grew suspicious of my behavior, my intentions. They forced me into a church, and when that didn't take, they shunned me. They told me I killed my brother. The only place I was welcome was in my bedroom. In the mornings, I would leave my room to go to school, and when school was over, I went straight back into my room. I took my meals alone with television as my companion. Dishes came in and out like a prison cell." Liam tried to move his fingers with no luck.

"One day, I had enough. I started painting my room, stacked up some flammable liquids next to the adjoining wall of my parents, and rigged their door shut, securing it with a rope. When I conducted an electric spark from the wall outlet to the combustible liquids, the place went up in an instant. No joy in my life has ever compared to my parents screaming for help in their room that night. The squeals of pain, the pounding on the door, I loved it all. They begged for my mercy, and it never came. When the fire ran its course, it burned away the string barrier leaving nothing but a sad accident. So, when you say that I carry guilt for their death, you're dead wrong, Liam," Robert said. The scraping started, and this time Liam knew the noise was a knife sharpened against a stone.

"Please, don't do this. I don't want to die," Liam cried.

"Oh? Wasn't that what you wanted for *yourself.* Jenny told me you threatened suicide—many times. Well, today you won't have to. I'll do it for you." The scraping stopped, and the sound of the passenger side door opening filled the car. It shut just as fast. Liam tried to move his body. The toxin was wearing off but not enough to give him any mobility.

Liam's fingers started to twitch, and he could sense some sensation. He felt the charcoal drawing that remained in his grasp. It was too late to warn Jenny about Robert, but if he could somehow hold the drawing—she might discover what Robert was hiding. It was the one chance he had left. Without notice, the car door swung open, the window went down, and the door closed again. Robert leaned in front of Liam with a knife.

"This is yours now. I just wanted you to know what ended your life," Robert said.

"Please *don't*, please, please," Liam said through tears.

"Sorry, but you did this to yourself." Robert pressed the blade to the right side of Liam's neck and slid its length toward him. He held tight to the charcoal drawing feeling the paper ripple and compress under his strength. Liam's eyes went wide as he began to choke on his blood.

CHAPTER 32

When Robert entered Reclamation, the stench of death was upon him. But the smell was too subtle for ordinary people to detect. Except for soldiers who experienced real action or a surgeon who watched as a patient went toward the light, no one understood the scent. Death to Robert was a mixture of adrenaline-filled sweat, acrid copper from the blood, and something elusive that he never understood.

He assumed it was the taint of their soul leaving the body—passing through him. It remained on his hair, skin, and clothes. Whatever the unexplainable was, he loved its afterglow with all his being. With each rendering of a soul, he felt baptized by the experience. The moment wouldn't last, but he didn't expect it to last. All good moments in life were bookends to the unhappy drudgery of daily life. He learned to appreciate the euphoria when it arrived and never mourned its passing.

Robert returned to his desk as always since the first time he set his eyes on the simple piece of furniture. His constant goal was to get back to the comfort of its glow. He felt happy. It was late, and the administrative staff left many hours before, leaving the office a ghost town. He moved down the hall toward his office. Anticipation for the desk rose in his chest until it felt as if it might burst. A few steps before entering his office and he spotted the glow spreading out into the hall. *How could everyone not see the desk's power?* It was beyond him. Through the doorway, Robert saw its glory, blazing with a fire unmatched by any flame he had ever witnessed. Sliding into the same comforting routine, he sat in the chair, pressed the tip of his shoe onto the loose board feeling it give then release, and bathed himself in the desk's glow. He closed his eyes, letting the smell of death enter his lungs like a sweet aroma. Robert recalled the drawing Jenny gave him at the dinner with Margaret. It was Zack's drawing of an electric chair with flames surrounding—he couldn't shake the image.

He opened a desk drawer, pulled the charcoal drawing from its resting place, and held it next to the desk. The picture didn't move, but the colors were vibrant, and the features so realistic that the flames seemed to dance on the paper as it did on his desk. Viewing Zack's electric chair drawing and the desk next to each other startled Robert—they appeared too similar. The sight caught him off guard, and it was clear he had to find out what Zack was seeing. He folded up the drawing and headed to the prison cells.

Robert made his way up each level of the prison with an officer waiting on each floor. He passed every guard with some offering to chaperone their warden. Robert waved their offers away. In minutes, he was on the highest floor, making his way into the lethal injection room—the same chamber he toured on his first day at Reclamation.

Robert touched the door handle, turned it in his grasp, and walked through the doorway. Energy, faint but constant, pressed down on his shoulders. The room was just as he saw it before, and just like the last visit, his intuition told him something was missing. Robert moved with purpose toward a wall to his left feeling the air, heavy in his chest. He began tapping on the drywall, hearing the hard thud of the stud behind, and then he heard a hollow sound. He continued to hit the drywall—he traced the shallow tone of the length of a large door.

His heart began to race with unlimited possibilities, hiding behind a thin layer of sheetrock. Robert tensed his body, pressed his arm close to his ribs, and barreled into the drywall. White chalky dust exploded everywhere as the wall crumbled with his weight. Before the dust had settled, a light shone on Robert so bright that he shielded his eyes from its radiance. His eyes soon adjusted to the light, and across from him in the tiny room was the electric chair identical to the one Zack drew.

Flames jolted upwards from the back and arms of the chair. Along with the chair, new flames rose from the wood planks that once connected to the chair. Robert saw that many of the wooden floorboards were missing all around the chair. The wood gave the mystery away. Joseph Hughes took the wood floorboards and made the desk with them. The desk he adored came from the planks, wood tainted by death. *Were souls trapped in the wood grains?* It made sense. *But why am I the only one who can see its shimmer or its flames?*

Robert pressed his foot to one of the remaining floorboards, watching it undulate up and down with his weight. An image struck him, crystallizing his thoughts. Darting from the injection room, Robert sprinted down the corridor, passing each level until he was once again standing in his office.

He moved, almost dancing to his desk, and kneeled behind it—pressing his fingers onto the loose board. Driving his house key into a crack, he pried the board up and away from the rest. There, lay several papers torn from Joseph's diary. He scooped them up in his hand, positioned himself onto his chair behind him, and clutched the pages like they were a long-lost child.

CHAPTER 33

Gage sat on his cot, staring through the bars feeling like a caged animal. The moonlight flooded through the window, making the shadows from the prison cell's bars dance with every pass of a cloud. He held the large stack of unopened envelopes from Marie. Gage turned them over and over in his hand, imagining what was inside, then pushing the thoughts away.

Damon watched from across the cell with curiosity, his eyes darting from the envelopes to Gage's somber expression and back again. Gage wondered what Marie might think about the plan he meant to perform that night. He didn't linger long on what she might think—he knew. Although Marie knew of Gage's criminal past, she would never tolerate the violence. With a little effort, there was no doubt Marie would forgive Gage for the woman's death during the robbery. She was with him long enough to know whether he would resort to brutality.

But Gage expected even more from himself. *I should have controlled Victor more that day*, he thought. On the surface of his mind, Gage blamed Victor for Ryan's death. If he hadn't killed Ricky before he gave Marie the money, his son would still be alive. Another part of him saw the robbery as a catastrophe that altered his life forever after. If he stayed on top of the situation, then his son would be alive. One thing was for sure—Gage couldn't bear to read Marie's disappointment in words.

Gage tossed the stack of letters onto his cot and folded his hands over his face. He wanted to cry, but again the tears wouldn't come, and he detested the emptiness that it brought. Gage replaced the hollow feeling with anger—a rage toward Victor. He wanted to experience love again, and he clung to the hope that killing Victor might lead him back to love after all the wounds had healed.

"The time is coming. Remember my bargain," Damon said. Gage glanced at the pristine letters with genuine remorse.

"Things are in motion. I can't turn back even if I wanted to."

"That's not true. Victor must remain alive."

"I heard you the first time around. Victor's fate doesn't concern you, Damon," Gage said almost as if he were talking to himself.

"It concerns me more than you know."

"After today, you will have another cellmate, and they will either take me to the cemetery or to the top level of Reclamation to await death," Gage said.

"The choice is still always yours to make," Damon said and stood just as Reginald walked to the cell. How Damon predicted he was getting a visitor confused Gage, but he let it go. Reginald nodded to Gage.

"Hello, Saint. I'm not here for you." Reginald looked toward Damon with eyes red and puffy. Gage passed the associate warden many times and thought of him as a pencil pusher, but that morning he seemed different. Reginald's face was menacing, and it was clear to Gage that he was wrestling with grave decisions of his own. Reginald dangled a pair of handcuffs in Damon's face.

"I've waited my entire life to put the memory of my family to rest," Reginald said with trepidation in his tone.

"Well, what are we waiting for?" Damon asked.

"Nothing at all." Damon extended his arms. Reginald secured handcuffs on him while Gage recognized the fury in Reginald's eyes.

"What are you going to *do* to him?" Gage demanded. Reginald trained his burning eyes to Gage.

"The best thing for you, Saint, is to sit back down," Reginald said in the coldest manner Gage ever heard. In a bar on the outside, Reginald was easy pickings, but a transformation took over the associate warden's demeanor. Gage sat back down as Reginald's gaze returned to Damon. Jake appeared from outside the prison cell.

"Where are you taking him?" Reginald looked at him for a long time.

"Back to his cell in the basement," Reginald said.

"I can't let you do that. The warden ordered *me* to keep him here under my supervision." Reginald turned from Damon to Gage and then to Jake. The bags under his eyes looked more pronounced in the corridor light.

"Just *like* Robert, I am also your superior. Remember that," Jake said nothing, "besides, I already cleared this with Robert." Reginald stared into Jake's eyes for a long time.

"So, you'll answer to Mr. Deville?" Jake asked.

"I will, Jake." Reginald pushed Damon toward the door.

"Are you sure you want to do this, Reginald," Gage asked.

"I should ask you the same," Damon said to Gage as he vanished from the cell. Gage stood there for a while—nervous for Damon's fate but preoccupied with his own for the moment. For Gage, the long walk down to the kitchen felt like a walk to an execution. Sometimes in his life, he used violence, but never was he prepared to murder with premeditation. He weakened under the burden of vengeance.

The anticipation or the sheer fantasy of taking a life proved far more complicated than Gage ever expected. He used every trick to bring back the anger that he needed to finish his task ahead. All images failed except one. He thought of Ryan just as he left him—small and helpless, clinging to his wife's shirt as he drifted off to sleep. Then he imagined his last painful days and his precious few remaining labored breaths slipping into oblivion. His engine was soon revving on all cylinders again. His tethered spirit floating over his body and settled into his skin.

When he reached the kitchen, the lights were already ablaze. Victor was sitting on a stainless-steel prep table with Stephen standing beside him. Victor plastered a smile upon his face like a child waiting to open a present. Gage witnessed a similar face before, often when counting out the split from a heist. Gage also recognized the nervous demeanor in Stephen, and how could he blame him for his apprehension. If Victor survived, they would pin a target on Stephen.

"There he is—my man. My man with the plan," Victor said when he first caught sight of Gage.

"Are you ready for this?" Gage asked, trying to hide his anxiety.

"Whoa, whoa, wait one minute. We aren't doing anything until I hear every detail of the escape." A stern mask replaced Victor's happy expression. That moment, above others, required Gage to convince Victor. If he didn't sell the escape plan, Victor would back out, and he might never get another chance to take him down. He threw away all doubt and dove right into his plan.

"First, we will shimmy up the heat duct from the industrial oven. Stephen will secure the door behind us—if guards discover our escape, they can't reach us the way we went." Victor listened close. "When we reach the top of the roof, we will have to climb down a drain spout until we reach the ground. We will crawl to the West where I have arranged for a hole cut into the fence, and just outside the fence is a car waiting with two sets of clothes and a car full of gas," Gage said, hiding any emotion.

"Your man on the outside cut the fence—and the car's there? How much do you trust the person you got for the job?"

"I trust them with my life."

"That's not much of a plan," Victor said with suspicion.

"You know me. I like to keep things simple so that not much can go wrong." Victor nodded.

"I don't know about this, man," Victor said.

"What's wrong?" Victor shook his head.

"Maybe this isn't such a good time."

"Not a good time? When will be a good time for you?" Gage asked with anger and panic rising in his voice. Victor shrugged.

"I always listen to my senses, and they are telling me that something's wrong," Victor said, fingering the handle on a kitchen knife like the one found in his cell. "Things aren't ever what they seem. Are you still angry about Eddie?" Gage glanced from the knives back to Victor. Sweat started to drain from Gage's pits.

"You came to *me*, Victor. I didn't come to you." It was Gage's moment to convince. "If you're happy here, then be my guest. After tomorrow, they will mend the fence, guards doubled, and the car towed away. Then it's over," Gage said, staring from Victor to Stephen, who began to sweat. "If you don't want to do this, I have a lot of prep work to do to get this kitchen ready for breakfast, so make your decision." Victor rocked his head, tapped his feet, and searched his shoes for an answer.

"Every time I ignore my intuition, things fall apart." Victor reached for a paring knife and pulled it off a magnet holding it secure. "I'll take this in case my instinct proves to be right," Victor said, holding the knife up to the light, "let's go, Saint."

The three prisoners walked to the immense oven at the back of the kitchen. Gage's body screamed to him *not* to go through with the plan, but his mind won out. If he canceled the escape, he would have to explain to Victor why. When they reached the oven, Stephen pulled down the heavy oven door, and then another opening just at the back. Gage looked to Victor and hoped Victor's mistrust would force him up the vent first. If not, the plan would fail.

"After you," Gage said, bluffing.

"I think I'll let you go first if you don't mind." Victor pointed the knife to Gage's chest. "Just in case."

"Whatever you say." Gage touched his pants pocket slow to make sure the matchbook was there. It was where he put it, and the reassurance relieved him. He reached for Stephen's hand and shook it.

"Thanks for your help."

"Good luck," Stephen said. Gage hopped into the oven. Gage couldn't help but think of the big bad wolf climbing down the pig's chimney. He folded his body at the waist, pushing his top half into the heating duct. Gage loaded wood planks into the duct the day before, leaving less than an inch on either side to move. It was tight, but not too close to cause much anxiety. He propelled himself up with his feet on the planks like a homemade ladder. In minutes, he was a body's length up, and Victor was inside but below him. Without notice, Stephen closed the opening to the oven with a loud clink. *That* made Victor jump.

Along with the construction, the duct was hot enough to suffocate. Gage inched his way up with Victor following close enough to scrape against his shoes with each handhold.

"What if someone starts the oven? We'll fry," Victor said. *Don't worry, give me a minute, and you'll know what it feels like to die*, Gage thought to himself.

"We will have beers in our hands by the time the ovens ignite for the day," Gage said and shuffled upward with more speed. The cramped space was dark except for the moonlight that shone from the opening above Gage.

"I'm not so good with tight spots, Saint," Victor said. Gage could tell he was nervous, and that was a good start.

"Take a rest, Victor. There's no race to the top." In Gage's mind, it *was* a race to the top. If he wanted to ignite the wood inside the duct and lock Victor inside, he needed to get some distance between each other.

"I'll catch up in a second, Saint." Gage moved faster, thrusting his arms up in the tight space, each hand and foot synchronizing on the wood planks. Victor noticed the sudden acceleration, and it put fear in his mind.

"Why are you moving so fast? I thought it wasn't a race?" Victor asked. Gage said no more. He focused on his mission. When he separated himself three body lengths from Victor, Gage slid his arms down into his pocket, which turned out to be harder than he expected. Scraping his arm across the wooden planks, Gage brought the cardboard matchbook to eye level, pulled one matchstick from the book, and flattened the matchbook. He lit the lone match, slid the thin matchbook between pieces of wood, and touched the lit match to the whole matchbook. Fire came to life.

"What's that?" Victor called from below. Gage was not sure how long he had before the wood spread the fire, so he hurried up past the initial spot of ignition.

"What in the hell are you doing?" Victor called in a panic.

"This is for my son—this is for Ryan. I hope you feel everything."

Gage glanced downward to ensure that the fire stayed lit. He saw the flame of the matchbook engulf the wood plank, and he saw Victor coming up faster than he thought he could. As the duct's opening came closer and the fire's intensity increased, Gage saw the first flaw in his plan. The smoke from the fire had nowhere to go but up to him. A thick cloud of acrid smoke encased him as it sought its freedom to the surface. In a faster time than Gage calculated, the blanket of smoke entered his lungs. He coughed hard to expel the black intruder. He reached for another plank and missed it with the tips of his fingers.

Misjudging his hold sent Gage plummeting down the shaft eliminating the precious distance he made between him and Victor and put him in the fire's path. He stalled his progress by holding out the bottom of his shoe onto the oncoming planks. When he gathered his senses, he felt a sharp pain as Victor drove his knife into the back of his heel.

The attack took him by such a surprise that he screamed out in agony, not caring where the cries might drift into the prison. Victor pulled the blade out to strike again, causing more pain sliding out than its entry. Gage used the opportunity to find his footing and move back up toward the top. Victor kept pace, thrusting the knife with every new foothold. The flames were all around both men by now. Gage's shirt caught fire twice each time he smothered the flame with his bare hand. Victor coughed from below, telling Gage how far he was from him, and by his estimation, Victor was just a few feet down. Gage was one body length from the top and fresh air when the smoke began to overtake him. He coughed hard to remedy the problem, but it was no use. A hand clutched Gage's foot.

"If I'm dying in here, then so are you," Victor said in a smoke-filled gruff voice. Gage didn't want to die with Victor. He waited too long for the moment to see Victor take his last breath. Gage kicked his leg hard with all the strength that the smoke in his body would allow. The kick landed on Victor's jaw, breaking his grasp.

Gage grabbed the planks with more fervor with a reserve he wasn't aware he possessed. He reached the top of the duct pulling his head out into the air as if he emerged from an ocean. Weakly, Gage wrenched himself from the mouth of the duct. The flames were spreading fast below Victor. He closed the duct grate and watched Victor's last moments through the slots in the grate.

With each step up the duct, the fire engulfed the remaining planks. The fire chewed into the fibers of Victor's clothes. He batted at the fire in a panic, putting out one while another began.

As he held on, the wood turned to smoldering embers in his hands. Victor ignored the burning pain and hurried up the duct to the top where he could go no further. He punched at the vented barrier with the fiery path of destruction heading his way. Victor felt the immeasurable heat when the fire reached his foothold and began melting his shoes.

"Help me. Please, help me. I don't want to die like this," Victor said, continuing to slap at the vent blocking his progress. Gage watched everything with indifference at Victor's helpless demeanor, the flames that threatened to overtake him, and the possibility of witnessing him burn down to the bone. "I'm sorry . . . sorry for everything." Ryan's face slipped into his mind. What would Ryan think of his father torching a man for any reason? A frightening thought popped into his head, and the thought somehow never occurred to him during all his scheming for revenge. *What if there is a heaven? Could I see him again?* The answer was clear. Not if you let Victor die. Gage didn't care if he died himself, but he couldn't let the man who helped cause his son's death to rob him of seeing Ryan again. Victor saw Gage's eyes looked back at him through the vent. Without notice, the wood under his feet gave way in smoky ash. Victor held onto the vent as his last refuge, at least until his strength failed. The fiery embers waited below.

"Please . . . help," Victor said in a weak voice. Victor felt the vent tremble against his fingers. Twice his muscles begged to let go, and twice he fought off the urge. The smoke was growing thicker when Gage opened the grate with Victor still holding onto its steel body.

"Give me your hand," Gage said. The last act before the smoke took his consciousness was a lunge with his hand to Gage's own. Gage pulled Victor from the duct and hard onto the roof. They both watched the world fade as guards rushed with weapons drawn to their location.

CHAPTER 34

When Jenny left Morris's home, she felt empty. Sweat, fear, and familiarity mingled on her skin. She didn't feel the need to wash clean like a shower scene in the movies—but the smell brought to the surface many bad memories.

Jenny took a sick pride in how the night ended with Morris. He wasn't the child abductor as she thought, and she solved none of Zack's problems, but what she did was remove her conflict with Morris forever. Her days of having Robert picking Zack up and dropping him off were over. The situation was the same as standing up to the bully and gaining his respect, or maybe it was fear that she gained.

Jenny made Morris respect her, and she would never hesitate to make another visit. As brutal as the confrontation was, her mind was already turning toward the image of her mother's shed. *How did Liam's death connect to the shed?*

Her instincts told her to walk away and forget everything about the night, except the loss of Liam, was too painful to let slide. It was the not knowing that would always do her in. Liam's death was in her mind, not unlike her father, leaving town without so much as a goodbye. Margaret Salvo was unfinished business, and she would finish it. She hated herself for not seeing the signs. Margaret always hated Liam from the first moment he showed up at her door to visit with Jenny. She could feel the bottom of her stomach as it churned, reminding her that no matter the circumstance, she would always be a little girl to her mother.

Jenny pulled into the driveway, heading past the house until it dead-ended at the garage. She turned off the car and sat motionless in her seat. Her homecoming was different this time as she craned her neck to her left and saw the shed. *Why would Zack draw the shed?* She didn't have the luxury of believing that her son's drawing meant nothing anymore. The world changed, and she couldn't deny any longer. Whether Zack's drawings were mystical or based on logic didn't matter anymore. What mattered was that they were right—

that they meant something or maybe that her son wasn't as bad as her frenzied reaction led her to believe.

Maybe Zack could see the injustices in the world in a way that others couldn't or wouldn't. Jenny hated herself for thinking the worst of Zack. She always had a good handle on people, their intentions, and their capabilities. But she realized that she was a child lost in the woods, no longer listening to that voice that says everything is fine because it wasn't okay anymore. Right didn't always win over wrong. The truth, she found out, was that the people with good intentions in life pretended that everyone thinks as *they* do. *What a crock*, she thought.

She hadn't talked to Robert for days, and she hoped to see him there when she arrived and soon realized that she would have to go it alone. She exited the Jeep, and instead of heading for the back door to her mother's house, she walked to the shed beside the garage. A breeze blew hard behind her, and with it, the smell of turning leaves. The seasons brought with them new hope to her until that night—the dying leaves and the chill in the air seemed to mirror her troubled state. Discolored leaves clung to the trees and fell to the ground. The leaves withered too soon like her friend Liam.

What Jenny noticed when she reached the shed was a broken latch with a missing padlock. *Somebody has been here before me*, she thought. She pulled the latch to the side and opened the door. What stuck out to her was that someone installed electricity to the little shed.

In her estimation, the shed wouldn't hold more than a large riding lawn mower and a few tools. *So, why the electricity?* She reached into the dark as if an animal might strike and flipped up the light switch. Neon lights above flickered and became constant in the small space. She believed from the beginning that her eyes were playing tricks on her. In the tiny shed, a stairway led down. She descended the steps fast.

She felt her insides squirm as if they belonged to a different organism. Something broke, something monumental that was the basis for her entire being. When she studied the larger room under the shed, she lost all hope, and her life disappeared. Margaret Salvo, the woman who was always the lighthouse in her life, was something else. Jenny scanned the walls of the shed.

"There has to be a mistake," she said with little hope. Hung on every inch of the walls were tools. Stainless-steel tools gleamed in the neon light. Of the hundreds of surgical tools that lined the space, Jenny recognized just a few. The scalpel she saw many times before. Also, the reciprocating saw for amputating limbs she'd seen in movies, but the rest were a complete mystery. Jenny's best guess—they were autopsy tools for experimentation. Either way, the shiny instruments were grotesque in their potential for brutality. If they flew from the walls, trying to make their way to her, it wouldn't surprise her a bit. They seemed to give off heat from their wicked past.

After a few moments, she realized that she stopped breathing, holding her breath as a self-defense mechanism. Her chest still burned from the broken ribs as she exhaled. At first examination, she didn't see them hanging next to the tools. Their black color pushed them into the background, but there they were, dog collars identical to the one Toby wore in the spectral vision of him.

There was a half dozen just like it and another half dozens of various sizes. Jenny marked in her mind how meticulous each tool hung from the wall. Jenny couldn't imagine her mother organizing a shed like that. She thought of Robert's tools at home and how he made a spot for everything. Jenny stepped into the room, feeling the floor dip. And when she looked down, she saw a large area rug, not unlike one decorating her living room.

She took each step one by one and noticed wood beams jutted up and down the mud wall in every direction. The room reminded Jenny of a coal mine with it supports surrounding the entire lower room. *Someone had to dig this out by hand, and it wasn't Margaret Salvo*, she thought. To her left was a metal shelving system that sat what looked like body bags and next to them was yards upon yards of chains.

She continued until she saw a shadow, which made her stop in her tracks. A man was sitting motionless in a chair opposite her. When her eyes began to distinguish what the form was, she was in the grip of real terror. She forced herself to look back at the stairs in case she needed to run.

She stood frozen between the prospect of moving forward to the stranger or retreating to safety. The sensible part of her mind begged her backward, but she didn't listen to that steady voice and pushed onward. As she got closer to the man, she could see that he was sitting in an armchair with his back to her.

"Who are you?" her voice echoed in the small confines. "Why are you down here? How do you know my mother?" She received no answer from the stranger resting in the chair. Jenny remembered her gun in her waistband, slid it out, and leveled it onto the back of the man's head. Jenny shuffled her feet side-by-side, circling the chair with her gun aimed at him. "You sit still, or I'll pull this trigger," Jenny said.

She finished her circling the armchair until she caught sight of the stranger's face. Her gun fell to the ground. Her eyes opened wider than would seem possible. She slapped her hand to her mouth and gripped her face until blood drained from the area.

Tears filled her eyes as she recognized the face. The man sitting in the chair was wearing a button-up, sleeveless dress shirt with an eyeglass case fastened inside his front shirt pocket. His long gray scalp accented his deep widow's peak on top of his head. The man was dead for a long time, which accounted for his long hair and fingernails that now resembled claws. The man was Darren Salvo, Jenny's father.

Jenny started whimpering, sliding into sobs. She moved to an empty chair next to Darren.

"I come out here to sit with your father every night," a female voice said from behind. Jenny whipped her head around to stare at her mother. "I don't miss a night with him," she said, stepping in front of her daughter. Jenny kept crying, trying to stop but failed at every attempt. Her eyes full, Jenny stared through her mother, not knowing what to say. "I know how this must look."

"Do you, Mother?" Margaret folded her hands into each other and gazed at the floor. "You said he left you, Mother. That he just walked out of our lives. You made me believe that my father abandoned me," Jenny screamed.

"I know. I know," Margaret said.

"Why did you say he left you, Mom? Why?" Jenny asked, with eyes flowing. Margaret turned away from her daughter.

"Jenny. Your father was leaving me—us both. He was walking out the door. After forty years of marriage, he said he didn't love me anymore, that he couldn't pretend anymore." Margaret turned back to her daughter. "Do you think I would let him walk out on me after all the years I spent on him?"

"That's what you should have done. Dad needed time to cool down, and he would have come back to you, Mother," Jenny said as she wiped at the tears with her hand. She tried not to look toward her father's body, but she still felt his presence. Margaret was already shaking her head.

"No, no, he had another woman he was running to, I know it."

"How do you know that, Mother? Did he tell you that?" Jenny asked with outrage.

"He didn't have to. Why would he leave after all those years without a bed to run to?" It was Jenny's turn to shake her head.

"It wasn't about him or whether he had another woman, it was about you. You would never let someone leave you—abandon you." Margaret was quiet for a while.

"Yes, fine, you're right. Your father had no right to leave me. If not another woman, he would someday end up with one. I invested the years with him—why should I allow someone to walk in and take him from me?" she asked with a scowl.

"How did Dad die?" Jenny stared at Margaret, and she stared back.

"After your father said his peace and was walking toward the door . . . I picked up a brass lamp, and I hit him—I brought it down on him—on his head. I never saw someone go down so fast, and when he did, his head hit the ceramic floor. There was so much blood—I mean, it was everywhere, in every crevasse of the tile. Do you know how long it took me to remove the stains?"

"You gave me the lamp you killed Dad with?" Margaret nodded.

"You always told me how much you wanted it. And I couldn't bear to see it anymore."

"So, you just left him there to die."

"I did until I got the courage up to call the police. And you want to know who arrived?" Jenny nodded, still thinking of the lonely, sad way that her father died. Drained of blood one drop at a time until he turned cold, then lifeless. Her eyes went wide, and she looked to her mother.

"Robert?" Margaret nodded and almost smiled but stopped just short.

"He was my knight in shining armor. He forgave me. Robert knew that it was a crime of passion. I didn't plan it. He offered me a way to keep the . . . deed to myself."

"What did you do, Mother?" Jenny asked, not wanting an answer.

"Well, when he came into my house to examine Darren, he saw a picture of you and Morris and Zack in a frame I had on a nearby table—"

"You didn't, Mother." Margaret looked agitated for the first time that night.

"I saw you leave Morris so many times. I knew you wouldn't stay with him much longer so, I told Robert to wait a little longer, and I would introduce him to you," Margaret said.

"That's how it happened?" Jenny held her jaw tight.

"That was close to it. Robert saw your picture and wanted to know if you were available."

"And you said yes? I was in a bad marriage already."

"I saw him as a protective husband and father. The moment he saw Zack, he fawned over him, telling me how much he loved children. Most men run away from a mother with a child—he wanted to be a part of both of your lives." Jenny threw her face into her hands and cried much harder.

"The surgical tools, the collars, the chains, are they yours?" Margaret shook her head and was clear where her questions were heading. "When you introduced Robert to me, did you know what kind of man he was?"

"No, I swear I didn't, Jenny," Margaret said in a panic-stricken voice.

"But you know now?"

"I have an idea—"

"And you let him live with me in my home, in my bed, with my child," Jenny screamed. Margaret put her head down and nodded to the floor.

"Robert made the arrangements. I couldn't get out of it. Believe me, Jenny." Margaret grabbed hold of her daughter's hands. Jenny pulled away.

"Did you hear some of that?" Jenny asked. Three men walked behind Darren Salvo's chair, and Scott Sedge was one of them.

"Yes, we did, Jenny," Sedge said. Margaret looked up in shock and back to her daughter.

"I called Sedge just before I arrived. I'm sorry, mother. Detective Sedge and I made arrangements that I couldn't get out of *either*," Jenny said.

"Margaret Salvo? You are under arrest for the death of Darren Salvo," Sedge said. One of the two officers who came along with Sedge placed Margaret's hands behind her back, cuffing them in one motion while the other officer began to read her rights.

"I have another officer inside with Zack, keeping him occupied so he won't have to see his grandmother hauled off to jail," Sedge said.

"Thank you for that."

"So, where's Robert?" Sedge asked.

"I called, but he never showed. I don't know where he is now," Jenny said, wanting to cry, and thought she might anyway.

"Don't worry, we'll find him."

CHAPTER 35

Robert held both the diary and the missing pages in his hands. He raised them to eye level, inserted the pages next to the jig-jagged remnants, and saw that they matched. The pages came from the diary. *Why would someone tear the pages out and hide them in a floorboard?* Robert put down the diary and lifted the loose pages in his hand. He began to read: *Joseph's Diary*

My scheme to keep Damon alive seemed to exhaust every connection I ever made in the state of Ohio. I faced the daunting task of keeping Damon from the electric chair when so many loved ones of his victims couldn't wait to see him fry for his crimes. How was I to make it look as if he died from the chair and still lock him away for safekeeping?

I've concluded that I cannot fake Damon's death by electrocution. There are too many eyes upon this high-profile case. Too many people are relishing his death and want to see him sent to hell where he belongs. I seem at odds with my selfish desires. My instincts tell me Damon should feel the rush of electricity for his part in my wife's death, but God has a different plan for me, and I struggle on the inside like a boat tethered to a dock, longing to break free.

The mayor made an impromptu visit to my office yesterday as a show of compassion or solidarity, take your pick. He announced to me he planned to face Damon Torinson before they flipped the switch. His political wrangling in an election year will be my undoing. I must keep Damon alive even if that means breaking the laws I've worked so hard to uphold. I assured myself that faking Damon's death or taking a life to save hundreds of others was the right thing to do. I was all set for the sacrifice of a prisoner to hide Damon away under the prison.

I took great care to build a suitable solitary holding cell below. I spared no expense to furnish the apartment because of its importance. After the sacrificial prisoner has died, we will usher Damon into his everlasting home. We calculated every detail—we rehearsed every lie, and now the problem falls on my shoulders. I cannot bring myself to kill someone no matter what the higher purpose promises. I wouldn't dare elevate my ethics to among the most enlightened, but I hold life so precious after Katie's death, and I can't take a life. Damon's execution is next week, and I must let go of the plan.

Today was the worst day of my life, and I don't have the courage or arrogance to exaggerate the despair I've fallen into because of what I have chosen. I, along with my son Raylen, have felt the cold hand of Satan as he laid ruin upon our lives. There's no excuse for my weakness. I stood across the room from Damon on the day of his execution. He stared at me, and I stared right back. The mayor was there to do his dog and pony show as I thought he would. He even had the foresight to have a photographer there to capture his iron hand of justice, promised to the voters who elected him to office.

A crowd stood behind a pane of glass, expecting Damon's demise. The audience contained reporters from nearby areas and family members of the deceased who suffered by the hands of Damon. The spectators gasped when Damon screamed in rage at the priest assigned to his execution. He demanded the priest leave his sight at once even as the priest insisted that Damon needed his last rites administered. Damon began to spit on the man of the cloth until he left with his mission incomplete. Leroy, my most senior guard, charged with the execution, presented Damon to the onlookers, and asked him if he had any last words.

He said nothing for a long time, and I expected Damon to pass into the next life without as much as a heavy sigh. Instead, Damon turned and faced me alone. He told me I failed God. He would return one day, and he would meet Raylen and finish the job Roger couldn't. With that said, Damon turned away as if he never spoke to me at all. Leroy fastened him into the chair, and all the while, I realized I had failed. I allowed this thing to continue his mission to damn the souls of men. The lives of many more innocent people, including my son, will be in danger.

An urge to pull him from the chair and drag him off where no one would ever find him possessed me. The prison cell I built for him under Reclamation became useless. I was such a fool, thinking I knew better than God himself. When they secured Damon into the electric chair, he lifted his head and smiled my way. The gesture was more than I could take.

I bowed my head as three guards readied their hands upon three separate levers, with one sending Damon the violent current. On a three count, they dropped the levers. Damon's body tensed and relaxed as the guards repeated the ritual three times to send him to his grave. The prison doctor felt for a pulse and shook his head. And with that, my failure was complete. I promised myself I would spend the rest of my life searching for Damon when he returned in another form.

When Robert finished reading Joseph's diary, his hands shook. From the first moment, Robert caught Damon in his sights—his instincts told him the man was no killer. He understood the whole story. Joseph Hughes was an insane, guilt-ridden old man who thought he let the Devil get away from him. With the lingering feelings of failure, Joseph, close to death, gave some poor loser the rap for Damon Torinson. What Robert couldn't fathom was why the old warden would change the diary to hide the truth. *Did he think anyone would go along with the story of a captured devil and keep him locked away? Joseph's childish belief that he could get away with it was such a joke,* Robert thought. For Robert, the only devil that existed was Joseph Hughes himself. The one satisfactory conclusion that Robert reached. Joseph was so grief-stricken by his wife's murder that he was desperate enough to lash out at anyone he could find. If Damon died in the sixties, then Robert needed to know *who the prison held for Damon Torinson's crimes?*

Robert studied his desk, opened his eyes wide, and sprung to his feet. Within seconds, Robert was out of his office and into Agatha's. Robert recalled the first conversation he had with her on the day of his arrival.

He paced around the room with pictures lining every wall and scanned every inch of the parlor until he picked out a photo—he snatched it from its nail. Robert held the picture frame in his hands, studying every line in the faces.

"I got you, Joseph," Robert said with a maniacal smile already forming.

Jake Shoeman sat on the recreation room couch. The television blared as he opened a clear, zip-lock baggie containing several sticks of raw carrots. He let out a small sigh, shoved the vegetable into his mouth, and glanced at the flickering television show. Stomping feet pounded on the floor as Robert thundered into the room.

"Get your lazy ass off the couch," Robert screamed. Jake scurried to a sitting position, pushing off the couch cushions, and falling back into its crack. He righted himself and stood at attention in front of his superior. His healthy snack was all but forgotten between the folds of the couch pillows. "Why aren't you guarding Damon as I instructed you?" Robert asked. The question confused Jake.

"You gave permission." Robert didn't hide his agitation.

"Permission for what?" Robert asked. Jake looked to his feet.

"Damon is under the prison. In his holding quarters," Jake said, looking back to Robert.

"Who told you I gave permission?" Jake didn't offer an answer.

"Who?" Robert demanded.

"It was Mr. Williams."

"You left your prisoner alone with the man who thinks killed his family?"

"What do you mean, thinks?" Jake asked. Robert shook the question away.

"Take me to them now." Jake put on his uniform coat, turned a key in a steel cage, pulled out a shotgun from its resting place, and grabbed a stun gun. Robert was already moving several steps ahead, leading toward the basement and a deadly situation.

They maneuvered down the steep cement stairs. The darkness of the lower level washed over them. Light flooded from Damon's living quarters, with Robert and Jake hurrying toward the rustling that echoed off brick walls.

"Keep your rifle at the ready," Robert said. Jake didn't like the implications. *Does he expect me to shoot Reginald down if he is attacking Damon?* Jake wondered.

"Don't do it. Reginald." Robert called on the other side of mangled, rusty medical equipment. They dodged left and right between equipment from the former sanitarium, before reaching Damon's quarters. When they entered, they saw Reginald and Damon sitting upon the sixties style couch. Robert expected to interrupt a life and death struggle to survive. Instead, the two men sat next to each other like long-lost brothers about to have tea together and talk away the night.

"What is this?" Robert demanded. Damon lifted his arm and gestured toward a nearby chair.

"Have a seat, Robert," Damon said. Robert shook him away.

"I'm not sitting with you. I know who you are now, Damon," Robert said in a mocking tone. He pulled a picture frame from inside his jacket and threw it onto the floor. It landed face up, cracking the glass but still revealing the two smiling faces. Joseph was one of those faces, and Damon was the other.

"Well then, you know me, and I know you, Robert Deville," he returned with a mocking tone of his own.

"Raylen Hughes," Robert said with a smile falling away from his face. Raylen brought his arm up again with no malice in his gesture.

"Please, sit and allow me to explain," Raylen said. Robert relented, taking a seat without breaking his gaze from Reginald or Raylen.

"You are correct, Robert. My name is Raylen Hughes, and my father was Joseph Hughes. My father took in Reginald not long after

Damon Torinson killed his family." Robert looked to Reginald, who remained quiet. "He became my brother. We were closer than brothers, and we both shared something in common. Damon Torinson tore through both of our lives like a tornado," Raylen said and walked over to the opposite side of the living quarters. "It doesn't surprise me—you discovering who I am. Never would I underestimate your cleverness. More than that, I labored to give you *too* much credit. I promised myself not to repeat my father's mistake."

"Let me ask you this, Raylen. Do you share your father's delusion that Damon Torinson was the Devil?"

"You read my father's diary, Robert, and it didn't convince you?"

"It was an interesting story, I'll give you that, but the one thing I understood was you weren't Damon," Robert said with confidence. "So, why fabricate a whole diary?" Robert asked. Raylen returned to his seat on the couch.

"We didn't have to fabricate the diary. My father wrote it. We only changed the ending, so you would think Damon Torinson was still alive—and bring you here."

"We…who?"

"Reginald and I," Raylen said. "We were your victims."

"Why would you go to all the trouble? Why would I care?" Robert asked.

"Let's cut out the pretense," Reginald said, shifting in his seat, "We discovered how you spend your after hours." Raylen nodded.

"I don't know what you're—"

"That's a worthless lie, Robert. We know all about the children," Raylen said with judging eyes, "my question is why? Why go through the trouble of carrying on such a masquerade? It must have killed you all these years to pretend to be something you are not—wearing the sheep's clothing when all you ever wanted the world to know was that you are the wolf," Raylen said. Robert stared at Raylen for a long time.

"You're right. The world *should* know. I've hidden behind the law for too long. The smell of their fear—watching the submission in their eyes as I cut into their skin—feeling their souls pass through me as they leave this planet," Robert said. His coldness chilled the room. "How *did* you discover me?"

"You know better than I who tipped us off," Reginald said.

"Sedge." Raylen nodded.

"We didn't have any evidence of who you were before you killed Liam. That was your mistake. All the deaths had no connection to your life…until then. You made the same mistake that every killer makes. You allowed your personal life to bleed into your work."

Robert listened to Raylen's monologue while his mind walked through his escape. The two men in front of him couldn't handle him in an altercation, and Jake was a coward. He told himself that he just had to pick the right time, and he would overpower them, lock them down there, and walk away. "You found the evidence that I was not Damon Torinson, but you knew long before that picture. Do you want to know how you knew?" Raylen asked and waited with patience for Robert to acknowledge the question. Robert gave a distant nod. "The reason you are sure I'm not Damon is because you *are*. You're the Devil we've been searching for over the years." The response got Robert's attention.

"What are you talking about?"

"Did you ever wonder about the desk—your fascination in its presence, Damon?" Reginald asked.

"Don't call me Damon. I know who I am and who I'm not." Robert said.

"You were the last man electrocuted here at Reclamation. And when you died, Joseph took wood that surrounded the electric chair and constructed a desk for his office. The desk was a reminder of his failure—to let you die the first time. I saw you spend hours staring at your desk. There was a part of you stained on that wood. Wouldn't you agree?" Reginald asked. Robert did but wouldn't utter a word.

"After your death, my father waited for you to return. His assumption, which proved correct, was that you couldn't enter a body that already contained a soul. So, he searched out the births in the area nine months from your execution, keeping lifelong tabs on children born during that time, hoping that one of them would someday slip up and we would discover you, Damon Torinson—"

"Stop calling me that," Robert said.

"My father kept a close eye on those children for two decades with no evidence of your rebirth. He was desperate and nearing the end of any hope of finding you when a miracle entered his life. He befriended a young part-time infirmary doctor."

"Otis," Robert said.

"It was Otis. Your name came up in a conversation right before my father's death. Otis told my father of a weird incident that occurred many years before. He told a story of how he helped deliver a baby for a young couple on the same day as Damon Torinson's execution. He described how two babies came out of the young woman. One infant was healthy, while something pulverized the bones of the other. Something destroyed the infant from the inside. Although there were two births that night, and the children were not identical twins, there was only one amniotic sac—only one cord." Raylen began pacing around the quarters.

"Otis said that he never saw a case like it before or since. The young couple he helped deliver a baby for that night was Ben and Lily Deville, your parents. Did they tell you about the brother you had?" Robert was nodding before he stopped himself. "I thought so. And I'm sure that later when they realized what you were, they blamed you, didn't they?" Robert didn't answer. "Not even moments old, and you committed your first atrocity," Raylen said without humor. "It was after that story that my father realized his error in searching for a child born nine months after the execution." Robert flexed his arms and waited for his chance to strike.

"My father was searching in the wrong places. Perhaps the fire that killed your parents might have helped him find you if you weren't so proficient at murder or covering your tracks. Your skill at manipulating the truth is unrivaled. I can't imagine what your parents must have thought about you. They no doubt considered you a locust come down from the sky to destroy their lives," Raylen said.

"Sorry to ruin your plans, but I'm not the Devil. I'm just a man who gave in to his urges, and nothing more." Raylen looked to Reginald.

"That's what you thought when you were Damon Torinson, and before him Sean Spires I suspect. Revelations will come with the dreams that awakened before. When this facility experienced your dreams so long ago, you changed the lives of every prisoner at Reclamation. Guess how many convicts made a return visit after they shared your dreams—nightmares." Robert looked the other way. Reginald formed his hand into a circle. "None. I would say that was the miracle. Maybe that was part of God's plan to rehabilitate Reclamation's lost souls. He's using your evil ways to save his children," Reginald said. The nonsense enraged Robert. Reginald tapped into a nerve that was dormant but came to life in a passionate flash.

"You can't keep me in here. People will look for me," Robert said with all the fury of a child refusing his punishment. Like a scream from the dark, Robert's phone rang. He pulled it from his coat, and Raylen snatched it from his hand to see the caller's name. Raylen leaned down.

"Well, speak of the Devil," Raylen glanced from the phone back to Robert, "your Jenny's calling right now. Soon she will go to her mother's shed and find your secrets, find out what you are. Trust me—she won't try to look for you after that," Raylen said. "You will pay for the life of Karie Hughes."

Robert lunged for Raylen. A fire that once radiated the desk now blazed in Robert's eyes. His hands were upon Raylen's neck before he made a twitch. But before he squeezed his hands, a shock of electricity ran through his body, sending him to the ground. Jake stood above Robert with a stun gun in his hand.

"I've been waiting a long time to do that," Jake said with relief. The prison siren blared in the basement of Reclamation. All heads turned upward to the sound.

"That sounds like my old cellmate, Gage. We should deal with him," Raylen looked to Reginald, and he nodded. "Jake? Make our new guest comfortable—he will be here for a long time.

He is in your charge." Jake nodded with Raylen and Reginald returning to the surface.

CHAPTER 36

When Gage opened his eyes, Raylen, Reginald, and Otis were standing over his bed. His lungs screamed from the smoke that filled them. He coughed to clear them before attempting to speak. All the faces held smiles for the inmate. Gage pushed himself back against the headboard, lifting the top half of his body to a sitting position.

"I feel as if I was just born, with my doctor and parents watching over me," Gage said.

"There is more truth to that than you realize, Gage," Raylen said. Gage gave Raylen a double-take, noticing his street clothes.

"Did we die, Damon?" Raylen smiled.

"We're alive, Gage, or should I call you Saint? But please call me Raylen."

"Okay, Raylen, how did you get out of your cell?"

"The best way I can put it is I was undercover in here, Gage. And I was lucky enough to cross paths with you," Raylen said and keeping his smile. Gage rubbed his red and irritated eyes.

"I don't get it," Gage said.

"The opportunity that I had to spend with you was enlightening. You're a good man. That's hard to find. You don't belong next to the men in Reclamation."

"The state seems to think otherwise," Gage said with sad humor.

"But we'll do something about that," Reginald added.

"Because of our father's work, we want to see the world with different eyes." Gage lurched forward in his bed.

"Where is Victor? Is he okay?" Otis leaned close to Gage.

"He's fine. We treated him for smoke inhalation, the same as you, and minor burns on his hands. He's recovering," Otis said.

"You had every right in the world to kill Victor for what he has done to you, and I wouldn't blame you for going through with it, but you didn't. You showed mercy to your worst enemy who wronged you most, and for that act, I will grant you an act of mercy in return. Gage, if you had killed Victor, there'd be nothing I could do for you. Do you remember my promise to you?" Raylen asked. Gage nodded.

"You said that if I spared Victor's life, you would bring my boy back to me," Gage repeated with some hesitation.

"That's right, I did." Raylen took the stack of unopened letters hidden under Gage's mattress from behind his back and handed them to Gage. He took the letters with trembling hands.

"When your wife Marie couldn't reach you through letters, she began sending some to the administration here at Reclamation. Before Victor killed your friend Ricky, he gave Marie your share," Gage began to swoon, "Your son's alive, Gage. Marie used the money, and she saved Ryan," Raylen said with tears in his eyes. Gage found the letters from the earliest date and tore them open and read the precious words that backed-up Raylen's story. Pressing the letters close to his chest, he relinquished himself to a real cry. He rocked back to the headboard allowing the emotions to come through.

CHAPTER 37

Gage stood wavering in place, waiting to exit the same massive steel door he entered after his sentencing. This time he was facing outward toward freedom. Images continued to cycle through his mind as anticipation began to shake his nerves. Either through coincidence or a miracle, fate delivered to Gage the most improbable outcome of his life. He could hear prisoners behind him in the distance screaming out their objections about this and that. Footsteps just behind caused him to turn around in a hurry. Reginald rushed toward Gage with a hand extended. Gage took his hand, pumped it hard, and dropped all pretenses. Gage brought Reginald into his arms, hugging him tight for a long time before releasing him.

"Thank you so much, Warden Williams," Gage said with a cheerful expression.

"I hope you considered this a gift in your life. I'm positive you won't have a second one."

"You and Raylen have given everything important back to me. I won't blow this chance," Gage said. Reginald threw him a suspicious expression but saw the gratitude on his face. He pulled a business card from inside his suit jacket and handed it to Gage.

"Raylen will get you honest work when you get out."

"Thank you," Gage said and looked down at his feet. Reginald extended his hand once more.

"Good luck." Gage shook his hand and turned back to the steel door just as it opened slow. The sunshine streamed in, and he adjusted his eyes to the bright light. Standing together was Marie and Ryan. She beamed a smile with her arms around their son. When Ryan saw his father in the flesh, he bolted from his mom's grasp and ran as fast as his tiny legs could carry him into Gage's arms. Gage held his son tight. A trembling started in his stomach, moved to his chest, and finished with a smile on his face. The dam broke, and a rush of tears dampened his eyes.

"I missed you so much," Gage said in a whisper to Ryan.

"I missed you too, Daddy. Please don't leave me anymore," Ryan pleaded.

"Never will again, I promise." Gage motioned Marie to come over. She stood smiling at the happy reunion a moment longer and joined in a group hug.

"He's not the only one who missed you," Marie said with tears of her own.

"I love you both," he said. Reginald looked on from the other side of the steel door. A smile captured his face as the doors closed to protect the public.

CHAPTER 38

Jenny pulled plates and plastic silverware from her basket and arranged them on a blanket. The spot she picked for the picnic was one that she used to take Zack to when he was a small boy. To Jenny, it was the most serene place in the entire world. Under a tree overlooking a beautiful lake was their escape from Morris's angry tirades. She stacked plastic containers of food on top of each other and handed Zack a cola. He took the pop and drank it while staring out at the water as Jenny studied him.

"Do you like this?" Jenny asked. He broke his concentration.

"Oh yeah, Mom, I like it a lot," Zack said and returned to the water's majesty. Later in the day, she would have to deal with her father's burial arrangements, but for now, she was enjoying time alone with her son. She wondered if she learned the lesson of bringing men into her life. Jenny thought she might be happier without one, or at least for the time being. Zack was all that she needed, and she knew he needed her too. She couldn't ask for more. Zack turned to her and smiled a child's naïve smile that spoke in silence that he loved the moment.

"Mom?"

"Yes, Zack," she said, taking a sip of her drink.

"I made you a picture," Zack said, already reaching for a folded sheet of construction paper. Jenny's heart dropped in her chest. Sweat wetted her palms as she reached for his drawing. She didn't want to see the picture, but the duty of a mother persisted. The picture was not the realistic charcoal drawing that she saw in his bedroom closet or the one that showed Liam's finality. This one was a crude drawing in crayons that children made. It showed two stick figures under a bright yellow sun with a multi-colored rainbow arched just over the character's heads.

"That's you, and that's me," Zack said and pointed at his depiction. Jenny was so relieved that she got her son back, scooping him up in her arms, and squeezed him tight.

"I love you, little man," she said and kissed his cheek.

"I love you, too, Mom." They both gazed at the ripples in the lake. "Do you think Robert will ever come back?" Zack asked. Jenny took a long time to answer.

"I don't, Zack. I think he's gone for good." Jenny knew that there were many questions left unanswered about what Zack saw and experienced. But for now, spending time with her son gave her all the happiness she needed.

"What do you think he's doing right now?" Zack asked.

"I don't know, Zack. I don't know." They were quiet for a while, eating and enjoying the company.

CHAPTER 39

By the time Jake Shoeman reached the steel door of Robert's quarters, the prisoner was hungry. Robert never depended on someone else for his survival before.

"Where have you been? I'm starving to death," Robert screamed. Jake opened a compartment on the door, slid a tray into the slot, and closed the compartment.

"I know what a health-conscious person you are, Robert. God knows you helped *me*. So, I'm bringing you the best foods possible," Jake said with a smirk. On top of the tray, sat sugary snack cakes of every size and shape imaginable. "Eat up." Robert grabbed the junk food and stuffed his face as fast as he could shove it into his mouth. Jake smiled, walked away, and turned back. "Oh, I forgot, I have a gift for you." Jake slid a carton of cigarettes and a lighter into the compartment. "Maybe you can shorten your stay with these. See you tomorrow. If you're lucky."

As Jake disappeared, Robert snatched the carton, opened a pack, and lit a cigarette from it. He pushed himself to the wall and puffed hard. Thick smoke surrounded him, and he heard a sound—slight at first. It was the sound of chains. In the smoke the cigarette produced, a form began to appear. It was the form of Toby with a collar around his neck and chains binding him just as Robert left him in the basement. Robert slammed his spine onto the brick wall behind him. Other children emerged—victims of Robert coming alive in the smoke—moving toward him. Robert screamed in horror.

"God, help me!"

ACKNOWLEDGEMENTS

First, I would like to give my appreciation to Lawrence Knorr, Chris Fenwick, and everyone at Sunbury Press for their hard work and dedication, bringing new stories out into the world. Their guidance has been invaluable, and they are making dreams happen for a lot of talented authors.

I would like to thank my readers who take their time to read my work and make it worthwhile for me to continue this journey. There are so many worlds to explore, and I hope you will come along for the ride.

Thanks to my wife, *Tricia,* who has carried the load many days and nights as I made my dream a reality. I can never say thank you enough for all you do for me and our children.

I want to say thank you to my children. *Lea* for your eternal optimism and creativity—I wish I was half as creative as you. *Jesse,* for your passion for life—you see the world on your terms, and I hope you always will. *Nick,* for your sense of justice—I hope your moral compass leads you to a happy life.

Thanks to my parents, who took me to see the *Exorcist* at the drive-in theater way too young—this is your fault. (Bev, Jerry, Chastidy, Mindy, and Chad may not be writers, but they are all storytellers.)

I want to give a huge thanks to my writing role-model, *Stephen King.* When I was finally old enough to buy my own things, I stumbled across your paperbacks, and my world changed forever. Watching your career and reading your books taught me that no matter what genre you write, a remarkable story can break through any barrier.

ABOUT THE AUTHOR

Jerry Roth is a graduate from The Ohio State University studying English Literature. He has written for Ohio newspapers and sports articles for the Disc Golf Pro Tour. His fiction career began as a screenwriter. He currently lives in Ohio with his wife Tricia and his three children Jesse, Lea, and Nick. After reading The Stand by Stephen King, he became passionate about creating his own work of fiction. Bottom Feeders is his debut novel.

You can learn more about the author at:
Jerryrothauthor.com
Facebook: @jerryrothauthor
Instagram: @_jerryroth_
Twitter: @_jerryroth_

Made in the USA
Monee, IL
10 June 2020